LINE OF DUTY

LINE OF DUTY

Michael Grant

DOUBLEDAY

NEW YORK   LONDON   TORONTO   SYDNEY   AUCKLAND

PUBLISHED BY DOUBLEDAY

a division of
Bantam Doubleday Dell Publishing Group, Inc.
666 Fifth Avenue, New York, New York 10103

DOUBLEDAY and the portrayal of an anchor with a dolphin
are trademarks of Doubleday,
a division of the Bantam Doubleday Dell Publishing Group, Inc.

Library of Congress Cataloging-in-Publication Data

Grant, Michael G., 1940–
Line of duty / by Michael Grant.
p.   cm.
I. Title.
PS3557.R2674L56   1991

813'.54—dc20   90-22387
CIP

ISBN 0-385-41967-8

Printed in the United States of America
June 1991
1   3   5   7   9   10   8   6   4   2
FIRST EDITION

To the three most important women in my life:
Barbara, Jennifer, and Amy.

Acknowledgments

The road to writing a first novel is long and dark. I am fortunate that the following people were there to light the way and make the journey easier:

Gerry McQueen, my "hook" in the publishing world.

Barbara Gelb, who cast the first light on the dark road.

Rick Feld, who was always there to offer encouragement and listen to me think out loud.

Bob Mescolotto, a good friend who was never afraid to tell me the truth.

Tom and Eileen Maloney, who, in spite of wading through several drafts, never wavered in their belief in me.

Kate Miciak of the laser pencil and cogent margin comments, whose bright spotlight lit the road so clearly.

Stephen Rubin, whose belief in me renewed my faith in myself.

David Gernert, whose blue pencil pruning proved to be not only on target, but relatively painless.

And a very special thanks to Kathy Robbins. Without her unwavering encouragement, gentle advice, and wisdom, I doubt this book would exist.

LINE OF DUTY

I

1

A COLD NOVEMBER RAIN BEAT DOWN ON THE DARK HARLEM STREET, rapping a staccato tattoo on battered trash-can lids and car roofs. Except for a wet, forlorn cat crouched under an abandoned Ford, vainly hoping to snare a careless rat, 128th Street was deserted.

A blue van turned onto the street and coasted down the block. It pulled to the curb and two men, one white and one black, got out. Sprinting through the rain, they ran for the entrance to a nearby apartment building.

Inside, the marble-tiled lobby smelled of pizza and fried fish. The two men got on the elevator and shook the rain off themselves as they ascended to the sixth floor. In the hallway in front of apartment 6N they paused for a moment and listened. When they were certain no one was coming, the tall black man pressed the buzzer. The sound of heavy footsteps was followed by the peephole snapping open.

"Yeah?" The voice was gruff. "What you want?"

3

The second, shorter man stepped in front of the door. "Police. We want to talk to you for a minute."

"Let me see your damn ID cards." The voice was petulant.

The two held their ID's up for inspection, exchanging quick glances when they heard him unlocking the door. From the sound of the rattling chains and sliding bolts, it was clear that Tiny Leonard took great precautions against intrusion. Like most drug dealers, Tiny had a customized steel door with reinforced frames and hinges that was as strong as a bank vault.

The door swung open and an enormous black man filled the space. He wore a pair of iridescent-green slacks and a white-on-white shirt that made his dark black skin appear almost blue. "Yeah?"

"We took down a dealer today," the short man said. "Claims he works for you."

"Motherfucker," the fat man muttered. "Every time you bust some chump, you think he work for me. What do I look like? General Motors?"

He turned and waddled into the living room. Following him, the tall black man signaled his partner inside and gently closed the reinforced door.

The room was decorated in early Woolworth, complete with plastic African figures, orange vinyl cushions scattered on the floor, and a fire-engine-red matador painted on black velvet. The floor in front of the stereo was littered with album covers, and on top of the color TV, which flickered soundlessly, a half-eaten sandwich and a can of beer were perched precariously on a pile of skin magazines.

Reginald "Tiny" Leonard, perfectly at ease in a dirty white velvet chair, squinted up at the two men standing over him. Like most criminals who came into daily contact with the police, he was not intimidated by them. "Okay, of-fi-cers, make it quick. I got a date tonight." He tried to lace his fingers across his ample belly but his arms weren't quite long enough and his hands slid into his lap.

The shorter man's eyes darted to his partner. "He wants us to make it quick." He turned to Tiny. "Who'd want to date a fat scumbag like you?"

Tiny's eyes narrowed and seemed to disappear into his wide face. "You best watch your mouth, cop," he said, jabbing a chunky finger at the short man. "You all are here as my guests. I don't have to take no bullshit from you. I got a good mind to make a civilian complaint against the pair of you."

In the past Tiny had indeed filed complaints. He'd learned it was a sure way to jam up a cop, and it was so easy it was ridiculous. All he had to do was walk into any police station in the city. Of course, he had to put up with the bad-ass looks from the chumps behind the desk, but they took the complaint anyway. Later, a sergeant or a lieutenant, looking real serious, would come to interview him. They were so polite—"Yes, Mr. Leonard. No, Mr. Leonard." Before they left they always solemnly assured him that the New York City Police Department did not condone such behavior and the officer would be dealt with. Tiny got such a kick out of the interviews that he made it a point to lodge a civilian complaint whenever he was arrested. One time he claimed he was missing money. Another time he swore the arresting officer stole his gold Rolex. To his delight, the cops investigated every one of his complaints.

He enjoyed telling the story about the time he got arrested by an inexperienced narc who forgot to give him Miranda warnings. In a loud voice he had indignantly demanded his rights. The flustered cop didn't have his Miranda card with him, so he recited the warning from memory. Tiny listened intently as the cop stumbled through his recitation. When he'd finished, Tiny asked, "Is that it?"

"I think so," the cop said.

"You forgot the one about the lawyer. You ain't never gonna be no sergeant, you dumb shit," Leonard roared as the cop blushed in embarrassment. He lodged a complaint that time too.

Tiny Leonard was afraid of many things, but cops weren't one of them. Unlike some of the bad actors he had to deal with on the street, he knew that cops were as predictable as the sunrise. They reminded him of the chained dog he used to taunt as a kid. The frustrated animal could only go as far as his chain stretched, so Tiny would stand just beyond that point and whack it with a stick. He felt tremendous power standing only inches from the snarling, foaming dog, safe from the slashing teeth; imagining himself a great bullfighter. Cops had chains and limits too, and he experienced the same feeling of power over them.

"Victor sent us," the short man said.

"What the fuck you talking about? I don't know no Victor. You must be smokin' some *bad* shit." Tiny started to laugh at his own joke but stopped when he saw they weren't laughing with him. He didn't know how they knew about Victor Cabrera, but it had been a mistake allowing these two ball-breakers in. Tiny's hooded eyes moved from the white man to the tall black. "Okay, joke's over. Get outta here before I call my lawyer." He started to push his fat body out of the chair, but the cops didn't move.

The taller man, who had said nothing thus far, now took his hand out of his pocket. The silencer attached to the barrel made the gun look like a high-tech toy, something from *Star Wars*.

Fear surged through Tiny, but just as quickly subsided as it occurred to him what they were after. It was a shakedown, and that was something he understood. He laughed nervously. "Hey, bro. Best put that thing away before someone get hurt." He took out his wallet and tossed it on the coffee table. "There's about two grand there. Take it and get out." Unable to resist the opportunity for sarcasm, he added, "If you look in the kitchen you might find some empty bottles. Why don't you take them for the deposit, you thieving motherfuckers."

His custom-made silk shirt clung to his sweaty back. Man, he thought, am I gonna lay one big civilian complaint on these crazy bastards.

The tall man cocked the pistol and brought it up to Tiny's fat face.

"You can't shoot me," Tiny snarled.

He died believing that.

THE TELEPHONE RANG FIVE TIMES BEFORE DENOTO HEARD IT OVER the din of typewriters, screaming complainants, and protesting suspects. Wearily, Detective Sal DeNoto picked it up, spraying ashes from the cigar in his right hand across his desk. "Two-six squad, DeNoto."

"Salvatore, how are you this fine evening?" It was Lieutenant Flynn, the desk officer on duty downstairs. "Are you catching tonight?"

DeNoto squinted through the cloud of cigar smoke to the clock on the far wall. "Yeah, Loo, but only for the next twenty minutes. Can it wait?"

" 'Fraid not. It's a homicide." Flynn pronounced it "hamicide." "Address is 531 West 128th Street. The sergeant and the sector are already there. Crime scene has been notified and is on the way."

DeNoto angrily ground the stub of his cigar into the Volkswagen hubcap that served as an ashtray. "Loo, the tour is almost over. How about we wait for—"

"Not this one, Salvatore. Your client's name is Tiny Leonard." Flynn chuckled and hung up.

DeNoto whistled as he put the phone down. Leonard, one of the biggest narcotics dealers in Harlem, had a reputation for being one mean son of a bitch. "Who'd have the balls to ice Leonard on his own turf?" he said to his partner at the adjoining desk.

The other cop, intent on pecking out an arrest report with two fingers, didn't look up. "The Lord works in mysterious ways," he said.

Rain lashed the windows, and DeNoto cursed softly. "Just what I need," he mumbled as he slipped into his battered raincoat. "Another homicide and it's raining like a cow pissing on a flat rock. I don't have enough to keep me busy."

The other detective ripped the form out of the typewriter and scrawled his signature across the bottom. "Look at the bright side, Sal. Another world-class scumbag has been scratched. With miracles like that, it's hard to believe there are still atheists in this world."

DeNoto tugged on his raincoat belt savagely. "You know, Crowley, you got some kinda sick religious streak in you."

On their way out the door, DeNoto stopped to straighten the squad room's pathetic Charlie Brown Christmas tree. Although it was only the second week in November, Sergeant Conklin, the squad's second whip, had put it up "to brighten up this fucking hovel," as he delicately phrased it. It hadn't been one of Conklin's better ideas. After getting knocked over three times by cops scuffling with unruly prisoners, the tree had developed a permanent list to port. Only seven ornaments survived, and the two light sets refused to stay lit for more than a five-minute stretch.

DeNoto regarded the tree with a jaundiced eye. "What a piece of shit. When did we take it down last year?"

Crowley looked over DeNoto's shoulder. "May. Remember, the lights came on three days after Christmas and we were afraid to touch it?"

"Yeah, that's right. Ten bucks says the fucking tree don't last till Christmas Eve."

DENOTO AND CROWLEY STEPPED OFF THE ELEVATOR AND INTO THE usual homicide-scene chaos. The narrow hallway was jammed with uniformed cops, ambulance attendants, Tiny Leonard's neighbors, and even a couple of reporters who'd been monitoring the police band. Three young cops with raincoats dripping water over the filthy floor jockeyed for position at the door, hoping to get a glimpse of their first homicide victim. They should have been on patrol, but when it came to gawking at carnage and gore, cops are just as voyeuristic as the next guy.

Years before, when DeNoto was in recruit school, each rookie had to tell the class why he became a cop. The class clown got up and said he became a cop because he was tired of always getting chased away from accident scenes by cops. Now he could do the chasing and see the action at the same time. Everyone thought it was funny except the sour-balls instructor.

Watching the rookies craning to see into the apartment, DeNoto decided that his classmate's answer had probably been closer to the truth than all the other altrustic bullshit he'd heard that day fifteen years ago.

Many of the apartment doors were opened a crack, and shadowed faces peered out. As DeNoto came closer, each door closed quickly, reminding him of fiddler crabs disappearing into sand holes on the beach. They could close their doors, but it didn't matter. He, Crowley, or another detective would talk to them eventually. A canvass of the building and neighborhood was mandatory in a homicide investigation. Usually it produced nothing, but every once in a while it uncovered *the* perfect witness. Because of that one-in-a-million chance, a canvass was SOP.

DeNoto stopped about ten feet from the open door of Leonard's apartment and ground his hissing cigar into the wet tile floor. With conscious effort he cleared his head of all distracting thoughts. He knew from experience that his first impression of the murder scene could yield valuable insights. There could be only one "first" look at a crime scene. After that it was never the same. It was like that Chinese proverb: "You can never enter the same river twice."

While Crowley began collecting information from the first officer on the scene, DeNoto squeezed past the rookies, nodded to the uniformed sergeant who was doing a pretty good job of keeping unnecessary people out of the apartment, and stepped through the door. Two crime-scene cops were already busy at their tasks. One snapped pictures with a beat-up camera while the other, on his hands and knees with tweezers and eyedroppers, methodically went about the business of collecting blood, hair samples, and anything else that might explain why Tiny Leonard was dead.

Cranking the film advance on his camera, the younger of the two glanced up as DeNoto came in. "Sal. You catching this one?"

DeNoto nodded to the kid and let his eyes sweep the room.

The homicide scene, a freeze-frame of the victim's last moment on earth, is often paradoxically serene. The violence and furor spent, what's left is a silent tableau of death. Tiny Leonard, now only a mountain of dead flesh, slumped in his filthy armchair with his head resting on the back, as though the effort of being murdered had exhausted him. The eyes, looking toward the stained ceiling, stared vacantly into eternity, and his pudgy, sausagelike fingers gripped the arms of the cheap chair. There was, DeNoto saw, an expensive-looking diamond pinky ring still on Leonard's left hand. A thin ribbon of blood had trickled from the neat black hole in Leonard's forehead and had ended in a gelatinous puddle on Leonard's white shirt. The stench of feces hung in the air.

DeNoto scowled, and his eyes swept the room once again. "Hey, Friedman, you want to be a detective. Notice anything unusual?"

The crime-scene photographer looked around. He'd taken more than a dozen pictures since they'd arrived five minutes earlier, but he hadn't noticed anything out of the ordinary. "Nope. The usual regulation murder scene."

DeNoto eyed the wallet flipped open on the coffee table and the beer can and sandwich on the TV. Carefully avoiding a small puddle of blood at Leonard's feet, he stepped in for a closer look at the body. "Someone came in here and snuffed Tiny while he sat there peacefully in his chair looking like the goddamned Lincoln Memorial."

Friedman took a second look around the room. "You're right, Sal. Not a thing out of place. What's it mean?"

DeNoto moved away to inspect the bedroom. "How should I know, Friedman? What do I look like, a detective or something?"

2

BRIAN SHANNON'S CRAMPED OFFICE ON THE THIRTEENTH FLOOR OF One Police Plaza resembled the bottom of a hamster cage. Every available flat surface was covered with precariously stacked piles of NYPD reports and folders. Pinned to the walls were charts whose blue, red, and black jagged lines tracked the ebb and flow of major crimes in the city.

A cigarette dangling from his lips, Shannon sat with his feet up on the desk and squinted at the sixty-one. The Complaint Report—or ''sixty-one,'' as the old-timers called it—was the basic workhorse form in the department. Its companion, the Complaint Follow-Up, or DD5, which detectives used to record additional information, was the next most important form. Shannon's desk was littered with sixty-ones and DD5's from the previous twenty-four hours.

He read the Leonard Complaint Report again, then dialed the Two-six squad. "Lieutenant Shannon, Chief of Detectives Office. Is DeNoto still there?"

A tired voice came on the line. "DeNoto here."

Shannon glanced at the wall clock. He knew the detective had been working nonstop since he'd "caught" the homicide nine hours ago. The SOP was to stay with a homicide while witnesses and leads, if any, were fresh. If the initial investigation determined that the case was going nowhere, things settled back to normal and the homicide became just one more for the overworked detective to solve. It was early in the case. DeNoto would still be digging for witnesses.

"I just read the Leonard sixty-one. It doesn't say much. Got anything else yet?"

"Not a hell of a lot, Loo." All lieutenants were called Loo. "This one's kind of wacky. Tiny was a major dealer up here. I figured he got hit in a dispute over drugs, but from what we're hearing from people on the street, it wasn't a mob hit. Right now there's nothing to explain it, but the junkies up here are shitting Hersheys. We've been rousting dealers all over Harlem, and the junkies are having a real tough time copping a buy this morning. The inconsiderate bastard who hit Tiny really fucked up business around here."

"What about the Medical Examiner?"

"Just the preliminary—death by bullet hole in the head."

"Drug ingestion?"

"The autopsy will tell, but I doubt it. Tiny didn't use the shit, he only sold it." DeNoto paused. "There was one thing . . ."

"Yeah?"

"The scene wasn't disturbed at all—no furniture knocked over, nothing spilled, nothing missing. His wallet was on the table with twenty-six hundred bucks in it. Tiny had a rep as a violent dude. What I can't figure is how he got his brains blown out without making a fuss. I've never seen such a neat homicide scene. It's really weird."

Shannon agreed: it was weird. He didn't tell the detective that the M.O. was exactly like another homicide sixty-one he had tucked in his drawer. "DeNoto, let me know if you come up with anything else."

"Okay. Hey, Loo, I don't usually get calls from the Chief of Detectives Office about routine homicides. There anything special I should know about this case?"

Shannon wished he knew the answer to that question. "Naw, I'm just trying to decide which chart Tiny belongs on." He hung up.

Shannon unlocked his drawer, took out a folder and reread the other sixty-one again. Then he gathered up his papers, lit another cigarette and went to see Bennett.

Deputy Chief Hugo Bennett, six-foot-four and close to three hundred pounds, was the Executive Officer of the Detective Bureau. It was the considered opinion of everyone in the bureau that Chief Bennett—or "Baby Huey," as he was irreverently called—was the sloppiest dressed and most accident-prone man alive. His one lumpy blue suit looked like he stored apples in the pockets, and the huge knot in his tie ensured that it would reach no more than midway down his enormous stomach. He usually wore scuffed brown shoes with his blue suit, and when he was feeling particularly adventurous, white socks. The rumpled man-mountain was topped off with a large crop of unruly red hair that looked like it had been combed with a Weedwacker. All in all, Bennett's general appearance suggested he was dressed by a committee of palsied blind men. His notorious garb was especially onerous to detectives who prided themselves on dressing and looking the part of a detective. There wasn't a cop in the bureau who didn't have at least one horror story concerning yet another example of Baby Huey's lack of sartorial sophistication.

But under that disheveled, disorganized, accident-prone exterior was the sharpest, shrewdest, don't-give-me-any-bullshit administrator in the department. Bennett had come on the job before a high school diploma was required. But even with his eighth-grade education, he was a better administrator than most of the young college-educated paper pushers in Headquarters. He had a talent for writing reports in police-amatic razzle-dazzle that brought tears of joy to the eyes of his bureaucratic superiors. He could make a weather report sound like an innovative community-relations program.

He was busy mopping up the coffee he'd just spilled when Shannon came in. "Jeez, what a mess! Goddamn cup just fell over. What's up?"

"I'm not sure, Chief. I got a couple of homicides that look a little strange."

Bennett dabbed at the soggy blotter, but only succeeded in spreading the puddle to the rest of the desk. A thread of coffee dribbled onto his tie. "Most homicides are strange. What makes these different?"

"Last night a big-time drug dealer named Tiny Leonard was murdered in Harlem. No robbery, no struggle, no apparent motive. He was shot in the head execution style. Two weeks ago"—Shannon opened his folder and read from the sixty-one—"Nelson Marbridge, male, fifty-two, was shot in the head execution style. Again no motive, and nothing taken from his Park Avenue apartment." He looked up. "The same M.O.—one shot to the head—was used in both homicides, but there doesn't appear to be a motive for either one."

Bennett gave up mopping his desk and sat back. "Any connection between the two men?"

"Negative. Marbridge was an art dealer. They traveled in very different circles."

"What about weapons?"

"Different guns."

"What do you think?"

"It may be just a coincidence, but I've got this hunch they're connected. They're just too similar."

"Are there any more?"

"I checked back to the beginning of the year. There's a couple that we know are mob-related, but only these two with the same M.O."

Bennett tossed the soggy napkin into the wastebasket, leaving a trail of brown drip spots across the typed reports in his in-basket. "You'll do anything to get out of this felony project, won't you, Shannon?"

"I won't lie, Chief. I think this project sucks. What's the point? All I'm gonna find is that crime in this city is getting worse. We already know that. I feel like I'm trying to prove that birds fly."

Bennett rested his elbows on the wet blotter. "I know how you feel, but things are heating up in this city. There's an election coming up next year, and that guy Pickett has really been sticking it to us in the press."

"Pickett's just another loudmouth politician looking for some free publicity."

"It's not that simple. You know the scuttlebutt. The mayor may take a shot at running for governor. If that happens, the P.C. may run for mayor. Either way, a lot of careers are on the line here. The only way to muzzle Pickett is to be out in front of him on crime issues. That's why the P.C. personally mandated the project, and that's why I brought you up here. You're one of the few men in the bureau who can add more than twenty numbers without opening your fly. I've known some tough men in this department who are afraid of nothing except some simple arithmetic."

Bennett's face reddened as he launched into his favorite tirade. "If it wasn't for those goddamn graph questions they always put on promotional exams"—his fist struck the desk perilously close to the coffee container—"a lot of good detectives would be bosses today! With your accounting background, there isn't another boss in the bureau who can handle this project as well as you."

"But I'm a squad commander," Shannon protested, "not a bean counter. There are plenty of guys who can do this."

"But not in the bureau. You know Larson—he doesn't like outsiders doing our work."

"Larson'd never know. He's not around long enough to know what's going on."

It was a well-known fact that Timothy J. Larson was an absentee Chief
of Detectives who spent most of his time with politicians, and anyone else
who could further his career. His greatest pleasure was seeing his picture in
the *Daily News,* arm draped around a prominent person. He left the day-to-
day bureau operation to Hugo Bennett.

Bennett sighed and reached for what remained of his coffee. "Listen,
Brian, I know how you feel. How long have you been up here?"

"Five weeks."

"How much more time do you need?"

"Three or four weeks."

"As soon as this project is finished, you go back to your squad. Swear
to God."

Shannon saw there was no point in continuing the discussion. He was
going to be stuck here until the felony project was completed. "Okay, boss,
but what if there is something to these homicides?"

"Forget it," Bennett snapped.

Shannon had touched on a sore point. The ability to identify similar
crime patterns was still the weakest link in the bureau. With more than
fifteen hundred murders investigated by scores of detectives every year, it
was a logistical nightmare. Without a coordinated reporting system, there
was always the chance that crimes with similar M.O.'s might not be
linked—especially if they occurred in different boroughs.

Bennett fought constantly with Larson about revamping inter-bureau
communications. In the past the bureau had gotten burned for failing
to recognize crime patterns, and Bennett didn't want it to happen again.
He wanted to centralize the bureau, set up a computer network that
would help identify crime patterns and M.O.'s. But Larson, who was
too busy campaigning for Police Commissioner, wouldn't sit still long
enough to listen.

In a more conciliatory tone, Bennett said, "Let me think about it, Brian.
In the meantime, if you find another one, let me know."

As Shannon rose to leave, the Executive Officer swung his arm across
the desk and knocked the cup over again. The coffee still in the cup flooded
the desk and dribbled onto his lap. "Goddamn it!" he muttered and grabbed
for another napkin.

Back in his office, Shannon adjusted the vertical blinds and watched a
red tugboat pull a sand-laden barge down the East River. By the time it
disappeared under the Brooklyn Bridge, he'd made up his mind. The hell
with Bennett and the felony project. He'd do a little checking into these
cases on his own.

Behind him the door opened slowly. A slightly built young man with an
enormous mustache slipped quietly into the tiny office. *"Perdone me,
señor. Mi—"*

Shannon, still looking out the window, said, "Cut the wetback bullshit, Velez. You're two hours late."

"I know, boss, but the subways in the Bronx are a disgrace—"

"Bullshit." The lieutenant sat down. "What's your excuse this time?"

Velez hung his head and his mustache seemed to droop even more. "Okay, I tried to get out of her apartment, but she wouldn't let me go! She's a bitch, man. A real bitch! Boss, you should see the body on this lady. I'm telling you . . . ." Words failed him, and he stood there shaking his head.

Shannon lit his fifth cigarette of the morning. "Someday her husband is going to come home early and use your gun to give you another asshole."

Velez winced and grabbed his crotch. "Jesus, Loo. Don't say that. *Madre mia!*"

Shannon watched the carefree young officer turn on the computer and arrange his work for the day. Most of the time he was an overgrown kid, but when he sat down at the computer, he was transformed. Velez had to be the smartest Puerto Rican in New York City. He was certainly the smartest cop—white, black, brown, or yellow—in the police department. A graduate of Bronx High School of Science, he had gone to MIT on a computer-science scholarship. While there, he baffled professors and fellow students alike with his uncanny mathematical talents and analytical mind. At the same time he infuriated them with his I-don't-give-a-shit street attitude. After a year, to the satisfaction of all concerned, he dropped out. He came back to the city and took the test for the police department. At the Academy he racked up the highest marks ever recorded, while simultaneously receiving more demerits than any rookie in recent memory.

The word of his mathematical skills spread, and before Velez graduated from the Academy, he had offers to work in every major administrative division in the department. But he turned them down. He wanted to be "a real cop." This flippant reproach of the administrative corps so infuriated the Chief of Personnel that he sputtered, "Fuck that little spic. He wants to be a real cop? I'll show him real cop." And so Probationary Police Officer Luis Velez, shield number 5612, was assigned to the infamous "Four-four" precinct in the Bronx—probably the closest thing to Dodge City in the twentieth century. Among its many distinctions, the Four-four boasted the highest homicide rate in the city.

Velez loved it. He made arrests, traded shots with felons, and screwed every foxy chick within reach. If even half of what Velez said about his sex life was true, he had to have the stamina of a water buffalo. When Shannon found out about Velez's computer talents, he knew he wanted him for the project. The negotiations, however, were not easy. Velez was having far too much fun fighting crime in the Bronx. Shannon appealed to his love of computers: "You'll design and write your own programs." No reaction. Finally he appealed to his basic instincts: "I'll cut you loose two hours early every day." It was the first time Shannon was to see Velez's patented weasel grin; a grin sincere and mocking at the same time. The final item in their verbal agreement was that Shannon had to swear on his mother's grave—never mind that she wasn't dead yet—to send Velez back to the Four-four as soon as the project was over. The Chief of Personnel would never have understood *that*.

Today, watching him across the confines of the cluttered office, Shannon asked, "Luis, why did you come on the job?"

Velez pried the lid off his coffee container and dumped three packets of sugar in before answering. "I dunno. I had enough of school. There was nothing else they could teach me that I wanted to know, so I quit."

"But why the police department?"

"It was either the P.D. or the French Foreign Legion. I took the P.D. because I get to go home every night and I don't have to go AWOL."

"What's your I.Q.?"

"I dunno. One thirty? Something like that."

One sixty-seven. The highest in the department. Shannon had looked it up in his personnel folder. He came to a decision. "Luis, I have something I need analyzed."

Velez's eyes lit up. A challenge. Anything unusual stimulated him. "Sure. What have you got?"

Shannon briefed him on the two homicides. "I want to know if there's a correlation between them."

Velez became thoughtful. "In computer circles there's a term—GIGO—garbage in, garbage out. What kind of data you got?"

"Just the sixty-ones and the DD5's."

"That won't tell us much."

"What do you suggest?"

"Let's get everything we can—M.E. reports, rap sheets, arrest reports, the works. If the correlation you're looking for isn't evident now, you're gonna need a lot more data for comparison."

Shannon reluctantly agreed. He was hoping to keep this simple, but Velez was right. If there was a link between the Marbridge and Leonard homicides, it was buried somewhere in the mass of material collected by the investigating officers. "Okay, we'll do it. By the way, what I want to do has to be done in addition to the felony project. And I don't want anyone to know what we're doing. Deal?"

"You got it, boss. I'll take the shit home and work on it if I have to."

"You live in the South Bronx and you have a computer in your apartment? Aren't you afraid of someone ripping it off?"

"Naw, the dumb bastards who burglarize my neighborhood will think it's a TV, and when they can't get a picture, they'll think it's busted and leave it alone."

3

As soon as Brian Shannon turned into his driveway, the tension from the long, tedious trip began to drain from him. Driving fifty miles every day in stop-and-go traffic in cold and heat on the Long Island Expressway, one of the world's worst highways, was physically, mentally, and emotionally exhausting. And his '74 Volkswagen Rabbit—a mechanical nightmare—was no help. Lately he'd been experiencing strange electrical problems. Sometimes the engine wouldn't start, while at other times it would suddenly die while he was on the expressway with cars whizzing by at sixty miles an hour. This car doesn't need a mechanic, he thought as he yanked the door open, it needs an exorcist.

It was at times like this when the same nagging question popped into his head: Why in God's name did I move all the way out to Smithtown? Of course he knew the rational answer: to make a better life for his wife and daughter.

Like thousands of other young newlyweds born and raised in the crowded tenements of the city, Brian and Eileen Shannon migrated east to Long Island in the sixties looking for a home in a paradise of quarter-acre lots and pseudo-colonial homes with stately pillars in front—a suburban Tara. The only thing missing was Scarlett O'Hara and Rhett Butler standing at the front door.

Smooth-talking real estate salesmen emphasized that here was a place you could let your children play outside without fear of crime or traffic. Plenty of room, big houses, low taxes, and good schools were also part of the allure. But all that soon changed. It wasn't long before the poisons that infected the city slowly oozed all the way out to paradise. Property taxes skyrocketed as harried officials built more schools to keep up with the burgeoning population. Houses sprang up on every available lot; the open spaces began to close in.

Then came the oil embargo, and Rhett and Scarlett discovered it was expensive to heat even a modest Tara. Some cops, part of this early migration, were caught in such a squeeze between their soaring oil bills and static salaries that they sometimes found it necessary to take sick days because they couldn't afford to gas up their cars.

On top of everything else, crime—the main reason for leaving the city—found its way into the cul-de-sacs and tree-lined streets of suburbia. In a few short years these suburbanites were dismayed to find themselves surrounded by most of the problems they thought they'd left behind, except that now they were fifty miles farther from work.

Eileen was just finishing up in the kitchen when Brian came in. One look at him and she knew he was in a bad mood. She kissed him and massaged the back of his neck, still tight with tension. "Have a bad day, Junebug?"

The pet name, which she only used when they were alone, was a result of their first meeting. Eileen Duffy had been a nurse at Lincoln Hospital, and her first sight of Brian was when he came slamming through the doors into the emergency room with a bloodied, handcuffed man in tow. Brian's uniform was covered with blood and she thought he'd been shot. But it turned out that the man in handcuffs had killed another in a knife fight, and Brian, who'd tried to break up the fight, had gotten their blood all over him. From his solemn demeanor, it was obvious Brian was a rookie. His shiny leather gear was so new it squeaked. It was love at first sight.

He had handcuffed the man to a radiator and sat down to write in his memo book. Eileen stood over him with her clipboard. "Name and command?" she said curtly.

"Shannon. Four-one."

"Patient's name?"

"He's not a patient," he said grimly, still not looking up. "He's a prisoner."

"Prisoner's name," she repeated, trying not to laugh.

Brian fumbled through the prisoner's wallet looking for ID. "Junebug Jenkins," he read from a crumpled driver's license. "One twenty Tremont—"

"Junebug!"

"Yeah," Brian said in growing annoyance, "that's what it says." He looked up and saw her for the first time; his frown dissolved into a smile and he started to laugh too. And together, as though they were the only people in the world, they laughed at their own private joke, oblivious to the moaning, bleeding victims of South Bronx mayhem surrounding them. They didn't see the forlorn man handcuffed to the radiator, they didn't see the child coming out of a treatment room proudly displaying a brand-new cast on her arm to a weeping mother. They saw only each other.

After that night, whenever she was working, Brian would manage to find some poor soul in need of medical attention and drag him into the emergency room. His sudden interest in the health and welfare of the citizens of the South Bronx didn't go unnoticed by the other cops in his squad. Ignoring their jibes, he'd bring in the sick, the lame, and the injured, and she'd whisper in his ear, "What have you got tonight, Junebug?"

One year later they were married. Brian had wanted to invite Junebug Jenkins to the wedding, but he was doing a fifteen to twenty in Attica and was, regrettably, unavailable.

Brian looked over her shoulder toward the stove. "Anything to eat?"

"We already ate. I was expecting you hours ago."

"Yeah, I'm sorry. Something came up, and by the time I left, I got caught in a world-class traffic jam on Delancey Street." He opened the refrigerator and peered inside. "Took almost an hour just to get to the Williamsburg Bridge. I thought the damn thing had finally fallen into the river."

She pushed him away from the refrigerator. "Get away before you break something. I have some sauce left over. Want me to make you some spaghetti?"

"Yours or make-believe?"

"Mine, of course. Since when have I ever served you tomato sauce from a can?"

"Never, my love," he said, grabbing her from behind. "I don't understand how an Irish girl learned to make such terrific Italian food."

"Did you marry me for my sauce?"

"Nope." He slipped his hands up and over her breasts and gave her a playful squeeze. "I married you for these."

She smacked his hand. "Stop it. Not in the kitchen. Do you want the spaghetti or not?"

"Okay." He sat down at the kitchen table and flipped through *Newsday*. "Where's Kathy?"

"I thought this headquarters assignment meant you'd be home on time for dinner every night."

"Something always comes up and—"

"You mean you always look for something to come up. My husband, ace detective, can't even relax with a cushy job."

"Cushy job my ass. I'm drowning in a sea of paper, and guess what I've discovered so far? Crime in New York City is increasing. Surprise, surprise."

Eileen set a place in front of him. "I'm impressed. Maybe you should retire and become a crime consultant."

"Yeah, I could charge a thousand bucks a day to tell them crime is on the rise. What a crock."

"Speaking of retirement—"

"Please, Eileen, not again. I don't want to talk about it now."

"You never want to talk about it." She stirred the congealed sauce and in a softer voice said, "It's time, Brian. You said you'd retire when you got your time."

"Let's not get into that again."

Before she could respond, Kathy came barging into the kitchen. "Hi, guys."

Brian looked up from the paper at his daughter. Her face, under all that teased hair, was a carbon copy of Eileen's when his wife was younger. At seventeen Kathy had reached that twilight age that drove parents to distraction. One minute she was a little girl padding around the house in an old bathrobe and enormous, furry bear-feet slippers; the next minute she was dressed like someone twice her age and begging her mother for the loan of her best pearls.

She gave her father a peck on the cheek, and her overpowering perfume made him sneeze.

"Daddy, I think I'm going to sing the solo at the Christmas concert. Mr. Dutton says it's between Marie Rubino and me, but I think Mr. Dutton likes me better." The sunny smile faded. "Dad," she said sternly, "you have *got* to come to this concert. Okay? Promise?"

"Okay, okay. I promise."

"Good. Gotta go, gang. Melissa and I are going to the mall."

"Dressed like that?" Brian eyed her mini. The skirt was at least five inches too short.

"Oh, Daddy. You're so old-fashioned. You think anyone who wears a skirt above the knees is a hooker."

"Hooker?" Brian looked at Eileen. "Where does she get that language from?"

"You," Eileen said. "Every time you see a girl in a short skirt you say she looks like a hooker."

"Well, they do. You're only going to the mall. Why do you have to dress like that?"

Kathy rolled her eyes. "Last year you were complaining because I was always in jeans. Face it, Dad. I'm growing up."

"Well how about growing up one year at a time? You just went from seventeen to twenty-five."

"You don't like it because it makes you feel old. Gotta run. 'Bye."

Brian unfolded his newspaper and propped it against the salt and pepper shakers. "Does she have a boyfriend?"

"Sort of. That boy Tommy."

"Is that the skinny one with acne or the one with the thirty-inch neck?"

"Tommy's on the football team and he doesn't have a thirty-inch neck."

"He looks like he should be playing for the Dallas Cowboys. He must eat a side of beef a day. Don't ever invite him to dinner."

"You're just jealous, Brian. Your little girl is growing up and she's interested in the opposite sex. You're just feeling old."

"Oh, yeah? What about you, 'Wendy'? I don't care what Peter Pan told you, you're getting old too."

Eileen's smile faded. "I know."

Brian was engrossed in the headline story about a homicide in Huntington and didn't notice Eileen had become quiet. Finally, he became aware of the silence and looked up. "What's up, hon?"

She stirred the sauce furiously. "You come waltzing in here at eight-thirty; you don't call . . . I feel like I'm running a hotel. You come and go while I stay home and cook and take care of the house. Boy, am I lucky." She started to cry.

Befuddled by her outburst, Brian went to her, but she pulled away. "Brian, it seems like yesterday we were a couple of kids with a brand-new baby. And now? I don't know. I feel so . . . useless."

"You're not useless, honey. You make a great tomato sauce. I always—"

She threw the wooden spoon in the sink and rushed out of the kitchen in tears.

Brian realized his stupid attempt at humor had backfired. He knew getting home in time for dinner was a sore point with her. After all these years, she still couldn't accept the fact that a cop's job was not a nine-to-five proposition. . . . Well, that wasn't exactly true. Most of the cops in headquarters worked an eight-hour day to the minute. At quitting time they put away their little pile of papers, locked up their staplers, and filed out of the building like a bunch of robots. But that wasn't his style.

He turned off the fire under the sauce—he wasn't hungry anymore—and rummaged in the refrigerator among the diet sodas and leftovers, looking for a beer. Finding none, he went to the cabinet under the sink and took out his special bottle of Black Bush. He poured a generous amount of the aged Irish whiskey into a Ronald McDonald glass and sat down at the kitchen table. Except for the muffled sound of the TV coming from the bedroom upstairs, the house was silent. For a long time he sat there absentmindedly running his finger around the smooth rim of the glass.

He made a decent living; his family was healthy. Still, something was wrong. Since their marriage twenty-one years ago, he and Eileen had had their share of arguments, but lately the arguments were getting more frequent. They'd developed an uneasy, fragile truce that could be broken by a careless word, a look, or a neglected telephone call.

All those TV sitcoms he grew up with were never like this. Harriet never stormed out of the kitchen on Ozzie. Robert Young never sat in his kitchen drinking whiskey alone. If he resembled any TV father, it was William Bendix's Riley, the guy who made a mess of everything.

Shuddering, he stood up and carried his drink into the den. He flipped on the TV and sank into his old reclining chair. He kicked his shoes off and, with half-closed eyes, watched the Islanders and the Penguins chase the puck up and down the ice. Soon the whiskey was gone and he was snoring softly, bathed in the blue light of the TV screen.

4

CAPTAIN PATRICK STONE CONCENTRATED ON THE FALL OF HIS FOOT-steps as he jogged around the perimeter of the basketball court. The high-pitched squeak-squeak of his sneakers on the smoothly varnished floor echoed in the cavernous Police Academy gym.

Stone glanced at his watch—only twenty-two minutes left to his daily morning run. He wiped the sweat from his forehead and focused on the dull ache in his calves and the tightness in his chest. His entire body sent alarm messages to his brain, but he ignored the signs and continued to run. He had entered into the realm experienced by athletes where pain and discomfort became almost pleasurable, and he felt the inner triumph that came from conquering fatigue. He put his head down and concentrated on the gleaming floor. The effect was hypnotic; the floor passing under him in a dizzy blur gave him the illusion of running very fast—almost like flying. The timer on his watch buzzed; the hour was up.

As he walked around the gym to cool off, Stone reveled in the rush of well-being that flooded over him. Once again he had overcome the physical barrier of pain, and had even run an additional five laps. Always competitive, he instinctively sized up the other policemen working out in the gym. At thirty-one he was in better shape than most of the younger, overweight cops who huffed and puffed their way around a couple of laps. Patrick Stone had nothing but contempt for men who refused to push themselves to the limit. His obsessive need to excel was one of the reasons he was the youngest captain in the department; he'd gone from cop to captain in only four years—a record in the New York City Police Department. He was also the commanding officer of NET—the elite Narcotics Enforcement Team.

Stone stopped to towel off in front of the Universal weight machine, where a muscular young cop was straining to finish his last bench press. "How's the shoulder, Charlie?"

"A lot better, Cap." The cop wiped the sweat from his face with the end of his tee-shirt. "Hey, Cap, I'm thinking of going into clothes. Think it's a good idea?"

"Sure. Plainclothes is a good experience. Just don't forget to keep studying. Remember, it's a boss's job."

"Were you in clothes?"

"No. Two years in a precinct and the rest of my time in Narcotics and NET. That reminds me. Did you hear the one about the two rabbis—"

A rookie dressed in Academy blues approached rapidly and cleared his throat. "Excuse me, Captain Stone, I have a telephone message for you, sir. The Police Commissioner wants to see you right away . . . forthwith, I mean."

Twenty minutes later Stone was ushered into the Police Commissioner's office ahead of a surprised Deputy Commissioner and his three assistants, who'd been waiting in the outer office for thirty minutes.

The P.C. sat behind his desk, engrossed in a report. "Sit down, Captain," he said when Stone walked in, not looking up. "I'll be with you in a minute."

Joseph P. Mara was an outsider whom the mayor had hired away from the Philadelphia Police Department five years ago—much to the dismay and consternation of several NYPD chiefs, who all but had their desk nameplates printed up.

Mara was young and Ivy-League educated—traits that made him an asset to the mayor and a threat to the old guard. What the old chiefs wanted was a team player—someone to perpetuate the status quo; someone to whom they could give the elbow, a wink, and say, "You know how things are? This is the way we've always done it." But to their eternal frustration, Mara didn't know how things were; furthermore, he didn't want to know. Most of his predecessors as P.C. saw the job as a capstone to their careers; Mara saw it as a stepping-stone. The old guard, sensing this, looked upon their commissioner as an unexploded shit bomb who in a careless moment could detonate their own carefully orchestrated careers.

Mara, hoping to force his senior commanders to look at their responsibilities in a fresh light, had immediately issued a policy of strict accountability. In response, the frightened commanders had retreated into a defensive mode and simply issued a flurry of new orders and procedures that did nothing except create obfuscation in the ranks and an illusion of reform. But nothing changed.

Fed up with their entrenched ideas, Mara always attended executive development conferences for probationary captains, where he let it be known that he was looking for people who were innovative and receptive to new ways of doing things. At one such conference, a young, newly promoted captain had stunned his fellow conferees when he said that all officers above the rank of captain should sign a one-year contract stating their goals and objectives. If these objectives were not met, the commander should be made to resign or face demotion. Politically the policy was unworkable, but Mara had enjoyed the look of consternation on the faces of the others in the room. Later, Mara asked his Chief of Personnel who the young captain was.

"Patrick Stone," the chief said dryly. "He marches to a different drummer."

Mara's retort had shocked his Chief of Personnel. "I wish more of my commanders marched to a different drummer. Then maybe we could drag this department out of the nineteenth century."

From the beginning, Patrick Stone had guessed correctly that the commissioner, a new breed of administrator, was looking for fresh ideas and ways to run a department mired in generations of bureaucracy and the status quo.

Stone's high profile, plus the fact that the twenty-nine-year-old captain achieved the highest mark on each of his promotional exams, kept bringing him to the new commissioner's attention. Three months later Stone had been given a "forthwith"—an immediate summons—to the P.C.'s office. "As you know"—Mara tugged at his ear, an unconscious gesture that had already become the butt of jokes among the brass—"from time to time the department selects a candidate for the Criminal Justice fellowship program at Harvard. It's my distinct pleasure to tell you, Captain Stone, that you have been selected for this honor. I've been watching your career with great interest. You're intelligent, innovative, and I believe you have a great future in the department."

Shortly after Stone's return from Harvard, the commissioner summoned departmental brass to a press conference in the cavernous Police Headquarters auditorium. The P.C. had chosen the occasion to announce his response to the shocking increase in drugs and drug-related crime in the city. Bathed in the unnatural glare of the TV lights, Mara stood at the lectern, a dour, lanky man with prematurely white hair. He addressed the audience of high-ranking police officials, but his message was directed toward the assembled press corps crowded below him.

"Today, I am pleased to announce the formation of a new unit. The Narcotics Enforcement Team—or NET, as it will no doubt be known—has been given one mission: to wage all-out war against the drug dealers in this city. NET has a mandate to pursue, arrest, and convict the high-level dealers and suppliers—these purveyors of death—who are killing our children, our city, and who are rending the very fabric of our society.

"The mayor and I are determined to crush this plague on our city, and NET will be in the vanguard of this all-out attack. To command this elite unit I have chosen Captain Patrick Stone, a dedicated police professional with an exemplary record of achievement. Captain Stone, who has just returned from his studies on a year-long fellowship at Harvard, has been given the authority to select personnel for his unit from anywhere in the department. And NET will crush the bloodsuckers who have been bleeding this city dry. Ladies and gentlemen, Captain Patrick Stone!"

As Patrick Stone rose to approach the podium that day eighteen months ago, two rows of chiefs, the shakers and movers of the department, turned their stony gaze on the handsome young upstart. When a superior officer who has been given a new command approaches the podium, it is customary for chiefs who know the man to shake his hand and wish him well. No one reached for Patrick Stone's hand that day.

Promotions, the old guard was convinced, should be a function of loyalty and longevity, certainly not something as esoteric as talent and potential. In his short, iconoclastic career, Patrick Stone's reputation as a loose cannon had earned the enmity of these chiefs—most of whom did not know him personally. And that was only the beginning of the threat Stone posed to the established order and their comfortable way of life.

Characteristically, Stone set about the task of building NET with the single-minded purpose that was the hallmark of everything he did. Most commanding officers in his position would have begun staffing the unit by honoring "contracts," that is, transferring friends and relatives of high-ranking members of the department into his unit. The "contract"—an unwritten tradition in the department—was of course reciprocal. But Patrick Stone, ever the maverick, refused to go along with the program. NET was the first major step in his career, and he was not about to jeopardize the opportunity for the sake of a handful of future favors. Independent and self-sufficient, he needed no one else's help. This had been his creed thus far, and he saw no reason to change now.

The first man Stone selected for NET was Sergeant Tim Hardy, whom he'd known since they'd been in the Narcotics Division together. For the rest of his staffing needs he went to the Personnel Bureau. There, a sergeant, a middle-aged man with a look of terminal boredom from doing the same mundane job for too long, stared up at Stone. "Let me get this straight, Captain. You want a printout of eligibles to draw from for staffing this new unit of yours?" Stone nodded. The sergeant didn't know what to make of it. Most commanding officers used department roster printouts as a *last* resort after the supply of friends and contracts was exhausted. "What kind of people are you looking for?" he asked warily.

Stone tossed a typed sheet on the desk, and the sergeant scanned the brief list of requirements: I.Q. 110 or better, active arrest record, male or female. The sergeant slid the list toward Stone. "This ain't complete. What about time on the job? What's the minimum time on the job you'll accept?"

"It doesn't matter," Stone said, sliding the list back to the sergeant, "as long as they're out of the Police Academy and under sixty-three."

The sergeant, scowling at what he considered to be a flippant response, studied the list again. "What about disciplinary record? Will you take a guy with trial-room convictions, command disciplines?"

"No felony convictions," Stone said with a straight face. "I draw the line there. I don't want any felons in NET."

The sergeant's face reddened. He threw the list into his overflowing in-basket. "This is gonna take some time. With these requirements, you practically got the whole job to choose from."

"Exactly," Stone said, heading for the door. "But I don't have a lot of time. I'll be back in the morning. Have the printout ready, Sarge."

The sergeant started to say something, but remembered his boss's explicit instructions: "Stone is a schmuck, but he's got the P.C.'s ear. Give him whatever he wants. I don't want no grief from the fourteenth floor."

The next day, in his new office in the Midtown South Precinct building, Stone gave Hardy the list of people he wanted to interview and proceeded to drive Hardy crazy with his seeming disregard for standard requirements. After a particularly promising candidate left, Hardy stuck his head in the door. "Pretty good, huh? Should I put in for him?"

Stone shook his head. "No, he's not right for NET."

Then a cop with a poor disciplinary record was interviewed. Again Hardy stuck his head in. "A real zero, right? That guy's been in mental retirement since he got out of the Academy. I'll tell him no good—"

"Put in for him. He's going to work out just fine."

After a few of these exchanges, an exasperated Hardy gave up in disgust.

Patrick Stone was enjoying himself. He had the entire department to choose from, and he was prepared to interview every cop in five boroughs if necessary. Methodically, he quizzed, cajoled, and joked with the interviewees, who hardly realized they were being subjected to a laser-sharp interview. They came in all shapes, sizes, and conditions. "I have only six felonies, Captain," one young cop bemoaned. "But I work in a quiet Queens precinct. There's only about six felonies committed in the whole fucking precinct in a year!" he blurted out. "Oh—excuse me, sir."

"Tim, put in for him."

A twenty-three-year veteran leaned forward, and said to Stone, "Why have I been in a radio car for over twenty years? Because I don't have a hook and I don't want to be a boss. But I'm the best sector car cop in my command."

"Tim, put in for him."

"You're pretty small," Stone said to the young woman sitting opposite him. "Do you think you could go through a door with a shotgun and vest with the big guys?"

"Captain," she answered in a strong voice that belied her slight stature. "I got two older brothers on the job, and I can still beat the shit out of both of them."

"Tim—"

"I know. Put in for her."

Stone studied the muscular cop in front of him. "You've been on the chronic sick list three times in the past five years. What's the matter with you?"

The cop met Stone's level gaze. "I've been jerked around a lot in this job, Captain. I won't bore you with the gory details. But I'll tell you one thing. If you give me a chance to be a cop, I'll never go sick another day again."

Stone closed his folder. "I'll take your word for it. Just remember, if you die, we hold the wake right here. Tim, put in for him."

Finally it was done. After days of selecting, rejecting, and in some cases reinterviewing, it was finished. NET had its full complement of people— one lieutenant, four sergeants, and twenty cops.

Stone, looking satisfied, pushed his chair back and put his feet up on the desk. "Tim, I'm bushed. I feel like Lee Marvin in *The Dirty Dozen*."

Hardy stared glumly at the roster. "Lee Marvin only had one dirty dozen to worry about. You got two."

Stone chuckled. "These people may not be recruitment-poster cops, but they'll do the job. I could have picked the hotshots and the contracts, but what good would it do me? Half of them would sit on their asses waiting for a better detail to come along, and the other half would run to their rabbis every time I yelled at them. Every man and woman I picked owes me loyalty. You watch, Tim. They're going to break their asses for me."

Hardy studied his boss sitting with his feet up on the desk as though he didn't have a care in the world. "I don't get it. Your future in this department depends on the success of NET." He looked at the roster again. "Yet you've picked rookies, oddballs, and castoffs that no one else wants."

"I like living dangerously."

Hardy suddenly smiled, remembering some of Stone's wild exploits when he was still a cop in Narcotics. "You don't have to convince me. I was the guy standing behind you, wringing my hands every time you pulled some crazy stunt."

As Hardy was leaving, Stone called after him. "Hey Tim, how many chiefs' brains can you fit on the head of a pin?"

Hardy grinned. "I don't know."

"All of them," he said and threw his head back and laughed.

Stone's assessment of his recruits was right on target. In the first month of operation he sent only two people back to their commands for lack of performance.

His unorthodox leadership style further earned their respect and allegiance. Instead of directing operations from behind a desk, Stone went out on the streets with his people. He didn't just show up for the arrest; he went on the interminably boring surveillances, the wiretaps in damp, roach-infested basements; he shivered in hallways with them, waiting for a drug bust to go down. Wherever an NET cop was, he could expect to see Captain Patrick Stone there too. The arrests—and the headlines—quickly mounted.

NET got so good, they were beginning to snatch major drug busts from under the noses of the better-equipped and better-financed federal narc units, who promptly called the police commissioner to register their indignant complaints. Publicly, Commissioner Mara commiserated with the feds; privately, he told Stone to keep up the good work.

Now, Mara scrawled his signature on the bottom of the report and tossed it into a basket. "Captain, I received a call this morning from the U.S. Attorney's office," he said grimly. "He wanted to thank me for the splendid assistance you and your men gave them with that drug arrest."

Stone relaxed. The commissioner was referring to the arrest of Cuban Pete the previous night. Usually there was fierce competition between federal, state, and local narc units. Cooperation between them was nonexistent, or minimal at best. Through his many sources, Stone had gotten word that the feds had a fistful of warrants and were frantically running around town trying to find Cuban Pete, the linchpin in a powerful drug-distribution network encompassing three states and Colombia. Thanks to Stone's talent for organization and detail, NET intelligence-gathering sources were able to keep tabs on most of the heavy hitters in the city. Stone knew where Cuban Pete was. The question was: Did he want to share this information with the feds?

After checking with several informants and his sources in the Drug Enforcement Administration, Stone discovered that the case was far beyond

NET's scope and authority. Not one to waste good information, he went to see the supervising agent in charge of the DEA office, a ruddy-faced man from Hastings, Nebraska, named Frank Keller.

"I hear you're looking for Cuban Pete," Stone said.

Keller tried to mask his surprise. That information was supposed to be confidential. Like many federal agents from out of town, Keller had a love/hate relationship with the NYPD. He had a natural distrust of the street-smart, wisecracking, irreverent NYC cops, but at the same time the DEA agent was in awe of their ability to wade through the unbelievable cesspool of the city's drug world. To him, most of these cops were ignorant and crude, but they always miraculously managed to come up with an arrest or the information they needed. It was damned frustrating.

"Why do you ask about Cuban Pete?" Keller replied.

"Because he's in the city," Stone said, "and I know where he is."

Keller, abandoning all attempts to appear disinterested, shot forward in his chair. "Jesus, we thought he'd skipped out of the country! We haven't been able to get a smell of him."

"I can tell you where he is. I'll even give you a couple of my guys to help take him down."

Keller lit a cigar with a wooden match. "What's in it for you? We don't do joint news conferences. This is strictly a federal operation."

Stone laughed. Keller hadn't a prayer of locating Cuban Pete, but his biggest concern was getting upstaged at a press conference. To Stone, and other New York cops, it sometimes seemed the feds got paid by the column inch of news copy. Extra for photos. "No strings," Stone said. "Honest."

Keller leaned back in his chair. Other agents who'd had dealings with the hotshot head of the NYPD's most exclusive unit had nothing but good things to say. Stone was a straight shooter and always delivered as promised. Nevertheless, Keller, his midwestern skepticism firmly in place, was still inclined not to take Stone up on his offer of free information. Then he remembered the U.S. Attorney, Nat Levine—another New Yorker—who was the pain-in-the-ass prosecutor on the case. Levine had been on Keller's back all week about Cuban Pete. Without Pete, Levine reminded Keller about a dozen times a day, there was no case.

Keller snapped his burned match in two and flipped it into his ashtray. "Okay. Where is he?"

At four A.M. the next morning a DEA team, accompanied by two of Stone's men, hauled Cuban Pete out of bed in his sister's Bronx apartment. It went so smoothly they didn't even wake the kids sleeping in the next room. Keller and Levine were ecstatic. Patrick Stone had made two more friends. And Mara's grim tone this morning merely masked his delight at upstaging the feds with another example of NET's superb intelligence network.

"We've been snatching a lot of collars from the DEA," Stone said to the commissioner. "I thought it would be a good idea to give them a hand with this one."

Mara closed the report in front of him and leaned back in his leather chair. "Captain, I assume you know who Nathan Pickett is?"

"Sure. The publicity-hungry state senator from Brooklyn."

"You underestimate him. He's more than a headline hunter. Nathan Pickett has his sights set on the White House, and he just might get there. Unfortunately, he intends to use this city's drug problem to propel him to national prominence."

Now Stone knew why he'd been summoned. He had seen Pickett's interview two nights ago on the six o'clock news. The black senator had ignited a firestorm of criticism by charging that higher-ups in the city's administration were purposely aiding and abetting the drug problem in the city. Without saying it, he implied that the police department was directly involved, citing an order issued by Mara six months before, forbidding uniformed police officers from making street drug arrests. Stone knew Mara's intent had been to keep his cops away from the corrupting influence of the free-flowing drug money, but Pickett had told the pretty-boy journalist who was interviewing him that the order was just one more example of the establishment's disregard for the safety and welfare of inner-city residents.

Pickett's allegations hit the headlines overnight and sent shock waves through the police ranks. Painfully sensitive to outside criticism, the department reacted in predictable fashion. Borough chiefs on down to precinct captains scrambled to issue orders and gather statistics to prove that *they* were tough on drugs. But the dismal statistics released by Pickett sabotaged their efforts; the indisputable fact was that drug use and drug-related crime *were* increasing.

"Pickett is going to head a demonstration in front of this building next week," an unhappy Mara told Stone. "He has a permit for three hundred people."

"This has been a cold November, sir. Can he turn out that many people in this weather?"

"I'm afraid so. But," Mara said, invoking the policeman's universal prayer, "maybe it'll rain."

As Mara was speaking, Patrick Stone had been trying to think of a way to turn the commissioner's discomfort to his own advantage. He'd thought of a solution, but he wasn't sure he wanted to use it. He preferred to present his major arrests as a fait accompli. Too many things could go wrong. But he knew that Mara desperately needed something to derail Pickett. And if all went well, he'd have that something. "Sir," Stone said, "I'm working a case that may result in a tremendous seizure of cocaine."

The P.C. looked cross. "What? Why the hell wasn't I informed sooner?"

"I just received the information myself," Stone lied. "We've had a wiretap on an East New York operation for two weeks. They've been quibbling over price and quantity. This morning they came to an agreement. They're bringing in four hundred and fifty keys."

"How much is that worth?"

"Street price as crack? Over sixty million."

Mara released his breath in a hiss. "Good God. When is this going to happen?"

"I'm not sure. They're still finalizing the delivery arrangements, but it has to be soon. The seller is threatening to call the deal off. My men have already begun to stake out the apartment." Stone could almost hear the wheels turning in Mara's head. He added a note of caution. "Sir, you have to understand that these drug deals can evaporate in an instant. If the bad guys suspect anything, they call it off."

"I understand, Captain, but we'll proceed on the assumption that it will come off. The minute the arrest is made, call Operations. They'll notify me immediately. I'll want to hold a press conference." The commissioner's grim expression finally gave way to a smile. "Pat, I knew you were good when I gave you this job, but you've performed beyond my expectations. I won't forget this."

"Thank you, sir. You'll be hearing from me," Stone said with an assurance he didn't feel.

5

As usual, the noonday traffic on Third Avenue was snarled by spillbacks at every intersection. Brian Shannon, his mind occupied by the mysterious phone call he'd received from DeNoto earlier that morning, weaved around the honking cabs and trucks. DeNoto had been evasive, but it was clear from his tone that the detective had something on his mind that he didn't want to discuss on the telephone. Shannon had made arrangements to meet him at the Automat at Forty-second Street and Third Avenue.

Parking a vehicle in midtown, even a police vehicle, was damn near impossible. Unmarked police vehicles were issued police-identification plates, which authorized parking in certain areas. But there was a long list of restrictions, and a cop who parked in one of these prohibited areas did so at his own peril. If caught, he risked becoming a victim of the dreaded Parking Enforcement tow trucks whose operators took great delight in snapping up errant police cars.

34

Shannon was forced to circle the block three times before he found a suitable illegal parking space. Walking past a row of stores on Third Avenue, he noticed that several had begun to put up Christmas decorations. It was still two weeks till Thanksgiving, but the New York merchants, rushing the seasons as usual, couldn't wait. Taking no chances, one enterprising stationery-store owner displayed a cardboard cutout of Santa Claus riding a turkey.

At one time, cafeteria-style Horn & Hardart Automats were as common as McDonald's. Coffee poured from dolphin-headed spouts, and a handful of nickels could buy you everything from club rolls to baked beans, which were displayed behind rows of gleaming glass-doored compartments. But the Automat, built for another era, was unable to compete with the ubiquitous fast-food restaurants. In the time it took to feed ten nickels into the coffee machine, you could order a cheeseburger, fries, and a Coke at McDonald's and be on your way. The Automat wasn't for people in a hurry. It was for tourists and people with no demanding timetable. All of which made the Automat on Third Avenue a perfect place for Shannon to meet DeNoto, since no self-respecting detective would be caught dead here.

Shannon carried his coffee and club roll to an empty table where he had a clear view of the door. He reached for the sugar and, remembering a favorite childhood prank, automatically tightened the top. When they were kids, he and his friends often loosened the tops of the salt-and-pepper shakers. Then they'd sit at another table and wait for some unsuspecting victim. Eventually the manager caught them and threw them out, but the story about the poor jerk with the mound of salt in his soup would be told and retold for days.

Shannon spotted DeNoto the minute he came through the revolving doors. The aging detective was fleshy around the middle, and his loud sport jacket did nothing to conceal his ample bulk. Like most men with thick necks, DeNoto looked uncomfortable wearing a tie, and his was pulled away from his collar. With hair bushy on the sides and thinning on the top, he reminded Shannon of one of the Three Stooges—was it Larry, Moe, or Curly? Shannon could never remember who was who.

The detective's experienced eye swept the faces at the tables and rested on Shannon. He walked over and sat down. "Been waiting long, Loo?"

"Just got here myself. Want some coffee?"

"Naw, I drink so much of that crap, I got permanent heartburn. Damn, I didn't know there were any of these joints left in the city."

"That's because you guys up in the wilds of Harlem don't get down to the big city very often."

"The wilds is right." DeNoto pulled a stubby cigar from his coat pocket. "I got a caseload would choke a horse."

Ignoring the dagger looks from an old man slurping soup at the next table, the detective lit up and squinted at the lieutenant through the smoke. "We got a mutual friend—Jimmy Conklin."

So DeNoto had been checking up on him with the second whip in the squad, Shannon thought. A typical gambit between two cops who didn't know each other. DeNoto wouldn't have told Conklin why he wanted to talk to him, he would simply have asked if Lieutenant Shannon could be trusted. Was he "okay"—a word that spoke volumes.

"I just spoke to Jimmy the other day," Shannon said. "Told him I'm holding him personally responsible for the squad's clearance rate."

"He told me to tell you he's keeping your in-basket clean."

Shannon put down his coffee. "DeNoto, I'm not a professional head-quarters paper pusher. You can talk. What's up?"

DeNoto hunched over and spoke out of the side of his mouth in a voice so low that Shannon had to lean over the table to hear. "I've been so busy the last couple of days, I just caught up to an old lady I missed on the original canvass." He looked down and prodded a crumpled napkin with his finger.

"And?"

"I dunno, Lieutenant. She's an old broad. Lives across the street from Tiny's building. You know old-timers—not exactly reliable. Well anyway, I asked her the usual bullshit, ya know?" Instinctively, he looked around, avoiding eye contact with Shannon. "Personally, I think she's half blind . . ."

"DeNoto, what did she see?"

The detective looked like a kid caught with his hand in the cookie jar. "She saw two guys go into Leonard's building the night of the murder. One was white." The big detective seemed to sag. "The other was black."

Brian Shannon blinked as though he'd been hit in the face with cold water. "Black and white?"

DeNoto nodded glumly.

They both knew what that meant. The only blacks and whites who traveled together in Harlem were cops.

"There's something else." DeNoto ground out his smelly cigar and spread his beefy hands on the table. "I got this informant . . . he says he's heard there are cops up to their asses in the Harlem drug trade. Loo, he's probably wrong. I'd hate to see a witch-hunt start on the word of a half-blind old lady and a stone junkie. Tiny Leonard was a piece of shit. He deserved to—" The detective stopped. They both knew he was about to suggest it was okay if cops murdered Leonard.

"How good is your C.I.?"

"How good is any junkie? He's had some good information in the past."

"Did you put any of this on paper?"

"You're the only one I told. My boss is on vacation. I know I shoulda called IAD, but . . ." DeNoto finished the sentence with a shrug.

Shannon knew the department procedures too; he should call IAD himself. He should also direct DeNoto to immediately submit a written report to his supervisor of what he'd just told him. If the department found out a superior officer was withholding information in a homicide investigation, Shannon would be flopped from the bureau, and his career—what was left of it—would be finished. But he needed time to think this through.

"DeNoto, listen to me. No DD5 on this. Tell no one, not even your boss. Understand? If this leaks out, you'll be back in uniform so fast it'll make your head spin."

The detective, already feeling miserable, needed no reminding. He'd seen detectives flopped back to the bag for a lot less. "I'm sorry I dropped this on you, but I didn't know what else to do."

"Go back and reinterview everyone on the block. See if you can find anyone else to confirm what you told me."

DeNoto sighed and lit up another cigar. "Okay, but it won't do no good. You know the people up there. They'd piss in my pocket and tell me it's raining. Half of them hate cops and the other half are scared shitless. It was a one-in-a-million finding the old woman. And the junkie? He's so fucked-up he don't even know when he's lying anymore."

"Maybe so, but check it out anyway. I want to know if you come up with anything. Understand? *Anything.*"

SHANNON RUSHED BACK TO THE OFFICE AND CAUGHT UP WITH BENNETT as he was about to eat his lunch. Briefly, he recounted what DeNoto had told him. Treating it like a packet of plastic explosives, the Executive Officer carefully unwrapped his egg salad sandwich. "The department procedures are clear," Bennett said. "We should report DeNoto's information to IAD right away, but in this case I have a problem with that."

"Why?"

"It's common knowledge that someone inside the department is feeding Pickett information. If that damn politician gets wind of this, he'll go straight to the press and blow it all out of proportion. Cops, narcotics, murder—I can just imagine the headlines."

"Aren't you jumping the gun, Chief? A black and white team and junkie gossip hardly make a case."

Bennett rotated the overstuffed sandwich, studying the best way to pick it up without losing any egg salad. "I know that and you know that, but the issue is tailor-made for Pickett. He'll pin us to the wall and we'll be on the defensive right from the get-go. We don't need any more adverse publicity.''

Bennett bit into the sandwich and a large glob of egg salad squirted out the back and cascaded down the front of his sauce-stained tie. It occurred to Shannon that it would be nice if someone invented Velcro bread just for Hugo Bennett.

"Leave it with me," Bennett said. "I want to run this by someone."

Shannon wondered who. The Chief of Detectives was out of town, and Bennett would be flirting with disaster if he made an end run around his boss. Larson would eat him alive.

MARGE WEBSTER, THE SHANNONS' GREGARIOUS NEIGHBOR, HAD everyone laughing as she recounted her hair-raising adventures as a school bus driver. Brian, sitting next to Eileen, squeezed her hand. Since their argument the other night, they'd called an uneasy truce. It had been a long time since they'd had company, and he was enjoying a night at home with friends.

The telephone rang as he was gathering glasses for refills. "It's for you, Dad," Kathy shouted from upstairs. "Someone from the job."

Angered by the intrusion, he stormed into the kitchen and grabbed the phone. "Yeah," he said brusquely.

"I hate to call you this late at night," Hugo Bennett said, "but I just got the call myself." Hugo Bennett's voice was gravelly, with the sound of sleep still in it.

"What's up, Chief?"

"We may have another one of your execution-style murders. I want you to take a look while it's still fresh."

Shannon was caught off guard. "Are you giving me the case?"

"No. The Six-eight has it. But after what you told me this afternoon, I figure your instincts about this are worth checking out. See if there's a connection."

"Where is it?"

"The Belt Parkway. A parking lot just west of the Verrazano Bridge."

"Yeah, I know where it is." He looked at his watch. "I'll be there in about an hour."

"One more thing, Brian. I don't want anyone to know why you're there."

Easier said than done, Brian thought as he hung up. It wasn't SOP for someone from the Chief of Detectives Office to show up at routine homicide scenes. They'd want to know what he was doing there, especially Howie Gabriel, the crafty Six-eight squad commander.

Eileen was standing in the doorway. "Who was that?"

"Bennett. There's a homicide in Brooklyn he wants me to take a look at."

"Why you? You're assigned to headquarters—"

"It's a long story."

"Brian, you can't leave now. We have company."

She was doing it to him again—making him feel guilty about doing his job. He avoided the hurt, accusing eyes. "I'm sorry. I have to go."

Eileen was about to say something when Marty Fedak, who lived next door, came into the kitchen waving an empty glass. "Hey, who do you have to kill to get a drink around here?"

Eileen rushed from the room.

Marty looked sheepish. "Did I say something wrong?"

Brian took his glass. "No. Everything's just fine," he said sourly.

AT THAT HOUR TRAFFIC WAS LIGHT. THE ONLY PROBLEM WAS THE Saturday-night drunks. Luckily they were easy to spot. They either crept along at thirty-five miles an hour with their noses draped over the steering wheel as they tried to decide if they were heading east or west, or they fishtailed at eighty miles an hour, convinced they were driving as straight as a laser beam. The trick was to give them plenty of room. With a little bit of luck they'd kill only themselves and not some poor bastard on his way to work.

Brian flipped on the radio. His favorite recording of *Tristan und Isolde* was just beginning. The erotic piece had a strange effect on him, especially when he was drunk. He turned up the volume and smiled, remembering the night he came home from a retirement racket smashed out of his mind. With the volume turned as high as it would go, he'd roared down the middle of the Long Island Expressway at a hundred miles an hour, singing along with the radio at the top of his lungs. The next morning he couldn't remember getting home, but he remembered the Wagner piece. And *that* was as close to Valhalla as he wanted to get.

As he sped west on the expressway, he thought about the look in Eileen's eyes. With Marty following him around like a puppy dog, he didn't get a chance to explain. But explain what? That he was back into police work because some poor schmuck got himself murdered? If he got involved in an investigation, that damn felony project might be put on hold. He was elated at the thought of shelving the project, even though he knew it would further upset Eileen.

Three years ago Brian and Eileen had entered into the "twenty-year-syndrome" zone experienced by most police officers and their wives.

A cop's wife, living in chronic fear for the safety of her husband, waits patiently for that magical twentieth year when a police officer is eligible for a pension. In order to maintain domestic tranquillity, cops traditionally placate their wives with mumbled promises about retiring. When the time comes, some do retire, but others, like Brian Shannon, who had allowed police work to dominate his life, couldn't cut the ties that easily. It wasn't that he couldn't do something else—he'd gone to school nights for a degree in accounting; Brian Shannon didn't *want* to do anything else.

Almost to the day of his twentieth anniversary in the department, Eileen had started nagging him about getting out of the job. He'd ignored her when he could, or made vague promises, and things quieted down. Then, a newspaper headline or the six o'clock news would sensationalize another cop murder, and it started all over again.

Brian had cut south to the Belt Parkway and driven through Queens and into Brooklyn. Red lights blinked up ahead. He eased off the parkway and pulled into the parking lot.

It was a picturesque spot to be murdered. With its spectacular view of the bridge and Narrows, the parking lot was popular both day and night. During the day it attracted joggers, salesmen with time on their hands, and old-timers with nothing better to do than watch tankers steaming slowly in and out of New York harbor. At night the parking lot attracted a different crowd. The view of the Verrazano with its ribbon of sparkling green-tinted lights spanning the Narrows between Staten Island and Brooklyn made this a favorite spot for lovers, cheaters, and voyeurs.

But no one lingered here tonight. Only radio cars remained, their red dome lights flashing across the gleaming surfaces of a late-model Porsche and the crumpled beer cans and trash that littered the cleared lot.

A footpath led to the water's edge about forty yards west of the parking lot. Shannon's heart sank when he heard Howie Gabriel's raspy voice.

"Hello, Lieutenant," Shannon said, approaching the cluster of men casually standing around a park bench with a magnificent view of the harbor. "How's business?"

"Brian Shannon! How the hell are you?" Gabriel, a broad-shouldered man in his late fifties, had the expectant look of someone perpetually hearing the punch line of a very funny joke. "What are you doing here?" The squad commander peered over Shannon's shoulder. "Got a bimbo in the car or what?"

"You're a dirty old man, Howie. Bennett gave me a call and invited me down to take a look at a real body. It's been a while since I've seen one. Gotta keep in practice."

Howie's big, uneven teeth gleamed in the darkness. "That's true. Being assigned to headquarters, you get to see plenty of stiffs but no dead bodies.

A squad commander should keep in touch—you'll excuse the pun. You wanna touch the body? Be my guest.''

"Why? So I can get my prints on everything, like you and your fumbling squad?"

Howie clutched his chest in mock horror. "My men get fingerprints on evidence? Impossible! I had all their fingerprints burned off with acid." The smile faded. "Why did Bennett send you, Brian?"

Shannon tried to look the long-suffering victim. "It's that goddamn felony project. Bennett wants me to show up at some homicides to find out if you hotshot squad commanders have any suggestions for the new sixty-one they're working on."

"I got a suggestion, but you and Baby Huey won't like it."

"Howie, don't break my chops. You think I like spending my Saturday night with you?"

"So Bennett sent you out to hold my hand. You shoulda brought him along. We coulda had a fucking DEA picnic. Naw, maybe it's just as well Bennett didn't come, he'd probably fall in the water."

One of the detectives pulled his collar up against the chill November wind. "This stiff's better dressed than Baby Huey, maybe we can strip him and send the clothes to Bennett." Gabriel guffawed.

"You guys oughta be on TV. Howie, do you think we can talk business? What've you got?"

The thirty-two-year veteran lit a cigar. He leaned against the railing and squinted at Shannon through the smoke. As the commanding officer of the squad investigating the homicide, he was not accustomed to sharing case information with another lieutenant from headquarters. Every instinct Gabriel had was hollering that Shannon was lying about his reason for being here.

"The ID in the wallet says he was Thomas Rowe, attorney. Gotta be worth a few bucks. He lived in Brooklyn Heights, and the shiny new Porsche in the lot back there belonged to him. He was found about twelve-thirty by a strolling couple." Howie flipped his spent match into the black water below. "They actually sat down next to the stiff. Took 'em a while to realize he was dead. I guess their first clue was the fact that he had three eyes. People are brain dead in this city, ya know? Must be all that fucking AIDS running around. We interviewed a parking lot full of people who all swear on their mothers' graves that they saw zilch. 'Course, there's not a whole lot to see when she's lying on her back with her feet on the ceiling and he's resting his ass on the steering wheel. . . . I must be getting old. I can't even imagine getting laid in the backseat of a car. My fucking back goes out if I sneeze the wrong way. Anyway, we'll talk to them again tomorrow."

Shannon was growing weary of Gabriel's vaudeville act, and a world-class headache—brought on by the combination of the few drinks he'd had earlier and the late hour—was forming behind his left eye. "Howie, do you think I could see the body before someone steals it?"

The bench was cordoned off with strands of bright yellow crime-scene tape. In the darkness Rowe looked like a drunk sleeping it off. It was only when Shannon looked closely that he saw the jagged stream of dried blood that ran from a small hole in the center of Rowe's forehead to the edge of his chin. The attorney was wearing an expensive jogging suit and a two-hundred-dollar pair of sneakers. A Rolex and a diamond pinky ring gleamed when the spiraling lights of the gumdrops on the police cars caught them. It wasn't a robbery.

Rowe's vacant eyes stared toward Staten Island. Shannon leaned close and peered into them. The eyes registered no fear, no surprise. The face was an enigma.

Like most cops, Shannon tried to read a victim's face. After all, the victim was his own best witness. The last thing he saw was his murderer. What had Rowe been thinking at the moment of death? Did he know he was going to die? Did he know the person who killed him? Shannon straightened up. It was no use. The lifeless eyes revealed nothing. One thing he did notice: there had been no struggle.

He walked along the path with Gabriel. "What do you think?"

"Probably a botched robbery. It doesn't look like anything's missing. I guess the perp was scared off before he could lift anything."

Shannon turned and looked toward the parking lot. "No one saw or heard anything? Someone should have heard a shot."

"I didn't say no one heard anything," Gabriel snapped. "I said no one admits to hearing anything. From this distance the whole fucking parking lot shoulda heard the shot. Besides, for all I know it might have been an amphibious attack." He jerked his thumb toward the seawall. "Maybe that French guy, what's his name—Cousteau?—came out of the water in a scuba outfit and popped the bastard. Hey, Reilly," he yelled to a detective standing nearby, "remind me to check Rowe's background. Maybe the son of a bitch was poaching seals in Brooklyn!" He turned to Shannon. "What do you think, Lieutenant Shannon, sir?"

In spite of the toothy grin, the hostility in the big lieutenant's tone told Shannon it was time to go. "Up yours, Gabriel," he said amiably, starting toward the parking lot.

Gabriel's smile vanished. "Don't pull my chain, Brian. What are you doing here? You're supposed to be crunching numbers in the Puzzle Palace, not helping old salts like me solve murders."

This was what Shannon had been afraid of. Bennett should have known better than to send him out snooping at a homicide scene. You couldn't bullshit an old-timer like Howie Gabriel.

"You're too suspicious, Howie. There's nothing more to it than I already told you." He turned, feeling Gabriel's eyes boring into his back.

"Hey, Howie," Shannon called over his shoulder, "maybe you're right. I'm gonna recommend to Bennett that this case be turned over to the Harbor Unit."

He could still hear Howie Gabriel's booming laughter as he drove out of the parking lot.

When he arrived home at two-thirty, the guests were gone and the darkened house smelled of alcohol and stale tobacco. Eileen was asleep.

6

Chief Bennett's voice on the telephone was formal. "Lieutenant Shannon, could you step into my office for a moment?"

That wasn't like Bennett. Most mornings he came into Shannon's office
to shoot the breeze and talk about the old days. Things were so much
simpler then—no IAD, no computers, no 911, and no Civilian Complaint
Review Board. Progress, Shannon thought ruefully, was not exactly welcome in the New York City Police Department.

"Oh, Brian, come in. I'd like you to meet Lieutenant Rose."

Rose stood up and shook Shannon's hand firmly. Shannon judged him to
be in his early thirties, six-foot-two. He had the lean look of an athlete.
Looking at the man, impeccably dressed in a gray suit with a perfect knot in
his expensive silk tie, Shannon felt uncomfortably seedy in his nondescript
sport jacket and baggy slacks. He took an instant dislike to this new
lieutenant.

44

Bennett was looking more uncomfortable by the minute. "Yes. Well, Brian," he began, "since the Rowe murder last night, there have been some discussions regarding the handling of these homicides. I, that is, we . . ." Bennett cleared his throat and started again. "You're going to investigate these homicides on a confidential basis—sort of a parallel investigation to the squad's—and Alex Rose here is going to be working with you."

"Chief, I appreciate the offer of help, but I don't need another lieutenant. I could use—"

"Brian"—Bennett brushed an imaginary speck of dust from his stained lapel—"I don't think you understand. I mean, Lieutenant Rose has already been assigned."

About to protest further, Shannon thought better of it. Obviously the chief had a bug up his ass, and this was not the time to start an argument. At least, he thought gratefully, he wouldn't have to work on the felony project for a while. He studied Rose. Judging by the way he was dressed, he was probably a hotshot from one of the specialized squads. "Where you from, Rose? Major Case? Joint Task Force?"

"Neither. I'm from IAD."

Shannon's heart sank.

Five minutes later a puzzled Velez watched Shannon storming up and down the cramped confines of the tiny office. "Goddamn IAD snooping son of a bitch! Why me? Why do I have to be teamed up with a dirt bag from Internal Affairs! Jesus H. Christ!"

"What happened, Loo? Where did this guy come from?"

"Who knows? Bennett talked to someone upstairs about the witness and the C.I., and then there was the Rowe murder last night. Now all of a sudden it's an IAD investigation."

Velez was puzzled. "Well, if IAD has it, why don't they take the whole investigation like they usually do?"

"Beats the shit out of me." Shannon slumped into a chair. He was so mad it took three matches to light his cigarette. "All I can get out of Bennett is that someone upstairs—I don't even know who—wants this handled quietly. Apparently I can't be trusted, so they've assigned me my own personal IAD snoop." He cradled his head in his hands. "I don't fucking believe this."

Velez felt as badly as Shannon but for a different reason. How was he going to come to work late and leave early with an IAD lieutenant right in the same office? *Maricón!*

"Hey Loo," he said weakly, "do you think you could get me transferred back to the Four-four now?"

Shannon shot him a murderous look.

"Just kidding, just kidding."

But he wasn't, and they both knew it. To most cops the Internal Affairs

Division, a unit whose sole purpose was to investigate the corrupt conduct of other cops, was poison. The headhunters—or scumbags, as they were called in the vernacular—had been accused of every heinous deed from betraying Jesus to selling atomic secrets to the Russians. It was universally understood that the best way for a cop to protect himself from IAD was to stay as far away from the headhunters as possible. And now they were going to have an IAD lieutenant in the same office with them. Velez began to feel genuinely depressed.

Late in the afternoon, after Velez had gone home, Alex Rose showed up carrying a cardboard box under his arm.

"Hi, Brian. I just brought a couple of things with me. Which desk should I take?"

Shannon eyed the box, wondering what mysterious IAD equipment it contained; probably thumb cuffs and miniature tape recorders. "Take that one," he said, pointing to a desk piled high with reports, and buried his head in a sixty-one.

Rose looked around the cramped room. Like most offices in One Police Plaza, it was decorated with metal desks that had been purchased early in the Lindsay administration and file cabinets that hadn't been locked in fifteen years. A bewildering collection of charts and graphs were haphazardly taped to the scarred walls, except for the area next to Shannon's desk. That wall was reserved for torn and faded department orders with telephone numbers scribbled around the margins.

Rose cleared a place and sat down. He looked inside each of his desk drawers, threw out a tea bag he found stuffed in one of them, then silently contemplated the room and the view from the thirteenth-floor window for ten minutes. Finally he glanced at his watch and cleared his throat.

"There's something you should know about me."

Shannon put down the sixty-one he had been pretending to read and eyed him warily. "Yeah, what's that?"

"I'm psychic."

"What?"

"Psychic. You know, I can read other people's minds. Not all the time of course, just when conditions are right."

"No one reads minds."

"I can. I'll give you a demonstration. I'll read yours." Rose leaned farther back; his eyes closed. "I'm getting it. It's starting to come in clearly. Oh, yes, it's very clear now. You're thinking that I'm a no-good scumbag from IAD who couldn't find his ass with both hands in his back pocket, and if I don't manage to lock you up for some petty violation of department procedure, at the very least I'll tarnish your reputation for the rest of your career." He opened his eyes and sat forward. "How'd I do?"

Shannon grunted. "Pretty close, but no cigar. I never thought about you locking me up."

Rose was suddenly serious. "Listen, we don't have to be foxhole buddies, but if we're going to work on this case together, we should try to get along. What do you say?" He put out his hand. "The name is Alex."

Shannon nodded, then shook his hand. "All right, Rose. Let's see what happens."

PATRICK STONE, ON HIS WAY TO A CONFERENCE AT THE LEGAL DI-vision office, stopped outside One Police Plaza to watch Senator Pickett's demonstration.

Chanting demonstrators shuffled around the interior of a rectangle of blue barriers set up on the promenade. The P.C.'s prayer hadn't been answered—it was a chilly but crystal-clear morning. To Stone's practiced eye it was clearly a well-organized demonstration. Section leaders with bullhorns led the chanting, shouting, "More cops, less drugs!" while the marchers, about three hundred strong, waved a variety of professionally printed signs. To stay warm, demonstrators took turns huddling around a fire burning in a fifty-five-gallon drum. Such creature comforts were denied the usual demonstrations, but the cops looking on ignored this transgression. An unusual number of high-ranking members of the department were in evidence. Apparently, extra brass had been assigned to keep the uniformed cops on duty in line. The last thing the department needed was a confrontation.

Stone scanned the crowd and saw Senator Nathan Pickett's tall figure surrounded by TV cameras and reporters. At forty-eight, Nathan Pickett still exuded the fluid grace of a superb athlete. An all-American basketball player at Temple, he could have had a successful career in the NBA. Instead, he chose to go into politics.

Since Pickett had been elected to the State Senate two years before, he'd been in the media spotlight almost daily. Championing minority causes with determination, with a voice that would have carried well from a pulpit, he acted like a man who was running for higher office.

His outspoken opinions on minority issues had made him a constant thorn in the side of Mayor Kessel's administration. Housing, Hospitals, and the Board of Education were but a few of the agencies that had experienced the uncomfortable scrutiny of the ambitious young senator's attention. Lately, however, it was the police department's turn, and Pickett clearly had Commissioner Mara reeling. He seized upon every issue—an alleged wrong-ful death, a stabbing on the subway, or a mishandling of an emotionally disturbed person—to savagely attack the department. But unlike some blus-tering demagogues who were little more than con men using political issues for their own personal gain, Pickett had facts at his disposal and could talk intelligently and persuasively on the issues that had brought the country's most powerful city to its knees. Underlying the pyrotechnics and histrionics of his speeches, there was always a real problem. His power base in the city had become so strong that he could call for a demonstration and within hours have hundreds appear. To add to the P.C.'s misery, there were persistent rumors that the senator was obtaining his devastatingly accurate information from someone inside the police department.

Curious to hear what Pickett had to say, Stone moved closer as the lights flashed on. The TV screen was kind to Pickett, but in person, under the harsh lights, he looked more his age. Nevertheless, he was a handsome man, with a neatly trimmed mustache and a smile that revealed even white teeth, and he radiated a magnetism that always attracted a crowd. Even cops on their way into One Police Plaza stopped and stood self-consciously on the fringe of the crowd to listen to what the man who castigated them daily in the media had to say. His resonant voice, which he used with great effect, was tailor-made for television press conferences.

A reporter, yelling to be heard over chanting demonstrators, asked, "Senator Pickett, do you think the Police Commissioner will rescind his order forbidding uniformed police officers from arresting drug dealers?"

"I don't see how he can do anything else and still claim to uphold the oath of his office." Pickett's easy, unhurried manner made it clear he was comfortable with the press. "The Police Commissioner has sworn to protect all the people, and that includes the poor in the inner city. But his do-nothing order repudiates that oath. It's absolutely ludicrous when drug dealers can conduct business in the street in full view of a police officer who has orders not to do his duty. The police department's refusal to stanch the flow of drugs into our inner-city communities is nothing short of genocide."

A pretty reporter with long blond hair pressed forward. "Senator, you have hinted that certain city officials are directly implicated in the drug trade. Will you now, or at some time in the future, name names?"

Pickett smiled grimly. "Linda, as you ladies and gentlemen of the press know, I've petitioned the governor to form a fact-finding commission to study the drug problem in this city. He has graciously consented, and the commission will begin hearings in the beginning of January, with me as chairman. Unlike the sham committees Barry Kessel is fond of forming, *this* commission will get to the heart of the drug problem. I assure you we will name names and point fingers. Our goal is to make New York a drug-free city. In the meantime, we're here to demand that Police Commissioner Mara withdraw his ridiculous do-nothing order and get back to protecting the people of this city."

A voice hissed in Stone's ear: "How'd you like to bust *that* nigger?"

Stone turned. It took him a second to recognize John Gannon, a class-mate from the Police Academy days, in the beefy, bearded man in a torn parka. Stone wanted to stay and hear what Pickett had to say but, masking his annoyance, he took Gannon by the arm and led him away from the crowd.

"Johnny, where are you now?"

"Narcotics. Been there for two years."

Stone hadn't seen Gannon since the Academy ten years ago, but he remembered him as being much thinner. Apparently Gannon, like many cops, spent too much time in gin mills, and it showed in the jowls and the gut. "Are you a boss yet?" Stone asked.

"Are you kidding? I'm still trying to pass the fucking sergeant's exam."

"What's holding you up?"

"Pat, we're not all brains like you. I always figured you were playing with yourself when you said you'd make captain before ten."

"I don't kid around about something like that, John. My career is right on schedule."

"If you don't get assassinated first."

"By who?"

"My boss, Chief Abbott, for one."

"I know of him, but I never met the man."

"Yeah, well he knows you. Christ, Pat, how do you think the C.O. of the Narcotics Division feels when you and your little band of merry men scoff up truckloads of narcotics while we run around with our fingers up our asses?"

"It's not that bad."

Gannon's eyes wandered to the demonstrators, who were now chanting: "Mara must go!"

"So maybe I'm exaggerating a little. We make some good collars, but nothing like you guys. You've made some humongous seizures. Where the fuck do you get your information?"

Stone watched Pickett fielding a battery of questions from the press. The politician's touch with the media was almost magical; he clearly had the designer-clad and manicured media eating out of his hand.

"We get our info the old-fashioned way, Johnny. We go out and look for it. By the way, what exactly does Abbott say about me?"

Gannon grinned and tugged his knitted cap over his ears. "You haven't changed. You always wanted to be the center of attention, even if it's the center of a dart board."

"Hey, I gotta know what my fan club is saying."

Gannon lowered his voice. "Abbott's been putting pressure on the districts to make more collars. He says you're making the Narcotics Division look bad."

"Then why doesn't the hump get off his fat ass and go out into the street like I do?"

"*That's* what drives him nuts! You should hear him. 'Stone's a commanding officer.' " Gannon's imitation of the raspy voice of Deputy Chief Abbott was superb. " 'He should act like an administrator and not like a goddamn rookie looking to get into the bureau.' "

Stone's smile was thin. "That's funny. Abbott's giving me advice and *he's* about to get flopped."

"No shit! We've been hearing rumors that Abbott was getting transferred. So it's true?"

"Yeah, but that's between you and me, Johnny."

"Sure, sure. Damn, now you're really going to be on Abbott's shit list. He'll blame you for the transfer."

"I don't give a fuck what Abbott thinks. Besides"—Stone nodded toward Pickett—"*he's* the one who's going to cause heads to roll. The P.C. is leaning on the borough commanders to get the crime stats down, but they can't. I'm the only boss doing anything around here, and the P.C. knows it."

Gannon regarded Stone in awe. "You got that right. A lot of guys in Narcotics would like to transfer into NET."

Stone shrugged. "The problem with Narcotics is that it's too unwieldy. Too many layers of bosses. By the time you get everyone's approval to make an arrest, the opportunity is gone. Do you know the P.C. wanted a hundred men in NET, but I talked him out of it? I told him I could do the job with twenty-five, and I was right. Now Mara thinks I'm the greatest thing since the microwave oven."

A cheer went up from the demonstrators and both men turned. Pickett, having finished his press conference, waved to the crowd as he headed toward the building entrance surrounded by aides.

"I heard him say he had a meeting with Mara," Stone said.

"Mara's a limp dick, but I wouldn't wish Pickett on my worst enemy."

Stone studied the senator's retreating figure intently. "Every cloud has a silver lining," he said softly. "Nathan Pickett is going to get me promoted."

Gannon's eyebrows went up. "How do you figure that?"

"He's putting a blowtorch to the P.C.'s ass, and I'm the only one around here with a fire extinguisher."

The beefy cop chuckled. "You're something else. Who else could use a cop baiter as a hook? Oh, shit. I'm late. Hey, take care, Pat."

Stone went on to his own appointment, a tedious meeting at the Legal Division, where the department lawyers—predictably—wrung their hands over some of NET's questionable warrant applications. The meeting ended with the red-faced Director of the Legal Bureau predicting massive lawsuits if Stone didn't curb his people.

In the hallway Stone pressed the down button. The elevator doors opened and he came face-to-face with Nathan Pickett. The senator smiled.

"Captain Stone, the commissioner and I were just talking about you."
Seeing the look on Stone's face, he added, "Are you surprised that I know
who you are? You shouldn't be." He pulled the startled captain into the
elevator just as the doors closed. "After all, you seem to be the only
policeman in New York City capable of arresting drug dealers."

Aware that the other passengers, mostly cops, were hanging on every
word, Stone smiled and shrugged. "Thanks for the compliment, Senator,
but that isn't true. The whole department wants what you want: a safe,
drug-free city."

Pickett threw back his handsome head and laughed. "Captain, you're in
the wrong business. With a line like that, you should be in politics. You're
much too modest. I just told your boss that if he had a hundred more
commanders like you, there would be no need for me to demonstrate in front
of his building."

Stone was uncomfortable with the way the conversation was going. On
one hand, he was pleased to be singled out for praise by Pickett, but on the
other, such attention was exceedingly dangerous. Notoriety made him an
easier target for disgruntled brass like Abbott. Even the P.C. might not take
kindly to having Stone's name thrown in his face by someone like Nathan
Pickett. Stone knew the value of a high profile, but only on his own terms.

"In spite of what you've heard," Stone said, "we're all doing the best
we can."

Pickett's smile faded. "I'm afraid the NYPD's best is not good enough.
The department is riddled with incompetence. You seem to be the one bright
shining light."

Stone, looking up into Pickett's face, wasn't certain if the senator was
serious. Mercifully, before Pickett could say anything else, the doors opened
and they were separated by the flow of people getting on and off the
elevator.

7

SHANNON ARRIVED AT THE OFFICE EARLY AND WAS SURPRISED TO see the IAD lieutenant, decked out in a well-tailored blue blazer and gray slacks with razor-sharp creases, already behind his desk. He'd half hoped that he'd come in this morning and find that Rose wasn't here—that somehow Bennett's announcement yesterday had all been a big mistake.

Shannon managed to stay out of the office for most of the first hour. When he came back, Rose, eyeing the computer, said, "Do you play that?"

"No. Luis Velez. He works eight to four . . ."

As soon as he said it, he realized he'd made a mistake. Involuntarily, he glanced at the wall clock. Twenty-five after eight. Goddamn him! He'd told him to be on time this morning. "We were working on a felony-trends project when I came across these murders with the same M.O. They seemed related, so . . ."

Rose waved a yellow legal pad in the air. "I've made a few notes about how we should proceed with this thing. I think—"

"Hold it, Rose. Let's get something straight. I'm in charge of this investigation."

Rose tossed the pad on the desk and nodded. "Okay. I just made a list of things we should do first, that's all."

Before the discussion could escalate into a heated argument, Velez mercifully came barging in. "Oh boss, she did it again! That foxy bitch—" He froze.

Shannon cleared his throat. "Velez, this is Lieutenant Rose. He'll be working with us for a while."

Velez smiled weakly at the tall lieutenant. "Hi, Loo. Nice to meet you."

Rose returned the smile; his eyes flickered toward the wall clock. "Nice to meet you, Velez. You're thirty minutes late."

For a moment there was a stunned silence. Then Rose began to laugh. He slapped the speechless Velez on the back. "Had you going for a minute there, didn't I? Have a seat. Lieutenant Shannon is about to tell us how to proceed with this investigation."

A dull headache began to form in Shannon's temple. Still, he decided to ignore the sarcasm. He sat down and pulled his notes toward him irritably. "Let's look at what we have. There are three homicides. First, the art dealer, Nelson Marbridge—no motive. Then there's Leonard. Motive? Possibly—*probably*—drugs. And finally, there's Rowe. Again no motive. The only common thread between the three is the M.O.—shot execution style. There's one questionable witness, and a junkie who says cops are involved in the Harlem drug trade. It's not much. So where do we go from here?"

Rose began to read from his list. "We reinterview the old lady and the junkie. Then—"

"For Chrissake," Shannon snapped. "I wasn't finished."

Trying to keep a straight face, Velez said, "Lieutenant Rose, I think that was a rhetorical question."

Rose leaned back and folded his arms. His green eyes studied Shannon amicably. "Okay, tell us. What do we do?"

Shannon flipped a page of notes. "We'll reinterview the old lady and the junkie." He realized he was repeating Rose, and quickly added, "But there's a lot more. For instance, Rose, you could check with IAD to see if they have an investigation involving cops and drugs in Harlem."

"No."

"No what?"

"No, there's no investigation."

"How do you know that?"

"I already checked."

Velez thumped the desk. "All right, Loo! You must have been working overtime." His broad smile vanished when he saw the withering look he was getting from his boss.

Shannon, holding his temper, continued. "We'll have to collect all the paper on these homicides. Velez, you can start with that. But first run a background check on Rowe. Rose, why don't you go up to the Marbridge Gallery and take a look around. I'm going uptown to reinterview DeNoto's witness tonight."

Clearly Shannon was planning to keep himself and Rose as far apart as possible. "It's okay by me," Rose said. "If you don't mind going up to Harlem alone, I'll risk a Madison Avenue art gallery."

Later, as Rose was dusting off a picture of a smiling brunette which he had pulled from his cardboard box, Velez looked over his shoulder and said, "That your wife, Loo? She's a very pretty lady."

"She's not really my wife." Rose neatly aligned the photo on his desk. "Cops in IAD don't have any real family, so the department issues us albums of fictitious family members. I have a whole collection of photos— aunts, uncles, grandparents—you name it. It makes us seem like real people."

Velez didn't know what to say, so he smiled weakly and turned back to his computer.

The telephone rang. Velez grabbed for it, listened for a moment and hung up. "That was Bennett. Larson's back and you two are wanted in his office forthwith."

The Chief of Detectives, who'd been at a law-enforcement seminar in Washington, had returned just that morning. Bennett had briefed him on events, and the chief's first comment was vintage Larson: "How the fuck did an IAD scumbag get into my bureau?"

Bennett, Shannon, and Rose filed into Larson's office with a guilty silence worthy of three truants going to see the principal. Bennett and Shannon sat on the couch, while Rose sat on a chair, apart from them. With a commanding view of lower Manhattan, Larson's office was large by department standards. Sitting behind his shiny oak desk, bracketed by the American flag on one side and the flag of New York City on the other, Timothy J. Larson looked more like a bank president than the Chief of Detectives of the nation's largest police force. On the wall behind him were the obligatory photographs of the Police Commissioner and the First Deputy Commissioner. On another wall was a staggering collection of photos showing the Chief of Detectives shaking hands with a wide assortment of people from the Boy Scout of the Month to three presidents of the United States.

The chief's desk showed no sign that it was the workplace of a busy executive responsible for more than two thousand detectives. The leather-handled letter opener was lined up parallel to the desk blotter, and the marble pen and pencil set inlaid with a row of miniature police shields—symbolizing Larson's meteoric rise from policeman to Chief of Detectives—was flanked by a set of empty in and out boxes. His desk blotter, unlike the cheap department issue, was made of expensive leather and gold trim.

"All right," Larson said brusquely, glancing pointedly at his watch, "who wants to tell me what the fuck is going on around here?"

Bennett realized he would have to speak first. "Well, Chief, you were out of town when Lieutenant Shannon here uncovered what he feels could be a pattern to these murders. Brian, why don't you summarize for the chief what you have so far?"

Larson's pale face colored slightly.

"I don't need a summary, for Chrissake, Hugo. You gave me that already. What I want to know is why you think these homicides are related and why you figure cops are involved?" His eyes bored into Shannon as though he were solely responsible for the murders.

Larson knew very few of the men who worked for him. Although Shannon had been working within spitting distance for five weeks, he had barely seen the man except for a couple of times as the Chief of Detectives hurried out on his way to lunch with an influential politician. Shannon knew Larson only by reputation—which was that he was a vicious son of a bitch, especially when crossed.

Shannon cleared his throat. His instinct told him that the homicides were related, but he was far from convinced cops were behind them. "Chief, we have a witness who saw two men—a black and a white—going into Leonard's building the night of the murder. Then there's a junkie who swears that cops are involved in drugs in Harlem. The three murders all have the same M.O."

Larson glared. "That's it?"

"We're just getting started. Before we came in here I told—"

"You got shit." Larson looked at Shannon as though he'd just announced the Russians were in Newark. "What the fuck is the matter with you? Where's the hard evidence? Fingerprints. Motive. Physical evidence." He adjusted his ruby cuff links. "A black man and a white together? Jesus Christ! What is this, Selma, Alabama, 1950? What's so strange about a black and a white together in Harlem? These days even the mob's an equal-opportunity employer! They were probably running numbers to the bank. Let me tell you something, Lieutenant. I don't need people in my bureau who see ghosts hiding behind every tree. Lieutenant, you're playing with yourself."

"Percell doesn't think so," Rose said softly.

The ensuing silence that accompanied this statement was deafening.

Mario Percell, the First Deputy Commissioner, was the department's second-in-command. Before that he'd been the Chief of Inspectional Services for sixteen years. As the man overseeing the Intelligence Division, the Inspectional Services Division, and the Internal Affairs Division, Percell was the only man in the department who knew where all the bodies were buried. He knew which chiefs were drinkers, the names of their girlfriends, and who was on the take in pre-Knapp days. And what was more, he had the dossiers to prove it. As the central repository for all this sensitive information, he was the most feared man in the department—for the same reason the Kennedys were afraid of J. Edgar Hoover—he knew too much. As everyone in the room was acutely aware, Mario Percell and Larson were mortal enemies. They'd come on the job together and had continually bumped heads ever since. To add to his dislike of Percell, Larson was convinced that the First Dep wanted to be the next P.C.

Up to this point the Chief of Detectives had studiously ignored Rose, but now he trained his pale blue eyes on him with a grimace that suggested he'd just spotted a turd on his new rug. "You must be the lieutenant from IAD?"

"Right, Chief," Bennett interceded nervously. "Lieutenant Rose here was sent to—"

"I know why he was sent here, Hugo." Larson didn't take his eyes off Rose. "He was sent here to spy. Ain't that right, Lieutenant?"

"Gee, not as far as I know, sir," Rose answered, smiling.

Rose's disingenuous attitude further infuriated the Chief of Detectives, who was accustomed to intimidating everyone below him in rank. He was also furious with Percell for taking advantage of his absence to transfer an IAD lieutenant into the bureau. In fact he'd already called the P.C. for an appointment. He'd straighten this out forthwith! In the meantime he would let this back-stabbing bastard from IAD know who was boss.

"Let me tell you something, Lieutenant. While you're here—and I don't expect that will be for long—you will work under the direction of bureau supervisors only. And you will report only to them. Is that clear, Lieutenant? If you don't like the ground rules, you can go back across the river to Poplar Street with the rest of your kind."

Rose never broke his smile. "You're the boss, Chief. I always do what I'm told."

Larson scowled. "And don't you forget it. Hugo, you're in charge of these two. And for Chrissake make sure they come up with some hard facts. Another thing, I don't want anybody to know what you're up to; not even the detectives handling the cases. When you come up with something beyond mere speculation, let me know. In the meantime . . ." He looked at his watch. "Christ! I'm gonna be late for Councilman Becker's luncheon!" He looked up at them in surprise as though he'd forgotten they were there. "All right, all right, get the hell out of here, all of you."

Back in the exec's office, Shannon slammed the door and threw himself into a chair. "I don't believe that hump! I'm trying to develop a case, and he acts like I'm an hysterical old maid looking for rapists under the bed."

Bennett sighed. "Take it easy. You don't know Larson like I do. That's just his way. He likes to keep everyone off balance. Haven't you ever gotten a 'Larsonphone'?"

Shannon shook his head. "I thought that was just bullshit."

"Nah, you're just one of the lucky ones. It's kind of like a hobby with him. When he's bored, or between luncheons, he reads up on a case and then calls the squad commander to break his balls. Ten minutes later he can't remember the name of the lieutenant he raked over the coals, but the poor bastard on the receiving end is left a mass of quivering jelly. For weeks he'll jump out of his seat every time the phone rings, thinking it's Larson again."

Rose laughed. "He's a chameleon. Just now he sounded like a union organizer, but I've heard him speak at conferences. He can sound like Winston Churchill when he wants to."

"How did an asshole like that get to be the Chief of Detectives?" Shannon asked.

"Let's not get philosophical," Rose said. "The real question is: What do we do next?"

"Start digging," Bennett said. "Look for a connection between the three homicides. And for God's sake keep this quiet. Larson's right. If it turns out there are killer cops on the loose, the shit will hit the fan. If Pickett gets wind of this, he'll crucify us."

"Politics as usual," Shannon said in disgust.

"You got that right." Bennett stood and slapped Shannon on the back. "Cheer up, Brian. Aren't we lucky to be down here in the trenches where none of this affects us? They could make Mickey Mouse the Police Commissioner and the job would go on."

TINY LEONARD'S APARTMENT BUILDING WAS A CUT ABOVE THE OTHER tenements on 128th Street, but not by much. The broken mosaic-tiled floors told of a time when this building was more than just another run-down Harlem tenement. But now the rickety elevator reeked of urine and the gloomy hallways had a sour smell—a combination of stale food, poor ventilation, and chronic decay.

With his money, Leonard could have lived anywhere in Harlem, including Sugar Hill. But he chose to live here. He wasn't alone in this regard. Mafia dons, who could easily buy and sell most corporate CEOs, often lived in shabby Little Italy tenements or modest homes on Staten Island.

For the past two hours Brian Shannon had been knocking on doors in the

Leonard building, hoping to pick up some shreds of information. But he wasn't optimistic. It had been a week since Leonard's murder, and homicides didn't get much colder than that. Nevertheless, still smarting from his meeting with Larson, he was determined to come up with something—even if he had to knock on every door in Harlem.

He wasn't having much luck. Most of the tenants refused to open their doors, and from those who did he received little more than sullen stares and mumbled lies. He put his ear to a door and heard a TV and rattling dishes. The occupants were getting ready to have dinner—something he should have been doing. He knocked and the sound ceased. Then he heard the telltale creaking floor as the unseen occupant inspected him through the peephole. Silence—then the TV volume came up and life inside continued. There wasn't a resident in Harlem who couldn't spot a cop, and whoever was behind the door had nothing to say to a cop.

He stopped in front of the last apartment on Leonard's floor. Situated at one end of the corridor, the door presented an unobstructed view of the entire hallway. Again he knocked and instinctively stepped to the side. Footsteps shuffled behind the door. Then silence. Shannon knew he was being watched through the peephole.

"What do you want?" a woman demanded.

He held up his ID. "I'd like to talk to you for a minute."

"What about?"

"The murder in apartment 6N. I—"

"I talked to the police already. I don't know nothing." Behind her a baby's piercing wail erupted. "Hush your mouth," she said, more weary than angry.

Shannon disliked conducting interviews like this. He had only seconds to make contact—to touch a chord of interest. If he failed, this woman would walk away and that would be that. He needed to see her face-to-face, to see her eyes, assess her body language. "It's important," he whispered, conscious that his voice carried in the hallway. She wouldn't want her neighbors to know she'd spoken to him. "A man was shot only a few doors from you." He struggled to find the right words to make her open up. "If shooting had started . . . there's a lot of kids in this building . . ." He left the rest to her imagination.

There was a pause, long enough for Shannon to remember he'd forgotten to call Eileen and tell her he wouldn't be home for dinner. Then he heard the sounds of chains and bolts being undone. The door opened. A rail-thin woman holding a squirming infant regarded him with hostile eyes. He guessed she was in her late twenties, but she looked forty. She was wearing a housedress that was so worn he could see her thin legs through the material.

Shannon's practiced eye took in the apartment behind her. He'd spent his early years as a precinct cop in the ghetto neighborhoods of the South Bronx. Certain things never changed; the poor lived the same now as they had twenty years ago. The only difference was that now the color TVs and VCRs were more attractive targets for the burglars who victimized the poor with depressing regularity.

Behind her two small children with their thumbs stuck in their mouths stared at him. Above their heads was a gaping hole in the ceiling, the result of a chronic water leak. Watermarks spread an abstract design from the crumbling ceiling to the worn linoleum floor. Dirty dishes were piled haphazardly in the sink. Against one wall, the TV, the best piece of furniture, had jagged black lines running across the screen.

"A white cop goin' to tell a black woman how dangerous it is here?" Her tone was more mocking than angry.

Shannon grinned disarmingly. He'd been caught trying to bullshit her, but at least she opened the door. "You're right. You know better than I do."

He was hoping she'd invite him in. If she had anything to say, she sure as hell wouldn't say it out here in full view of the staring peepholes. "Were you home that night?" he asked.

"Yeah."

"Did you see or hear anything?"

"I already answered them questions. Why you askin' the same questions again?"

"Because sometimes, after people have had a chance to think about it, they remember things."

"I don't remember nothing."

Her expression was blank, but his instinct told him she had something to say. Taking a chance, he gently pushed the startled woman back into her apartment.

"What you doin'—"

"I'm sorry, I just want to show you something." He closed the door firmly behind him. Now they were out of sight of the prying neighbors.

"Well?" Her initial surprise was giving way to anger. "What you gonna show me?"

Shannon had no idea. He just wanted to get out of the hallway. He turned and peered through the peephole. Damn! What a view. It was better than expected. "If you were looking at the right time," he said softly, "you could have seen who went into Leonard's apartment."

"Even if I was lookin', I couldn't of seen them in that dark hallway."

A jolt went through Shannon. "Most of the hallway is pretty dark," he said, with his eye still to the opening, "but there's a light over Leonard's door. What'd they do, knock or ring the bell?"

"I told you I didn't—"

"You see them step out of the shadows and stop in front of Leonard's door. Then they—what?" He held his breath.

"Rang the bell," she said in a small, flat voice.

"They rang the bell," he repeated. Hunched over, eye to the peephole, his back was beginning to hurt, but he was unwilling to turn around and risk breaking the delicate connection they'd made. "Then what?"

"I don't know. I didn't look no more."

"They ring the bell and then . . . ?"

"I told you I don't know."

She was getting angry; he was losing her.

"Okay. You didn't look again. Did you ever see them before?"

"No."

Short answer, no elaboration. She was getting ready to clam up and throw him out. "How would you describe them?"

"I only looked for a second. They stopped at Tiny's door and I looked away. I was scared of that man. We all was."

"I know." Shannon straightened up, relieving his protesting back. The sleeping infant's peaceful expression was in sharp contrast to the fear in his mother's eyes. "Mrs. . . . ?"

"Little. Wanda Little."

"Mrs. Little, I want you to know that anything you tell me is just between you and me. You saw the men who killed Leonard, and I'm looking for them. I need your help."

Gently, she rocked the sleeping infant in her arms and glared at him. Physically they stood no more than three feet apart, but the distance between them—black vs. white, cop vs. Harlem resident—created a chasm over which it was sometimes impossible to reach. Shannon wanted to tell her that he was on her side; that they both wanted justice. But they didn't speak the same language. It was up to her.

She wiped a dribble from the baby's chin. "I didn't hear nuthin', but the tall one," she said, still looking at her baby, "was black, and the shorter one was white with blond hair."

Suddenly exhausted, Shannon leaned against the door. DeNoto's witness had been right.

AT SEVENTY-THREE MRS. RAMONA GORDON HAD THE SHARP-EYED look of a much younger woman. With her crisp white blouse and hair pulled back in a severe bun, she looked like a Sunday school teacher.

Shannon shifted on the chintz-covered couch and tried to look natural balancing a dainty teacup in one hand and a plate of homemade cookies in the other. He'd come to see DeNoto's witness right after he'd left Wanda Little's apartment.

In contrast to Little's shabby apartment, this one was meticulously clean. Starched curtains hung from the windows, and the hardwood floors gleamed. The room smelled of furniture polish and cookies.

"Trash. That's all that's here nowadays. Trash." For the past half hour Mrs. Gordon had been giving Shannon a running account of the decline and fall of Harlem since 1930, the year she came up from South Carolina.

"When I came to Harlem, I was only fifteen, but you could walk the streets with never a thought of a body hurting you. Why, the men tipped their hats and said 'good morning' and such. Today, the good Lord knows a decent woman can't walk these streets of Sodom. Since my husband Clarence died ten years ago—he was with the Post Office, did I mention that?"

Shannon, his mouth stuffed with his third cookie, nodded.

"I seldom go out. My whole life is right there." She pointed to an ancient black-and-white TV set. "Although the Lord knows there ain't much to watch, what with all the sex and violence."

Shannon, seeing the opportunity to short-circuit her oral history of Harlem, interjected, "I understand your TV wasn't working the night of the murder?"

"No, it was not. I'd called the man to come fix it, but it takes forever for them to do anything. If I'm not watching TV, I'm looking out the window."

"Was it raining that night, Mrs. Gordon?"

"Yes it was, and the streets were empty. Then I saw this van I didn't recognize. I won't lie to you, young man, I'm a nosy old woman. I look out that window all the time and I know most of the cars that park on this block."

"I'm nosy too," he said, smiling. "That's why I became a cop. Go on, what did you see next?"

"Not much. It was raining cats and dogs. Two men got out. As I told that detective, one was a Negro and the other was a white man. They went into the building across the street."

"That would be Leonard's building?"

"Yes, that spawn of the devil."

"Could you describe them?"

She pursed her lips. "It was so fast. They got out, and the next thing they were gone."

"Can you remember anything about them? Height? Clothing?"

She shook her head. "Too dark for that."

"Did you see them leave?"

"Yes. But I almost missed them. I went to make myself a cup of tea. I came back just as they were getting into their van."

"How long would you say you were away from the window?"

"Maybe ten minutes."

Shannon wanted to see the view from her window. In his struggle to get up from the soft couch, he almost upset his teacup. Rescuing her delicate china, she efficiently took the cup from him. "Can I get you more tea, Lieutenant?"

"No," he said a little too abruptly, then added, "but it was delicious."

The lighting outside her window was good. He could read the license plates of the cars parked across the street. "Mrs. Gordon, exactly where was the van parked?"

She pushed the curtain aside. "Right there where that white car is."

The spot she'd indicated—almost directly across the street—was well lit. From this angle she could have seen the plate number. "Mrs. Gordon, can you read the license plate on the white car?"

She leaned forward and squinted. "L-H-M-six-nine-one," she said triumphantly. "Eyesight's almost as good as when I was a child."

"I don't suppose you happened to notice the plate number of the van?"

"Lieutenant, I'm a nosy old woman, but I'm not *that* nosy."

"How about the van? Can you describe it?"

"It was hard to tell the color under those new funny-colored lights. All I know is it was a dark color."

"Anything else?"

"The windows were real dark, the windshield too. A body couldn't see a thing inside."

Shannon was pleased. Although it wasn't much, it was something; he had two witnesses who saw the murderers. When the time came, he'd show them a photo array or conduct a lineup. He had no doubt that Mrs. Gordon would cooperate. Wanda Little? He'd cross that bridge when he came to it.

He gave her his card. "Thanks for your time, Mrs. Gordon. If you think of anything else, please give me a call."

On the way out the door Shannon mentioned how delicious the cookies were. She wouldn't let him leave until she'd given him a napkinful to take with him.

8

Over coffee and bagels, supplied by Rose, Shannon recounted his interviews with Wanda Little and Mrs. Gordon.

"So it's definite." Rose rested his hand-sewn shoes on the desk. "There were two killers—a black and a white. Now we need something concrete—a name, or a license number."

Shannon bridled at Rose's less than enthusiastic response to his information. "That's all they could tell me."

Velez spoke up. "Wait a minute, Loo. From what you said, there's a chance the old lady could have seen the license-plate number. Right?"

"I said the lighting was good and her eyesight is good. But she didn't make a point of looking at the plate."

"How about hypnosis? Last year in the Four-four we had a homicide in a social club. The witnesses wanted to cooperate, but they couldn't agree on the description of the perp. The squad took them to the department hypnotist and came up with some good information.''

"You might have something," Shannon said. "I've never used them myself, but I know people who have."

"What the hell," added Rose. "It's worth a shot."

Shannon looked at his watch and stood up. "I'll call them this afternoon and see if I can set up an appointment. Right now I'm on my way to the morgue to see an M.E."

Rose shuddered. "Go without me, pal. Dead bodies marinating in formaldehyde are not some of my favorite things. Besides, I didn't get a chance to get up to the Marbridge Gallery yesterday, so I'm going this afternoon."

Velez tugged on Shannon's sleeve. "Hey boss, take me."

Shannon looked at the young cop's desperate face and recognized the signs—he was getting restless. With the felony project on hold, and all the available homicide information fed into the computer, Velez had nothing to do. "All right, but I'm warning you, you horny bastard. There are laws against necrophilia."

The Medical Examiner's building, an unassuming edifice on First Avenue, was indistinguishable from the other medical buildings in the area. Only the Latin inscription, carved on the marble wall at the entrance, defined this building as something unique. In English it would have read: "Let conversation cease. Let laughter flee. This is the place where death delights to help the living."

Some detectives liked to believe that all murders were solved by brains and old-fashioned legwork, but the good ones knew that just as many cases were solved on a marble slab by the probing instruments of a medical examiner.

Inside, the air was oppressively heavy with the smell of chemicals and decay. Shannon and Velez stopped at the front desk and were told Epstein was in the back performing an autopsy. They wandered down the labyrinth of somber corridors past rows of shining stainless-steel drawers, which housed the remains of bodies. They stopped outside the autopsy room and peered through the glass.

Inside, Epstein was leaning over a cadaver. He made an incision in the shaved scalp, starting behind the left ear. Swiftly, he drew the scalpel across the top of the head to the base of the right ear. Then, carefully, he pulled back both sections of the scalp, the way a child might peel an orange. He bent close to the exposed skin and examined it for a moment. Satisfied, he picked up a stainless-steel saw and prepared to open the top of the cranium. Shannon tapped the glass. Epstein looked up, smiled, and motioned them in.

Dr. Sidney Epstein was one of the best medical examiners in the city. Shannon had worked with him on several cases and had been impressed with the pathologist's meticulous professionalism. Where many M.E.'s were content to run one test, Epstein ran two. He always went the extra mile, and as a result often uncovered more evidence than his less enthusiastic colleagues.

Mercifully, Epstein lacked the ghoulishness of most medical examiners. Some M.E.'s, who weren't wrapped too tightly to begin with, took great delight in scaring the hell out of unsuspecting cops by extracting arms out of chest cavities and lunch bags. If an M.E. knew it was a cop's first autopsy, he really pulled out the stops with macabre antics that would bring tears of joy to Vincent Price.

"Lieutenant Shannon, how are you?"

"Fine, Doc, how's business?"

"Couldn't be better." Epstein put the saw down and patted the cadaver's bare stomach. "He can wait. That's what I like about this business—the patients never complain." He pulled off his rubber gloves and shook hands with Shannon and Velez.

Velez stared at the corpse on the slab—a middle-aged black man with a gaping gash in his throat that ran almost ear to ear. "Holy shit," Velez whispered, "what'd he get hit with? An axe?"

Epstein regarded the body benignly. "Actually, he was cut with a very sharp razor."

Velez nodded mutely, then walked around the table, inspecting the assortment of gleaming steel knives and saws. "This a murder, Doc?"

"Yes."

Velez couldn't take his eyes off the stripped skull. "How do you know?"

"Because people who commit suicide with a knife or razor always make tentative cuts—we call them hesitation marks. Even at that point a person isn't sure he wants to die, or at least he doesn't want to feel any pain. When it's murder, the cut is usually deep and deliberate. This one is murder for sure. His windpipe and carotid artery are cleanly severed. Someone was very upset with this fellow."

"Hey, Doc"—Velez moved his attention to the scale used to weigh organs—"how do you determine the time of death?"

"Maggots. Depending on the temperature, they hatch anywhere from twelve hours to three days. We just figure out how old and how many maggots there are in the body."

Velez's face said he was sorry he asked.

The morgue wasn't a place you stayed in any longer than necessary, and Shannon wanted to get out as soon as possible. "I don't want to take up too much of your time, Doc. Did you get a chance to review the autopsy reports?"

"Yes, and I spoke to the people who performed them."

"What do you think?"

The pathologist lit a cigarette. Shannon was dying to do the same, but he'd given up smoking for the second time this week.

"Actually, they're all very boring pathology-wise. Nothing unusual. All shot in the head with different-caliber guns. Nothing unusual in the blood, organs, or tissue tests."

"Aside from the head shots, did you notice any other similarities?" Shannon pressed.

Epstein pondered a spiral of smoke. "Well, there was something a little peculiar."

"What was that?"

"There were no defensive wounds and no tissue or hair under the fingernails."

"Meaning?"

"In most violent deaths the victim puts up a struggle. He raises his hands to ward off the blow, the knife thrust, even the bullet. We expect to find cuts, bruises, or bullet holes in the hands and arms. There were none on your three victims. At first I thought they might have been drugged, but there was nothing in the blood and tissue-test results to suggest they were incapacitated in any way."

"Is there a chance that one or more of them committed suicide?" Velez asked.

Epstein shook his head. "For one thing, when people shoot themselves, they generally aim for the temple or the heart, seldom the forehead—much too awkward. Besides, the wounds were abazed with no tattooing."

"What does that mean?"

The young cop was acting like a goddamn schoolkid on a field trip. "It means," Shannon answered curtly, "that the gun wasn't held up against the temple."

"Which," Epstein concluded, "is usually a good indication of suicide."

"How far away would you say the shooter was?" Shannon asked.

"Maybe two or three feet, judging by the condition of the entrance wounds. The angle of entry indicates that the victims were sitting down and the shooter stood in front of them."

"A victim sits still while someone stands over him and pumps a bullet into his head. He doesn't stand up, he doesn't run, he doesn't offer resistance. And it happened three times! What the hell does it mean, Sidney?"

"I don't know, Lieutenant. My job is to find out how they died." He flipped his cigarette into the floor drain. "Yours is to find out why."

*   *   *

NEW YORK CITY HAS MANY EXCLUSIVE RESIDENTIAL AREAS, BUT the one area that personifies true wealth more than any other is Park Avenue above Seventy-second Street. No flashy towers of Babel here, only tall, stately buildings constructed in the first half of the century, when architecture made a statement about elegance, not ostentation. This was not the habitat of movie stars and rock idols. Indeed, the few who tried to crash Park Avenue were told politely, but firmly, that they and their kind were not welcome. Park Avenue was reserved for investment bankers, international lawyers, and art dealers like Nelson Marbridge, whose old-family money could afford to install the black sheep of the family on Park Avenue, far from the family compound.

Alex Rose parked across the street from a massive, ornate structure on the northeast corner of Seventy-sixth Street. The doorman, dressed like a Prussian general, flagged down taxis, held limo doors open, and patted fluffy poodles with the practiced grace of a ballerina. Rose pondered on how two killers—assuming there were two—had gotten past the general. He made a mental note to return some night to see what kind of security the building offered.

The Marbridge Gallery, a narrow two-story building sandwiched between two larger galleries, was located on Madison Avenue near Eightieth Street. When Rose entered, a middle-aged man with short-cropped hair and a neatly trimmed mustache looked up from a hardcover book. "Yes, may I help you?"

"Is Mr. Marbridge in?"

The man pursed his lips. "Mr. Marbridge, I'm afraid, is dead."

"Oh, I'm terribly sorry. Was it an accident?"

The man regarded him suspiciously over his Ben Franklin reading glasses. "Yes."

"How awful. I met Mr. Marbridge several months ago in . . . my goodness, I travel to so many countries in South America, I can't remember which one."

"Peru," the man offered. "Mr. Marbridge traveled there often. As you can see, we specialize in Peruvian art—both pre-Colombian and modern."

Rose eyed a canvas depicting a screaming man with three eyes and a nose growing out of an ear. "Marvelous." He stepped back, the better to view the masterpiece. "Wonderful lines, such . . . zest."

"Yes, it is." For the first time, the man smiled. "Mister . . . ?"

"Rodney Winfield. And yours?"

"Stephen Pyne. It's a Del Gado." He nodded at the canvas. "Perhaps you've heard of him?"

"I don't believe I have."

Pyne's smile faded some. "He's a wonderful new talent from Mollendo. Nelson is—that is, *was*—helping him along in his career."

The door opened and an elderly couple came in. Pyne quickly sized them up as browsers and returned to his more promising conversation with Rose. "We have nine Del Gados, ranging in price from one to thirty thousand. A real bargain."

Rose resisted asking if that was in pesos or American money. "Mr. Marbridge and I had such a lovely time when last we met. So knowledgeable. Was he in the business long?"

"I've been with him for ten years. Before that—"

"Excuse me. How much is this?" The woman waved an ugly ceramic jug over her head.

Pyne gasped. "Please, madam, don't touch the objets d'art. That urn is worth nine thousand dollars!"

"Well, *excuse* me." Chastised, she gently returned the urn to its pedestal. In a stage whisper she said to her husband, "Who's he kidding. I've seen the same thing at garage sales for ten dollars."

Pyne rolled his eyes and looked to Rose, who dutifully shook his head in commiseration. "So," Rose continued, "this gallery has been here for a long time?"

"Oh yes. Mr. Marbridge opened the gallery in 1961."

Rose turned his attention to a canvas that looked suspiciously like the bar codes used in supermarkets. "A Del Gado?"

"Actually, that's a Salinas. I'm afraid he's not selling well at all."

"Really? I can't imagine why. There's such . . . strength, such . . . vitality in the brush strokes."

"Do you think so?" Pyne, apparently not a fan of Salinas, inspected the painting again. "Hmm, I think I see what you mean. There is a certain primitive immediacy to the work. It's amazing, I've looked at that painting a hundred times and—"

"Excuse me. How much is this?" Proud of her newly acquired knowledge of gallery protocol, the woman pointed at, but didn't touch, a squat statue of a female with huge breasts.

Pyne pursed his lips. "That statue," he said in low, measured tones, "is twenty-five hundred dollars."

The price prompted a raspy giggle.

"You said Mr. Marbridge traveled to Peru often?" Rose asked.

"Several times a year. He was always bringing back new pieces. Nelson had a very special feel for South American art."

"Yes, I can see that. Looking at all these lovely pieces, I imagine there's a brisk turnover."

Pyne frowned. "Actually, no." He dropped his voice. "If the truth were to be told, we gross very little. Always have."

"Really? How in the world do you manage to survive? The rent and overhead must be outrageous."

"It certainly is. But actually—"

"What's it called?" It was the woman again. She seemed bent on inquiring about the price of every item in the shop.

"It's a fertility goddess," Pyne said through clenched teeth.

"But what's its name?"

"What's *its* name!" Rose bellowed, frightening both the woman and Pyne. "Madam, you are not talking about an *it*. This priceless piece of ageless art is not a dog. It's the love goddess, Tico Tico. She was used in ancient fertility rites where the most unspeakable sexual perversions were performed—using that very statue, I might add—by men, women, and llamas."

The woman gawked at the statue in horror.

"Furthermore," Rose continued to shout, "a shaman put a curse on her. Anyone defiling her will become pregnant in the most violent manner imaginable!"

It worked. She had her husband's arm and was dragging him toward the door.

"Come on, Fred," she declared indignantly. "Obviously, these two perverted homosexuals want to be alone."

Rose winced. Pyne giggled. The door banged.

"That was marvelous, the way you got rid of her. Tico Tico, indeed. How clever."

Rose assumed an indignant air. "They were probably just killing time until the movie matinee. You were saying something about the high rents?"

"Yes. Dreadful. This shop," Pyne confided, "has never turned a profit all the time I've been with Nelson. Actually, Mr. Marbridge is—there I go again—*was* a man of independent means. Fortunately, he didn't have to make a profit."

Rose contemplated Pyne's sincere face and tried to decide if he was jerking him off or if he was really that naive. He decided on the latter.

"Really? Well, we can be thankful that a fine man like Nelson Marbridge supported the arts without tainting it with the crassness of commercialism."

Pyne gazed at Rose with new respect. "What a wonderful thing to say. You're absolutely right, Mr. Winfield."

"Well," Rose said, "I really must be going. By the way, what's going to happen to the gallery now?"

The scowl on Pyne's face told Rose he'd hit a nerve. "It's to be sold by the family. Of course, no provisions have been made for me. The family lawyers have made it abundantly clear that I am of no concern to them."

"That's too bad. Well, I really must fly."

Pyne winked at Rose. "Perhaps you'll drop in again before the shop closes."

Rose, momentarily struck dumb, mumbled, "We'll see," and fled.

9

BRIAN SHANNON AND MRS. CLARENCE GORDON, DRESSED IN HER finest dress and hat, took the elevator to the eighth floor of the Police Academy, where the department hypnotist was located. Mrs. Gordon thumbed through an old *Time* magazine, while Shannon went into another room to review the procedures with the hypnotist.

Detective Maria Garcia, who looked young enough to be his daughter's classmate, was delighted to explain what she was about to do. "As I said on the phone, Lieutenant, not everyone is a good candidate for hypnosis. Drug addicts and alcoholics are definitely out. Little kids and old folks are iffy. What we like are young, intelligent people who are very suggestible."

Shannon regarded the detective skeptically. "It's hard to get witnesses to fit that bill."

"I know. I gave you my list of druthers. I just want you to understand that the further we get away from these parameters, the less our chances of success.''

"What about Mrs. Gordon?"

"She's seventy-five, Loo, that's two strikes right there."

Shannon, remembering the old lady's quick mind, said, "Mrs. Gordon is not your ordinary seventy-five-year-old."

"How long ago did this take place?"

"A week."

The detective looked less than enthused. "Loo, I don't want you to get your hopes up."

"Garcia, I've been investigating homicides a long time. I don't even know what the word optimistic means."

"Okay. We'll give it a try."

Shannon, curious about the procedure, asked, "What are you going to do?"

"Nothing exotic. I'll do a simple test to check her suggestibility level. If she's a good subject, I'll put her under. That part is fairly straightforward. It's the recall technique that's important. Some individuals respond to certain techniques better than others. For instance, you told me she's a big TV watcher. When I put her under, I'll suggest she's watching TV. I'll place her back to that night and get her to see the vehicle as she saw it. Then I'll ask her if she can see the license plate. Now this is the tricky part. If she didn't see the plate, there's no way she can give me a number. On the other hand, if she looked at the plate—even momentarily—there's a chance I can get her to 'see' it again."

"How do you do that?"

"Using the TV metaphor. I ask her to zoom in on the plate—just like a TV camera."

"That simple?"

"That simple and that difficult. The mind is a very complex piece of machinery. We don't understand the half of it. Hell, there are some who say hypnosis doesn't exist."

"Probably the same people who say bees can't fly."

"Yeah, I guess so. I'm only a technician. What do I know."

"So you're saying that if Mrs. Gordon saw the plate, she'll be able to recall it?"

"I didn't say that. Think of this way. The mind is like a camera. It records everything it sees. It's all there—pictures of everything we've ever seen—roaming around somewhere in the recesses of the mind. But we can't always retrieve that information. There are mitigating circumstances—age and mental deterioration, to name just a couple. That's why we like to work with the profile I mentioned earlier.''

The more she talked, the more pessimistic Shannon was becoming. "Let's do it," he said sourly.

He waited outside while Mrs. Gordon and Garcia went into another room. Twenty minutes later the old woman emerged and Shannon went in to get the results from the detective.

"You were right about her, Lieutenant. She's one sharp lady."

Shannon felt a surge of excitement. "What did she tell you?"

"I got some good news and I got some bad news. The good news is that she saw the plate. The bad news is that she can only recall part of it."

Shannon's enthusiasm for hypnosis quickly waned. "How could—"

"I don't know. Maybe the plate was obscured by a shadow. I just don't know. She's certain the last three numbers are 598, and she's pretty sure there are three letters before the numbers. It's a New York registration."

"Shit, there's got to be hundreds of plates with that combination."

"The van is blue, if that helps."

"Sure it helps. Does she know the make?"

"No. We worked on that. Trouble is, all those vans look alike."

Shannon studied the numbers written on the paper. So near and yet so far. He had two witnesses who had seen Tiny Leonard's killers. He even had a witness who'd actually seen the vehicle they'd arrived in. But all he had was a partial plate of a blue van, make unknown. "The plate is probably stolen anyway," he mumbled.

They had so little to go on, that every clue, no matter how insignificant, had to be checked out. He stuffed the paper in his pocket. Maybe Velez could do something with it.

VELEZ FLASHED HIS WEASEL GRIN. "LET ME SEE IF I GOT THIS STRAIGHT, Loo. You want me to ID the owner of a blue van—make unknown— based on a partial plate?"

"Something like that."

"What do I look like, the Wizard of Wang?"

"I already narrowed it down for you," Shannon said, sounding more confident than he felt. "It's a New York registration."

Velez studied the partial plate. "Assuming there are three letters in this plate, there are 17,576 possible combinations. Then all I have to do is match those up with all blue vans registered in New York State."

"You're breaking my heart. Can you do it or not?"

"Sure I can do it. I just don't think it'll do any good. I'm going to wind up with a shitload of possibilities. If I knew the make of the van, it would help."

"We tried. Mrs. Gordon doesn't know the make."

"Loo, you realize the van, and/or the plate, is probably stolen."

That thought had indeed occurred to him. It probably was stolen. But then again, maybe it wasn't. "These guys may not be as bright as we think."

"Using your own van to drive to a hit? Come on, Loo, no one's that dumb."

Again, Shannon had to agree. No one was that dumb. Especially if they were cops.

Shannon came in early the next morning and was surprised to see Velez already working at his terminal.

"What happened, Luis? Couldn't find anyone to shack up with last night?"

"Even I need to get some rest once in a while."

Shannon peered at the screen. "How're you doing?"

"I'm going nuts. Since six I've been querying DMV for all plates ending in 598, but their computer keeps going down. At this rate, it'll take forever to get the data. I can't wait to ask for the blue vans. Their computer will probably explode."

Five minutes later Velez stood up and let go a string of Spanish curses.

"What's the matter?" Shannon asked.

"The goddamn computer is down again! They don't need technicians up in Albany to fix that thing, they need body and fender men!"

Shannon stood up. "Keep trying. I gotta go see a junkie. Tomorrow morning," he added with mock seriousness, "I expect the name of the van owner on my desk."

"Señor Lieutenant," Velez deadpanned, "if their fucking computer keeps crashing, tomorrow morning you may find my heartbroken body hanging from a light fixture."

BRIAN SHANNON AND DET. SAL DENOTO WERE THE ONLY TWO PEO-ple in Carl Schurz Park without a dog. DeNoto eyed a tiny Yorkshire terrier being walked by a fur-coated woman. "What the hell is that?" he said out of the side of his mouth.

"I don't know. It looks like a dust mop with feet."

"I bet that thing costs more than my car. Look around you, Loo. There must be a million dollars' worth of dogs crapping in this park every day."

The tiny park overlooking the East River was the site of Gracie Mansion— the home of the mayor. Unlike Central Park, which attracted an eclectic mix of New Yorkers, Carl Schurz was frequented mostly by expensively dressed and well-coiffured East End Avenue residents walking the latest in designer dogs.

Earlier that morning DeNoto had called Shannon to tell him he'd finally found his C.I. The detective had resisted setting up a meeting, but the lieutenant prevailed. Now they were in the park to meet Ernest "Sticks" Wallin.

It was late afternoon, and the cold November air smelled like snow, but DeNoto had a bead of perspiration over his upper lip. "Tell you the truth, Loo, this whole thing makes me real uncomfortable."

"Why?"

"My boss asks me what's new on the case and I tell him nothing. Now you want to meet my C.I. and talk about crooked cops. Maybe I shoulda called IAD," he added glumly.

"Sal, I know how you feel, but I have to talk to this guy. Just make the introductions, I'll ask the questions. You don't even have to hang around."

In fact Shannon would have preferred to meet the C.I. alone—the less DeNoto knew the better. But DeNoto said Sticks wouldn't go for it.

As they climbed the large horseshoe stairs leading to the pedestrian walkway overlooking the East River, DeNoto described his week-long search for Wallin. "Sticks just vanished. I looked in all the usual places, but no one had seen him. I figured he'd climbed into a hole and OD'ed, in which case they wouldn't find him until he started to stink. Then I caught up to his girlfriend at a neighborhood methadone clinic. She's a beaut, a methadonian with the I.Q. of a cauliflower. Last she'd heard, he'd been busted. I checked with central records and tracked him down at Rikers. He got sprung yesterday. Carl Schurz is his idea—said he wouldn't have to worry about running into anyone he knew." The detective glumly surveyed the park. "That's the understatement of the year. Probably only knows about this place from mugging rich old ladies and their dogs."

"What did he get busted for this time?" Shannon asked.

"Boosting car radios in midtown. The complainant was a girl from Jersey. The dopey ADA—a new kid—made the mistake of giving the radio back to her *before* she signed the complaint. Naturally, once she got her radio back, she didn't want to be a good citizen no more. Without the complainant, the charges were dropped and Sticks walked." DeNoto tugged at his tie. "What a fucking city. You have to hold a citizen's property hostage to get them to do the right thing."

"Can you blame them?" They both knew the complainant would have spent more time in court than Sticks would have spent in jail—assuming he was convicted.

"Yeah," the detective conceded, "that's true."

By the time they got to the top of the stairs, they were both puffing. "There he is," DeNoto said.

Standing by the railing overlooking the river, an agitated, skeletal-thin black man hopped from one foot to the other.

"Look at that fuck. He's just out of the can, and he's back on the shit already. Looks like he needs another hit, and guess who he's gonna ask to pay for it?"

While Shannon waited by a bench, DeNoto went to talk to Wallin. The bearish detective towered over the diminutive junkie. DeNoto spoke briefly. Wallin shook his head. DeNoto jabbed a beefy finger into the man's bony chest. Wallin glanced over at Shannon and again shook his head. Apparently he didn't want this meeting either. The detective's hand shot out and grabbed the smaller man by the collar. He half dragged him over to Shannon. "Sticks, I want you to meet a friend of mine."

Wallin's eyes darted about but he refused to make eye contact with Shannon. "I don't know what I'm doin' here," he whined. "I didn't do nuthin'. Sal, I'm tryin' to get straight, I swear to God. I'm gonna beat the drugs. All I need—"

DeNoto pried the man's hand off his arm. "Please, Sticks, don't make so many promises. You're beginning to sound like a fucking politician."

Sticks Wallin was a study in uncoordinated animation. His drug-ravaged brain fired erratic commands to his nervous system, causing him to blink, jerk, and shrug uncontrollably. Just watching him was exhausting.

"I hear you know something about cops involved in drugs," Shannon said.

Wallin's leathery face collapsed. "What cops? I never said nuthin' like that."

DeNoto threw an arm around the man's thin neck and squeezed. "Sticks, Sticks, I want you to calm down. Get your shit together or I'm gonna throw you in the fucking river. You understand?"

"Sal, I don't feel so good. My stomach hurts real bad. I think I got the flu or somethin'."

"Okay, okay," the detective said soothingly. "As soon as we're finished here, I want you to rush home and make an appointment to see your internist. In the meantime tell my friend here what you told me."

Wallin, seeing he wasn't going to get any sympathy from DeNoto, turned his attention to Shannon. "Sir, excuse me, sir, are you a policeman?"

DeNoto smacked the back of Wallin's head with his open hand. "What the matter with you, Sticks? We'll ask the questions; you give the answers."

"Sure, sure, Sal. I just wanna know who I'm talkin' to, that's all."

"Yeah." DeNoto shook the man. "So you can sell that information to someone else."

Wallin started to protest, but Shannon cut him off. "Sticks, I'm not a social worker, don't try to shine me on. Just tell me what you told Sal."

Wallin stuffed his hands in his pockets and shivered. It was beginning to get dark, and the cold, damp air was getting to the emaciated junkie. "I heard some stuff. Just talk, you understand?" His watery eyes fastened on Shannon's left shoulder. "They say cops is arrestin' some people and lettin' others do their thing. You know what I'm sayin'?"

"Are you saying the precinct is protecting drug dealers?"

"No, man, I ain't talkin' 'bout no street peddlers and chump precinct cops—excuse me—I mean officers. I'm talkin' the big dudes—the distributors and the downtown cops."

"Where are the cops from?" Shannon asked.

"I don't know. I don't even know if they is cops or feds. I swear to God. You know what I'm sayin'? It's just talk, that's all."

"What's the deal? Are the cops partners, or just getting paid for protection?"

"I don't know, but there's a lot of bitchin' from certain individuals. Some big shipments is gettin' snatched by cops, but others is gettin' onto the street with no trouble. They say it's more than coincidence. You know what I'm saying?"

"Who is 'they'? Do you have a name?"

"No, sir, I don't know no one specifically, you understand? It's just general talk, that's all."

Shannon looked at the shivering man and decided he probably didn't know any more than he was saying. Even if he did, the junkie would never tell him, or even DeNoto for that matter. Revealing that kind of information could get him deader than the leaves swirling around their feet. "Okay, Sticks. Thanks for your help."

Like a kid who's been kept after school, the junkie turned to DeNoto. "Can I go, Sal?"

"Yeah, take off."

Wallin's voice dropped and he leaned close to the big detective's chest. "Sal, I'm busted. Could you give me something . . . you know what I'm saying?"

DeNoto took his wallet out of his pocket. "What are you going to do with the money, Sticks?"

The junkie smiled, revealing a mouthful of wrecked teeth. "Get some food, man. I ain't eaten right in weeks. You know they don't feed you right at Rikers. I want to get me some good food."

"You're full of shit. You're going to spend it on smack."

"No, Sal, I'm off that shit. You know what I'm sayin'?"

Shannon recognized the turmoil on DeNoto's face. Like most cops, DeNoto had ambivalent feelings about his informants—especially if they were drug addicts. Junkies were the living dead. They'd sell their mothers for the price of a fix. They were untrustworthy, disloyal, and for the most part, incapable of rehabilitation, yet they were indispensable to cops who needed the kind of information that only a street junkie could provide. Cops and junkies developed a peculiar relationship; the junkie came to rely on the cop for advice, money, and sometimes protection, while the cop, in spite of himself, sometimes came to genuinely like his pitiful source of information. Fortunately for the emotional well-being of the cop, the dangerous, violent life of a junkie precluded any long-term commitment.

DeNoto stuffed two twenty-dollar bills into Wallin's jacket pocket. "Sticks, if I find out you spent this money on drugs, I'm going to break your useless neck."

"Sal, I'm gonna buy some food right now. You know what I'm sayin'?"

DeNoto silently watched the retreating figure, then yelled after him, "Sticks, don't mug anyone in this park. The mayor lives here." He wiped his forehead and turned to Shannon. "That lying fuck's on his way to cop a score. He can't wait. Would you believe he's only twenty-eight? He looks like he's fifty. He's got hepatitis, jaundice, ulcers all over his body, and Christ knows what else. But he can't wait to pop some more of that shit into his veins. I give him another year, tops." The detective leaned on the railing and gazed into the inky water below. "What do you think, Loo, about what he said?"

"You know him better than I do, Sal. You tell me."

"Sticks is all fucked up. His information has been good in the past. But I don't know, I just don't believe him."

"Why? Because you don't think he's telling the truth, or because you don't want to believe that cops might be dirty?"

The big detective sighed. "I don't know, Loo. I just don't believe him. I gotta be getting back. Can I drop you somewhere?"

"No. I'm going to walk. I can use the exercise." Knowing DeNoto was unhappy in his role as an IAD surrogate, Shannon decided to take him off the hook. "Listen, Sal, if you hear anything else, call me. Otherwise you and I won't be speaking anymore."

Relief flooded DeNoto's face. "Thanks, Loo. I'll call you if I hear anything."

Shannon, buttoning up against the wind, walked south along the pedestrian walkway. The streetlights on Roosevelt Island sparkling across the water reminded Shannon that Christmas was a little more than a month away. He was unhappy and frustrated by their lack of progress. Velez was working on the plate combinations, but Shannon didn't hold out much hope that he'd be able to identify it; there were just too many combinations. After seven days they didn't have very much—two witnesses, a partial plate, and a junkie who was pointing fingers at cops.

Unlike DeNoto, Shannon believed Sticks. But was there a connection between these corrupt cops and the deaths of the three men?

Three men were already dead. If they didn't solve the puzzle in a hurry, maybe a fourth would die. They needed a break. Soon.

10

IT WAS ALMOST SIX O'CLOCK WHEN THE TELEPHONE COMPANY TRUCK pulled up to the corner of New Lots and Alabama avenues. Stamping their feet to ward off the cold, three workmen began setting up barriers around a manhole. Two pried the cover off and the third, carrying a toolbox, descended into the cavity. At the bottom of the shaft he opened the box and took out a radio. "T.C. to Base," he whispered.

In a vacant apartment on the fifth floor, overlooking the intersection, Patrick Stone looked down on the telephone truck. In the rapidly fading daylight he could just make them out. "Base. Go ahead."

"We're in position."

"Good. How does it look?"

"If I did wiring like this when I was with the company, they would have canned me."

Stone and the other two cops in the apartment chuckled. Sgt. Paul

Radlicki, who'd worked for the telephone company before he became a cop, was a perfectionist. When Stone had assigned him and two of his men to the truck, Radlicki had insisted on giving the men a crash course in how to behave like telephone repairmen.

The cop standing next to Stone at the window peered at the truck through binoculars. "If he's got the time, he's probably going to correct that wiring," he said.

Stone's sharp eyes detected something amiss. "T.C.," he said into the radio, "you don't have your four-way flashers on."

"Ten-four," Radlicki answered in a tight voice. Before he released the mike, Stone and the others heard the beginning of an indignant roar. Below, Stone saw one of the men dive into the truck and switch the lights on.

"Those poor bastards," the cop with the binoculars said. "It's gonna be a long night if Radlicki has his tight pants on."

Another voice crackled over the radio. "Sky to Base."

Stone looked across the street at the roof opposite him. Two men huddled in the shadows of a sprawling pigeon coop. "Go ahead."

"We're all set."

"Ten-four."

The two had chosen well. They'd positioned themselves at one end of the row of rooftops so their backs were protected and they had a clear view of the other roofs. Stone reviewed his plans. It was imperative that nothing go wrong—especially tonight. All the escape routes were covered. When it got darker, more men would be sent to each rooftop. Below, additional men hid in trucks and doorways. If necessary, Radlicki was prepared to pull the truck into the middle of the street and block it. Another truck at the other end of the block would do the same. Kakavos and his team were in the basement of the building across the street, monitoring the apartment and the telephone. Soon he'd have to go into the cellar to join them. But not until it was absolutely necessary.

"Foley," he said to his communications man, "I'm going to take a nap. Wake me when you hear something."

Stone stretched out on a torn, moldy couch—the only piece of furniture in the stripped apartment—and promptly fell asleep. His unusual behavior didn't surprise the two cops; Patrick Stone had a reputation for pissing ice water at times like these.

An hour later Foley shook Stone awake. "Cap, we got the word. The buy is going down at nine."

Stone sat up quickly, instantly awake. "What time is it now?"

"Almost seven."

"Who's covering the backyard?"

"Beals."

"I'm going to pick up some doughnuts. Tell him I'll call him on the radio when I get into the block."

Ten minutes later Stone, standing in a darkened doorway a block away from the target building, whispered into his radio, "Hawk to Nest."

"Nest. Go ahead."

"Come get me."

"Stand by."

Moments later a tall black man wearing a shabby Army fatigue jacket slid out of the shadows. "Come on, Cap," he said. "I'll take you in the back way."

Stone followed him into a hallway lit only by a filthy yellow bulb, down cellar stairs, and across a garbage-strewn yard into another cellar. Once in the cellar the black man led him through a maze of narrow, dark corridors. A cat darted past them, making them both reach for their guns. Finally the black man stopped in front of a storage room and knocked. "It's Beals," he whispered. "Open up."

The door opened and a squat man with fierce, bushy eyebrows pointed a shotgun at them. Sgt. Aristotle Kakavos lowered the weapon and smiled. "Come on in, Cap. It ain't much, but it's home."

Silently, McKay Beals slipped back to his post in the rear yard. Stone stepped inside. The large room, lit by a naked electric light bulb hanging from the ceiling, was half coal bin and half storage area. It stank of coal dust and cat urine. Billy Callahan, wearing a shoulder holster, sat at a table laden with tape recorders and electronic equipment. He was monitoring the wiretap and the bug that had been placed in the apartment five floors above. Five other cops were playing seven-card stud on top of a cardboard box.

Stone handed the bag of coffee and doughnuts to one of them. "Here, Teddy, I know you guys are always hungry."

Teddy Gibson gratefully accepted the bag of goodies. "You got that right, boss. You can't get a decent cup of coffee within ten miles of this shithouse."

The men had come to expect Captain Stone at these raids, and it made them feel better knowing that their boss was going to go in with them—ahead of them, more often than not. Even the sergeants liked Stone. He asked a lot of questions, but as long as he heard the right answers, he didn't interfere.

Stone wiped the seat of a filthy chair with a handkerchief and sat down. "Fill me in, Ari. What's happening?"

"We intercepted a call forty minutes ago. The shipment's coming at nine. They're supposed to call when they're on their way."

"Everyone in place?"

"Yep. Hardy and his team are covering the roof and the backyard;

Radlicki has the trucks, and O'Neill is covering the street. My team is making the arrest.''

"How many in the apartment now?''

"Two.''

"What's the latest on the delivery?''

"The same. Four hundred and fifty kilos.''

"Good.'' Stone could almost see the P.C.'s smiling face. "What kind of hardware do they have?''

Kakavos addressed the cop monitoring the tape recorders. "Billy, what's the latest on their ordnance?''

The cop, who wore a sweatshirt that said KILL THEM ALL, LET GOD SORT 'EM OUT, slipped his earphones off. "I heard one guy say he had a nine mm. I've also been hearing a bolt action sliding in the background. Could be an Uzi.''

"Shit.'' Stone and Kakavos spoke in unison. The card players glanced uneasily at each other.

There was no such thing as an easy bust anymore. No more sawed-off shotguns, or Saturday Night Specials that seldom worked. Now the bad guys were armed with state-of-the-art firepower—"nines,'' Uzis, machine pistols, and flak jackets. Many of these gangs were better equipped than some NATO countries. They were certainly better equipped than the New York City Police Department, which only recently had begun to arm narc assault teams with automatic weapons.

Even with better firepower, however, it was still an unfair fight. The perps, unencumbered by legal requirements, didn't hesitate to shoot at the slightest provocation. And that was why so many cops got killed; that extra second a cop took to assure himself that he was within his legal and moral rights to use his weapon was sometimes one second too long.

"What are Hardy and O'Neill's call signs?'' Stone asked.

"Hardy is Bluebird; O'Neill is Polecat.''

Stone reached for his radio. "Bluebird, are you in position?''

"Affirmative. Doors and fire escapes covered.''

"Is Tecci ready?''

"That's an affirmative.''

In order to neutralize the drug dealers' expected superior firepower, Stone had thought of an unusual diversionary tactic. Just before they were to go through the door, Tecci was to set off an M-80 outside the window of the apartment. It was hoped that the explosion would distract the drug dealers long enough for the battering ram to take the door down.

"Polecat. Are you ready?''

The high-pitched voice of Sgt. Brenden O'Neill came back. "The street's covered.''

"The street's covered," Kakavos mimicked O'Neill's voice. "Jesus, you'd never know that weenie voice belonged to a gorilla."

Brenden O'Neill, all six feet, seven inches and 270 pounds of him, had gone to Fordham as a pulling guard. But a chronic knee condition made it impossible for him to continue and he left school. Fordham's loss was the NYPD's gain. O'Neill, the most fearless man in NET, was still irked at Stone for giving him the street assignment tonight. He always wanted to be the first one through the door.

Stone looked at his watch. Eight-thirty. From experience, he knew that these people were seldom prompt. Nine could mean four A.M., noon the next day, or never. Now came the wait.

Stone watched Billy Callahan monitoring the wire. From time to time he adjusted the gain to pick up something being said upstairs. Suddenly the cop grabbed a fly swatter and slammed it against the side of the desk. "Got you, you little bastard." He scooped up the dead roach and deposited it in an ashtray full of other dead roaches. Without looking up from his dials, he said, "Is that a confirmed hit, Sarge?"

Boylan threw his cards on the table. "Bullshit! That's illegal," he protested. "He's feeding them, Sarge."

"I am not. I'm eating a crumb bun, for Chrissake. Can I help it if a few crumbs fall?"

Kakavos inspected the table and blew the rest of the crumbs off. "I'll confirm that one. But you keep the area clean downrange or you're disqualified."

He turned to Stone. "A roach-hunting tournament," he explained. "A roach counts as one and a water bug counts as two. High man wins the pool. Billy's an ace. He's won so many pools, the guys are accusing him of breeding them at home and sneaking them in."

"The cocksuckers wouldn't trust Mother Teresa," Billy muttered into his dials.

Stone, looking into the darkness just beyond the pool of yellow light, saw the reflection of several pairs of tiny red eyes watching him. Involuntarily, he shuddered. He didn't mind the roaches, but rats spooked him. Looking at his outwardly calm appearance, there wasn't a man in the room who would guess how hard it was for Stone to sit in a cellar with rats that close to him.

Kakavos followed the captain's gaze. "It kinda reminds you of the movie *Snow White*, don't it? Like when she wakes up in the forest and all those eyes are staring at her. Only these beady little eyes don't belong to rabbits and chipmunks, they belong to fucking rats." He tossed a bottle cap toward them and the eyes blinked off simultaneously. Stone tried not to listen to the scratching feet scurrying across the coal.

Kakavos whispered out of the side of his mouth. "I hope these guys don't get the bright idea to hold a rat-hunting tournament. We'll have to bring in fucking bushel baskets for the bodies.''

Just then the tape recorder hooked up to the telephone activated. A telephone call was coming into the apartment. Billy, listening, gave the thumbs-up sign. "They're on the way," he announced.

Kakavos keyed the mike on his radio. "Heads up, everybody, incoming mail.''

Abruptly, idle conversation ceased. The cards were abandoned as each man silently rechecked weapons and bulletproof vests. Kakavos fed a round into the chamber of his shotgun and stuffed extra rounds into his jacket pocket. Everyone, including Stone, put on blue jackets that had POLICE emblazoned across the backs in large yellow letters. If the shooting started, it was critical to tell the good guys from the bad guys at a glance.

"Ari, let's go over it one more time.''

Kakavos spread a drawing of the apartment's floor plan on the table and everyone gathered around. They'd reviewed the plan a dozen times before in the last two days and each man knew exactly what he was to do, but no one complained about doing it again.

"To the right of the front door is the kitchen." Kakavos pointed with a stubby finger. "There's a hallway—about twenty-five feet long—leading into the living room straight ahead. Two bedrooms to the left. Stein and Vigna will be on the ram. When the door comes down, Gibson, the automatic-weapons man, goes through first, then me with the shotgun. Sakash, Boylan, and Callahan will follow to subdue and cuff.''

Stone studied the drawing grimly. Under the circumstances, the plan was as good as it could get, but he didn't like the long hallway leading to the living room. It was like a funnel. Anyone shooting from the living room couldn't miss. "It's a lousy setup," he said.

The length of the hallway hadn't escaped the sergeant either. "I know. We have to get in fast.''

"What kind of door?''

"The usual. Reinforced steel. But we may be in luck. Sakash got a chance to examine it earlier. The frame on the lock side is made of wood and it wasn't replaced. It's the weakest part. Stein and Vigna will concentrate on that side of the door.''

O'Neill's high-pitched voice broke the silence. "Truck pulling into the block. Three getting out . . . they're going into the building . . . two left in the truck . . . we'll take them.''

"Three?" Kakavos swore in Greek. "There was only supposed to be two coming. Now we have five targets to worry about.''

Billy looked up from his dials. "Cap, they're inside the apartment.''

"Okay." Stone was glad to be getting out of the cellar. "Let's go.''

At the first landing they met one of O'Neill's men. "Have the people in the truck been neutralized?" Stone whispered.

"Yeah. O'Neill didn't even wait to open the door. He yanked one poor fuck right through the window."

Silently, the group crept up the five flights of stairs. A small child was crying in an apartment on the second floor; a wisp of black smoke swirling at the ceiling betrayed that someone had burned the ribs on the third; a family fight was in progress in apartment 4D. And everywhere was the rank, eye-watering stink of urine.

When they reached the fifth-floor landing, Boylan tiptoed down the hall and unscrewed the light bulbs, plunging the hallway into darkness. Using pencil flashlights, they moved into position in front of the door.

Stone hissed into the radio, "Bluebird, do it now."

All flashlights switched off. They waited in the darkened hallway, lit only by the cracks of light coming from under other apartment doors, listening for the sound of the explosion—the signal for the men on the battering ram to hit the door with everything they had.

Stone rubbed his forehead. There were so many things that could go wrong with an operation like this. He tried to plan for every eventuality, but there was always the unexpected. In his mind he reviewed the plan again. It was as good as it could get.

It seemed like an hour since he'd given the order that should have sent Tecci scurrying down the fire escape with the M-80. Where the hell was he? Had he been spotted? Had he dropped the damn thing? Did he have matches?

The explosion was deafening.

"Holy shit!" someone muttered. The noise momentarily stunned them into inactivity. Kakavos was the first to react. He slapped Stein on the back. "Go! Go!" he hissed.

Overcoming their initial paralysis, Stein and Vigna lunged forward, striking the door below the lock. The door shook but held firm. Inside, Stone heard screams and curses. It was working. They had the advantage of surprise on their side, but they were still in the hallway on the wrong side of the door. "Come on!" he shouted. "Get that goddamn door down!"

Grunting, the cops lunged and again bounced off. "Fuck me," Vigna muttered. "Goddamn door's a lot stronger than it looks."

Every second they delayed gave the people in the apartment the chance to recover. Stone pictured the long hallway on the other side of the door. In his mind's eye he saw a man standing there with an Uzi. "Come on, for Chrissake. Do it!"

Galvanized by the urgency in his voice, Kakavos and the others threw their weight behind the men holding the battering ram. There was a loud crack and the doorjamb split. By now there was total confusion. All the carefully drawn plans on the chalkboard back in the office were out the window. With four cops piled up in front of the door, Gibson couldn't get through.

In an effort to get out of the way, Sakash ripped his hand on an exposed nail and screamed out in pain. Stone saw the whole operation collapsing. Not only were they losing the element of surprise they so desperately needed, they were in real danger. Bunched up in front of the door, they were an easy target. One burst would take them all out.

Stone, his .38 in hand, shoved his way through the door. Thick blue smoke hung in the air, which was heavy with the acrid smell of cordite. Suddenly a man covered with red paint stumbled out of the smoke toward them. Stone crouched and brought his gun up. But then he froze. It wasn't paint, it was blood. The man's face and chest had been shredded by glass. Unable to see, he bounced off the walls, his bloodied hands leaving streaks of blood. *"¡Estoy ciego!"* he screamed. *"No puedo ver."*

Boylan swept the injured man's legs out from under him and snapped a pair of handcuffs on him almost before he hit the floor. More moans came from the direction of the living room; Stone waved Gibson forward. The cop shoved past Stone and advanced in a crouch toward the living room. Suddenly he stopped and stood up. "Holy shit!" Stone heard him shout.

Furious at Gibson for not covering himself, or anyone else, Stone bolted toward him. Then he saw what the cop saw. The living room window frame was in splinters and the tattered curtains were smoldering from several small fires. One man lay sprawled on the floor, unconscious. His clothes were soaked in blood. Cut and bleeding from flying shards of glass, three others, still dazed and disoriented from the violence of the explosion, stumbled around the room. The acrid smell of gunpowder filled the air.

Gibson shouted, "Police! Hands over your head!"

One man held a bloodied handkerchief against a flap of skin hanging from his cheek. The front of his sixties-style double-knit sport jacket was drenched in blood. The others, looking equally incongruous dressed in lightweight tropical clothing, stared at Gibson dumbly.

Gibson, waving the gun barrel for emphasis, said more slowly, "Put your fucking hands over your head!"

Kakavos hissed, "Save your breath, Teddy. These fuckers are shell-shocked. They think they're still in Miami."

Glass shattered. Tecci, kicking out the remaining panes, climbed through the window. *"Marone!* What a racket. I think I'm deaf."

"Let's get them cuffed," Stone said, surveying the chaos. "Call for some ambulances. Someone put out that fire."

Kakavos ripped the curtains down and stamped out the smoldering fires. "Stevie, what the hell did you use?"

Tecci looked at the sergeant blankly. His ears were ringing and he couldn't hear. "What?"

Kakavos repeated the question more loudly.

Tecci looked sheepish. "I figured more was better than less," he shouted.

"How much more?" Stone asked.

"I tied five together."

Kakavos tore the rest of the smoldering curtains down and flung them out the window. "Five M-80's! You crazy bastard, that's about a pound of dynamite. You could have taken this whole goddamn building down!"

Callahan tried to give his prisoner the Miranda warnings, but the man simply squinted at him and shook his head. "Hey, Sarge," Callahan called to Kakavos, "I don't think this guy speaks English. We need a Spanish interpreter."

Kakavos stooped and looked into the prisoner's dilated pupils. "You don't need a Spanish interpreter, you need someone who can give the Miranda in sign language. Anybody got Helen Keller's telephone number?"

Stone, beginning to feel the intoxicating rush that came from putting one's life on the line, started to laugh. He felt invincible. They'd made mistakes, but they'd done the job. They had five under arrest, and judging from the duffel bag on the couch stuffed with money, a truckload of cocaine. Except for Sakash getting caught on a nail, no one was hurt. A few stitches and he'd be as good as new. All in all, it had been a good night.

By now the others were crowding into the apartment. An excited O'Neill rushed up to Stone. "Boss, wait'll you see the load of shit in the truck! There's enough coke there to keep the entire population of Manhattan high for a year."

It was over.

O'Neill, surveying the devastation, kidded Tecci. "Hey, Stevie, next time why don't you call for a napalm drop?"

Everyone laughed, except Tecci, who was slapping the side of his head. His ears were still ringing.

Stone crunched through the broken glass to the door. "All right, people," he said. "Let's start moving the bodies out. As soon as the paperwork is done, it's to Mulrooney's we go. Drinks on me. But don't keep me out too late. The P.C. and I have to do a dog-and-pony show for the press in the morning."

IT WAS ALMOST TEN A.M. WHEN PATRICK STONE ARRIVED AT ONE Police Plaza. He was hung over, but still floating from the residual effects of last night's adrenaline high. Too keyed up to get to bed early, he'd closed Mulrooney's at four that morning.

He was looking forward to the press conference. Unlike some of his colleagues, who became paralyzed at the thought of speaking before TV cameras, Stone relished the exposure. It gave him a chance to impress the P.C., and anyone else who might be able to further his career.

Inside the bricked lobby he flashed his ID at a bored security officer and went directly to the auditorium on the ground floor. The increased security in and around the auditorium was immediately evident. Emergency Service cops with flak jackets and shotguns were stationed at all doors and exits. Officers, standing at the entrance to the auditorium, checked IDs carefully. Only people with authorized press credentials were admitted.

The additional security was the direct result of an idea Stone had given the commissioner during a telephone conversation earlier that morning. For maximum impact, Stone had suggested that they have the cocaine on hand to display to the press. The commissioner's horrified staff, thinking of all the things that could go wrong, objected strenuously, but they were over-ruled by their delighted boss, who thought it was a splendid idea.

The harried inspector responsible for the security of the auditorium spotted Stone and pulled him aside. "I understand this was your idea," he said, tight-lipped. "This evidence should be locked up in the Property Clerk's office—not on display like a goddamn circus."

Stone knew why the inspector was upset. Property, especially narcotics whose street value was worth over sixty million, was a hot potato. Nothing could jettison a career faster than losing important evidence, and the inspector wasn't happy being saddled with that responsibility. He stuck a finger in Stone's face. "You're a grandstander, Stone. You figure this department is a fucking vaudeville show, but be careful, pal—the vaudeville stage is full of banana peels."

Mara and his entourage were coming into the auditorium. "Think of it this way," Stone said, patting the red-faced inspector on the back, "if I land on my ass, at least it'll give you a good laugh."

After a last-minute briefing from the Deputy Commissioner of Public Information, Mara stepped up to the podium. While he waited for the stragglers to find seats, he studied his audience, and was satisfied by the turnout he'd gotten on such short notice. All the networks and every major paper were represented. It was ironic, but he probably had Nathan Pickett to thank for that.

In front of him two cops lined up the last row of clear plastic envelopes containing the cocaine. When they'd finished, the commissioner began.

"Ladies and gentlemen. What you see on these tables in front of you is four hundred and fifty kilos of cocaine—the fruits of an arrest made by NET early this morning. If this cocaine were turned into crack, it would have a street value of over sixty million dollars."

Now that the harmless-looking white powder had a price tag, it took on a whole new meaning for the photographers. The room lit up from the explosion of flashes as they snapped pictures of the tables.

"Eighteen months ago," Mara continued, "the Narcotics Enforcement Team was created to go after high-level drug dealers. Under the capable command of Captain Patrick Stone, who is sitting behind me, they have done so with admirable aggressiveness. In spite of what some may say, this"—he swept his hand over the tables—"is an example of what the New York City Police Department is doing about the drug problem. Twenty-four hours a day dedicated police officers risk their lives to arrest and confiscate the money, drugs, and weapons of drug dealers in this city.

"As any responsible person knows, there is no easy solution to the insidious drug problem that plagues not only our major cities, but our small towns as well. But I can assure you that the New York City Police Department stands second to none in its desire to make this a drug-free city. What we need at this time is the support and confidence of our citizens. Divisiveness and groundless allegations can only lead to a lowering of the morale of the very men and women who are doing the most in this war against drugs." He paused, sweeping his audience with his eyes, then said, "I'll take questions."

A reporter in the back shouted, "Is this display your response to Senator Pickett's charges?"

"No," Mara shot back angrily. "This is the culmination of an investigation that has been ongoing for several weeks." He pointed to a tiny woman in the front row, whose hand was raised.

"Commissioner, will this seizure have an effect on the city's drug supply?"

Mara tugged at his ear. "Absolutely. The law of supply and demand applies to the drug business as well. As a result of removing this large amount of cocaine from circulation, there will be less available."

Stone studied the reporters' faces and waited for someone to challenge the commissioner's statement. The reality was that the supply of cocaine seemed endless. Any confiscation, even one this large, had little impact on price or availability. But no one spoke up.

"Commissioner, how do you respond to Senator Pickett's allegation that what he terms your 'do-nothing' order is an act of genocide against minorities?"

Stone saw Mara's knuckles whiten as he grasped the sides of the podium. The allegation, which the press had begun to call "Pickett's charge," infuriated the commissioner.

"That order merely spells out the proper procedures for drug arrests. It's imperative that the department coordinate its efforts. The last thing we want is for a uniformed officer to arrest someone who might be under surveillance by the Narcotics Division. Besides, we've found that too many street arrests made by the uniformed force are being dismissed in court because the officer failed to establish a prima facie case. Drug arrests require a level of expertise that the average officer on the street doesn't possess. It is not a do-nothing order. It specifies that the officer will call the Narcotics Division and report his observation. Specially trained members of the Narcotics Division will be immediately dispatched to evaluate the information and make a summary arrest if warranted.''

Stone was amazed at the gullibility of the press. No one challenged the massive flaw in Mara's argument. Drug dealers were fluid. A few stayed in one location, but the vast majority moved from street to street. The Narcotics Division, overwhelmed by their own crippling workload, didn't have the manpower to respond to the dozens of calls logged in every day by enthusiastic cops looking to become detectives. By the time the narcs arrived, often days later, the dealer was long gone.

A red-nosed reporter who wrote a column for the *Daily News* got to his feet. ''Commissioner, Ted Farrell, the head of the PBA, agrees with Pickett. He says you've handcuffed the cops on the street and they've become frustrated because they can't do their jobs.''

Mara paused before answering. It was one thing to attack Pickett, it was another to go after the powerful police union. He'd gotten as much mileage as he could expect from this press conference. There was no point in getting sucked into a media war with the PBA. It was time to end it here. ''The PBA has a right to its own opinion,'' he said reasonably. ''But they don't make policy; policy is my prerogative. That's all the time we have. Thank you, ladies and gentlemen, for attending.''

Stone was stunned and angered by the abrupt end of the conference. He'd planned to describe the arrest and the role NET had played in it. He knew a story about breaking down doors made good copy, but Mara had deliberately hogged the spotlight. Before he had the chance to express his disappointment, however, the commissioner was rushed out the door by his aides, leaving the commanding officer of NET alone to watch the camera crews pack up their equipment.

11

IN THE SIX DAYS SINCE ROSE HAD BEEN ASSIGNED TO THE INVESTI-
gation, Shannon did his best to avoid the lieutenant from IAD. By tacit
agreement, each had gone his own way, conducting interviews and collecting information. They communicated by scribbled progress notes and an
occasional conversation, but mostly they communicated through the medium
of Velez. The arrangement wasn't perfect, but it suited Shannon—until an
unhappy Velez told him that he felt like an only child in the middle of an
especially dirty divorce war. Faced with a rebellious subordinate, Shannon
had to concede it was time to stop acting foolishly. Like it or not, he'd have
to work more closely with Rose.

Fortified with a second cup of morning coffee, he lit a cigarette and went
back into the office.

"All right," he said, clearing a space on his cluttered desk for his coffee

cup, "we've collected a lot of paperwork, let's see if it means anything."
He started to take off his jacket.

"I brought some coat hangers from home," Rose said. "They're behind
the door."

Shannon glared at him and dropped his jacket on the desk. "What have
you found out about Marbridge?"

Rose shook his head and reached for a folder on his desk. If he was
surprised by this sudden change in routine, he didn't show it. He opened his
folder and scanned his notes. "Yesterday I interviewed Marbridge's assistant, Stephen Pyne. Our friend Nelson Marbridge was a fifty-two-year-old
homosexual art dealer."

Velez grinned. "Isn't that redundant?"

Rose looked up. "Velez, you're a bigot."

"Yes, but a *heterosexual* bigot."

The lieutenant continued. "He came from a wealthy family in Connecti-
cut, who gave him a liberal allowance to stay far away from the family. In
1961 he opened a small gallery specializing in South American art. Some
pre-Colombian stuff, but mostly really bad modern stuff. Pyne said they
didn't make any money selling that shit."

"When you come from a wealthy family," Velez pointed out, "you
don't have to make a lot of money."

"Keep making sage observations like that, and we'll have to make you a
detective." Rose returned to his notes. "Lived in a classy condo on Park
Avenue, where he met his untimely demise. As we all know, there were no
witnesses."

"No witnesses?" Velez asked incredulously. "On Park Avenue? That's
not exactly an abandoned part of town."

Rose shook his head. "It's also not the South Bronx. People on Park
Avenue don't sit on their front stoops drinking beer out of little brown paper
bags."

"Anything else?" Shannon asked.

"I ran a criminal-record check on Marbridge and came up with zilch.
But I have a feeling he was arrested sometime in his life. For faggery if
nothing else. I've been trying to get in touch with a contact in Customs so I
can run Marbridge's name through their system. Maybe there was a glitch in
our computers and his record isn't coming up."

Shannon studiously ignored Velez. "It happens. Computers are only as
good as the assholes who feed them."

"Thank you very much, Señor Lieutenant," Velez said indignantly.

"Another thing, Pyne said Marbridge practically commuted to Peru."

"So? You said he dealt in South American art."

"Yeah, but if he bought art every time he went, there wouldn't be
anything left in the whole country."

"What are you getting at?"

"Maybe he was a mule."

"Running drugs into the U.S.? No way. If he was a professional mule for any length of time, he'd have gotten locked up at least a couple of times."

"Not necessarily. He imported a lot of stuff. Plenty of places to hide it."

"We're not talking about smuggling a couple of bottles of booze, for Chrissake. We're talking about big time drugs. There's no way he could have been doing that and not have a record."

"You're wrong, Brian. My roommate at the FBI Academy was from Customs. He said—"

"*You* went to the FBI National Academy?"

"Yeah. What about it?"

"I put in for that three times and I'm still waiting. It always seems the guys in IAD get the choice assignments."

"Christ! You're unbelievable. Not that it's any of your business, but I was a *patrol* sergeant in the Two-oh when I went to the Academy."

Shannon shrugged. "Whatever. The point is, Marbridge would have a record if he was involved in transporting drugs."

"Customs can barely keep up with their known targets. Most of their information comes from informants. If no one blew the whistle on Marbridge, and he wasn't careless, he could have been doing it for years. The gallery didn't make any money, but Marbridge lived extremely well. I'm sure his family allowance couldn't have paid for all that." It was clear from the look on Shannon's face that he wasn't buying it. "Anyway," Rose continued, "I'm going to check him out at Customs." Rose slapped Velez on the knee. "How about you, amigo? Did you find out anything about Mr. Rowe?"

"I thought you'd never ask." Velez grew serious. "Mr. Thomas Rowe was an example of the American dream come true. Born in New York on February twenty-third, 1939, he graduated in the top ten percent of his class at Brooklyn Law. Relocated to Miami, and bounced around a few law firms. He finally opened up his own practice in 1975, where he struggled to put food on the table. Then, in 1984, he seemed to hit his stride. Suddenly he was making lots of money. Life was beautiful"—Velez paused dramatically— "until that fateful day in 1984."

"What happened?"

The weasel grin appeared. "He was busted for laundering money through a Bahamian bank."

"Drugs!" Rose snapped his fingers. "That's the connection. I knew it."

"Before you close the case"—Shannon's voice dripped sarcasm—"you might want to establish that Marbridge, Leonard, and Rowe were connected."

"Brian, Brian"—Rose shook his head—"you take all this too seriously."

"Maybe, but we're not going to get anywhere playing armchair detective. I have a contact in the DEA. I'll call him later to see if he can get me more on Rowe."

"How did you make out with DeNoto?" Velez asked Shannon.

"No brass ring. DeNoto's informant was vague. He says some big drug dealers are left alone, while others are getting hit all the time."

"Sounds like a pad," Velez said.

Rose poked the young cop. "We're getting ready to make you a detective and already you're talking like a boss."

"I can't help myself. This shit is so fascinating. When I grow up, I want to be just like you guys."

"It *does* sound like a pad," Shannon said. "Unfortunately, DeNoto's informant doesn't have any details. Just a lot of scuttlebutt. He's not even sure if it's city cops or feds."

Shannon scribbled the three names on a piece of paper and idly drew lines connecting them. "So where does that leave us? A major drug dealer, a crooked lawyer, and an art dealer." He drummed the pencil on the desk. "How the hell do they tie in?"

IT WAS EARLY AFTERNOON WHEN BRIAN SHANNON WALKED INTO THE Three Deuces bar, but even at this hour it was crowded. The Three Deuces, on Lexington Avenue and 102nd Street, was a carbon copy of a hundred other bars in Spanish Harlem. Its clientele—people who lived in a four-block radius—went there to drown the frustration of working in menial, dead-end jobs in the garment center and hotel kitchens.

No one turned to look at Shannon when he entered the stuffy, smoke-filled room, but conversation stopped in mid-sentence and more than one pair of eyes followed his progress in the bar mirror. A buxom woman, wearing a red dress that was two sizes too small, danced in front of a jukebox blaring a salsa record. Behind her a man clapped his hands in drunken encouragement.

Shannon sat on a stool at the far end and ordered a beer. A few minutes later a man wearing a tattered windbreaker and torn jeans shuffled in. He wiped his nose on his sleeve and moved toward Shannon. It wasn't until the man was almost upon him that Shannon recognized his friend Ray Santos behind the scraggly beard. He followed the stoop-shouldered figure into the back and sat down at a dusty leather banquette.

"Jesus, Ray, you look like shit."

The derelict sitting opposite him grinned. "Thanks, man, I'll take that as a compliment."

"You DEA undercover guys take your work too seriously."

Santos winked. "In this line of work you better take it seriously or you wind up fucking DOA."

"What does Marie think of it?"

"Apparently not much. She walked out on me six months ago."

"I'm sorry."

"Occupational hazard. UC work is tougher on the women."

"You've been at this for a long time. Why don't you pack it in?"

"What, and give up show business? It's in my blood, man. I love this shit."

Shannon couldn't tell if Santos was serious or just being sarcastic. He himself loved being a cop, but he couldn't understand a man wanting to spend most of his life acting the part of a junkie. Not only was it dangerous and dehumanizing, but it usually wrecked their personal lives as well. A lot of the undercover people he knew in the P.D. and the DEA were divorced, borderline alcoholics, and in a few tragic cases had even succumbed to the drugs they had sworn to eradicate. "Did you find out anything for me?"

Santos eyed the dancing woman. *"Marone*, what an ass!"' Reluctantly, he turned his attention to Shannon. "Yeah, right after you called, I checked with a buddy of mine in the Miami office. He told me Rowe started out as a shithouse lawyer chasing ambulances. There was no money there so he started representing small-time drug people—arranging bail, copping pleas, the usual shit. Then Rowe got lucky and made a connection with some big players. In 1983 he started laundering money for them. Somewhere along the line he made a connection for a big-time operator in South America. When we caught up to Rowe, he had so much money he was storing it in bushel baskets. Brian, do you ever get the feeling that we're in the wrong end of this business?"

"Only when I hear stories like that. Who was the guy from South America?"

"We never found out. We tried to turn Rowe, but he was too scared. He said he'd do life before he'd hand up his associates."

"What about Tiny Leonard?"

"You got bingo there. On at least two occasions Rowe brokered deals between Leonard and the guy in South America."

"Nelson Marbridge?"

"Nada. No one ever heard of him." Santos cocked his head and studied Shannon. "One out of two ain't bad."

"Yeah, but I was looking for the whole enchilada. Ray, thanks. I owe you."

"You're in my black book. Brian, what the hell are you working on? You could have gotten this information through channels."

"I know, but it's more fun this way."

Santos scratched his beard and studied the stained ceiling. "It's a devious fucking world we live in. I'm beginning to think no one tells the truth anymore.''

"You've been under too long, Ray. Your head is all fucked up.''

"Yeah, probably. Do me a favor, Brian. Let me leave first. I don't want to be seen walking in the street with a cop. It'll ruin my reputation.''

Shannon looked at his watch. If the traffic wasn't too bad, he'd be home in time for dinner for a change. He waited for five minutes and then got up to leave. As he was passing the bar, the woman in the red dress pushed her drunken partner aside and tried to dance with Shannon. He sidestepped her and spun her back into the arms of the man. Again, no heads turned, but the resentful eyes watched him in the mirror. As he was going out the door, a voice shouted, *"Maricón!"* And there was a burst of nervous laughter.

12

SHANNON SPENT THE MORNING COLLECTING COURT RECORDS IN MAN-
hattan and Queens, while Rose was at the Identification Section making
copies of arrest reports.

Before noon Rose dropped a bulging manila envelope on Shannon's
desk. Its contents represented the culmination of eight tedious days sifting
through court-records rooms, precinct files, and dusty storage areas. "This
is a complete set of files on each of the murders," Rose announced. "Each
folder has a set of sixty-ones, DD5's, forensic reports, M.E. reports, the
works. Your homework for tonight." He tapped the envelope. "When you
come in tomorrow, there will be a quiz. No multiple choice."

Shannon hefted the weighty material. He still didn't trust Rose, but he
had to admit the lieutenant from IAD was efficient. All the more reason he
was determined not to let him take over the investigation. It was still

the bureau's case, unless they found cops at the bottom of it. Then . . . who knows?

Rose stood up and stretched. "Come on, Brian, I'll buy you lunch."

They stopped at the OTC, a small pub in the heart of Wall Street. Rose ordered scotch and Shannon inspected the array of bottles behind the bar. "Do you have Black Bush?" he asked.

"A fine whiskey that," the small ferret-faced Irish bartender answered. "But we don't carry it. The owner's too goddamned cheap, he is." Shannon settled for a scotch.

"What's Black Bush?" Rose asked.

"An Irish whiskey made by Bushmills in Northern Ireland. I first tried it when I was there a couple of years ago with the Emerald Society."

"What were you doing, selling guns to the IRA?"

Shannon ignored the jibe and watched Rose polish off his scotch. "I thought Jews didn't drink," he said.

"They don't. That is, they don't drink at all or they drink too much. I," Rose said with a self-deprecating smile, "count myself among the latter. Of course I blame that on my upbringing."

"Your old man drink?"

"God, no." He laughed at the thought. "I grew up in an Irish neighborhood in the Bronx. I was the only Jew on the block, so I had no choice but to assimilate. Now"—he shrugged—"I'm a ruined Jew. I drink too much, listen to the Clancy Brothers, and eat ham. My very first girlfriend was Peggy Flynn—a nine-year-old flaming redhead. I thought my mother was going to have a stroke. She still curses the day we moved to the Bronx."

"Do they still live there?"

"No. They live in Great Neck now."

They drifted into the innocuous small talk men engage in when they're trying to feel each other out. They talked about sports, women, and the job—all the while trying to discover something meaningful about the other. But both being shrewd interrogators, they offered little information of value, and of course received none in return. What they did discover after three drinks was that they agreed on absolutely nothing.

Finally Shannon turned to the subject that was bothering him. "Rose, what if it turns out that cops are involved?"

"What about it?"

"Well, I mean I guess you guys will take it from there."

Rose twirled his ice cubes. "What do you mean by 'you guys'? My shield says City of New York. What does yours say? Hoboken?"

He knew what Shannon was getting at. If cops were involved, Detective Lieutenant Brian Shannon wanted nothing to do with it. Hunting cops, even murdering cops, was best left to the scumbags in IAD.

"You consider yourself a good cop, don't you, Brian? You can spot a felon at five hundred yards, but you'd trip over a rotten cop and never notice him. Why is that? Because you don't want to admit that cops go bad? Well I got news for you, pal. They do."

Shannon said nothing.

"Let me tell you how it happens, Brian. When a cop's a rookie he's willing to tilt at windmills, but after a few years he begins to get cynical— too many plea bargains, too many suspended sentences, too much exposure to the bullshit in the world. After a few more years he's totally fed up with police work. At this juncture he has several choices: he can go into mental retirement, finish up his twenty years and get out, or he can develop an interest outside police work. Cops are very enterprising; they've become lawyers, writers, musicians, carpenters, undertakers—you name it and cops have done it. But if the burnout is too severe, or if his moral equipment isn't what it should be, a cop may turn to crime. It starts small—robbing DOAs of loose change and cheap jewelry—but eventually he moves up to the big leagues—drugs, robbery, and extortion.

"These guys don't operate in a vacuum. Other cops see and they know what's going on, but of course they won't say anything because we have a code of silence—just like the Mafia and the medical profession. The conspiracy of silence prevails. In a way, we're all responsible for them. We didn't create them, but we let them exist. They thrive on our silence and self-imposed impotence."

Rose was annoyed that he'd let Shannon's question get to him. He'd handled enough corruption investigations to know by heart the sorry chain of events that led to the destruction of otherwise good cops, but he also knew better than to preach, especially to another cop. In a more conciliatory tone he added, "The way I see it, *you* are the good guys and *I* am the good guys. The people who committed the murders are the bad guys even if they carry shields."

Rose's speech had hit a nerve. Rationally, Shannon knew Rose was right. But emotionally—that was something else. Shannon had spent most of his adult life as part of the police family, and during his twenty-three years he had come to trust and rely on his brother officers.

He was also ambivalent about these murders, which came wrapped in their own seductive logic. Didn't Leonard, a purveyor of certain death, deserve to die? Weren't he and the others like him in the drug trade parasites, sucking the lifeblood of society? But in spite of his indignation, he had to admit it was not for him to say what should be done with people like Leonard. As a cop the best he could do was arrest them. The rest was up to the courts and the lawyers.

"What I meant was," Shannon said lamely, "if cops are involved, it's department procedure to turn the case over to IAD."

"Not this time, Brian. We're stuck with it because no one wants it. You and I are neither fish nor fowl. We're not IAD and we're not the bureau either. We're just two unfortunate guys who have been tagged to handle a very hot potato. Hey,'' he said sarcastically, ''you'll get used to it. You handcuff cops just like everyone else—behind the back. We even use the same arrest reports.''

Shannon wasn't happy with Rose's description of them as a team. ''I don't think there are cops involved anyway,'' he said with little conviction. ''A cop would have to be nuts to get involved in murder.''

Rose downed the rest of his third drink. ''From my particular perspective,'' he said, ''I've seen cops do some crazy things; don't look for rational reasons for irrational behavior.''

PATRICK STONE TURNED OFF WEST STREET ONTO A DARKENED PIER. During the day the pier was a parking lot filled with the cars of people who toiled in the forest of high-rise office buildings in lower Manhattan. After dark it was used for more sordid purposes. Not far from a cluster of West Village gay bars, it was the meeting place for cruising homosexuals out for a good time—or a bad time, depending on their sexual proclivities.

Stone, picking the quietest part of the lot, coasted to the edge of a bulkhead and doused his headlights. On the black, oily waters of the Hudson River, a brightly lit dinner-cruise ship steamed north returning from its tour of the Statue of Liberty and the lower bay. The sound of music and laughter wafted over the water.

Out of the corner of his eye Stone saw movement to his left. Thirty yards away a figure in a white leather jacket and tight stone-washed jeans emerged from the shadows. Like specters, the gays who prowled the West Side waterfront seemed to have the ability to appear and disappear into thin air. The man walked slowly across the open space. He studiously ignored Stone until he was less than ten feet from the car. Then he turned and his eyes locked on Stone's. In the space of a heartbeat he knew he hadn't found a kindred spirit and he veered away. A moment later he melted into the darkness and was gone.

Stone glanced at the dashboard clock. It was ten minutes after eleven. His confidential informant was late again. He looked in his rearview mirror and saw a set of headlights coming up behind him. A silver Mercedes convertible glided into a spot next to Stone. The last time he'd seen Eddie Dumont, he was driving a BMW. Either business was picking up or Stone's informant had gone into the used-car business.

Dumont slipped into the front seat next to Stone, and the interior of the car was immediately enveloped in a powerful cologne.

''Jesus, Eddie, you smell like a French whorehouse.''

Dumont's droopy eyes widened. "Are you kidding? This shit costs over a hundred bucks an ounce! Is it really bad?"

Stone, seeing the hurt spread across his informant's pockmarked face, said, "I'm only kidding, Eddie. It's okay."

An unfortunate combination of a large nose and an undercut jaw made Eddie Dumont look remarkably like a rodent. But at thirty-five he was as successful as an amoral, not terribly bright, criminal could hope to get. He had it all—money, expensive cars, and the beautiful women who went with money and expensive cars. He did, however, have one peculiar flaw—he was pathologically insecure. Despite possessing the best that money could buy, he needed confirmation that everything he owned was first-class. If Stone were to tell him his new Mercedes sucked, Dumont would probably drive the car off the pier without a second thought. Fortunately for the little neurotic, his financial resources permitted such extravagant solutions.

Stone had only a vague idea of Dumont's full range of illegal activities. Most big-time criminals specialized in one type of crime, but not Eddie Dumont. A rare breed of criminal, he successfully dabbled in whatever opportunity presented itself—sort of a one-man underworld conglomerate. Not one to pass up an opportunity, Dumont earned a good living from a wide variety of ventures ranging from con games to drugs. Stone *knew* he was into drugs; that's how they'd met. Dumont was swept up in one of NET's first arrests—a complicated deal involving a four-way transaction.

Stone, who knew the value of a good informant, especially in a brand-new narcotics enforcement unit, had been on the lookout for a suitable one. Sensing Dumont's insecurity, he took the terrified man aside and pointed out the facts of prison life to him. In the joint, Stone explained in elaborate terms, a slightly built man like Dumont was destined to become someone's wife. The only question was whose—a big black buck, or a sadistic iron-pumping murderer? Either way, Stone explained in graphic terms, Eddie Dumont's plumbing would never be the same.

It was the easiest flip Stone ever made. The man rolled over like a puppy and proceeded to hand up his associates so fast that Stone had to tell him to slow down.

For over a year Eddie Dumont had been one of Stone's most productive C.I.'s. Theirs was an unusual arrangement. Unlike most cop-informant relationships, Stone never paid Dumont. Eddie didn't need the money. The little man's reasons for becoming a confidential informant were much more complex. Of course, he was grateful to Stone for keeping him out of jail. But as a negative proton is inexorably attracted to a positive one, Eddie Dumont, the essence of insecurity, was drawn to Patrick Stone, the supreme example of self-confidence. When Dumont was in Stone's presence, he exhausted himself trying to read his idol's disapproval, real or imagined.

"Eddie, you're late again. Why don't you get yourself a decent watch?"

Dumont held up his wrist with the offending watch; the gold Rolex glistened in the darkness. "This fucking thing cost me five thou." He stared at it, wondering how anything so expensive could be bad. "You're right." He started to take it off. "It's a piece of shit."

Stone stopped him. "It's not the watch. *You're* the problem. If you looked at the damn thing once in a while, maybe you'd be on time. Where have you been? I haven't heard from you in three months."

"That's because nothing's been going on, Pat. Everyone on the street is in a panic. That fucking nigger, Pickett, has been beating the drum and stirring up a hornet's nest. He's got the cops nuts. They're locking up people for jaywalking, for Chrissake. How can anyone do business in such an atmosphere?"

Stone was amused at Dumont's indignation. "Sounds like police brutality to me."

"Seriously, I haven't heard a thing. Until last night." He leaned toward Stone, causing the gold chains dangling from his neck to jangle. "Pat, you're gonna love this." Even though no one was around, the little man glanced over his shoulder out of habit. "There's something big coming down. A group in Peru bought a *canning* factory and they're going to ship a ton of coke disguised as *canned peas!* Can you *believe* that shit?"

"Where did you hear that?" Stone asked sharply.

Dumont's eyes narrowed. "Pat, you know better than to ask me that. If the word got out I was talking to a cop, I'd end up in that river nailed to a fucking plank."

"I don't mean names. Just be more specific."

Dumont, nervous when Stone was angry, licked his lips. "I'm getting to it. They're going to ship the peas, I mean coke, from Peru to another South American country first. From there they'll ship it into New York. Clever, huh?"

"What South American country?"

"I'm not sure. Honduras, I think."

"Eddie, that's *Central* America."

"Hey, so my geography ain't so good. Maybe it's Central America."

Stone slammed the steering wheel with his palm. "Goddamn it. If you're going to give me information, get your facts straight."

Dumont cowered against the door. "Take it easy, Pat. These people don't invite me in when they're talking about this stuff. I only get bits and pieces, ya know?"

Stone relaxed his grip on the wheel. "I'm sorry. When is this going down?"

"The peas is—" He stuck his finger in his mouth. "Is it the peas is, or the peas are?"

Stone glared at him.

"I'm trying to improve my vocabulary. I wanna talk more like you."

"The peas are."

"Okay. They're on their way to . . . Honduras. I'm sure about the country, even if I don't know where the fuck it is." He grinned, and his protruding front teeth completed the rodent image.

"How is it coming in?"

"Freighter. Probably one of those piers on the East Side where they dock the banana boats."

"When?"

"Mid-January." He saw the look on Stone's face and added, "I'll try to get a better fix on the date."

"Who are the players?"

"Some guy from Peru, that's all I know. From what I hear, he's got big bucks and a big operation."

"Do you have a name?"

"Naw. You know this business. No one uses real names. Everyone is called Carlos, or Mr. Big, or some shit."

"Okay. When you hear more, call me."

Dumont studied Stone's face in the dim light, looking for a sign of approval. "You don't seem very happy. I thought you'd be doing cart-wheels, for Chrissake. I'm talking a ton of coke!"

"I know. It's good information. Thanks."

Dumont sulked. "I'm beginning to think you're not grateful."

"Sure I am."

"Yeah, well, you didn't do anything about the last info I gave you. They landed a planeload of shit right in Kennedy Airport. It was a ground ball, for Chrissake! What happened?"

"Don't question me, Eddie."

Stone's harsh tone lashed the sensitive little man. "All right, all right. It's just that I want to see you do good, that's all."

"Do well," Stone said automatically.

"What?"

"Do well, not do good."

Dumont knitted his thin eyebrows. "I'll try to remember that."

"Eddie," Stone said in a softer tone, "about that Kennedy job—you don't understand police work. Sometimes we get our wires crossed and things don't turn out the way we want."

"Sure, I understand. Hey, come to think of it, the pea caper is being run by the same guy from Peru who ran the planeload of shit into Kennedy. Maybe *this* time you can ruin his fucking day."

"Yeah, maybe. Do you have anything else?"

Dumont frowned. "That's it. Ain't it enough?"

"Yeah." Stone looked at his watch. "It's getting late."

The informant got out, but before he got into his car, he stopped and hurled something into the water.

"Was that your watch?" Stone yelled out the window.

"Yeah," Dumont said sheepishly. "It was a piece of shit. Next time you see me, I'll have something better."

When Stone got back to the office, Sergeant O'Neill and three of his men were just finishing up their activity reports.

The big sergeant knew Stone had gone to see a confidential informant. "Hey, Cap. How'd it go? He give you anything good?"

"Naw," Stone said, going into his office. "You know C.I.'s. They all have active imaginations."

13

THE BIG MAN CAME AROUND THE DESK AND CRUSHED ROSE IN A BEAR hug. "How the hell are you, Alex? Still chasing cops for a living?"

Tom Muller, Rose's roommate at the FBI National Academy, had changed very little in five years. If anything, he'd gotten taller. "Yeah," Rose said, untangling himself from the bear hug. "How about you? Still looking through ladies' underwear for undeclared jewelry?"

When they'd met at the National Academy, Muller was a Customs agent assigned to Kennedy Airport. Every night over a case of beer he'd entertain Rose and their classmates with tales of horny Customs agents in pursuit of contraband. His descriptions of strip searches and exotic hiding places left his audience shaking their heads. They never knew if Muller was telling the truth or making it up.

"Ah, the good old days," Muller said wistfully. "Now I'm a boss and I'm supposed to stop these guys from doing the things I used to do."

Rose glanced around the office. "Very impressive. What are you boss of?"

"Drug investigations out of Kennedy. Not as much fun as ladies' underwear, but what the hell. How about some coffee?"

After Muller got the coffee, he and Rose reminisced about the National Academy, where they and a few hundred other law enforcement officers spent eleven weeks as the guests of the FBI. The purpose of the National Academy sessions, which the FBI ran four times a year, was to expose future police administrators to the most current thinking in law and police science, but for the attendees the greatest benefit came from meeting and developing contacts with fellow law enforcement officers across the country. As a result, National Academy graduates developed their own "old boy network," through which they could obtain information quickly, or information that couldn't be gotten through regular official channels.

"Alex, remember Wally Ford, the screwball with the Arizona State Police?" Rose didn't remember, but he nodded anyway. "Called me last year; said he was taking his family to Europe for a vacation and wanted to know if I could expedite him through Customs when he got back." Muller put his head back and laughed. "The son of a bitch came home with so much booze and gifts, I still don't know how the goddamn airplane got off the ground. 'I picked up a few extra things,' he says. 'You think you can get me through Customs?' I'm amazed he didn't get us both locked up. Then he invites me to come out to Arizona. Said he'd show me a good time. Arizona, for Chrissake! What the hell's in Arizona besides rattlesnakes?" Muller downed the rest of his coffee. "How about you, Alex? Going on vacation?"

"No, this is police business. I need some information on someone."

"No problem. Did you submit a request for a background check?"

"I can't use official channels."

Muller's jovial smile vanished. "I don't suppose you can tell me why?"

"It's tricky, Tom. I can't say much."

Muller leaned back and put a size thirteen shoe on the edge of the desk. "I don't know, Alex. They're getting pretty touchy around here about unauthorized computer checks. We've had a couple of scandals involving selling of information. Are you sure you can't go through channels?"

"Positive. I wouldn't ask you if there were some other way. I ran a name check through my computers and came up with zip. I have a hunch this guy's taken a bust somewhere, sometime, for narcotics."

Muller's face was immobile, but Rose knew that he was weighing the pros and cons of his request. A great deal of sensitive information was stored in law enforcement computer banks, some of it extremely valuable to certain people, not all of them on the side of the angels. The sale and misuse of this information had created a whole new electronic-age headache for law enforcement administrators. Violation of their strict guidelines was dealt with severely.

The foot came off the desk. "What the hell, I owe you one. I've never forgotten that term paper you wrote for my personnel administration course— even if it was only a B-minus paper . . ."

"Bullshit. That was an A paper."

Muller stood up. "Maybe it was. Come on."

They entered a large room with glass walls on three sides. Rows of men and women hunched over computer terminals. Some fed information into the insatiable memory banks, where it was sorted, indexed, and catalogued, while others queried the same memory banks for information on the many and complex illegal activities the Customs Service was charged with preventing.

Muller scanned the room until he found the person he was looking for. A middle-aged black woman with a sixties-style Afro looked up from her console as they approached. "Hi, Muller. Haven't seen you in the fishbowl for quite a while. What'd they do, demote you?"

"Naw, Millie, they're not on to me yet. I hate to disturb your afternoon nap, but I need a name check."

"Sure." She put on her reading glasses and typed a code. A display appeared on the screen. "What's the authorization number?"

Muller leaned down close to her ear. "Millie, this has to be unofficial."

She glared at him over her glasses. "You know better than that, Tom. I can't—"

"I know, I know. You don't have to quote the rules to me, but this guy—an old friend of mine from the NYPD—is working on some super-duper James Bond crap that no one's supposed to know about. If I don't help him, he's threatening to have my driver's license revoked for life. How will I get to work? I live in Jersey, for Chrissake! I'll have to leave my house at midnight just to—"

"Stop it. You're breaking my heart. What've you got?"

He turned to Rose and winked. "I love this woman. If she weren't black, I'd marry her in a minute."

Millie, rapidly typing the code to enter the name bank, snorted. "I wouldn't marry you anyway, you big ugly honky. What's the name?"

"Marbridge," Rose said. "Nelson Marbridge."

"Thank God, an uncommon name." She looked up at Rose. "The last time this turkey requested a name check, it was something like John Smith. Took most of the week to get through the list." She typed the name. Two lines appeared on the display screen.

Muller peered over her shoulder. "Son of a bitch! Two Nelson Marbridges?"

Millie asked Rose: "You have a DOB?"

He looked through his notes. "September fourth, 1937."

She typed in the date of birth and one name popped up. "Bingo! You got a hit. Nelson Marbridge, September fourth, 1937."

"How do you figure it?" Rose said. "I ran the name and got nothing."

Muller squinted at the screen. "Not unusual. A lot of interagency information gets dropped through the cracks. He was busted in 1975. Millie, can you bring up the arrest report?"

Almost instantaneously the arrest report appeared on the screen. Muller frowned. "Receiving a shipment of drugs. I see an arrest, but no conviction."

"What does that mean?" Rose asked.

"Hard to say. This info doesn't say much. You'd have to review the case folder to get the whole picture."

"Is that possible?"

Muller shook his head. "Out of the question. Not without a formal request." From the look on Rose's face he knew that wasn't an alternative. "There's one more way." He looked back at the screen. "Steve Ward, the arresting agent, is a good friend of mine. He retired about a year ago and took a job as the security director for an oil company in the city. If you want, I'll call him and set up an appointment. When do you want to see him?"

"Right now."

"Okay. Millie, can you give me a hard copy of that?"

"Sure. Pick it up on your way out."

He put his huge hand on her narrow shoulder. "I want you to forget we ever had this conversation." He pointed to Rose. "You've never seen this man. In fact, you've never seen *me*."

Millie rolled her eyes. "How could I forget you, you hunk of man? I've changed my mind—I will marry you."

Muller kissed her on the cheek. "It's a deal. As soon as I figure a way to get rid of my wife and seven kids, we'll do it."

STEVE WARD WAS A THIN, SERIOUS MAN WITH SHORT-CROPPED GRAY hair. He gazed out the window of his thirty-seventh-floor office toward a hazy New Jersey.

"That was a long time ago. When Tom called and gave me the name, I gotta say I couldn't remember the case. But then he read the arrest report over the phone and it all came back to me. Marbridge was a dealer—antiques or art?"

"Art."

"Right. There was a shipment—statues and the like. Nothing unusual. He wasn't on our watch list. When they were moving the shipment in the freight warehouse, a pallet tipped and the boxes broke open. The warehousemen noticed some of the statues were broken. Turned out they were stuffed with several pounds of high-grade heroin. We got a search warrant and tossed his apartment and gallery, but came up with nothing.''

''What happened in court?''

''As I remember, his family had a lot of money. They hired a high-priced lawyer and he beat us. We didn't have him that good to begin with. Marbridge denied knowledge of the drugs. Claimed he was an innocent victim. Of course he was full of shit, but we lost the case.''

''Did you do a follow-up on him?''

''Sure. We put him on our watch list and gave him some special attention, but I think we spooked him. He was clean the whole time we dogged him. But you know how it is; the workload gets heavier, there are more promising cases to attend to. After a while we dropped him.''

''Do you think he was actively involved in drug running?''

''Not a doubt in my mind. In his line of work, he was perfect as a mule. After he was busted, I'm sure he never carried anything on him, but I'll bet my pension he was bringing in the shit one way or another.''

Ward thought about it for a moment and added, ''That was a frustrating case. I put a lot of legwork into this guy—talking to informants and the like. The info I got was that Marbridge was connected to some big-time players in Peru. I don't know who—I never did get a handle on that.''

''So you think Marbridge was still involved in the drug business even after his arrest?''

''Yeah. Big bucks, minimum risk. Why not? My experience has been that once these guys get a taste of the big money, they can't let it go. On the other hand, the drug business isn't something you get to retire from voluntarily. If my information was correct, Marbridge was tied into a major distributor. They look unkindly on anyone who wants to call it quits. One way or another he was up to his eyeballs in drugs.''

Rose had his connection. The art dealer, like Tiny Leonard and Thomas Rowe, was in the drug business. ''Thanks for the information, Steve. Oh, one more thing. Does the name Thomas Rowe mean anything to you?''

''No.''

''How about Tiny Leonard?''

Ward thought for a moment. ''Nope. Should it?''

''He was a Harlem drug dealer.''

''Plenty of those around.''

''Yeah, too many.'' Rose stood up and inspected Ward's retirement plaque. He'd been a Customs agent for twenty-eight years. ''How do you like retirement?''

Ward's gaze wandered around the plush office. ''I still can't believe it. A year ago I was freezing my ass off on stakeouts at Kennedy; now I'm a director of security and everyone calls me mister instead of hump.''

''You like the job?''

"Yeah," he said unconvincingly. "I don't know what I'm doing yet, but they don't know what I'm doing either, so we're even. I'm glad to be out, but I still think like an agent. I still say 'we' instead of 'they.' I wonder when that will change?"

Ward walked Rose to the elevator. As the doors were closing, he said, "Hey, Alex, if you need anything else, give me a call. I'd be glad to help."

Maybe it was the eagerness in his tone, or the animation in his face when he spoke of past investigations, but to Alex Rose, Steve Ward, retired Customs agent, didn't look like a very happy director of security.

ROSE BARGED THROUGH THE DOOR AND ANNOUNCED, "MARBRIDGE was dirty!"

Velez looked up. "Well, are you going to tell us about it, or do we play twenty questions?"

Rose slid into his chair. "Nelson Marbridge was bagged in 1975 on a drug charge."

Shannon slammed a file drawer. "Was he connected to Leonard or Rowe?"

Some of Rose's enthusiasm waned. "Ah, I don't know. But he was tied to some big dealers in Peru."

"So what?" Shannon tossed a folder on his desk. "There are plenty of big drug dealers in Peru."

"So we know Rowe brokered deals between Tiny Leonard and a South American."

"And you're saying that Leonard, Marbridge, *and* Rowe were dealing with the same guy?"

"Yes."

Shannon put his scruffy loafers on his desk. "Rose, you oughta be a fiction writer. You couldn't get a conviction in the *department* trial room with that flimsy evidence."

"For Chrissake, will you forget I'm IAD and listen. I know it takes a stretch of the imagination, but it's entirely plausible. It's obvious from the M.O.'s that all three were killed by the same perps. The perps, or whoever hired them, had to know all three. Why couldn't it be the Peruvian? Marbridge spent a lot of time in Peru. Why couldn't he have been the mule for the same guy Rowe laundered money for?"

"Okay," Shannon said, "let's suspend disbelief for a moment. We'll assume all three knew each other and dealt with this South American. Why are they DOA?"

Rose slumped in his chair. "I don't know."

Velez held up a copy of the *Daily News*. The headline on page five said: CRUSADING SENATOR VOWS TO UNEARTH NARCO CORRUPTION.

Velez tossed the paper to Shannon. "Pickett's launching a commission in January. He says he has witnesses who will expose a major drug network in the city."

Shannon had read the story. "Pickett is stirring up the pot, and it must be pissing off a lot of people." He tossed the paper on the desk. "Maybe these deaths are just general housecleaning."

Velez looked at his watch and flipped on the portable TV he kept in the office. "It's almost five. Pickett is going to be interviewed by Wes Blackburn."

"That hump," Shannon said, echoing the sentiment of most of the cops in the department. The failed actor-turned-TV-journalist had built his celebrity on a format of tacky, sensational interviews featuring a wide variety of weirdos, most of whom had an axe to grind with the New York City Police Department. "I wonder why he's interviewing Pickett?"

"Probably ran out of baldheaded Armenian transvestites," Velez offered.

The handsome but very serious face of Wes Blackburn filled the screen. "Today, we have in the studio with us, State Senator Nathan Pickett. The senator, completing the second year of his first term, could have made millions playing basketball in the NBA, but he chose instead a life of public service. Nathan Pickett has become the champion of the little people in this town, and in this role has earned the acrimony of many city officials. More recently, the senator has stirred up a hornets' nest with his allegations of widespread narcotic-related corruption."

Blackburn swung his chair and leaned toward a dour-faced Nathan Pickett. "Welcome to *Spotlight on New York,* Senator. Let's not beat around the bush. There are those who say you have your sights set on the White House and all this talk about corruption in the city is just that—talk. How do you respond?"

Pickett flashed an engaging grin. "Wes, you must have been talking with Mayor Kessel or Commissioner Mara. It is true that there are some city officials who say my charges about narco corruption are unfounded, and *that,* I submit, is part of the problem. This head-in-the-sand syndrome is one of the reasons why the city is in the shape it's in. Decent people afraid to walk the streets—day or night—small businesses closing at dark, a stampede of major corporations away from the city to safer environments. This hemorrhaging of our essential tax base must stop, or we will be faced with problems that will make the fiscal crisis of the seventies pale by comparison."

"Senator, you have been very critical of Joseph Mara, the Police Commissioner. Is it fair to blame him for the city's economic problems?"

"I don't blame Joe Mara for the failing economy. That's within the mayor's province. However, the commissioner's abysmal handling of the narcotics problem has certainly contributed to this city's economic woes."

Blackburn, sensing an opportunity for controversy, perked up. "Ah, the famous 'Pickett's charge.' "

Pickett smiled. "You ladies and gentlemen of the press have chosen to call it that, but yes, the commissioner's order regarding narcotic-related street arrests has hamstrung the police officer on the street."

"How do you know that, Senator?"

"Because, Wes, I have a continuing dialogue with many police officers who tell me so."

Blackburn's penciled eyebrows shot up. "Are you saying that police officers actually confide in you?"

"Yes. Does that surprise you?"

"Well, it's no secret that your attacks on the police department have made you public enemy number one at One Police Plaza."

" 'Attack' is a harsh word. I *have* criticized the department when I felt it warranted, and perhaps the hierarchy in the department isn't fond of me, but I have the support of the honest, dedicated cops on the beat. They want what I want: a safe city. If the Police Commissioner would just let the cops do what they're paid to do, we'd all be much better off."

"Is there no one in the police department doing the job?"

"Yes. Captain Patrick Stone, the young commander of the Narcotics Enforcement Team, comes to mind. He and his men have been doing a splendid job arresting drug dealers. Unfortunately, they are few in numbers. We need every police officer in this city to become imbued with the tenacity and dedication of Captain Stone and his men."

"Your commission, which you promise will expose corruption in this city, is due to start in January. Will police officers testify?"

Pickett took off his glasses and wiped them with a handkerchief. "I'd prefer not to say at this time. Suffice it to say there will be several witnesses, directly connected to the narcotics trade, who will testify about the extent of the narcotics epidemic in this city."

Blackburn grinned slyly. "Will Captain Patrick Stone testify?"

Pickett slipped his glasses on and smiled. "Wes, I think I've already answered that question."

Blackburn, sensing he wasn't going to get a headline revelation from Pickett, sagged in his swivel chair. "Unfortunately, Senator, we've run out of time. Thank you for appearing on *Spotlight on New York*. In your usual forthright manner, you've pulled no punches, and we thank you for your candid frankness."

He swung his chair toward the camera. "Tomorrow on *Spotlight on New York* we'll have—"

Rose turned the TV off. "Son of a bitch. It sounds like he knows a hell of a lot more about what's going on in this town than we do."

Shannon wasn't impressed with Pickett's performance. "He hinted at a lot, but he said nothing."

"Do you think he has Stone in his pocket?" Velez asked.

"I doubt it," Rose said. "Stone's too smart to get involved with someone like Pickett. It'd be the quickest way I can think of to jettison a promising career."

Shannon stared at the darkened screen. "Maybe so, but I wouldn't be surprised if this program puts Captain Stone on the P.C.'s shit list. For him it'll be like trying to answer the question: When did you stop beating your wife?"

"Why don't we talk to Pickett?" Rose said suddenly.

Shannon snorted. "Are you kidding? He won't tell us shit. He's going to save it for his commission."

"Maybe, but if even half of what he said is true, he's got to be a good source of information. Brian, three people, all connected to the drug trade, have been murdered. There's something going on in this city, but we're not putting the pieces together. Maybe Pickett has some answers."

Shannon picked up the newspaper and tapped a photo of Patrick Stone standing alongside the Police Commissioner. "*This* is the guy I'd like to talk to. Right now Patrick Stone knows more about major drug dealers than anyone else in the city. If there's something going on, he'd know about it."

"He's a great boss too," Velez said. "I'm thinking of putting a fifty-seven in for NET."

Shannon gave him a dirty look. "You're not transferring anywhere until you're finished here."

"I know. I wouldn't leave now. This shit is too exciting."

"Maybe we *should* talk to Stone," Rose said.

"And tell him what? What reason could we give him for wanting information about drug dealers?"

"How the hell do I know? But you're right about Stone. It's uncanny how effective NET has been. I have a friend in Narcotics, and they can't believe some of the arrests those guys have made. Even discounting the hype press Stone gets, he's been nailing a lot of major players in the city. He must have one hell of an intelligence network to do that."

Reluctantly, Shannon had to agree with Rose. But he doubted Larson would allow them to bring Stone into the investigation. "If I get the chance," he said, "I'll bring it up with Larson."

"We still haven't answered the sixty-four-million-dollar question," Rose said.

"What's that?" asked Velez.

"Are the murderers cops?"

Shannon shook his head. "I don't think cops are behind these killings."

"Jesus, you're stubborn."

"Maybe it's because I'm not as quick as you IAD guys are to jump to conclusions."

"Bullshit, Brian. Look at the facts. What's the one thing about these murders that's most puzzling? Three people—including a streetsmart drug dealer—are murdered, and there's not the slightest sign of a struggle. Three people let their killer in, and just sat there when he put a gun to their heads and fired. Think about it. Who could lull three people into that position?"

A troubled look clouded Velez's eyes. "Damn, Loo, you got a point. If the killers *were* cops, once they ID'ed themselves, the victims would relax. They'd figure they might take a bust, but they'd never expect to be blown away. It'd be like shooting fish in a rain barrel."

The office fell silent as each man imagined the unimaginable scenario—a policeman standing in front of his victim and executing him in cold blood.

14

WHENEVER THEY COULD, SHANNON AND ROSE STILL WENT THEIR separate ways. Rose obtained a copy of the tenants' list in Marbridge's apartment building, which Velez fed into a computer. Shannon spent a Saturday night, alone, sitting in the parking lot by the Verrazano Bridge jotting down license-plate numbers. Later, every plate was run through the Department of Motor Vehicles and the names of the drivers were run through the state computers. The results were fed into Velez's computer and cross-checked for a match with names already entered. No results.

And so they continued in the same slow, tedious way, looking for a break, hoping for something that would open up the investigation. Unlike movies and popular detective stories, there were no dazzling feats of deduction in smoky squad rooms, none of the convenient clues that led TV detectives unerringly to the murderer. Real detectives canvassed neighborhoods, ran license plates, and collected endless lists of names in the hope that just one bit of information would provide an answer, or part of an answer.

When Shannon and Rose started snapping at each other, Velez distracted them with his tales of nocturnal adventures with cheating South Bronx wives. Rose started to refer to Velez's expanding computer file as the *Book of Lists*. "Hey, Luis," he said. "When this is over you can apply to the *Guinness Book of World Records* under the most names compiled with the least amount in common."

Velez swore softly in Spanish and tossed another thick but useless printout on the desk. "Damn, how did they ever catch anyone in the old days?" He'd been running variable searches on names and addresses, and each time the results were the same. No correlation.

"It was easy," Shannon answered. "They didn't have computers to drown them in useless information."

"Yeah, and they had investigative tools not available to us," Rose said.

"Like what?" Velez asked.

Rose smiled slyly. "They could beat the shit out of a suspect until he told them what they wanted to know."

"And there was no IAD in the old days either," Shannon added icily.

Late in the afternoon Brian Shannon said he was going uptown to take a look at Marbridge's apartment. To his dismay, Rose said he'd go along.

They parked across the street from the ornate building. Outside, a doorman dressed in a greatcoat with gold buttons and piping stood guard under a dark green canopy.

Shannon shut off the motor and opened the window. After a two-week stretch of biting November weather, the temperature had risen and it was a mild, pleasant night. "The first question is: How did the killer, or killers, get past the doorman?" Idly, he reached over and turned the radio on. Itzhak Perlman was just launching into Vivaldi's "Winter."

Rose said, "What the hell is that?"

Shannon adjusted the volume. "Vivaldi."

"You? The big-time homicide detective likes classical music?"

"Let me guess, you like country and western."

"Jazz."

Shannon made a face. "There's no structure to jazz. It's a free-for-all. Everyone plays his own thing."

Rose groaned. It was the same old story. Anyone who didn't understand jazz always said that. "That's not true. Jazz happens to have a very rich harmonal structure. They're not making it up as they go along, they're improvising on a given chord structure—"

"Come on," Shannon countered, turning the volume up. "You can't compare jazz to classical music. How many jazz tunes are going to be around two hundred years from now?"

Rose reached over and turned it down. "Listen, let's compromise. If you must listen to that, how about keeping the noise level down to a dull roar?"

Shannon sighed, but made no further move to raise the volume.

Neither spoke as they watched the building across the street. Finally, Rose broke the silence. "How about witnesses? You got results by going back to Leonard's building. Maybe we should interview everyone here."

"No point. I know the squad commander who's supervising this case. He's a stickler for canvassing. I guarantee every one of Marbridge's neighbors has been interviewed more than once. Besides, people who live on Park Avenue are a lot more willing to cooperate with the police. I read all the DD5's—no one saw anything. Most of Marbridge's neighbors weren't even home. "I don't understand these people. They buy million-dollar condos in Manhattan and then spend most of their time someplace else."

"Maybe the killer lives in the building. Did the squad look into that possibility?"

"Look at the size of the place. Must be at least fifty apartments. Investigating everyone in there would take more time than the department's willing to spend on one homicide. I don't know about IAD, but real detectives don't have time to piss into the wind."

"My, aren't we touchy."

"Well don't ask stupid questions."

"What's stupid about it?"

"Let's face it, chasing cops for a living doesn't qualify you as a detective."

"Ah, now I get it. You're ticked because you think I'm impersonating a detective."

"Well what do you know about being a detective?"

"What did you know about being a detective before you became one? Or were you to the bureau born? Tell me, was this ancient honor bestowed on your family for some honorable service to the queen?"

"Don't break my balls, Rose. You know what I mean."

"Yeah, I know exactly what you mean. You think you have some kind of lock on being a detective, as though the bureau were a religious sect whose secrets are known only to a chosen few. Give me a break! Being a detective is nothing more than common sense, intelligence, and reasonable powers of observation. For example, Detective Lieutenant Shannon, do you see what that doorman does? When he can't find a cab on Park Avenue, he goes around the corner. Someone could easily slip into the building while he's away."

Just then, a second uniformed man came out and spoke to the doorman. The doorman looked at his watch and said something to the other man, who hurried off.

"Yeah, but the lobby door must be locked."

"So?"

"So, you won't be able to get in."

"I say we can. Loser buys dinner?"

Shannon yanked the door open. "You're on."

They huddled in a doorway down the block from the entrance. Finally, the doorman went around the corner to look for a cab and they scurried into the lobby. Shannon rattled the locked door. "Now what, Sherlock?"

Rose ran his finger down the list of names and pressed a bell. A cultured female voice answered. "Yes, what is it?"

"I got flowers for Mrs. Talbot," Rose answered in his best Brooklynese.

"You have the wrong apartment. I believe Mrs. Talbot lives on the eighth floor."

"Yeah, but she ain't home and I got instructions to leave these flowers right by the door. It's a surprise, ya know?"

"Why don't you leave the flowers with William?"

Rose looked at Shannon. "William? Oh, the doorman. He's out getting a cab for somebody and my truck's double-parked. You know how these cops are around here—always looking to shake you down. If I get another ticket—"

"Oh, all right, for heaven's sake." The buzzer sounded and they slipped into the lobby.

Rose chuckled. "Being rich is no guarantee that you're not a schmuck. They pay big bucks for security, then give it away to a stranger on the intercom. You take the stairs, I'll take the elevator. It's apartment 412."

When Shannon came puffing up the stairs, he found Rose waiting outside the door of 412 with a big grin on his face. "Meet anyone interesting?"

Shannon was too out of breath to speak. It was times like these when he realized he was out of shape: too many cigarettes, too much coffee, and not enough exercise. Once again he promised himself, halfheartedly, to start jogging and lose some weight.

"Okay," Rose said. "We got in here without being seen. Let's see if we can get out."

Before Shannon could say he'd take the elevator, Rose was already inside and the doors closed. Muttering obscenities and breathing hard, Shannon hurried back down the stairs. The lobby was deserted and the doorman still hadn't returned. Shannon slipped out the front door.

They were in the car for five minutes when they saw the other uniformed man scurry around the corner and dart into the building. "Let's see what the doorman has to say," Rose suggested.

The doorman was a pleasant-looking man with a wide red face and a full head of snow-white hair. He carefully studied Shannon's ID. "Yes, Officers, what can I do for you?"

"We're investigating the Marbridge murder," Shannon said.

"Terrible thing, that. Terrible." He took off his hat and wiped his brow with a handkerchief. The weather was too warm for the heavy winter uniform he was wearing.

"Were you working that night, Mister . . . ?"

"Bill Clancy. I was. So was Denny, my elevator man."

"Did you notice anything out of the ordinary that night? Strangers? Suspicious people?"

"No. Not a soul. Some detective, a great big fellow, asked me the very same thing."

"Mr. Clancy," Rose asked, "is there any way someone could have slipped by you that night?"

"Not at all." He seemed hurt that anyone could even think such a thing. "I'm always here. When I go to dinner, Denny takes over for me. I've been here over thirty-five years and never a complaint about my services."

"What about Denny?"

"He runs the elevator, that's his job. Except for his dinner hour and the time he relieves me, he's always in the elevator."

"Does he ever leave the building?"

"Not at all."

"I see." Shannon had heard all he needed to hear. "Thanks for the information."

"Any time, Officers. Say, my son's in the department. Works in Brooklyn he does. Liam Clancy. Maybe you know him?"

Rose and Shannon suppressed smiles. With over thirty thousand cops in the department, it was highly unlikely they'd know him. Shannon was reminded of the time in Ireland when a farmer, discovering he was American, asked him if he knew his cousin in Chicago.

"The name sounds familiar. I might have worked with him at one time," Rose said.

The old man beamed.

Crossing the street, Rose said, "You owe me a dinner, Lieutenant, and I'm starved. I know a terrific little Italian joint not far from here. A mite expensive, but the food—"

"Rose, will you shut up?"

ARI KAKAVOS, THE LAST SERGEANT TO ARRIVE IN RESPONSE TO A hurried telephone call to report forthwith, walked into a very quiet NET office. Hardy and O'Neill were sitting at their desks with their heads down.

"What's up?" Kakavos asked.

Hardy, intently reading a Personnel Order, didn't look up. Kakavos sat on the edge of O'Neill's desk. "Brenden, you want to tell me what's going on?"

The big sergeant pointed to Stone's closed door. "He's on the warpath. Radlicki's team blew a surveillance, and Stone's been chewing his ass out for half an hour."

"Mr. Precision? How?"

"I don't know, but I have a feeling we're going to find out."

The door opened and Stone stuck his head out. "Lieutenant Carlin, is everyone here?"

"Yes, sir," the administrative lieutenant answered.

John Carlin, a funereal, pinched-faced man, was responsible for running the everyday administrative functions of NET. Supervising roll calls, time cards, overtime reports, court appearances, and a host of other record-keeping functions demanded someone with a careful eye for detail and organizational ability. John Carlin was more than qualified on both counts.

"Everybody in my office. Now."

The three sergeants filed in behind Carlin, who, as usual, carried a yellow pad for note taking.

Stone slammed the door, hard. He began in a low voice. "I've called you in because I'm beginning to see some sloppy police work and it's going to stop right now. Radlicki's team blew a case they'd been working on for three weeks."

"Captain—" Radlicki started to protest, but thought better of it when he saw the look on Stone's face.

"You blew it, Paul." Stone slammed his hand on the desk. "No excuses. You either do the job right or you do it wrong. There's no in-between here."

Kakavos, the unofficial spokesman for the sergeants, spoke up. "Cap, what happened?"

"Kileen and Herbert were scoping the drop location. *Three* days in a row, they parked in the same spot. Christ! A blind man would have made them. This morning the wire went dead and all the players scattered. It was going to be at least a two-hundred-key delivery."

Radlicki, pale from the effort of controlling his temper, said, "I'll admit they screwed up, but they're two of my best men. Nobody's perfect."

Stone leaned forward. "Anyone who expects to work for me," he said evenly, "better be a hell of a lot closer to perfect than that."

The sergeant's gaze never wavered. "Will you reconsider their transfers?"

O'Neill and Kakavos, hearing about the transfers for the first time, stole glances at each other.

"No. Kileen and Herbert are history. And I'm putting you all on notice. If you fuck up, you're out of here too. This is NET, not a goddamn Laurel and Hardy movie. You wanna screw up cases, I can arrange to have you transferred to Narcotics with the rest of the fuck-ups. Pass the word to your teams. You blow an investigation, you're gone."

Without another word Stone rose and left the office, leaving a shocked silence in his wake. Radlicki was the first to speak. "Fuck him," he said bitterly. "I'm putting in a fifty-seven."

"Take it easy." Hardy nervously reached for a cigarette. "There's no reason to transfer. He'll cool down."

Kakavos turned to the administrative lieutenant, who thus far had said nothing. A standoffish man to begin with, Carlin's role as the office administrator separated him from the sergeants who worked in the field. "Hey, Loo, is he serious about transferring them?"

The lieutenant got to his feet and adjusted his old-fashioned horn-rimmed glasses. "I've already begun to process the paperwork," he announced and walked out of the office.

"This sucks," Kakavos said. "Herbert and Kileen are good cops. They don't deserve to get flopped. If he starts chopping guys, they're going to start bailing out."

"He's a friend of yours," O'Neill said to Hardy. "What's the matter with him?"

"I'm not Stone's keeper," Hardy snapped. "How the hell should I know what's biting his ass?"

The big sergeant's face reddened. "I didn't say you were."

"Hold it, hold it," Kakavos interjected. "Why are we yelling at each other? Tim, you're his buddy. If anyone can talk to him, you can. He's got a bug up his ass. What's the problem? Our arrest stats are going through the roof, we have a ninety-percent conviction rate, and our seizures have been getting bigger and bigger. We're doing better than the whole Narcotics Division, for Chrissake. What does he want from us?"

"Maybe the P.C. offered him inspector if he doubles the numbers," Radlicki said dryly.

"That's bullshit," Hardy said in defense of his friend.

Kakavos scratched his heavy five o'clock shadow. "He used to piss ice water, but he's been real touchy lately: snapping at everyone, criticizing everything. Come to think of it, he hasn't been the same since he came back from that Florida vacation last September."

Radlicki's grin was evil. "Maybe he didn't get laid."

"Or"—O'Neill winked—"maybe he did, but he got more than he paid for. The gift that keeps on giving—"

Hardy stood up. "Will you guys grow up?"

Hardy's tone had broken the playful mood, and Radlicki was once again somber. "It's true, Tim. Stone is turning into a world-class hard-on."

"It's just that he doesn't tolerate mistakes, that's all."

O'Neill shook his massive head. "For Chrissake, Tim, *nobody's* perfect. Not even Patrick Stone."

"Maybe not. But he's never gotten over the time he was transferred because of what some cops did to him."

Kakavos's bushy eyebrows rose in anticipation. "Stone flopped? What happened?"

"Nothing. It was a long time ago." Hardy, wishing he hadn't brought up the subject, rose to leave, but O'Neill's powerful hand clamped down on his forearm.

"Tim, we all have to work together here. There shouldn't be any secrets between us. Why did Stone get flopped?"

Hardy didn't want to discuss Stone's problems with them, but the big sergeant's tone, and the expectant expressions on the others' faces, left him no choice. Reluctantly, he slid back into his chair. "Stone had just been promoted to sergeant and transferred back to Narcotics. He was assigned to a team he'd worked with as a cop. They were all friends so he figured he could trust them."

"What'd they do?" Radlicki asked.

"One night he had a lot of paperwork to do. You know the rules: a sergeant is always supposed to be in the field with his team. But Stone sent them out to do a surveillance on a promising drug location while he stayed in the office to finish up."

"Let me take a wild guess," Kakavos grinned. "They didn't go to the surveillance location. Right?"

"They spent the tour in a bar. One of them got into an argument with a drunk. A couple of punches were thrown. The guy pulled a knife; one of the cops pulled a gun." Hardy slumped in his chair as though he were personally responsible for the incident. "Before the night was out, the cops were suspended and Stone was transferred back to patrol."

"Where did they dump him?" Radlicki asked.

"Central Park."

Radlicki winced. "A buzzsaw like Stone flopped into the *park* to count squirrels! The poor bastard."

Hardy nodded. "It was tough. You know him—always has to have all burners going. I talked to him a couple of days after his transfer." Hardy's eyes locked on the dirty tile floor as he recalled the conversation. "I'd never seen him so angry. He always hated being in uniform. Said it made him feel like a security guard. He talked about packing in the job."

Kakavos broke the silence. "So what happened?"

Hardy, brought out of his reverie, looked up in surprise. He'd almost forgotten about the others in the room with him. "You know the job. When something goes wrong, the first reaction is offer a human sacrifice. Most of the bosses in Narcotics knew Stone had been given a bum rap, and went to bat for him. It took a while for the C.O. to finally calm down, but when he did, he realized he'd dumped his best sergeant. Three weeks later, he brought Stone back.''

Hardy stood up slowly. ''Stone swore he'd never let someone else's actions hurt his career again. That's why he reads every arrest report and warrant application. He doesn't want anything, or anyone, to stop his rise to the top.''

Radlicki chuckled, but there was no mirth in it. ''If Stone thinks he can do twenty years in this job without making mistakes, he's playing with himself. Your buddy's an egomaniac, Tim. He gets a kick out of doing a high-wire act without a net. Thing is, when he falls—and sooner or later he's gotta fall—he's gonna make one helluva splat.''

Hardy blinked. ''That won't happen to Patrick Stone.''

''All I know,'' Ari Kakavos added, ''is that I came into this unit to work for a guy like Stone, because he's one of the few bosses in this job who doesn't have his head up his ass. But that seems to be changing. I don't know what's wrong with him, but if he isn't careful, he's going to fuck up a great outfit.''

''I don't know what's going on,'' O'Neill said, ''but he's getting worse. It seems the more we do, the more he wants. Tim, will you talk to him?''

Hardy looked into the concerned faces of his fellow sergeants and saw what Patrick Stone's unyielding drive for more and more arrests was doing to them. ''All right,'' he said softly, ''I'll see what I can do.''

15

THE VISIT TO DR. ABRAHAM ALTMAN'S OFFICE BEGAN WITH A QUES-
tion from Velez. "Who would do something like this? If cops are doing
these murders, they gotta be nuts. If they're nuts, maybe they've come to
the attention of—what's the name of that unit?"

"The Early Intervention Unit," Rose said. "The EIU's supposed to
identify the problem cop before he gets into serious trouble."

"I've never heard of it," Shannon said. "How do you get on their
list?"

"A lot of ways," Rose explained. "A C.O. can make a recommenda-
tion; the guy can have too many civilian complaints; unnecessary force
complaints. Even being chronic sick can get you on the list. There's some
kind of point system they use." He turned to Shannon. "Maybe Luis has
something. Right now we're looking for a needle in a haystack of thirty

125

thousand cops. If we could define the type of person we're looking for, we might be able to narrow it down.''

"A personality profile," Shannon said. "I know just the man who can give it to us.''

Abraham Altman was a successful psychiatrist with a large, wealthy clientele. Financially, he was in a position to offer his services free from time to time to select members of the police department, a fortunate happenstance because there was no line in the department's budget for two-hundred-dollar-an-hour consultations with Park Avenue shrinks.

A certified police buff, Dr. Altman enjoyed talking to detectives about the psychological implications of murders. On more than one occasion he'd canceled appointments with distraught blue-haired matrons in furs and Gucci shoes to discuss a murder with a detective in a sports jacket and forty-dollar loafers.

In spite of some personal peculiarities, Altman had an impressive track record. More than one detective had been startled to discover upon making an arrest that the suspect fit Altman's profile right down to the clothes he was wearing. Some cops dismissed psychiatric profiling as little more than black magic, but Shannon's experience was that it could be very helpful. Besides, if it would help solve these murders, he was prepared to consult with a whole platoon of witch doctors.

Dr. Altman's nurse escorted Shannon and Velez into his office. When Shannon had said he'd made an appointment to see Dr. Altman, he'd expected Rose to jump at the chance to talk to a psychiatrist. Instead Rose declined. "I'm not real fond of shrinks. My mother has been going to one for so long, my father claims him as a dependent.''

Velez, seeing the opportunity to escape from the office, volunteered to go. "Why not?" Shannon said. "If we have time, maybe we can ask Altman about your raging hormones.''

"I already have the answer to that, Señor Lieutenant. It's all that cheap rice we Latinos eat. It makes us strong like bull.''

Altman, a small, chubby man in his late sixties, sat behind a huge mahogany desk with the dimensions of a helicopter pad. He rummaged through his tweed jacket until he found his pipe. He carefully tamped the tobacco into the bowl, then lit a wooden match and, without putting the pipe in his mouth, waved the flame over the bowl. Next, he put the pipe in his mouth, lit another match, and held it so far above the pipe that it didn't look like the tobacco had a chance of igniting. Velez glanced at Shannon and crossed his eyes.

Shannon, who had seen Altman's pipe-lighting ritual before, took the opportunity to inspect the oak-paneled office. In addition to the usual collection of degrees and awards, there was an extensive collection of framed photos showing Altman at various police picnics and fishing trips. In one photo an ecstatic Altman struggled to hold up a huge striped bass. Knowing cops, Shannon suspected that the smiling men standing alongside Altman had probably "arranged" for Altman to catch the biggest fish.

When the doctor was assured his pipe was properly lit, he leaned back in his overstuffed chair and stared at the ceiling with a look of supreme contentment. "There are two secrets to a good smoke," he said in a low voice with just the trace of a German accent. "First, the tobacco must be packed just so. Second, the match must never, never be applied directly to the tobacco. It sears it. The flame must be held at precisely the correct distance so the tobacco is allowed to combust naturally." He took a few puffs and continued staring at the ceiling.

The psychiatrist, his bald head enveloped in a cloud of blue smoke, stroked his beard and puffed his pipe contentedly. Velez was beginning to think he'd forgotten about them. Velez thought he looked like Sigmund Freud. Then he realized that *all* psychiatrists looked like Sigmund Freud. Finally the chair swiveled toward them.

"Well, Lieutenant Shannon, what have you brought me today?"

After cautioning Altman about the confidentiality of what he was about to tell him, Shannon recounted everything he knew about the three murders. Altman listened intently, squinting through his smoke screen and showing neither surprise nor shock. By the time Shannon had finished, Altman was done with his pipe and was using a pocketknife to scrape the ashes into a Waterford crystal ashtray. To Velez's relief—he didn't think he'd be able to stand another pipe-lighting routine—Altman slipped the pipe into his pocket.

"Interesting. Very interesting," he said noncommittally.

"We were wondering, Dr. Altman, if you had any ideas about the personality type we should be looking for."

The psychiatrist gazed at Shannon with a quizzical expression, as though he'd been addressed in a foreign language. "How many policemen are there in the department?" he asked abruptly.

"About thirty thousand."

"Then there are thirty thousand people in the department capable of committing murder, minus," he added with the hint of a smile, "you two, of course."

So far Velez wasn't impressed. Altman seemed to be just another quack mouthing cryptic pronouncements while making a lot of money on other people's misery. A witch doctor with a diploma.

"Do you mean because all cops have authoritarian personalities?" Velez asked.

The doctor peered intently at him. "Is it Detective Velez?"

"No." Velez gave Shannon a baleful look and his mustache seemed to droop even more than usual. "It's still police officer."

"No, Officer Velez, the authoritarian-personality business has been done to death. No one gives it much credence anymore. Lieutenant Shannon, understandably you'd like a nice neat profile. But, alas, this scenario is not as simple as that for a rapist or a child molester. They at least fit into certain predictable aberrational patterns. But your assassin policeman?" He shrugged elaborately. "He's everybody. Policeman, truck driver, student. We are all capable of murder."

"I don't believe that," Shannon said. "Maybe a lot of people are capable, but not everyone."

"It's an impossible hypothesis to test, I'll admit. But maybe you and I differ on definitions. Let me ask you a question. When a soldier kills the enemy, is he a murderer?"

"No, of course not. There are rules of war."

"I see. What if the soldier is Abu Nidal and the enemy is a planeload of innocent civilians?"

"That's different. Abu Nidal is a terrorist and there's no declared war."

"Oh? By whose definition? You say he's a criminal terrorist, but I'm sure he sees himself as a freedom fighter and whatever he does is justified by his cause. The point is, man defines his terms to suit his purpose, and the key is rationalization.

"One can convince others to do almost anything if one presents it in the proper manner. Didn't we convince more than forty thousand men to die in Vietnam? We simply told them it was their patriotic duty. All nations do the same. Throughout the ages men have been made to give up their lives for God, king, and country. A policeman could be made to commit murder if the concomitant circumstances were right."

"Such as?" Shannon asked.

"Perhaps he's someone who is frustrated by the ambiguities of society's justice. We put a man in prison for stealing a car, but heads of corporations steal billions and get away scot-free. Incidentally, the ambiguity of society toward capital punishment doesn't help. You said the three murdered men were all involved in drugs. Your murderer could rationalize that all drug dealers are essentially murderers anyway."

Velez spoke up. "But how could a sane cop kill someone in cold blood?"

"Ah, we're talking about definitions again. Sane is a legal term, not a medical one. Like most legal definitions, it is not very satisfactory. Sane and insane imply only two choices, like a light switch—on and off. In psychiatry we prefer to think of normal and abnormal as imprecise points on a continuum. To build on the same simile, the concept of normal and abnormal is like a rheostat switch. If you slowly turn a rheostat switch, at what point will you reach a 'normal' light level? If you are reading the fine print in a contract, you will want the lights turned all the way up. If, on the other hand, you are having dinner with a beautiful woman, you will want the lights turned down low.''

"In other words," Velez interjected, "what we call normal is subjective."

"Exactly. And normal changes from culture to culture and century to century. In sixteenth-century England, for example, they threw their excrement out the window. Perfectly normal behavior in a culture where there was no indoor plumbing."

"I got news for you, Doc," Velez said dryly. "In some parts of the South Bronx they still throw their shit out the window."

"Is that so?" Altman said, staring at Velez over his glasses. He was silent for a moment; probably considering Freud's reaction to people in the South Bronx throwing excrement out the window.

Then he continued. "I recently read a study done on the dynamics of torture. Some of the findings may be applicable to your case. The question— similar to yours, Officer Velez—is: How can normal, civilized people maim and kill other human beings in cold blood?

"Surprisingly, the study's conclusion suggests that the torturers studied are very much like you and me. Hollywood notwithstanding, they are not grotesque, drooling hunchbacks living in dungeons and bell towers. From personal interviews and diaries it appears that certain dynamics come into play which allow them to do these terrible things without damaging their psyches."

"What are we talking about? The Spanish Inquisition? The Middle Ages?"

Altman's smile was patient. "Amnesty International has identified almost ninety countries which at this very moment engage in torture as a routine part of the administration of their governments."

Shannon sat forward in his chair. "I can understand barbaric acts in time of war, but how can someone engage in torture day after day and remain normal—or whatever we call it?"

"It appears the torturer has the ability to split the personality—not in the psychotic sense, but in a rational way—in order to preserve his sanity. At the end of the day he leaves his work behind him and goes home to his family. He eats dinner and watches TV just like the rest of us."

Shannon was growing more and more exasperated. "But how can he do that and remain normal?"

"How can he *not* do that and remain normal?" Altman countered. "You policemen use this split-personality technique every day. Have you not seen horrors and misery in your work? Have you not seen children mutilated, people butchered—the worst aspects of society?''

"Sure," Velez said. "What cop hasn't?"

"Do you take this home with you?"

"Some do," Velez answered. Then he added, "But they end up wacky."

"Exactly. To maintain stability one must learn to leave these horrors behind. One must learn to separate these experiences from one's personal life, or risk psychological destruction of the psyche. There are many mechanisms for forgetting the horrors of police work. But the point is that policemen, doctors, or anyone else who daily witnesses terrible events must be able to separate these experiences from their personal lives. A policeman can go from the scene of a mutilated baby to his own child's birthday party and keep the two environments separate and distinct. Is he normal or abnormal?''

"Then you're saying a cop—a normal cop—could take part in these murders and at the same time lead a normal life?" Velez asked.

"Yes, and more than likely he would look and act just like the rest of his colleagues.''

The room was silent except for the soft ticking of the antique grandfather clock in the corner. While Velez and Shannon mulled over the implications of what had been said, Altman once again began to rummage through his pockets in search of his pipe. To Velez's despair, he started the pipe-lighting ritual again.

Shannon waited until he'd finished and then resumed his questioning. "What are some other dynamics?"

"Remember, I said rationalization was the key. The three men killed were not really human, they were vermin that had to be destroyed. Your killer may only be doing what the courts should be doing."

"Goddamn, Doc, you got that right," Velez said. "You don't know how many times I've arrested bad guys only to have them walk in court or wind up with an S.S. I gotta admit, summary execution has crossed my mind more than once.''

Altman's eyes narrowed. "What's an S.S.?"

"Suspended sentence," Shannon explained. "Luis has just admitted that he has considered killing some of his prisoners, but he wouldn't actually do it. It would take more than just rationalization."

"Yes, that's true. It would take something more. Perhaps fear or intimidation. If I knew something terrible about Officer Velez, something that he didn't want exposed, I'd have a hold on him. The strength of that hold would be in direct proportion to how terrible was his secret."

"Hey, Doc," Velez said, "I may screw around with the ladies a little, but I'd have to murder somebody before—" He stopped and glanced at Shannon; they were both thinking the same thing. The only secret terrible enough to make a sane person commit murder was that they'd *already* committed murder. Or something close to it.

The two cops stood up. "Thanks for your time, Doc," Shannon said. "You've given us something to think about."

Altman, puffing on his pipe, made no effort to rise. "This is a very interesting case. I wish I could be more specific." He looked at their perplexed faces and smiled his sad smile. "As policemen you dwell in the dark regions of man's psyche, but you still can't accept the darker nature of mankind. You are prepared to believe that a particular individual is evil, but not that mankind possesses a strong capacity for evil. Remember, in terms of evolutionary time we have barely fallen out of the trees. What we euphemistically call civilization is just a thin veneer separating us from our savage past."

Shannon, his mind preoccupied with what Velez had said, hardly heard him. "Yeah, I guess so."

Altman saw the look on Shannon's face and mistook it for disappointment. "There is one ray of hope for you, Lieutenant Shannon."

"What's that?"

"Remember, I said the key was rationalization? The human mind has an unlimited capacity to rationalize, but rationalization is a defense mechanism—a temporary barrier against an unpleasant reality. A great deal of energy is required to maintain this charade. After a while it becomes debilitating and the body can no longer sustain it. Your policeman, like an Atlas in blue, has the weight of his guilt on his shoulders. But he can't go on forever."

"Something has to give," Velez said.

"Exactly."

"And when the world comes tumbling down, he'll make a mistake."

"Or," Altman offered, "in order to expiate his guilt, he may feel compelled to confess his crime."

"That's the best news I've heard in a long time," Shannon said. But his euphoria was short-lived.

"However," Altman cautioned, "if they stop their activities, the pressure subsides and it's conceivable that they could live with what they've done for the rest of their lives."

On the drive back to the office Shannon said, "I think you hit on something, Luis. Murder would be the only secret that would make someone commit another murder."

"Either being the actual murderer, or part of it somehow. I liked that term he used."

"What was that?"

"Blue Atlas. He said you're looking for a blue Atlas. Hey, Loo, did you notice Altman never came from behind that big desk? He reminded me of a frightened rabbit hiding back there. The pipe and the beard, they're all barriers. Something else for him to hide behind."

"You're too much, Velez. Just one interview with a psychiatrist and you're ready to hang up a shingle."

"Hey, that's an idea. I could specialize in sex therapy."

16

When Shannon and Velez got back to the office, Rose was waiting for them.

"Well, how did it go?"

"You're looking for a blue Atlas," Velez said.

"A what?"

"Loo, this shrink is off the wall, but he said a few things that make sense. He said these guys are probably under a lot of pressure and one of them may crack. If he does, he'll make a mistake and expose himself. He may even give himself up."

Rose looked at Shannon. "Is that right?"

"I'm not as optimistic as our young friend here, but it's a possibility. Luis said something that makes more sense. Altman thinks these guys might be forced to do these killings because the leader has something on them.

Luis said that only the threat of exposing a murder could make someone commit another murder.''

Velez added, ''Or, if not the actual murder, then a witness to one.''

''Or, if not murder,'' Rose embellished the theory, ''how about an unjustified wrongful death?''

''Typical IAD,'' Shannon mumbled.

''Wait a minute, Loo, he's got a point. Imagine you're with one of the guys in your squad. He shoots the wrong guy and he finds some way to cover it up. And you do nothing about it. Where does that leave you?''

''If it comes out,'' Shannon answered, ''I'm out of a job and face criminal charges for concealing a homicide.''

Rose's initial enthusiasm waned. ''Naw, it's not good enough. A threat of exposure still wouldn't make me commit murder.''

''There's more to it than that,'' Velez explained. ''Altman said there are a lot of ingredients in the mix—rationalization, fear, and the emotional and intellectual stability of the man himself.''

Rose put his arm around Velez. ''Damn, we *are* going to have to make you a detective. So what are you getting at, Luis?''

''Maybe these guys were involved in a job-related shooting that wasn't righteous and they covered it up.''

Shannon scowled. ''I still don't buy it.''

''That's because you're looking at it from your middle-class viewpoint,'' Velez said. ''You don't have the capacity for that kind of rationalization.''

''And you think others may?''

''That's what Altman said. Hey, don't look at me. He's *your* expert.''

''So you think these guys might have been involved in a shooting that was bad?''

''Yeah.''

''It's worth a look,'' Shannon said. ''Start collecting data on all cop shootings within the last two years. We'll see if any names pop up in your computer.''

''I'll take care of the Early Intervention Unit,'' Rose said. ''I know the C.O. I'll tell him it's for an IAD investigation. Those are the magic words. Once you mention an IAD investigation, no one asks any more questions.'' He looked at his watch. ''I have to meet my wife at a cocktail party at six. It'll be a squeeze, but I'll pick up the list on my way.''

Rose met with the commanding officer of the Early Intervention Unit, but between interruptions from frequent telephone calls and gossip about who was transferred to where, he didn't get out of the captain's office until after seven. He was late for the party, but he had the list in his pocket.

He was hardly in the door when Rachel materialized at his side. "Where have you been?" she hissed.

"I'm sorry, babe. I had to pick something up and I got delayed."

"Thanks a lot. I've had to make all sorts of excuses for you."

"Rachel, no one cares if I'm here or not."

"That's not the point. I don't want to discuss it now. The bar's over there. I'll see you later."

At the bar a tall, distinguished man held his glass up to the light and squinted. "This wine is almost *too* assertive."

"A bit too *masculine* for me," agreed the woman in the oversized fishnet sweater and riding boots.

Rose, in no mood for *meshugge* wine mavens, grabbed his scotch and drifted away. It was another of those must-go-to cocktail parties with the same people, the same gossip, and the same plastic hors d'oeuvres. While Rachel flitted about scoring points with the right people, he was awash in yuppie account executives and models with frontal lobotomies.

The apartment, located in an elegant building on Fifty-fifth Street, belonged to a client—the CEO of a Fortune 500 conglomerate. The twelve-foot ceilings gave the apartment character and the potential to be truly spectacular, but the owner favored starkness. The interior, done entirely in black-and-white tile, marble and patent leather, reminded Rose of a huge men's room. At any moment he expected an old gent to dust him off with a whisk broom.

Several large—and no doubt expensive—abstract paintings, highlighted by strategically placed track lights, hung from the massive walls. To Rose the paintings looked suspiciously like a housepainter's drop cloths. He wandered over to the stereo and examined the records, hoping to find some decent jazz to replace the audio Valium oozing from the speakers. He thumbed through the collection in disgust. No such luck. This guy had enough shlock music to stock a dentist's office for a year.

"Well, if it isn't my favorite gendarme!"

Rose turned to face an elfin-short man wearing large pink glasses. "Hello, Van. How are you?" Van—no last name—was an art director at Rachel's agency.

"Marvelous, simply marvelous! Tell me, have you shot anybody lately?"

"No, Van," Rose answered with a straight face. "Have you blown anybody away yourself lately?"

The little man giggled. "Oh, you policemen are all the same. So violent!" He touched Rose's sleeve. "Nice material. Where ever did you get it?"

Rose pulled his sleeve away. "Rachel dresses me. I have no idea."

"Well I'd like to undress you."

"Van," Rose whispered softly, "go away."

"My, aren't we huffy," the art director said, and headed for the bar.

Rachel slipped up to him. "Having a good time?"

"I think Van wants my body."

"Oh, don't pay any attention to him. He's harmless."

"Maybe to you," he said, holding a stirrer like a Groucho cigar, "but you don't have a body like mine."

She squeezed his hand and melted into the crowd. Rose backed into a corner and watched how easily she glided from one group to another. Strikingly beautiful—even in this glitzy crowd she could have been a model. In fact last year she'd had an offer from an agency, but she'd turned it down. She'd been on the other side of the camera with the photographers, the art directors, and the sponsors and had seen firsthand what models went through. Except for the handful of super models, who could demand special treatment, modeling was a short-lived, dehumanizing, highly paid career as a mannequin.

Rachel was interested in something more lasting and important—power and control. In some ways she was very much like his workaholic father. Her intolerance for less than perfection made her quick to anger, and like his father, there was the unstated but tangible need to succeed. She loved the advertising business, and more than once, unable to sleep from the excitement, had kept him up half the night describing how she'd convinced another rich sponsor to spend millions to advertise his product the way she envisioned it. From what everybody told him, she was a natural. Her success still bewildered him. When they'd met six years ago at a singles weekend in the Catskills, she was no more than a glorified secretary working at a small ad agency on Madison Avenue.

The weekend had started out a disaster. Rose had talked his friend and radio-car partner, Jack Burke, into going to Grossinger's for the weekend, and it had been a mistake. Burke, who looked like a six-foot leprechaun, didn't fit in with the predominantly Jewish crowd. At the bar, hours after dinner, he was still complaining. "I ask for pork chops, for Chrissake, and he brings me six different kinds of fish. What do I look like, a fucking penguin?"

"It's kosher," Rose explained for the third time. "Besides, we didn't come here for the food."

"I didn't come here to starve either." Burke looked around the bar. "Alex," he whispered, "*everyone* here is Jewish! Even the Puerto Rican chambermaids are Jewish, for Chrissake. People are staring at me. I feel like a jig at a KKK convention. I gotta be the only goy within a hundred miles of this place."

"Maybe it's that advertisement you're wearing around your neck."

Burke fingered the large crucifix. "You think so? Maybe if I saw the arms off, it'll look like a mezuzah."

"While you're at it, you'd better put a paper bag over your big Irish face."

A dejected Burke signaled the bartender for another round. "If I'm not going to get laid this weekend, I might as well get loaded."

Rose was the first to see her coming through the door. "Those two by the door," he said, poking his partner. "Let's meet them."

Burke turned and looked. One was strikingly beautiful; the other, slightly overweight, was plain. "Don't tell me." He tucked his crucifix inside his shirt. "Let me guess which one is mine."

Alex and Rachel were married less than a year later.

She advanced rapidly in her job and was given more responsibility and more money. One day she came home and, to his amazement, announced she was quitting. Alex had protested; she was already making more money than he was. But she merely laughed and said she could do better. And she did when she got the job with her present employer. Now she was responsible for several major accounts, and other agencies were trying to pirate her away with offers of ridiculous salaries.

He never dreamed she'd fit so comfortably into the knockdown, drag-out business world. Instead of being exhausted from her hectic schedule, she seemed to draw energy from the routine of frantic late-night telephone calls from art directors, weekends at the office hurriedly redoing a presentation, and the daily pressure that comes from capturing million-dollar accounts.

When they were first married they talked about having a family. But there had been no talk of children recently. Her job had taken precedence over everything else. Rose had to admit it was exciting; at least in the beginning. The occasional opening-night tickets, the private museum parties, and the junkets to Las Vegas and Europe were just some of the perks of a rising star in the advertising business.

He enjoyed straddling both their worlds—even though his Academy instructors said it couldn't be done. As it was explained to him, the kinds of hours a cop kept weren't conducive to a normal social life, and a cop quickly grows weary of meeting strangers—and surprisingly, friends—who insist on telling him in great detail about the ticket they'd gotten, not because they were speeding, but because they wouldn't pay off the cop. As a result of these unpleasant encounters, cops retreated and stayed among their own kind—people they were comfortable with. To his dismay, a rookie soon found he had little in common with his old friends. It was hard to relate to someone who complained about having a hard day at the office when that same day you'd found a decaying body at the bottom of an air shaft. And so cops socialized together, and in the process became more and more isolated from the rest of society—caught in the vortex of increasingly smaller and smaller concentric circles.

This bleak scenario was not for Rose. He made it a point to cultivate both police and civilian friends, but lately Rachel's world was beginning to wear thin. Perhaps because the investigation made the trivial machinations of advertising pale by comparison. He'd conducted many investigations, but nothing like the one he and Shannon were working on. He was beginning to understand the allure a murder investigation held, and he was beginning to understand Shannon's dedication. A murder investigation got under your skin. It took on a life of its own and made extraordinary demands on you. It stayed with you twenty-four hours a day; it was a new experience for Rose.

Ted Trotman, a V.P. in Rachel's firm, grabbed his elbow. "We were discussing the concept of yin and yang in Western experience," Trotman explained. "You're a policeman, Alex. In your line of work you must see some interesting contrasts and opposing forces."

The others seated around the couch looked up at him expectantly. Normally Rose didn't discuss police work with civilians, but a memory from long ago came to mind. He sat on the arm of the couch. "Years ago, I was still a rookie assigned to the West Side . . ." He paused and waited for the memory to come back. "At that time the *Daily News* was calling Eighty-fifth Street between Amsterdam and Columbus avenues the worst block in the city. It was claimed there was more crime per square foot there than anywhere else in the city, and they were probably right. My partner and I were on a rooftop sitting on a shooting gallery—"

"What's that?" Trotman asked.

"Junkies use the top-floor stairway landings to shoot up," Rose explained. "It was a clear, cold October night. Not even the glare of the city's lights could dim the bright stars. We heard a piano playing and went to investigate.

"In those days the difference between Eighty-fifth Street and Eighty-sixth Street was like night and day. Eighty-fifth was row upon row of run-down tenements infested with rats, roaches, and junkies. Across the backyard—a distance of no more than fifty yards—was Eighty-sixth Street, a land of doormen, elevators, and stained-glass windows. From our vantage point we could see directly into the apartment across from us. It was like watching a movie. There was a party in progress and the guests were dressed in evening gowns and tuxedos. Waiters in short red jackets scurried about with silver trays of champagne. My partner and I were mesmerized. We sat on the edge of the roof, feet dangling over the side, and watched. These people might as well have been a million miles from Eighty-fifth Street. We were prowling the rooftops for junkies, and they were drinking champagne and talking about the ski conditions at Innsbruck. It was incredible! I always wondered if the people who lived in that building ever looked out their stained-glass windows and saw the other world in their backyard.''

For a moment no one said anything. Rose was suddenly conscious of the silence.

"Did you arrest anyone that night?" asked an attractive blonde sitting on the couch.

"What? Oh, no. No one came that night."

"Did you get a good look at the apartment?" an older woman with blue hair asked.

"Yes. I had a perfect view."

"Tell me, how was it decorated? It sounds like a marvelous apartment." There was a burst of nervous laughter from the group.

Suddenly Rose needed a drink. He excused himself and headed for the kitchen. On the way he met Rachel. "Let's get out of here," he said.

"I can't. Paul is starting to talk about a new project." In the flush of her excitement, she didn't notice he was seething.

"Screw Paul. I'm up to here with these phony bastards. Look around the room, Rachel. This group looks like the cast of a Fellini movie."

She brushed her hair back. "Oh, and I suppose those macho cavemen you work with are perfectly normal."

"I didn't say that."

"Alex, what's the matter with you? Are you having an anxiety attack because of Van?"

"Of course not. It's— I can't explain it. I guess everything seems like so much bullshit."

Rachel's eyes flared. "And a gathering of your friends isn't? Do you consider a night out watching a bunch of drunken cops guzzling beer and listening to their dreary wives discussing triple Waldbaum coupons a foray into a meaningful experience?"

"Rachel, you're a fucking snob."

"Don't insult me, Alex. This isn't all fun and games for me either. You may not realize it but a lot of business gets conducted at these 'superficial' parties."

"What are you trying to prove? Do you expect to be doing this for the rest of your life?"

"Yes," she snapped.

Her answer surprised both of them. "I'll tell you what, Rachel. I'm going to have another drink. If you haven't finished conducting your business by then, I'm leaving."

She started to say something, but Paul called to her. Without a further word she turned and walked away.

As Rose watched her in animated conversation with her boss, it occurred to him that he willingly shared her world but she wanted no part of his. She'd never liked cops and was clearly uncomfortable in their presence.

In the kitchen he dumped ice cubes in his glass and poured himself a very large scotch. The swinging door opened and the blonde who had been sitting on the couch came in holding an empty wineglass. "It must be very exciting being a policeman."

"Not much. I only hunt other cops." Rose drank deeply of his scotch. The blonde blinked, not knowing what to say.

"I'm sorry. I didn't mean to snap at you. I've had a bad day."

"We all have those days." She turned to leave.

"Wait. What are you drinking?"

"Some dreadful white wine," she said, handing him the glass. She leaned against the refrigerator and watched him pour the wine. "Inside there a minute ago, you were thinking the party you spied on was pretty much like this one, and you were wondering if anyone here ever thought about the great unwashed masses who live on the Eighty-fifth streets of the world."

Rose studied her more carefully. He'd assumed she was just another bubble-headed girlfriend of one of the guests. Maybe he had her pegged wrong. Like many of the women at these parties, she was attractive. But there was something in the way she fixed her gaze on him that he found pleasantly disturbing. He couldn't quite interpret its meaning. A come-on? Sincerity? Friendly?

"I guess I was making a comparison at that," he said.

There was just the trace of a smile on her lips. Mocking? "The danger with that kind of thinking is that you can come across as a pompous ass who thinks he's the only one who knows what misery is."

"Maybe I *am* a pompous ass."

Her smile widened. "I don't think so, because if you are, so am I."

It was Rose's turn to smile. "I'm a great judge of character. I'm sure you're no pompous ass."

She looked at him appraisingly. "You don't look like a cop."

"Well, to paraphrase Gloria Steinem, this is what a cop looks like."

Her hand went to her heart in mock pain. "Touché." She turned to leave, then stopped and handed him a piece of paper.

When she was gone he studied the note. Written on it was a name—Adriana—and a telephone number. It wasn't the first time a woman had given him her telephone number, but the decision to keep it or throw it away suddenly seemed very important. He stared at the writing—a bold, sweeping script—for some time. Then he crumpled it up and threw it in the wastebasket.

PATRICK STONE HERDED HIS HAPPY GROUP INTO A CORNER AND THREW two twenties on the bar. "Innkeeper, give these guys anything they want."

The three-hundred-pound bartender, sensing a long night of drinking and big tips, smiled, revealing a missing front tooth.

"Somebody's birthday?" he asked in a raspy voice that sounded like he'd been hit in the throat with a baseball bat.

"Naw." Steve Tecci pulled up a stool next to Stone. "Sort of a bon voyage party."

"Oh yeah? Where ya goin'?"

"Not me. A friend of mine, sort of. He's not going far though; probably Ossining, New York."

"But he's going for a long, long time," McKay Beals, the tall black cop, chimed in. "Twenty to thirty years."

Recognition flickered in the obese bartender's eyes and his smile collapsed. They were fucking cops, and cops, he knew, were lousy tippers—unless they were shitfaced. Once again he cursed his luck. Of all the gin joints in the world, why did his uncle Carmine have to open a bar around the corner from the Manhattan Criminal Courts Building? His clientele was mostly cops—and lawyers, the only people cheaper than cops. Even *when* they were shitfaced.

Patrick Stone and Sergeant Hardy's team had assembled at Carmine's, a filthy hole-in-the-wall bar on the fringe of Little Italy, to celebrate NET's latest triumph. After five weeks of trial-room warfare with two of the city's top criminal lawyers, NET, under the able leadership of Vincent T. Sorvino, the thirty-four-year-old ADA assigned to the case, had emerged victorious. Frank Rosetti, a major drug dealer who had managed to elude prosecution for years, had been convicted of all six counts, ranging from illegal possession of a firearm to a B Felony sale of drugs.

Stone picked up his drink. "Where's Vinnie?"

"He's coming," Tim Hardy said. "After that verdict, Sorvino's probably sitting on the D.A.'s desk demanding a promotion to the Homicide Bureau."

A baby-faced man wearing a baggy brown suit and scuffed loafers banged through the door. "Did someone use my name in vain?"

Stone inspected the disheveled Assistant District Attorney and shook his head. "Jesus, Vinnie, I think the jury voted a guilty verdict because they felt sorry for you. You're an ADA, for Chrissake, not a Legal Aid hack. You should have a better image."

Sorvino examined his stained tie. "This *is* my image. Unlike you overpaid cops, we ADAs barely make minimum wage."

Steve Tecci stuck a beer in Sorvino's hand. "Here, cry into that and spare us."

Sorvino took a long gulp and slammed the bottle on the bar. "*Goddamn, I feel good.*"

Stone grinned. "You should. You nailed that sucker with every count."

"Yeah, I did, didn't I. But I owe it all to you guys." Sorvino solemnly shook hands with each of them, beginning with Stone, then Hardy, Tecci, Beals, and finally Walt Cronin. "You guys were terrific on the stand."

Tecci leered. "You should see us in bed."

The young ADA loosened his tie and climbed up on a stool next to Stone. "Seriously, you guys have no idea how tough it is to get a conviction in this liberal fucking town. If I were trying Jack the Ripper, I'd be lucky to get him to cop a plea to disorderly conduct. I don't understand it."

"Maybe," Tecci suggested, "it's because most of the people on juries are dirty themselves."

Sorvino wiped his mouth with his sleeve. "Spoken like a typical cop." He turned to Walter Cronin. "You set the tone for the case, Walt. When you testified about the daily meetings Rosetti had with the others, I could see the jury's eyes lighting up. How the hell did you get so close to them?"

Cronin laughed self-consciously. "Probably because I don't look like a cop."

Sorvino studied the gawky, sandy-haired police officer. He knew Cronin was twenty-four, but he looked like a teenager. "You got that right. Pat, where the hell do you get these guys from? Central casting?"

Stone smiled. "Police work is all show biz, Vinnie. The bad guys play a role; we play a role. We're just better actors. Once you understand that, you have the key to running a successful sting operation."

Five hours later, long after the others had gone home, Stone, Sorvino, and Hardy were still occupying the same bar stools. Hardy, who had been drinking club soda the whole time, was the only clear-eyed one in the trio. Stone and Sorvino had slid into that comfortable zone where, anesthetized by alcohol, they were immune to the demands and pressures of the outside world. They floated in the pleasant sea of camaraderie known only to men who have shared the experience of combat and survived. As long as they remained in this state, they were brothers, and nothing—not skin color, rank, or political persuasion—made any difference.

Their little band had beaten the odds. Burdened by restrictive rules and procedures of law, they had taken on the best that the underworld could afford and won. Little Vincent T. Sorvino, sheathed in his baggy Sears suit, had tilted with a battery of high-priced lawyers in thousand-dollar London-tailored suits. But in the courtroom lists none of that mattered; only superior intelligence, careful strategy, and meticulous attention to detail prevailed. Sometimes.

That peculiar institution—the criminal trial—was, as cops and prosecutors knew only too well, fraught with danger for the good guys. The founding fathers, in their zeal to ensure that every man received a fair trial, bent over backward to guarantee impartial treatment. And the Supreme Court, continuing the tradition, broke its back refining these safeguards in the form of the Miranda warnings, the inadmissibility of hearsay evidence, and the pretrial evidence-disclosure rule. Intellectually, law enforcement people knew the reasons for these rules and applauded them. Unless they were directly involved in the case. Then, the primitive instincts for blood took over and these sacred safeguards were suddenly viewed with great suspicion; they weren't there to protect the innocent, they were there to fuck up the good guys! In the heated contest of good vs. evil, prosecutors and cops longed for something more practical—say, trial by ordeal.

Vinnie Sorvino, who'd been talking nonstop about the case since he'd sat down five hours before, signaled for another drink. "You know, there was one point when I thought they had us."

"When was that?" Stone slid his empty glass toward the bartender.

"When Rosetti's lawyer tried to make an issue about the amount of money seized."

"That didn't bother me. It just told me they had shit and were grasping at straws."

"Yeah, true, but I was watching the jury. When the defense said there was a fifty-thousand-dollar discrepancy, the jury started to squirm. Juries are funny animals. No one *wants* to vote for conviction, no matter what they may say later. So, they're always looking for an excuse to let the guy off the hook. What better excuse than cops taking money? If *cops* take money, so the thinking goes, why should I convict the poor bastard they took it from?"

"Yeah," Stone said, "I see what you mean."

"That's why I put you on the stand so early. When you reviewed your background—Harvard, youngest captain in the department, handpicked by the Police Commissioner to run NET—I could see the jury settle down. You

impressed the shit out of them, Pat. When you were finished, there wasn't
one of the twelve who could entertain a thought of you, Tim Hardy, or any
of your men taking a nickel. After that it was a piece of cake.'' With a
magnanimity spawned by victory, Sorvino added, ''What the hell, it was a
nice try, but it backfired. Not only didn't the defense-ploy work, it put the
jury squarely in our corner for the rest of the trial.'' He slapped Hardy on
the back. ''God, I love this job.''

''That's not what you said five weeks ago,'' Stone pointed out.

Sorvino scowled. ''That's because I'd just gotten my brains beaten in
trying a Narcotics Division case. Damn, what a difference between them
and you guys. The cop responsible for vouchering the cocaine got the shit
kicked out of him on the stand. He couldn't remember if he counted the
bags in the sitting room or upstairs in the squad room. It was no big deal—I
tried to signal him, but the dopey bastard wouldn't look at me. The defense
smelled blood and went for the jugular. The cop got flustered and said a lot
of crazy things. It was all over after that. By the time the defense got
through mugging the poor kid, I half expected the jury to convict the
Narcotics Division, for Chrissake! You guys are so professional. How do
you do it?''

''I handpick each man and train him myself.''

''How?''

''I teach him how to testify, how to take proper notes—''

''You mean you actually conduct classes?''

''That's right,'' Hardy said proudly. ''The captain runs mock trials and
we critique every case, whether we win or lose.''

''No shit! What a great idea. Stone, you ought to be the P.C.''

Stone smiled. ''That's the general idea.''

The drunken ADA regarded Stone. ''I'm not kidding, Pat. I've worked
with a lot of bosses in your job, but you're head and shoulders above
them. You have it all—smarts, drive, and the ability to lead people.
I've seen how your guys respond to you. If anyone can make it to the
top, you can.''

Stone stood up and put his arm around Sorvino. ''I'll bet you say that to
all the cops who get you a conviction.'' He looked at his watch. It was after
nine. They'd been drinking continually since four, and they'd exhausted
their supply of war stories. Even the glow of that afternoon's victory was
beginning to wane. ''That's it for tonight,'' Stone said.

Sorvino slid unsteadily off his stool. ''Yeah, me too. Tomorrow it's
back to the salt mines.''

Tim Hardy, thumbing through the bartender's *Daily News,* stood up
abruptly, knocking his stool over. Without a word he slid the paper in front
of Stone and pointed at a photo. A man's body slumped out of a Mercedes.
The sports car, roped off with evidence tape, was surrounded by uniformed

cops and detectives. Even though the photo was grainy, and the man's face was covered with blood, Stone recognized the rodentlike face of Eddie Dumont. The headline read: UNDERWORLD FIGURE MACHINE-GUNNED ON BROOK-LYN PIER.

Stone snapped up the paper and read the sketchy article. Suddenly pale, he sat down heavily. Sorvino had been reading the story over Stone's shoulder. "You know him?"

"What? Oh, yeah. One of my confidential informants."

"Was this the result of anything he was doing for you?"

"No." Stone quickly recovered his composure. "Actually, he gave me very little. I just feel sorry for him, that's all. He wasn't a bad guy. Just a little man trying to play hardball with the big guys."

Sorvino squinted at the photo again. "Fuck him. He's one less scumbag to prosecute. One down, Pat. Only two million to go."

II

17

TECCI AND BEALS WERE IN COURT ON A PROTRACTED TRIAL, AND Walter Cronin was assigned to go with "Big Ben" Hamilton to execute an arrest warrant.

Hamilton was probably the smallest cop in the department. After only eighteen months on the job, Stone brought him into NET because, like Cronin, Hamilton didn't look like a cop. Born and raised in Westbury, Long Island, the little black cop had never seen a slum until he was transferred to the Twenty-eighth Precinct in the heart of Harlem. No rookie was more shocked than he at the sights he saw there. It was hard to say who was more surprised by Hamilton's naiveté, the other cops or the residents in the Two-eight.

Cronin knew Hamilton slightly, but he'd never worked with him before. The one thing Cronin was sure of was that the short cop was quick to

149

laugh—unless someone mentioned his height. Like many short men, Hamilton was supersensitive to disparaging remarks about his diminutive stature.

It was dark when Hamilton pulled off the East River Drive at the 125th Street exit and threaded the car through the narrow, poorly lit Harlem streets chronically clogged with double-parked cars. "I've been trying to catch up to this dude for weeks," he explained to Cronin. "But he's always gone by the time I get there. But not this time. My informant says he's hiding out in his aunt's place on 118th Street. With a little bit of luck I should have him in the slammer before midnight."

The radio crackled. "Two-five Charlie . . . ten fifty-two at seven-three-two Lexington Avenue . . . meet the complainant in front of the building." Two-five Charlie acknowledged the job.

Hamilton adjusted the volume. "Hey Walt, you ever watch those L.A. police shows on TV?"

"What about them?"

"Ever notice how sexy their dispatchers sound?"

"Yeah, now that you mention it."

"How come our dispatchers always sound like someone's pounding salt up their asses?"

Cronin thought about that for a moment. "Beats me. Maybe it's the cheap speakers in these cars."

"Naw, it's this fucking city. Everything's falling apart—rickety bridges held up by a hundred coats of paint, potholes you could hide a fucking Greyhound bus in. Even our dispatchers sound like crap. I want to be a cop in L.A., where all the complainants are gorgeous starlets with big tits, the bad guys wear Bally shoes, and the buildings are only two stories high."

"What does the height of the buildings have to do with it?"

"Are you kidding? You throw a bathtub off a second-story building, it don't build up enough velocity to chip the paint on the radio car. When I was in the Two-eight they dumped one of them suckers off a ten-story building onto a radio car. The fucking car *and* the bathtub ended up in the subway!"

Cronin laughed. "Ben, you weren't in the Two-eight long enough to see a bathtub fall ten floors."

"True story, swear to God." He edged the car to the curb. "I was there when the cop made it up."

Once inside the tenement building, Hamilton ran his finger down the mailboxes, most of which had already been pried open by junkies looking for welfare checks, and found the name. "Lucinda McBride, apartment 6W. Shit! Why is it *always* on the top floor?"

Puffing, they made their way up the urine-stained stairs. From the moment they'd entered the hallway they heard the sounds of angry voices coming from somewhere in the building, but it was only when they got to the top floor that they discovered the racket was coming from the McBride apartment. "Great," Hamilton said, pausing to catch his breath. "We're going to have to adjudicate a family fight before I make the arrest." He listened at the door before rapping it with his jack. "Police!" he shouted. "Open up!"

There was the sound of a scuffle, followed by the thump of something hitting the floor. The two cops stepped back as the door smashed open and a man came hurling out. He crashed into the opposite wall and slowly sank to the floor. The door slammed shut with a bang.

"Holy shit!" Hamilton stared bug-eyed at the victim—a man about six-three and over two hundred pounds. Blood trickled down the side of his head and from a cut lip. Both cops looked at each other with the same thought—*If this big guy is the loser, what does the winner look like?*

Cronin cleared his throat. "Ben, is Ronald Paisley a big guy?"

Hamilton looked down at the man. "He ain't that big, I don't think. But I'll tell you what. If he did this, I may just grant him immunity from prosecution and forget the whole thing."

Cronin sighed and propped the woozy man up against the wall. "What happened?"

The bleeding man dabbed his head with a dirty handkerchief. "It's my wife. She drunk again."

The two cops tried unsuccessfully to suppress grins. "Your wife did this to you?"

"Yeah," the man answered, failing to see the humor. "She get nasty when she drink."

"I can see that. Hey, slick, is Ronald Paisley in there?"

The man dabbed at his bloody lip and frowned. "That no-account nephew of hers ain't welcome here."

"Yeah, but he's in there, isn't he?"

"No he ain't. I jus' told you that."

"Right. But if you don't mind, we'll just take a look for ourselves."

"Go ahead. It's your ass," the battered man said, and shuffled down the hall out of range.

Hamilton rapped the door again. "Open up, woman! Right now!"

The door opened and a tiny woman in a ragged dress glared at Hamilton with bloodshot eyes. His mouth dropped open. She was even smaller than him! "Hey sister," he said, launching into his ghetto-jive bullshit. "What's happenin'. Anyone else in der wit yo'all, mama?"

"Just me, fool," she said, and without warning let loose a kick to Hamilton's groin that would have been good for a sixty-yard field goal in a head wind.

As Hamilton went down like a punctured tire, Cronin lunged toward the woman, but he tripped over the prostrate body of his partner. Shrieking, she grabbed Cronin by the hair and propelled him across the room into the refrigerator door. And the fight was on.

For the next several minutes, or what seemed like the better part of the night to Walt Cronin, he wrestled and traded punches and kicks with the smallest and toughest female he'd ever seen. That was the problem—she was too small to hold on to. He grabbed her in a headlock, but she slipped out. He grabbed her wrists, but she seemed to melt from his grasp. It was like fighting a mirage, except a mirage doesn't hurt and this one was getting in some pretty good punches. At one point they tumbled into the playpen and rolled cursing and yelling among stuffed animals, sour milk, and baby turds. Fortunately, the youngster, watching Mommy duke it out with the nice policeman, had found a safe haven under the kitchen table.

A fistfight with a woman presents several problems for the average male cop. From childhood, boys are taught never to hit girls, and old habits die hard. It usually takes a couple of good beatings at the hands of females before a cop learns to override years of cultural training and coldcock a woman just like anyone else who is trying to beat the living shit out of him.

Cronin, who was beginning to tire, noticed with alarm that his opponent wasn't even breathing heavily. Finally he saw his opening. As she looked away for a moment to grab an empty bottle, he stunned her with a desperate right cross to the jaw. Her eyes turned inward, then she fell over backward into the playpen, unconscious.

Gasping for air, he dragged her out and handcuffed her hands behind her back. He propped her in a chair and leaned against the stove to catch his breath. By then Hamilton, who was no longer seeing stars, stumbled into the apartment clutching his groin.

"I got her," Cronin puffed. "This bitch is nuts. Call for a bus. We'll psycho her."

"Noooo!" the husband roared as he charged into the apartment. Hamilton didn't move fast enough, and the man—all two hundred pounds of him—came down on him like a jumbo jet falling out of the sky. They hit the floor in an explosion of bodies. Instinctively, Cronin swung his jack and caught the man square in the forehead. It sounded like that sweet, sharp *thwack!* you hear when a ball player hits a home run. The man's eyes glazed over and he slumped on top of Hamilton like a dead bear.

"What the fuck is going on here?" Hamilton squawked indignantly as he struggled to escape from underneath the massive inert body. "What am I, *shit*?" He elbowed the man in the ribs and staggered to his feet.

Cronin turned just in time to see the little woman stand up with the cuffs dangling from one wrist; her wrists were so small she'd slipped out. She waved the cuffs at them and his heart sank: there was murder in her eyes.

"Fuck this!" Hamilton yelled and drew his gun. "Sit down, you crazy bitch!'' he screamed, pointing the gun at her, ''or I'll blow your motherfucking head clean off!''

Even in her drunken state she could see that he was crazier than she was. In slow motion she slid back into the chair. ''Now throw those cuffs to my partner nice and easy.''

She slipped her wrist easily through the other cuff and tossed them to Cronin. On the floor her spouse groaned.

''Now don't either one of you move, or I'll blow your goddamn heads off. You hear me?'' Then he remembered why he was here. ''Oh, yeah. Where's Ronald?''

''He ain't here,'' she said, struggling to focus on him with bleary eyes.

Hamilton licked his lips. He thought about searching the apartment, but prudently decided against it. ''I'll take your word for it,'' he said. ''Come on, Walt.''

Slowly they backed toward the door. Hamilton, holding the gun in both hands, just like the girls in *Charlie's Angels,* swung it back and forth between the woman in the chair and the dazed behemoth on the floor. At the door he announced: ''We're leaving now. Don't come out for at least an hour. You hear?'' He slammed the door and they were out in the hallway. ''What the fuck did we just do?'' Hamilton asked incredulously.

Cronin, who ached all over, shook his head mutely.

''Jesus,'' Hamilton whispered, ''I feel like I just robbed a fucking bank!''

''Come on,'' Cronin said. ''Let's get the hell out of here.''

After the brawl in the apartment they stopped at a diner. As they talked about the incident their anger gave way to bewilderment and finally to laughter. Hamilton finally suggested, ''Hey, Walt, how about one more stop? Ronald's girlfriend lives nearby. Maybe I can catch him in the saddle.''

They parked around the corner and walked into the block. Hamilton explained the plan. ''We'll go into this building, cross the roofs and come down in her building.''

When they were on the roof, Hamilton whispered, ''Quiet and watch the clotheslines.''

''Easy for you. You're so short you can walk under them without bending over.''

''Very fucking funny,'' Hamilton hissed and melted into the darkness. Quietly they moved across the rooftops, avoiding clotheslines, garbage, and pigeon coops. At the third roof landing Hamilton stopped. ''This is it.'' Just as he was about to open the roof landing door, he paused. ''Someone's inside,'' he whispered. ''I hear voices. Gotta be junkies shooting up.'' He took out his gun and positioned himself in front of the door. Cronin stood to the side and grasped the doorknob. ''Now!'' Hamilton yelled.

Cronin yanked the door open, and for the second time that night all hell broke loose.

Three junkies were inside. One was on the floor, leaning up against the wall, working the needle in his arm, while the other two were cooking another hit in a bottle cap. The one with the needle in his arm was too far gone to react to the cops exploding through the rooftop door, but the others, already antsy from the need of a fix, bolted like frightened rabbits. The bottle cap, and its contents of liquid heroin, splattered to the tile floor as one junkie dove headfirst down the stairs and got away. Hamilton slammed the other man against the wall and stuck his gun in his ear. "Don't move motherfucker or you're dead."

"Okay, okay." The frightened junkie squirmed, then went limp. "I didn't do nuthin'."

Hamilton cuffed his prisoner and rolled him on his stomach for the search. But first he gave the traditional warning: "Listen, scumbag, I'm gonna search you and I don't want no AIDS or hepatitis. If I get stuck with one of your filthy needles, I'm gonna stick it up your ass sideways. You better tell me now. You got any needles in your pocket?"

"I ain't got nuthin'," the prisoner sputtered, his face pressed to the filthy tile floor.

Gingerly, Hamilton went through his pockets and came up with two glassine envelopes. "Bingo!" he said gleefully, waving them in the air.

While Hamilton was searching his prisoner, Cronin reached down and plucked the needle from the other junkie's arm. The man, dreamy-eyed, looked up at Cronin and smiled a toothless grin. "No problem, my man, no problem." Then he focused on Hamilton and said the wrong thing. "Damn, that's the *smallest* cop I ever seen."

Hamilton spun around. "What!" His eyes were on fire. "What did you say, you piece of shit?" This was definitely not Ben Hamilton's best day. He'd been kicked in the balls by a woman, jumped by a gorilla, and now insulted by a low-life junkie. He stepped up to the man, took his gun out and pointed it in his face. "You maggot shit," he hissed. "I'm gonna blow your fucking face off."

The junkie, still dancing in Elysian fields, looked up at the enraged cop and said softly, "That's cool, man. That's cool."

Cronin stood frozen in horror. The sight of Hamilton standing over the junkie with his .38 Special sent images of the people they'd executed flashing through his head. Suddenly, it became clear to him: he and the others were murderers, and all the rationalizations in the world couldn't change that.

Cronin saw Hamilton standing menacingly over the junkie sprawled on the floor. Instinctively, he lashed out with the butt of his gun. And for the third time that night Ben Hamilton went down.

Later, in the station house, Cronin apologized. "I'm sorry. I really thought you were going to kill him."

Hamilton rubbed the lump on his head. "Next time why don't you just say something? I wasn't gonna kill the dude. I just wanted to get a rise out of him. Damn, I go out to bag a felony warrant and I end up with a two-bit junk collar and a concussion." He looked at Cronin with baleful eyes. "You know, I think I shoulda been a fireman. This job is too fucking dangerous!"

Cronin didn't hear him. He was wondering what he was going to do if he was asked to take part in another murder.

THE MUSIC WAS SO LOUD THAT STEVE TECCI COULD FEEL THE VI-brations in the parking lot fifty feet away. Following the crowd, he entered the cavelike vestibule and waited for his eyes to grow accustomed to the purple and blue lights. Then he paid the cashier and went inside.

The interior of the Inferno, the current "hot club" in the Bronx, was an eerie kaleidoscope of lights, colors, and sounds. Multicolored strobe lights flashed from ceilings and walls, giving the dancers the stutterlike movements of people in a silent movie. More lights flashed up from the dance floor, casting grotesque shadows across the dancers' faces.

In the Inferno, one felt the music more than heard it. On a platform high above the dance floor, a D.J. wearing earphones and dark glasses bobbed his head and mouthed the lyrics to the song being blasted out to the dancers below. The music, ricocheting off the hard surfaces, seemed to come from everywhere at once, and the incessant, throbbing sound emanating from the banks of speakers was mind-numbing. In such an atmosphere there was no room for thoughts of narcotics arrests, courtrooms, or murder. The Inferno blotted out everything else.

Slowly, Tecci made his way toward one of several packed bars. With a practiced eye he surveyed the prospects scattered in self-conscious clusters. It was the usual assortment—college girls from Westchester, leather-clad punk types with rainbow-colored spiked hair, and straights, who came with wide eyes and nervous giggles to experience Bronx nightlife. The pungent smell of marijuana was everywhere.

Tecci continued his circuit and ended up back at the entrance. A steady stream of girls came and went, one group indistinguishable from the other—except for the facial expressions. Those coming in affected a look of studied nonchalance, while those who left, alone, wore expressions of desperate disappointment.

Two bouncers, rushing a drunk through the door, bowled over a group coming in, but no one protested. It was, after all, part of the excitement; the reason they'd paid twenty dollars to get into the Inferno.

Tecci, seeing no one who interested him, was about to leave when he saw her standing with three other girls. She was petite, but her modified punk hairdo and spiked heels made her look taller. Tecci guessed she was about twenty. She wore white leather pants, and even her loose-fitting top couldn't conceal the promise of a great body.

Although Steve Tecci was thirty, he looked much younger. His blond hair, which he kept short, gave him a boyish appearance that women found appealing. With his lean, muscular body, which he kept in shape by lifting weights, he blended in easily with the young crowd that frequented the Inferno.

A burly man festooned with gold necklaces was trying to get the blonde's attention, but it was obvious she wasn't interested. Tecci approached them.

"Hey, babe, I've been looking all over for you. Where you been?"

The girl looked at him with puzzled green eyes. The man, incensed at Tecci's attempt to cut in, pushed Tecci. "Fuck off," he said menacingly.

Without warning Tecci drove his knee into the man's groin. The man's eyes bulged and he slowly sank to the floor. Before Tecci could deliver another knee to his face, three bouncers converged on them.

"Okay, that's enough," the largest of them said; a massive black man who wore three earrings on one ear.

"Sure." Tecci stepped back. "This dude was trying to hustle my girlfriend. A guy can't even take a piss around here without someone trying to hustle his old lady."

The big bouncer smiled down on him. "Next time maybe you'd better make before you come in."

Tecci grinned. "Fair enough."

The big man looked down at the man writhing on the floor. "Get him out of here," he said to the others.

They lifted him easily and slipped unobtrusively into the crowd. People standing ten feet away didn't even know an altercation had taken place. Through it all the blonde and her friends looked on in amusement and the music blared on.

"I feel like a knight in shining armor," Tecci said, pulling the startled girl away from her friends. "Come on. You can buy me a drink for saving your life."

The blonde's friends, seeing he was interested only in her, moved on in search of their own knights in shining armor, or at least a guy with lots of gold chains and an expensive sports car.

They found a small table littered with empty beer bottles and sat down. "Where are you from?" Tecci asked.

"Yonkers."

She chewed gum and wore too much makeup. Still, her eyes were a beautiful green.

"What's your name?"

"Sharon."

"Sharon," he whispered softly, "get that goddamn gum out of your mouth. You look like a pizza waitress."

"What?"

"You heard me. Get rid of the gum."

Flustered, she obediently wrapped the gum in a tissue and stuffed it in her bag. Tecci felt a surge of excitement; he had her.

"Shit!" she said, suddenly angry. "Who do you think you are?"

"I'm your protector," he said soothingly. "I saved your life and now I'm responsible for you forever. It's an ancient Oriental custom."

She looked at him quizzically. She didn't know what to make of him. He wasn't like the guys she usually met here.

"Lighten up," he said. "In America it's different. I'm only responsible for you until midnight."

Over a beer and something called "The Gates of Hell," he learned she was twenty-four and worked as a secretary somewhere in Manhattan. In response to her questions, he gave vague answers about his background, but she didn't seem to notice, or care.

He looked at his watch. "Come on, let's get out of here."

Sharon eyed him appraisingly, trying to decide if she wanted to go with him, or wait for a better offer. He certainly wasn't the type of guy she usually left the Inferno with. He was good-looking—in a scary sort of way, but there was something threatening in his manner; his requests, which sounded like commands, made her vaguely uneasy. Still, it was exciting. "Okay," she said. "Let's go."

Like most girls who came to the Inferno, she wasn't as sophisticated as she thought she was. Movies like *Dirty Dancing* filled her with romantic ideas about dance clubs and mysterious strangers. But movie stars like Patrick Swayze didn't come to clubs like the Inferno. Sharon, and others like her, were more likely to meet potheads, fags, married men, or on a real bad night, someone like Steve Tecci.

Tecci's car was parked at the outer fringe of the lot, away from the lights and noise of the club. He reached over and stroked her hair. "You wear too much makeup. Do you know that?"

She pulled away from him and her angry eyes flashed in the darkness. "Who the hell do you think you—?"

"Hey, all I meant was you're very pretty. That's all. You don't need a lot of that crap."

Her anger turned to exasperation. "You certainly have a way with words."

Tecci shrugged boyishly. "I'm sorry, Sharon. Sometimes I say things and they don't come out the way I mean them."

He was watching her closely for her reaction, and saw that he still had her on the hook. When he'd been stationed in Japan, he'd once watched a man train a dog with an electric cattle prod. The dog jumped every time he was touched. Eventually, the man had only to point a stick at the dog and it would crouch on its belly and whimper. Tecci liked to have the same effect on his women. Only he didn't need a cattle prod. His was a much more subtle approach. By the simple method of alternating his moods between anger and gentleness, he was able to exert power over girls like Sharon.

He started the car. "My roommate's girlfriend is staying with us for a couple of days, so the place is a little crowded. Do you mind a motel?"

She cocked her head and tried to look shocked. "Who said I was going to bed with you?"

"I did." His hand poised on the gear lever. "Well?"

She ran her fingers through her hair and propped up her falling spikes. "What the hell, you saved my life tonight. I guess I don't have any choice."

Tecci smiled, revealing even white teeth. He knew this wasn't her first time going to a motel with a stranger, but it was certainly going to be her most memorable. He jammed the car into gear and stomped on the gas. The quick acceleration snapped their heads back and they both laughed as the car screeched out of the parking lot.

18

THE BOUNDARIES OF THE NINTH PRECINCT ENCOMPASS AN AREA euphemistically called the East Village. Since the turn of the century the neighborhood was known simply as the Lower East Side—a ghetto overpopulated by Eastern European Jews, Poles, and Ukrainians. It had everything a ghetto could offer—poverty, crowding, sickness, and rampant crime. But from this cesspool of humanity some managed to make successes of themselves. People like Eddie Cantor, the Gershwins, and Jimmy Durante were all products of the Lower East Side.

In the fifties the Jews, Poles, and Ukrainians saved their money and migrated to the suburbs and were replaced by the new minorities—blacks and Hispanics. In the sixties the influx of flower children and hippies became sitting ducks for drug dealers who welcomed them with open arms. It wasn't long before the Ninth Precinct gained the dubious distinction of having the highest crime rate in the city. Eventually the city administration hit upon the perfect solution for slums—they demolished the neighborhood. Block after block was razed, scattering the residents and roaches to distant parts of the city.

The gentrification program attracted a better class of people, who loved the neighborhood, but hated the name. Over on the West Side of Manhattan, Greenwich Village enjoyed a reputation as a quaint Bohemian area populated by writers, artists, and poets. So some clever developers started calling the Lower East Side the "East Village." What's in a name? Plenty, said the real estate developers, who jacked up the prices to fit the new image.

The East Village, still in transition, contained an interesting potpourri of artists, writers, yuppies, hippies, plus an assortment of minorities. Of course, each group lived in its own little enclave within the neighborhood. Moynihan and Glazer were right; the melting pot didn't.

The Ninth Precinct cops, the smallest minority of all, had carved out their own piece of the territory—Dinty's. Every precinct has a cop bar. They have no special qualifications except close proximity to the station house and a tolerant owner who doesn't require oxygen every time a drunken cop lets a round go through the ceiling.

"Bar popping," or "unauthorized discharge of a firearm"—as the official department statement of Charges and Specifications worded the event—struck fear into the hearts of police superiors. So it was comforting to know that if in a moment of exuberance a cop let one go through the ceiling, he was among friends.

During the hours when the cops are in residence—from midnight till closing—the usual clientele goes elsewhere. The sight of so many armed, glassy-eyed cops unnerves even the most hardened barfly, which is just fine with the cops. As one detective put it: "It's enough we have to work with civilians, it's too much to expect us to drink with them too!"

Stopping off at Dinty's after a "four-to-twelve" is so institutionalized that long-suffering cops' wives refer to the tour as the "four-to-four." Dinty's was the last sanctuary for the cop—a place where he could complain about the scumbag public, the lousy job, and the no-balls sergeant he worked for. Sometimes the no-balls sergeant sat on the next stool, but in Dinty's it is considered bad form to take umbrage at constructive criticism. Besides, cops seldom fight in cop bars. They save their energy for special occasions like weddings, bar mitzvahs, and exit ramps of parkways, where inebriated cops have been known to take on civilians—and other cops—with an admirable lack of discrimination.

Right around the corner from the station house, Dinty's was dirty, smelled of stale beer, and the owner even bought back on the few occasions when he was drunker than his patrons.

It was into this glassy-eyed, smoke-filled scene that Walter Cronin returned. He'd been assigned to the Ninth from the Police Academy, but hadn't been back since his transfer to NET. Nothing had changed. Dinty's only concession to the approaching Christmas season was to replace the burned-out bulbs in the dusty set he left draped over the cash register all year long.

Above the blare of the jukebox Cronin heard the foghorn voice of his old partner.

"Hey Walt, you old hump! Where the fuck you been?" Tommy Reilly emerged from the crowd and grabbed him in a crushing headlock. "Slumming, are we?" Reilly had an off-center smile that made him look like a degenerate altar boy. "Hotshot from NET don't need to mix with the trench cops anymore, huh? I'll bet you miss this place. Right?"

"Sure," Cronin answered, throwing some money on the bar. "Psychos, family fights, rats, leprous junkies—what's not to miss? I don't have any fun anymore."

Reilly had changed. Although they were the same age, his former partner looked much older. There was an edge of bitterness in his voice, and the impish gleam in his eye had gone out. Maybe the street does wear you out faster, Cronin thought, but he would willingly trade everything to be back in the Ninth with his old partner.

Reilly stuck a beer in Cronin's hand. "It's good to see you, kid." Reilly claimed the right to call Cronin kid, because he graduated from the Police Academy a class ahead of his old partner.

Cronin ducked Reilly's playful slap and looked around at the faces at the bar. Some he knew, but most were unfamiliar—evidence of the high turnover rate in a pressure cooker like the Ninth. He'd only been gone for eight months, but the smoked-filled Dinty's, the garbled conversations of half-drunken cops, even Tommy Reilly, seemed like memories from a distant past.

Reilly saw Cronin looking around. "Same old shit here, kid. Fighting crime and boredom in the Big Apple."

Reilly's eyes, Cronin noted, were already glassy. He'd started early.

"Hey, remember Tony Corvo? Son of a bitch made the bureau! Can you believe that shit? He couldn't find a nigger in Harlem and they make him a fucking detective! I got over two hundred felony arrests and I can't get shit. This fucking job's not on the level." He leaned close and Cronin smelled the beer on his breath. "What's the scoop, partner? How'd you get into NET? All this time you had a hook and you never told me?"

"I didn't have a hook. You know Captain Stone's reputation. He doesn't honor hooks."

Reilly nodded. "So I hear. You lucky bastard. I'd give my left nut to get into NET."

Cronin was struck by the irony. He'd do almost anything never to have been in NET. "It's not all it's cracked up to be," he said carefully.

"Hey, I hear Stone's a good boss. Not like Captain Toovey. Remember him? Maybe not. He must of got here just after you left. Only lasted four months before they had to evacuate him back to headquarters. He was getting the thousand-yard stare, the ball-less bastard."

Cronin knew Toovey by reputation. Newly promoted, he was a rising star who'd done all of his rising in One Police Plaza. It was suggested he get field experience, and some comedian in the Orders Section with a perverse sense of humor condemned poor Duncan Toovey to the Ninth Precinct.

"I don't think he shit the whole time he was here," Reilly continued. "I swear to God, his ass was so tight he turned brown. You know he insisted on a sector car to escort him in and out of the precinct?" Reilly dropped his voice. "Just before he left we had a little trouble in the station house. Freddy Dreebe, you remember him?" Reilly crossed his eyes. "Spaceman Dreebe from the planet Mongo? He worked Sector Adam.

"One night he makes a collar—don't ask me how—the skell must have jumped into the fucking radio car and given himself up. Anyway, Dreebe didn't give him a good toss on the street. He's in the sitting room writing up the arrest, and the skell decides he don't wanna do the court scene. He whips out a Saturday Night Special he had tucked in his crotch and tries to punch Dreebe's ticket to life.

"Well, Dreebe—I don't think he ever fired a shot in anger his whole life—yanks it out and lets six go at the skell at point-fucking-blank range! Naturally, being Dreebe, he misses. Meanwhile, the desk officer—you remember Lieutenant Connor, our resident Rambo?—and me and Guardino, who were just coming off meal, come charging into the sitting room. I'm telling you, Walt, it was like Beirut on a Saturday night! Everybody's pounding away. Dreebe, his gun empty, is trying to burrow his way under the fucking floor tiles. Meanwhile, the skell is running up and down the sitting room, dodging bullets and yelling 'Time out, time out. I'm out of ammo!' Can you believe that shit? Time out? Like this was the fucking Super Bowl or something!"

"What happened?"

Reilly looked disgusted. "We must have fired a couple of dozen rounds at the son of a bitch and he didn't even get powder burns! I'm surprised the fuck didn't die from lead poisoning just inhaling all that shit. Later, the lieutenant and Guardino claimed they couldn't get off a clean shot because Dreebe was in the way. But that was bullshit. Dreebe was dug in so deep under the table you couldn't have taken him out with a fucking mortar round. At least I was honest. I tried to kill the fuck, but I missed. Pure and simple."

Cronin shook his head in disbelief. "So he got away with trying to waste a cop?"

Reilly looked around. "Not exactly. Lieutenant Connor—that man's computer is missing a couple of chips—went bat shit. I don't know if he was mad because the skell tried to kill Dreebe or because he didn't succeed. Man, he did a number on him. I think the poor bastard would have preferred a bullet to the beating Connor gave him. That's when Toovey arrived on the scene. The little faggot was in his office when the firefight started, and he didn't come out until he was sure everyone was out of ammo. He comes into the sitting room, which by now has so much gun smoke drifting around, it looks like L.A. on a bad day. He spots Connor dangling the skell out the window by his feet, and his fucking eyes grow to the size of pizza plates."

"What did he do?"

Reilly signaled for another drink. "The dumb bastard gave his first and last order of the night. 'Lieutenant,' he says, 'put that man down.' Well, that was exactly the wrong thing to say to Connor, who didn't need too much encouragement to begin with. He lets go of the fucking skell and scores a direct hit on the garbage cans twenty feet below."

"Jesus! Did he die?"

"Naw. He must have landed on his fucking head. He was okay, just the usual contusions, intrusions, and protrusions. That night Toovey burned up the telephone wires to headquarters. Someone overheard him whining, 'I don't care if I stay a captain for the rest of my life, get me out of this lunatic asylum!' " Reilly looked hurt. "He's got some balls calling this a lunatic asylum. I hear this precinct used to be really bad a few years ago."

"Hey Walt!" Mark Goodstein, the community-relations officer, came up and pumped his hand. "How're you doing in NET?" Cronin mumbled something about it being great. "Hey," Goodstein continued, "remember José Marrero, the kid who lived on Avenue C? The one you were always trying to keep out of trouble?"

"Yeah," Cronin answered with a feeling of dread.

José was a headstrong kid who lived in Cronin's sector. Unlike so many others in the precinct, José was bright and ambitious. Cronin took the sixteen-year-old under his wing and did his best to keep the impressionable youth away from the thieves and junkies in the neighborhood. When the teenager learned Cronin was leaving the precinct, he gave the startled cop a going-away present—a medal of St. Michael the Archangel, the patron saint of policemen.

"He joined the Marines! How about that! He escaped from the neighborhood. On the other hand, as an old Navy man, I'm not so sure he wouldn't be better off staying in the old neighborhood."

"You fucking squid," said Reilly, the ex-Marine, "what would you know about it?"

Cronin didn't know what to say. He'd expected Goodstein to say José was dead, or in jail. Maybe he had made a difference. Maybe the frequent talks with the hard-nosed kid that seemed to go nowhere had made a difference. Unaccountably, tears stung his eyes. "That's great," he mumbled and downed his beer.

Goodstein slapped him on the back. "Score one for the good guys. Hey, Walt, take care."

Goodstein made his way down the bar and was buttonholed by the PBA delegate.

"NET must be a great place to work," Reilly said. "I hear Stone's good people. The brass don't like him, so he must be okay. I'd like to be locking up the big guys instead of chasing these mutts around the streets. Did you know we can't roust the fucking dealers no more? That wimp Mara put out an order saying street cops can't make drug busts in the street. Like I don't know what to do when I see a drug deal going down in front of me! Gimme a fucking break. Truth is, the job's afraid we're going to shake them down. The mutts know it too. Have you any idea what it's like driving around in your own sector and seeing these mutts dealing right in front of you and giving you the finger? Drives me nuts. Every now and then I grab one, drag him into a hallway and beat the living shit out of him." He shrugged. "It works for a while, but they come back and I have to do it all over again."

"Tommy, stay away from those guys. You're only going to get jammed up."

"Fuck them. A couple of them dropped kites on me already. I've been to CCRB for hearings. Cost me a few vacation days, but what the fuck." Cronin saw the anger and frustration in his ex-partner's eyes. "That's why you're lucky," Reilly continued, "you work in an outfit that goes after these scumbags."

Cronin wished he could tell Reilly what NET was really like—at least for him. Instead he said, "It's okay, but to tell you the truth, I'd rather be back here in a sector, going on jobs, making arrests, and helping people like José Marrero."

Reilly looked at him, aghast. "Are you outta your fucking mind? For every José there are a hundred kids who wind up in the can, or DOA from an overdose. You've been away from the streets too long, kid. You can't be St. Francis of Assisi out here—you gotta be Attila the fucking Hun. Walt, old buddy, do you think you could get me an interview with Stone?"

Cronin set down his beer carefully. "No, I can't," he said softly.

"Hey, I'm your buddy, remember? You won't speak up for me? I got plenty of collars—"

"It's not that, Tommy. You know Stone's rep. He picks his own people."

Anger crept into Reilly's voice. "I don't want you to kiss his ass in Macy's window, just see if I can get an interview. That's all."

"Okay," he lied. "I'll talk to him. But I can't promise anything."

Reilly grinned and thumped him on the back. "All right! Hey bartender, give me a couple of beers for me and my hook here!"

Cronin and Reilly continued to talk about old times, but it wasn't the same. The gulf between their lives was too wide. Finally, Reilly looked at his watch and stood up unsteadily. "Hey kid, I gotta go home. Got court in the morning." He leaned close. "You know what kinda case I got? An intox! Do you believe it? I just hope they don't ask me to take a breathalyzer." He pondered that possibility for a moment. "What the hell, I can testify as an expert! Right?" Then he hugged Cronin in a rare display of emotion that occurred between cops only when they were drunk. "Take care of yourself, kid. And don't be a stranger. All right? Hey, and don't forget to talk to Stone about me." Suddenly the forced, happy exterior was gone. "This place is getting to me, ya know? I feel like I'm drowning in a fucking cesspool. I gotta get out of here."

"Okay, Tommy. I'll see what I can do."

Cronin watched his ex-partner go through the door, and wanted nothing more than to be back working with him again.

"Hey kid, you look like your dog just died."

Cronin turned toward the smiling, craggy face of Billy Murphy, the real reason he'd come to Dinty's. Murph was a dutch uncle to many of the young cops who went to him with their problems. The scuttlebutt was that Murph had done some time in a seminary but had packed it in after a few years. There were a lot of ex-seminarians in the ranks of the New York City Police Department. As one ex-seminarian phrased it: "The two jobs are not totally dissimilar—one saves souls, the other asses."

Cronin trusted and respected Billy's commonsense approach to the job. Maybe Murph could give him some advice, some way out of this dilemma. But what could he say? He certainly couldn't tell him the truth.

"Billy, what do you think about those Field Associates?"

The Field Associates program was a product of the shocking revelations of the 1971 Knapp Commission. In the aftermath of disclosures of widespread corruption, the department instituted new programs designed to root out and discourage corrupt practices. The department recruited officers, mostly probationary cops, and convinced them it was their duty to secretly report corruption. If the cop agreed, he was given a code name and assigned to a precinct. From time to time he was debriefed by a supervisor from Inspectional Services. The program was successful because no one knew if there was one or a thousand Field Associates.

Billy's frown etched deep lines in his face. "Walt, don't get mixed up with those humps."

"No way," Cronin protested. "I was just wondering if they serve any useful purpose. Do they ever report anything important, or is it all just bullshit?"

Billy toyed with his Coke. Besides being an ex-seminarian, he was also an ex-drunk. "Who knows? But I'll tell you something. In my time in the job I've seen this department catch a guy with his hand in the till, turn him around, and use him to catch other guys. In the end, when they're through with him, they drop him like a bad habit. The poor bastard is like a man without a country. At first he thinks he's lucky because they didn't throw him in the can, but every cop in the job knows who he is and hates him, so where's he going to go? IAD? Even they don't like turnaround scumbags. Usually he puts in his papers and ends up driving a taxi, if the booze don't get to him first."

Cronin persisted. "But how does a guy deal with . . . you know, serious problems?"

A wariness crept into Murph's eyes. In the smoky light of Dinty's he studied the young cop seated next to him. He didn't like what he saw. Cronin had lost weight and there were deep circles under his eyes. He had all the earmarks of a guy in big trouble, and it wasn't the booze. Cronin, he noted, nursed his beer—not something a guy who was having booze problems would do. Murph suspected Cronin's problems were a lot worse than booze. "The best way to deal with serious problems," he said evenly, "is to avoid them altogether."

Murph's answer was frustratingly simple. But it was too late for avoidance. Cronin wanted Murph to tell him a way out of his difficulties. He knew he was treading on dangerous ground. He was approaching the fine line between idle bar talk and confession. But he was desperate. Murph was his only hope. "If a guy got into trouble . . . real trouble . . . but wanted to get himself out, how—"

"Kid." Murphy put his hand on Cronin's arm. He knew what was coming and he didn't want to hear any more. It was one thing to listen to tales of marital infidelities and losing bouts with the bottle, it was another to be on the receiving end of a confession from a kid working in a high-powered narc outfit like NET. He didn't want to be saddled with this kind of knowledge. "Walt, there are some things you gotta do for yourself. Every situation is different. I don't know what you were going to tell me, and I don't want to know. But I'll tell you one thing. You're gonna have to live with whatever you decide. No one else can tell you what to do." He gulped down the rest of his Coke, and for the first time in many years wished it were something stronger. Avoiding Cronin's anguished eyes, he squeezed his arm and said, "I gotta go. Take care, kid."

Cronin, alone at the bar, considered Billy's bleak words. The ex-seminarian was right. This job would use him to get to the others, and then they'd throw him away. He'd be crazy to go to IAD. But the question remained: What the hell was he going to do? He stared at the sad, blinking Christmas lights draped over the cash register until he was brought back to reality by a call for last round. Dinty's was getting ready to close.

19

THE BAR WAS LIKE ANY ONE OF THE HUNDREDS OF WATERING HOLES in midtown Manhattan, but on the night before Thanksgiving it took on a festive, almost feverish atmosphere. Clusters of yuppies with their ties open and vests undone drank foreign beer out of green bottles and hotly debated the future of the Jets and the Rangers. A couple of older executives—bleary-eyed from too many martinis—mumbled obscene propositions to bored secretaries, who in turn glanced seductively at the sports-distracted yuppies.

At the quiet end of the bar the few serious drinkers who came here after work to drown the day's frustrations and humiliations sat squarely on their stools, extra-dry martinis in hand, cigarettes and change neatly stacked in front of them, and paid attention to no one except their blurred images in the mirror opposite them.

Sgt. Tim Hardy squeezed past the yuppies, who'd moved on to arguing the morality of the Giants' move to New Jersey, and went directly to a table in the rear.

Sitting in a darkened booth was a young man who could have passed for any one of the hard-charging executives sitting at the bar.

"Hello, Chief," Hardy said.

Patrick Stone looked up and smiled. "Hi, Tim."

Only superior officers above the rank of inspector were called Chief, but Hardy, who'd been present the day Patrick Stone was promoted to captain, had said, half in jest, "If you keep getting promoted this fast, I'd better start calling you Chief."

Stone had smiled, but his tone was deadly earnest. "It won't be long, Tim. I'm going right to the top of this department."

After a few months Hardy began calling Stone "Chief" when they were alone.

The waitress came over and took their order—another scotch for Stone and a club soda for Hardy. After she left, Stone leaned forward. "Notify the others," he said softly. "A meeting at your place Friday, 2100 hours. We have another assignment."

Hardy stiffened. "It's only two weeks since the other one."

Stone twirled the cubes in his glass. "Something's come up."

"Victor?" Hardy tried to keep the anxiety out of his voice.

To Hardy and the others, Victor was just a name, a shadowy figure whom neither Hardy nor the others had met.

"Tim, I promise this is going to be our last assignment. But it's also our most important."

Hardy tried to ignore the knot forming in his stomach. "Chief, it's too soon."

"I'll be the judge of that," Stone said sharply. "Relax, there's nothing to worry about."

But the sergeant wasn't fooled by Stone's optimistic tone. He'd been watching Stone absentmindedly tearing off pieces of napkin and rolling them into little balls—something he did only when he was nervous.

Hardy, extremely uncomfortable in the role of dissenter, squirmed in his seat. For laconic men like him, putting thoughts into words was worse than physical labor. A bead of perspiration formed on his lip. "This is a mistake," he began tentatively.

"Tim, you know me. You know I leave nothing to chance. Everything is under control."

"Is it?"

The waitress returned with the drinks, and the two men fell silent. After she'd gone, Stone continued. "This assignment will be carried out just as carefully as the others."

Hardy had promised himself he'd clear the air, get it all out once and for all. "You needed the money, didn't you?" he blurted.

Stone's gray eyes locked on Hardy's. "What do you mean?"

With the greatest effort Hardy broke eye contact. "Right after NET started, before we got into this mess, I overheard you talking to your broker on the telephone. Did you lose much?"

"Let's just say I overextended myself. Unfortunately, when you play with commodities and options, you can get your ass kicked pretty quick. But it's nothing I can't handle. Everything is under control."

Hardy was frustrated. Stone, in his smooth way, was parrying all of his concerns and making them appear foolish. "What about this guy Victor? Who is he?"

"All right, Tim. That's enough. You don't have to know anything else."

"*Anything* else? I don't know a goddamn thing. All I know is that you came to some arrangement with a man named Victor, and we've killed three men. Now you're talking about killing a fourth. Things are getting crazy. We—"

"Do you want out?" Stone's voice was hard.

Hardy wiped a puddle with his napkin. "I'd like us all to get out. We've made some money. Why don't we just call it quits? You don't know what this is doing to you, Chief. All the sergeants are complaining, especially about your decision to transfer Kileen and Herbert."

Stone's eyes flashed. "Don't tell me how to run my outfit. They were incompetent, and I don't tolerate incompetence."

"You have to lighten up, Chief. The men are giving it everything they have. You've become obsessed with arrests. Why?"

"I have my reasons."

Stone studied the sergeant's worried face. He liked Tim Hardy, but even after all these years he wasn't quite sure why. Perhaps he needed the plodding deliberateness of a Tim Hardy. Stone, an impulsive risk taker, required someone to temper his reckless impetuosity, and Hardy, a man who wanted to go over everything "just one more time," was his perfect foil. Like a shark and a pilot fish, they formed the perfect symbiotic relationship, each providing a critical ingredient in the other's life.

On more than one occasion Hardy's fears—often unspoken—had prevented Stone from an unwise course of action. Without realizing it, he'd come to look upon Hardy as a litmus test for his actions.

"Tim," Stone said, betraying none of the doubt he felt, "this assignment will run as smoothly as the others."

Stone's patronizing manner had always been comforting to Hardy, but now he fought its seductive pull. "Are *you* willing to risk everything for money?"

Without answering, he turned the question on Hardy. "Are you doing it for the money, Tim?"

Hardy stared at the carbon bubbles rising in his glass. Why did he do it? He didn't know why. It had just seemed to happen. "But we're not talking about me. You have your career to think of."

Stone swirled the ice cubes in his glass. He *was* thinking about his career, and Tim Hardy was a critical component in his plans. He raised his glass to the unhappy sergeant. "To success."

STONE REMAINED IN THE BOOTH LONG AFTER HARDY HAD GONE. THE effort to maintain a facade was wearing him down, and the only time he could relax was when he was alone. He'd made a mistake getting involved with Victor, but now he was almost out of the woods. After this next and final assignment, he'd be free, and he could get on with his life and career.

He looked up as a couple passed by. The girl, a striking brunette, tossed her hair back and said something to her companion, and Stone was instantly reminded of Tina. Since that night, he'd tried to drive all thoughts of her from his mind, but it was impossible. There was always something to remind him—long, flowing hair, a certain perfume, a tanned body—and he was back on the yacht again.

In the bar's quiet back room, away from the laughter and blaring music, he relived the first time he'd met Victor Cabrera. It was just over a year, but it seemed longer; so much had happened. Stone, in the middle of a boring vacation in Puerto Rico, stood at a roulette table trying to decide which number to play next. He'd been wrong six times in a row and was running out of money. Listlessly, he dropped a chip on number 10 and watched the little ball settle on 25.

A voice next to him said, "Too bad, my friend. Lady Luck seems to have abandoned you."

The speaker was a nondescript, balding man in his late fifties. Except for a pair of dark, intense eyes, he was not the type one would give a second glance to, but his female companion—a willowy girl with gleaming mahogany skin—was something else again.

"Lady Luck doesn't seem to have abandoned you," Stone answered, his eyes on the girl.

"That, my friend, is debatable." The stranger dropped a stack of one-hundred-dollar chips on number 68. Stone played 72. The ball sped around the wheel, bounced, and came to rest on 68. The croupier raked in Stone's chip and placed a duplicate stack next to the stranger's.

"Here." The man slid the stack toward Stone. "It may bring you luck."

Stone was impressed. This stranger was offering him a pile of hundred-dollar chips as casually as one might offer a cigarette. "No thanks. I only lose my own money."

The man smiled and scooped up his chips. "Then at least let me buy you a drink. Perhaps it was you who brought me luck." He put out his hand. "My name is Victor Cabrera, and this is Tina."

They adjourned to the hotel bar. Stone, who never told strangers he was a cop, said he worked on Wall Street. Cabrera rambled on about himself. Talking a lot, but saying little, he claimed to be an importer of construction equipment. But Stone, who had heard plenty of snow jobs in his time, didn't believe him. More than likely Cabrera was into something illegal. Still, Stone could care less. He was on vacation; why not enjoy the taste of the good life for one night?

He'd worked hard over the last year turning NET into a smooth-running arrest machine, and in the process, making a name for himself in the department. Not one to delegate responsibility easily, he had worked sixteen-hour days juggling administrative matters in the office, while at the same time working in the field with his men. The hard work was paying off. NET's arrests and convictions were impressive, and NET had just concluded an intensive three-week investigation culminating in a half-dozen high-level arrests. But Stone's sixteen-hour days were wearing him out. At Hardy's insistence, he'd reluctantly agreed to take a week off.

While Cabrera made small talk, Stone tried to figure out the relationship between the older man and the girl. She was young enough to be Cabrera's daughter, but they didn't act like father and daughter. She was dressed too expensively, and too well, to be a call girl. After a couple of drinks Victor suggested they go to his boat for a nightcap. Stone, having nothing better to do but go back to an empty hotel room, readily agreed.

As the taxi pulled up to the darkened pier, he noticed there was only a tender with one man standing at attention. "Where's your boat?"

"Out there." Victor waved his hand toward the inky black water. Silhouetted against the city lights, a white hull, bobbing on a mooring, gleamed in the darkness. The boat was outlined with strings of small white lights which flickered and sparkled across the water.

"Christ!" Stone muttered. "How big is that thing?"

"About a hundred feet, I believe." Victor started down the gangway. "You can ask my captain."

They sat on the open rear deck, where they were served drinks by an army of quick-moving stewards in starched white uniforms. The hot, humid breeze carried the scents of the tropical land toward them. Music drifted over the water from a boat Stone couldn't see. In the darkness Stone watched the girl. The wind blew her soft hair in her eyes. She brushed it away and smiled back.

Finally, Victor yawned and got to his feet. "It is getting late. I can have you taken back to your hotel, but why not stay the night? Tomorrow we're going for a cruise. I would be delighted if you came with us."

Without hesitation Stone agreed.

A polite steward, who spoke little English, showed him to his cabin. Stone was disappointed that he didn't have a chance to be alone with the girl, but there was always tomorrow. He lay awake savoring the luxury of his silk-sheeted bed. It was a long way from the stinking, frigid streets of New York. Just before he'd come on vacation, he'd spent eight straight nights sitting on a wiretap in a cellar in Harlem.

Suddenly he heard a click as the doorknob turned. Instantly alert, he sat up and looked around the room for a weapon. The door opened wider, and he recognized Tina's exquisite silhouette. Softly, she closed the door and stopped at the foot of his bed. Her clinging white silk nightgown emphasized her lithe body underneath.

"We never got a chance to talk," she said. "May I sit down?"

Stone, leaning on an elbow, patted the bed. "Isn't Victor going to miss you?"

She pushed her long hair away from her eyes. "I am not Victor's mistress. We are just good friends."

"That's the best news I've heard all night," Stone said.

"Would you like a drink—or something?"

The pause sounded promising. Stone sat up and propped the silk pillows behind him. "Yeah. Let's start with a drink. Is there any scotch around here?"

She slid off the bed and opened a set of louvered doors, revealing a well-stocked bar. She poured a scotch for him. Then she opened a drawer and took out a small ivory box. Stone glanced at the contents and stiffened. He'd used marijuana on occasion, but never cocaine. "Tina," he said evenly, "I'd rather you didn't use that."

"Why? There is no one here to arrest us."

Her tone was teasing, but her chance remark jolted him. For a moment he thought she knew he was a cop.

"It's just that—"

"Try some, Patrick. It's excellent quality."

She held the box out to him, and he stared at the harmless-looking white powder. He estimated it to be at least 400 milligrams. Felony weight. "No," he said, and downed his scotch.

Ill at ease, but at the same time fascinated, he watched her carefully cut two lines on a glass tray. Jesus Christ, he thought, I arrest people for this. He got out of bed, took his drink, and went to look out the porthole. The moon, half hidden by clouds scudding across the sky, reflected a shimmering line of silver water—like liquid cocaine.

She came up behind him and slipped her arms around him. He turned and stared into her beautiful dark eyes, now luminous. "That stuff inhibits your sex drive," he whispered.

"Really?" She took his hand and pulled him back to the bed. "Let's see."

His memory of the rest of the night's events was an alcohol-induced blur. He vaguely recalled her going back to the ivory box, returning to make love, and returning to the ivory box again. Finally, exhausted, they both fell asleep.

Awakened by the throbbing engines and the sunlight streaming through the porthole, Stone got up to go to the bathroom. He'd drunk too much, but thankfully, had only a dull headache to show for it. He returned and stopped to admire Tina's magnificent, sleek body sprawled across the bed. He'd made love to many women, but none as uninhibited.

Suddenly the hair on the back of his neck rose. Something was wrong. Her mouth open, the exquisite body so still—too still. Stone dove across the bed and pressed his fingers to her carotid artery. No pulse. Throwing the pillows aside, he yanked the body into a better position to administer mouth-to-mouth. Her lips, which only hours ago were warm and demanding, were now cold. "Come on," he hissed with each savage blow he delivered to the inert body. "Come on. Wake up!"

Then the door opened and a steward, carrying a breakfast tray, was standing there. The steward's shy smile turned to horror as his eyes fell on the nude girl sprawled across the bed.

For a moment Stone's world came to a stop. Hunched over the body, panting from exhaustion, he tried desperately to restore order to a universe turned upside down. He didn't see a frightened man in a starched white jacket; he didn't see the tray with its gleaming sterling-silver covers; he didn't see the delicate long-stemmed rose in the crystal vase. He saw only one thing, and his mind screamed it: *Witness! The man was a witness!*

The steward, mumbling in Spanish, stumbled backward; the rose vase shattered on the floor. Stone snapped out of his paralysis. "Mr. Cabrera!" he yelled to the steward. "Get Cabrera. Pronto!"

Moments later Cabrera, still in his silk robe, appeared in the doorway. He took one glance and brusquely ordered the wide-eyed steward away. He closed the door. "What happened?"

"I don't know." Stone, unaware of his nakedness, ran his hand across his forehead. In spite of the air-conditioned cabin, he was bathed in sweat. "I woke up and she was like this—"

Cabrera shook his head. "I'm sorry, Patrick, it is all my fault."

The unexpected words of sympathy jolted Stone. He'd half expected Cabrera to accuse him of murdering the girl. "What? Your fault?"

"Tina had an uncontrollable drug habit. Her extravagant use of drugs has put her into the hospital on more than one occasion. When she is with me, I never allow her to use drugs. I don't know how—''

"I tried to tell her, but she wouldn't listen. Goddamn her!'' Feeling light-headed, Stone moved away from the body, once erotic—now obscene in death. "I'm a cop. Do you know what this will do to my career?''

Cabrera's raised eyebrows expressed his surprise at Stone's revelation. Then he became instantly solicitous. "Ah, then I can appreciate your concern.'' He handed Stone a robe. "None of this was your doing. You can't be held responsible for the actions of a foolish girl.''

"You don't know the police department. When they find out about this—'' Stone's imagination was already conjuring up the sensational head-lines and the humiliation of a department trial. "I'll lose my job. I—'' He stopped when he realized how selfish he sounded. A girl had just died and he was worrying about his career.

Cabrera said quietly, "They do not have to know.''

Stone's head shot up. "What? What do you mean?''

"I take full responsibility for this most unfortunate accident. There is no need for you to be implicated. I will take you back to San Juan and report the death when we are at sea. The authorities need never know you were even on board.''

"But the steward . . . he saw—''

"My employees are extremely loyal. Nothing will be said. I promise you.''

The relief of a drowning man who'd just been thrown a rope swept over Stone. "Are you sure?''

"Please.'' Cabrera's tone was gentle and insistent. "Everything will be taken care of.''

One hour later, shaken but grateful, Patrick Stone was dropped off in San Juan. He took the next available flight back to New York.

After the initial shock had worn off, the worry that he might have been set up by Cabrera began to gnaw at him. Dreading a sensational story about an unfortunate death on a luxury yacht, he scanned the newspapers daily. But he saw nothing. As days turned into weeks, the memory of that nightmare slowly receded, until he could almost believe it had never happened. He concentrated his energy on NET. His total immersion in his work left no time for brooding. Slowly, the old confidence returned. Patrick Stone was once more in charge of his destiny.

Then a telephone call came from Victor Cabrera. "My friend.'' Cabrera's voice was cheery. "How are you?''

Stunned by the familiar voice that brought the events of that night crashing back into his life, Stone mumbled a reply.

"I am in New York on business. Staying at the Plaza. Why don't you join me for dinner tonight?'' Cabrera's tone made the invitation almost a command.

Stone never wanted to see the man again, but he had to know what Cabrera wanted. Reluctantly, he agreed.

Dinner was an ordeal. Under better circumstances, Stone, who appreciated good food, would have enjoyed dining in the dark-paneled, high-ceilinged Oak Room of the elegant hotel. But now he picked at his steak and glumly gazed out the window at hansom cabs crammed with tourists streaming in and out of Central Park, while an ebullient Cabrera prattled on about the atrocious New York City traffic and surly cabdrivers. To a disinterested observer, Cabrera could have been a tiresome uncle from out of town boring his nephew with his adventures in the big city.

Finally it was over and they stood on the hotel steps to say good-bye. Tina's name hadn't come up. Outside, the musty, pleasant smell of horses permeated the evening air. Cabrera shook Stone's hand. ''Well, my friend, it's been good seeing you.'' Then the smile disappeared. ''By the way, that problem has been taken care of.'' He patted Stone's hand and went back into the hotel.

In spite of Cabrera's assurances, Patrick Stone went home troubled. Once again he began to wonder if he'd been set up. But if it was a setup, why hadn't Cabrera taken advantage of it that morning five weeks earlier?

The next day he set out to find the answers. After several days of discreet inquiries of his sources, a hazy picture of Victor Cabrera emerged. Cabrera was indeed a wealthy businessman from Peru, with interests in the United States, South America, and the Caribbean basin. He had no record; his references were impeccable. Yet doubt gnawed at Stone. Dissatisfied, he called a contact in the DEA and asked the agent to run a name check. The Peruvian wasn't in their computers. Evidently, he was what he claimed to be.

Still, Victor Cabrera remained a troubling enigma.

20

IN THE SIX YEARS SINCE HIS DIVORCE, TIM HARDY HAD LIVED ALONE. The apartment in Astoria was more than adequate for his simple needs; he spent more time at work anyway than he did at home. Such lack of attention to his personal life had been a major factor in his divorce. He and his wife Joan had had no children, and one day Joan, tired of being alone when Hardy wasn't home, and alone when he was, had exploded. He listened patiently to her long list of grievances without offering an apology or a defense. After a long, painful silence she began to cry. The next day she moved out and went to live with her sister in New Jersey. The only emotion he felt was one of relief.

He looked around the room to make sure everything was in order. As a last-minute thought, he took a pile of newspapers and tossed them behind the couch. Then he went into the kitchen to check on the coffee.

Within fifteen minutes everyone was there. Steve Tecci, blond and muscular, came into the living room carrying two beers. He tossed a can to the lanky black man sprawled on the couch. "Here you go, my man. Sorry, we got no wine. I know how you folk love wine."

McKay Beals barely smiled. "Keep talkin' like dat, white boy, and I'm gonna cut yo' ass."

Tecci flopped down on the couch beside him and slapped his knee. An unusual team, the two men were opposites in many ways. Where Tecci was outgoing and flamboyant, Beals was quiet, almost sullen. Tecci was a flashy dresser who wore gold chains and designer clothes. Beals usually dressed in jeans and sweat suits. But somehow the chemistry was right. The two streetwise cops worked well together.

The fourth member of the group, a boyish-looking Walter Cronin, sat apart from the others and said nothing.

Patrick Stone, the last to arrive, took a drink from Hardy and sat down. He looked at the four men, each so different, and wondered if they'd be able to handle this final contract. With each assignment they'd become more and more recalcitrant. In the beginning, Tecci and Beals were glad to get the money, but even they had balked at the Rowe contract. The strain was beginning to show. Hardy, the loyal soldier, went along in spite of his personal misgivings. Then there was Walter Cronin.

Cronin was unquestionably the weak link in the chain Stone had carefully forged. From the start he'd been the most frightened. Stone made sure he kept the young cop on the periphery. Cronin's job was to follow the subjects. Stone left the actual killing to Tecci and Beals, who were by temperament better suited to violence.

This final assignment would take his best sales pitch, but Stone was confident he could talk them into it one more time. After all, he'd orchestrated the others without a hitch.

From the beginning he'd thought it best not to tell Hardy and the others what he'd known from the start: there would be four killings. One by one he'd spoon-fed the targets to them, always offering suitable rationalizations why the victims should die. It wasn't too difficult convincing them that three men deeply involved in drugs deserved to die, especially after the Bay View Motel incident. But this next target would be different. Stone withdrew an eight-by-ten photo from a folder and tossed it on the coffee table.

Beals snapped up the photo of the handsome middle-aged black man wearing wire-rimmed glasses. "Motherfucker. You want to ice Nathan Pickett?"

Tecci put his beer on the table and took the picture from Beals. "Who's Nathan Pickett?"

"Where the hell you been, Stevie?" Beals said. "He's only that damn New York State Senator who's been all over the news."

Cronin spoke up. "Chief, is he into drugs?"

Stone looked at the puzzled faces. "McKay is right," he said. "Pickett is a state senator, and to answer your question, Walt, no, he's not in the drug business."

Tecci looked perplexed. "Then what's the beef? I thought the deal with Victor included only drug people?"

"That's been true up until now." Stone weighed his words carefully. "But Pickett is a special case. He's going to head up a special commission on narcotics. Victor thinks it may draw too much attention to his operation."

Cronin sat bolt upright. His face was ashen. "Is someone on to us?"

"Take it easy, Walt. No one knows anything. But Victor feels if they shake the tree hard enough, something's bound to fall out. Pickett is the catalyst behind this commission. If he's out of the way, it'll never get off the ground."

Tecci ran his fingers through his blond hair. "Chief, it's okay for Victor to order a hit. His ass is safe in Peru, but this Pickett guy is no two-bit drug dealer. If he's a high-profile politician like Mac says, all hell will break loose."

"And he ain't *just* a politician." Beals looked directly at Stone. "He's got ambitions for bigger and better things."

"How much are we gonna get for this?" Tecci demanded.

"I haven't discussed price yet, but it'll be a lot more than the others. This is also our last assignment."

"What's our time frame?" Beals asked. Stone saw that he would have no trouble with the lanky black cop.

"We have to do it before Christmas."

Hardy, who had been silent since the men gathered, spoke for the first time. "Yesterday was Thanksgiving! That leaves only a month."

"What's the rush?" Beals asked.

"A month is plenty of time," Stone said, keeping his voice calm. "But it has to be done before Christmas because the commission begins the first of the year."

Hardy got to his feet and moved uneasily to the window. He didn't understand Stone's uncharacteristic hastiness. If nothing else, Patrick Stone was thorough. Even though the other murders had been done in a matter of weeks, each was meticulously planned and orchestrated. From the beginning Hardy had been heartsick about the killings, but he implicitly trusted the Chief's judgment. As long as Stone was calling the shots, Hardy was confident everything would work out all right. But now he seemed to be rushing things. Later, after the others had gone, he intended to find out why.

"Walt," Stone said, "I want you to begin tailing Pickett Monday. We'll need to know his movements. Here's his home and office address. Okay, gentlemen, that's it for now."

*   *   *

THE SEAT AT THE FAR END OF THE BAR FACING THE DOOR IS WHAT the tactics instructors at the range call the "cop seat." A cop naturally gravitates to this spot because it offers the best tactical advantage—there's no one at his back and he has a clear view of the door. The problem is that people who make a living holding up bars know this. The first one they take out is the dope in the cop's seat.

Rookies were sufficiently impressed with this warning and they never sat there, but habits die hard, and the old-timers continued to occupy the tactical high ground. Tecci and Beals always sat in the cop seat, hoping for a stickup.

They'd stopped in a seedy, nondescript gin mill. Tecci dipped his bottle in a small puddle of beer and absentmindedly made overlapping rings on the counter. "What do you think, Mac?"

Beals frowned. "Man, this is bad. You ain't been reading the papers, but I'm telling you this guy Pickett is all over the headlines. He's been hammering the department about drugs in the city. You know what's going to happen if we kill this dude?"

"Yeah, the job will go ape shit and they'll put every fucking detective in the city on the case."

"And they'll all be looking for *us*. This is crazy shit."

"Mac, I don't think Stone was telling us everything tonight."

The black cop swiveled in his chair. "What do you mean?"

"Stone doesn't make mistakes, and he certainly doesn't do things half-assed. He knows killing Pickett is going to raise a ruckus, but he's going to do it anyway."

"What are you getting at?"

"I think this Pickett commission knows a lot more about Victor than he's letting on."

"Why wouldn't he tell us that?"

"I don't know. Maybe he thinks it would spook us. I know Hardy don't want any more of it, and Cronin looked scared shitless."

"Yeah, he almost puked when the Chief said we were going to ice Pickett."

"By the way"—Tecci lowered his voice—"the Chief grabbed me on the way out tonight."

"Yeah, I saw. What did he want?"

"He wants us to keep an eye on Cronin."

"Why?"

"Maybe he thinks Cronin's gonna crack."

"Do you think he'd blow the whistle on us?"

"Not a chance. He's up to his ass in this, same as us."

Fear flickered in the black man's eyes. "If we get caught, we're in deep shit. You know what they do to ex-cops in the slammer. Getting hit in the shitter ain't my idea of—''

"I'm telling you, we're not going to get caught." Tecci grew pale at the thought of being confined in a prison with men who wanted nothing more than to get a piece of an ex-cop. "I guarantee you, Cronin will never hand us up. And to make sure, we'll keep an eye on him."

"Man, we never should have gotten involved in this in the first place."

Tecci signaled the bartender for two more beers. "I don't like it any better than you do, but we're up to our asses in this already. Besides, you heard him. This is the last time."

"But this ain't like the others. This one ain't right. I got a bad feeling about it."

"Will you knock it off, for Chrissake, you're giving me the creeps." Tecci stuck a bottle in his partner's hand. "Look at the bright side. At least we're going to make a lot of dough on this. I can use it."

"Damn, Stevie, what the hell do you *do* with your money? Burn it?"

Tecci fingered his gold chain. "I got expensive tastes, and so do my women. I spent last weekend in Cancún with a gorgeous chick."

"Was it worth it?"

"Ain't no fuck worth two thousand bucks."

Beals whistled softly. "Man, that's what it cost you for a weekend?"

Tecci grinned. "You know me, I'm not the type to stay home and watch TV."

Beals looked at his watch and drained the rest of his beer. "Speaking of chicks, I gotta meet someone. Later, man."

"I'M GONNA HAVE A DRINK. YOU WANT ONE?"

"No." Eileen's voice was muffled by the pillow.

Brian stomped out of the bedroom and went down to the kitchen. He poured himself a full glass of Black Bush and gulped it down. The whiskey burned his throat and made his eyes water. It was good whiskey, but it wasn't meant to be drunk like Ray Milland did in *The Lost Weekend.* He smiled in spite of his anger. He felt so melodramatic sitting at the kitchen table in his skivvies with a bottle of whiskey on the table—trying to forget what happened upstairs, or trying to understand. He wasn't sure.

There had been tension since dinner when Brian and Eileen had had another argument about the hours he was keeping.

It was Friday night, and after dinner Kathy left to stay overnight at a friend's house. After an hour of stony silence, Brian went up to the bedroom to apologize. Given Eileen's mood, it took some coaxing, but he talked her into making love. It had been a mistake; there was too much anger between them. His gaze wandered to the crazy jagged pattern on the ceiling left from last year's leak, and he wondered what the hell was happening to them.

Eileen, her eyes red from crying, came silently into the kitchen. Her pink silk nightgown looked incongruous under her old terry-cloth robe. She padded over to the kitchen sink with the kettle. "I'm going to make tea. Do you want any?"

He downed the last of his drink. "Yeah, okay."

Neither spoke as she moved about the kitchen preparing the tea. Eileen placed a mug in front of him and sat down. Her robe opened slightly and he saw the gentle swell of her soft breasts. In spite of his anger, he felt a flicker of arousal.

Brian studied her face across the table. Except for the small lines around the mouth and eyes, she wasn't much different from the pretty young nurse he'd met in the emergency room twenty years ago. "Eileen, I'm sorry. What happened upstairs—"

"It's not just that." The hurt and anger in her voice stung him. "So you couldn't make love to me. Maybe I'm not attractive to you anymore." She pulled the robe tightly around her like a protective blanket.

"It's not that, Eileen."

She went on with no sign that she'd heard him. "There are times when you're like a total stranger. All you think about is the job." She took a deep breath. "When you got that transfer to headquarters, I was happy. I know you didn't like it, but I did. I thought maybe we could lead a normal life, but nothing's changed. You're involved in this investigation, and it's worse than before. Your mind's always someplace else."

"This is a big case, Eileen. One of the—" He stopped when he saw the expression on her face. Whenever he tried to talk to her about the job, she tuned out. It was ironic. Most cops made it a practice not to talk to their wives about the job; he was the exception. He wanted to give her some idea of the attraction it held for him. But she didn't want to know. "You wouldn't understand," he said lamely.

"You're right, I don't understand." Her eyes filled. "What are you trying to prove? You're only a lieutenant, not the Police Commissioner."

She flushed. "I'm sorry, Brian. That wasn't fair. Making lieutenant was an accomplishment. Most of your friends are still cops. I know how hard you studied for those promotions."

In spite of her efforts to soften the blow, her words had stung. He needed no reminder of his wrecked career aspirations. When he was a young cop he was full of enthusiasm and confidence. How many times had they talked about his future? Captain by twenty, then—who knows? Maybe Chief of Detectives, maybe even Police Commissioner! When you're young, the future has no limits, but eventually the pure, straight course becomes twisted and confused, until it's no longer recognizable. And one day . . .

"You're right, Eileen. I shot for the moon and landed on my ass." He sipped his tea; it was cold and bitter. "I've been thinking about things lately—the plans, the dreams. I don't know what happened. Things just seemed to get away from me. I never seemed to have enough time to do all the things I wanted to do. Maybe I haven't been a very good father and husband. I . . .'' He fell silent, unable to express the turmoil he felt.

He was so deep in the forest, he couldn't see the trees. Imperceptibly, over the twenty-three years he'd been on the force, he'd sunk deeper and deeper into the cesspool of crime and violence. Day after day he'd seen people steal, cheat, and kill one another and he'd become numbed to it; he'd lost his capacity to be shocked, to be indignant at the subhuman behavior around him. Worse, he'd come to expect it. To shield himself from these daily horrors, he'd carefully erected a shell, and it was effective—too effective, because it also isolated him from Eileen and Kathy. But he saw none of this because he'd become a cop junkie—addicted to the violence, the uncertainty, the adrenaline-pumping thrill of police work.

Eileen put her hand on his. "Brian, I love you, but the job is taking too much from you. In the name of God, give it up."

They sat at the table enveloped by an uneasy silence, each reflecting on what had been said and mentally editing what they might say next. Flashes of them as newlyweds, Kathy as a baby, and promotions all flickered in and out of Brian's mind in an endless, unwanted stream.

Seeing the distant look in her husband's eyes, Eileen felt utterly alone. Her husband sat less than three feet away, but it might as well have been three thousand miles. His mind was far away, wandering in the dark, frightening corridors of murder and violence. Eileen stood up. "I guess I'll go to bed."

"I'll be up in a minute."

She stopped at the door. "Nothing's changed, has it? We have these talks, but nothing changes."

Brian didn't answer. She turned and went upstairs.

21

WALTER CRONIN FOLLOWED NATHAN PICKETT AND HIS GIRLFRIEND to La Mansarde, the newest of the trendy French restaurants clustered on the fashionable East Side. These ubiquitous restaurants operated with the same infallible formula: small portions, high prices, and even higher wine prices. Restaurants like La Mansarde owed their existence to the corporate expense account which allowed businessmen to take clients and mistresses to dinner on the company tab; it was a rare patron who paid with his own money. It certainly wasn't the kind of restaurant Walter Cronin could afford to take his wife to even on a special occasion.

Parked up the block, he watched the steady procession of taxis, Mercedeses, and stretch limos pull up in front of the restaurant to disgorge elegantly attired patrons. It was a scene alien to the young policeman. His occasional night out consisted of hamburgers at a fast-food restaurant with the baby strapped into a plastic high chair.

It was ironic, now that he had plenty of money—he didn't even know how much he had stuffed in his closet—he had to be careful what he did with it. The Chief had cautioned him about putting money in places where they kept records. Consequently, he deposited only small amounts in a special savings account he'd set up. He didn't dare tell Nancy about the secret account, and he still didn't know what he was going to tell her when he'd saved enough for the down payment for the house she wanted so badly.

He'd almost begun to feel comfortable taking the money now. Not like the first time—in the room at the Bay View Motel.

The arrest was supposed to have gone down without a hitch. That's why Cronin was with them. Newly assigned to NET, he was just along for the ride. It was supposed to be a training exercise. Their information said a mule—a Mexican businessman with no criminal record—was to deliver four kilos to a Harlem contact in a motel near the airport. The deal had already been made. This was just going to be a simple exchange of drugs for money, with amateurs as the go-betweens.

Cronin and Beals picked up the Mexican as he left Kennedy Airport and followed the cab to the Bay View Motel, a block off the Belt Parkway. By prearrangement with the motel management, Stone, Hardy, and Tecci occupied the room bracketing the one where the exchange was to go down. Stone monitored the wire in the room and, when he'd heard enough, gave the signal to go in. As Beals, armed with a shotgun, came through the door, the Harlem contact, a middle-aged black man, jumped up. Beals clubbed him with the butt and he went down. The Mexican, either because he was frightened or didn't understand enough English to know what was happening, stepped back and stuck his hand inside his jacket. Tecci, the second one through the door, saw the move. He brought the shotgun up and fired. The blast caught the man in the chest and slammed him across the bed.

After the deafening roar, there was a sickening silence. Beals, the first to react, dove across the bed and flipped the Mexican's jacket open to retrieve his weapon. But there was nothing inside but the dead man's passport. In that instant they all knew Tecci was in serious trouble. He'd killed a man without justification.

Stone quickly sized up the situation and tossed his car keys to the tall cop. "Mac," he said, "there's a black briefcase in the trunk of my car. Bring it back here. Fast."

Hardy's eyes were wide with fright. "What are you going to do?"

"I have a throwaway gun. We're going to flake him."

"Captain," Cronin said, his voice shaky, "there'll be an investigation. We'll never—"

"There will be an investigation," Stone replied icily. "Let's make up our minds now. Do we flake the DOA or do we let Tecci take the heat for wasting a shithead?"

Tecci, still shaken from the encounter, looked down at the bloody remains on the bed. "Fuck him. He coulda had a gun. Right, Cap?"

Stone turned to Hardy. "How about it, Tim? What do you say?"

"Can we cover this?" he said in a tight voice.

"Damn right we can. The department won't look too closely at the justified shooting of a drug dealer. Besides, we're the only witnesses. It's up to you, Walt. It's your call. Do you side with a DOA drug dealer, or one of our own?"

Cronin licked his parched lips. When he was a recruit in the Academy, the instructors spent hours talking about corruption, until the rookies were all bored to death. The party line was always the same. The road to corruption was a slow slide into lawlessness. It often started with a free cup of coffee. Then came payoffs from gamblers, then robbing DOAs, and if you sank low enough, money from the drug trade. Walt was certain he'd never get involved in anything that would jeopardize his career. He had too much to lose. From the first moment on the street, he was ever vigilant for the first encroachment of corruption, determined to stop it before it started. He was so scrupulous in his behavior that he often fought with restaurant owners to take his money.

But the Academy instructors were wrong. It didn't happen slowly. One minute he was as excited as a schoolboy taking part in his first major drug arrest, and the next minute he was being asked by a man he trusted and respected to lie—to put his job on the line to protect another cop. The Academy hadn't prepared him for this. He couldn't take his eyes off the dead man on the bed.

Stone put his hand on Cronin's shoulder. "I know how you feel. No one likes to see a man die. But who is this guy? Some scumbag from Mexico who came here to poison the poor skells in this city. Am I right?" He flipped open the Mexican's suitcase, exposing neat stacks of bills—more money than Cronin had ever seen. "You know where this money goes? Back into the business to buy more drugs and more power. Some of this money may buy the deaths of good cops. If we handle this by the book, Tecci is going to be put through the wringer. The grand jury and the D.A. will have a field day. Why did he shoot if he didn't see a gun? Why didn't he shoot to wound the man? Why was he so exposed that he felt he had to shoot the man? You know the kinds of questions they'll ask. If he's lucky, the department will only flop him from NET; if he's unlucky, he may lose his job. For what? For that piece of shit on the bed? Article Thirty-five states a police officer can take a life to defend the life of another. Isn't that right?"

Cronin nodded numbly. Like every police officer, he'd been drilled in the provisions of the Penal Law, especially Article 35—the legal justification for the use of deadly physical force.

The most serious action a police officer can take is to use his gun. The department went to great pains to ensure that every police officer knew when he could, and could not, use deadly physical force. But like most laws, which try to encompass every conceivable contingency, Article 35 was ambiguous. It was the most important section in the Penal Law, but it was also the least understood.

"Walt," Stone continued, "let's suppose you see a man about to take the life of another, and the only way to stop him is to kill him. Under Article Thirty-five, are you justified?"

Cronin nodded.

"All right, so this skell wasn't going to kill Tecci *now*. But what about next *week*? Next *year*? Sooner or later this scumbag was going to kill a cop. Wasn't Tecci justified in blowing him away first?"

Cronin's head was spinning. He felt sick. He just wanted to get out of the airless room. But Stone's words pinned him to the seat, forcing him to make a decision. What the captain said was true—in part—but then again . . . Oh, God, he thought, what is right?

Beals, sweaty and out of breath, burst into the room with the briefcase. "We're getting a crowd out there."

"All right," Stone snapped. "Make up your mind. We gotta do something now."

Cronin didn't remember answering. As if in a fog, he saw Stone smile. Overwhelmed and disoriented, the young cop stumbled into the bathroom. He threw up until his throat was raw and his body ached. When he came out, he slumped in a chair, physically and emotionally drained. Numbly, he watched as Hardy wiped the prints from the gun and threw it next to the body. Stone was on the telephone, requesting an ambulance and precinct personnel to respond. After Stone hung up, he reached into the suitcase, took out a stack of bills, and walked over to Cronin. "Here," he said softly, holding out the money to the stunned cop, "this is for you."

Cronin looked first at the money and then at Stone. His mouth worked but nothing came out. Stone's smile was understanding. "It's okay, kid, take it. Otherwise it'll only go to the Property Clerk's office, where it'll rot."

"I can't take it, Captain. It isn't right."

"Sure it is. Look at that bum on the bed. Expensive clothes, flashy jewelry. Do you think he ever worried about paying bills and feeding a family? You're saving for a house, aren't you?"

Cronin nodded dumbly.

"On your salary that's going to take a long time. Don't your wife and child deserve something better?"

Again, Cronin nodded. He seemed to be hypnotized. Stone's voice poured over him like warm liquid. As long as Stone spoke—it didn't matter what he said—Cronin felt safe. Was the captain speaking the truth or lying? Cronin was no longer sure. He heard Stone's voice, as if from far away. ". . . it wasn't his money anyway."

He didn't remember taking the money, but he remembered the hard, unfamiliar feel of it in his pocket. Later, when the room was filled with cops and ambulance attendants, he felt as though he were naked and everyone in the room could see the money he'd taken.

He barely remembered going to the precinct, answering questions, filling out endless forms. Finally they let him go home. He stuffed the money in a shoe box and buried it in the bottom of a closet. It was months before he took the first five hundred dollars and opened a bank account.

The money was one thing; the killings were something else. They were on his mind constantly. The thought of what he'd done—was still doing— gave him chronic stomach pains that woke him in the middle of the night.

He poured more coffee from his thermos and waited for the couple in the French restaurant to reappear. It was just past eleven when Pickett and the woman came out. Cronin got a good look at her as they waited under the lighted canopy for a taxi. In her late thirties, she was reasonably attractive, but no knockout. Well-dressed, but not flashy. And she was white.

The taxi snaked through the narrow streets of Greenwich Village and stopped in front of a row of brownstones on Charles Street. Cronin watched the lights come on in the second-floor apartment. He thought Pickett's companion might be a prostitute, but when he ran a name check, on the name he found on her mailbox, he discovered that Julia Nussbaum was an assistant professor of political science at New York University.

Returning to the car, Cronin rested his head on the back of the seat. It was 11:35. Fifteen minutes after one Pickett came out and walked quickly up to Seventh Avenue. There he caught a taxi back to his home in Brooklyn Heights. From there, Cronin headed for his own apartment in Queens.

Cronin reviewed what he'd learned about Pickett in the four days and nights he'd been tailing him. The senator maintained a busy, but fortunately, well-publicized schedule. The two times Cronin had lost him, he'd called the senator's office and was told by a helpful staffer where the senator could be found—usually a public event where he was making a speech. As helpful as Pickett's staff was, Cronin doubted that they knew about Julia Nussbaum; it was fortunate he didn't lose the taxi that took the senator to Charles Street earlier that evening.

If Nathan Pickett was like the others Cronin had watched, he probably did the same thing week after week. Cronin was amazed at how regular and monotonous people's lives were. The other targets he'd watched were equally predictable. Marbridge had been like a machine—from home to gallery to home again. Even Leonard, who Cronin thought was going to be difficult to follow, was surprisingly routine. The drug dealer seldom left the neighborhood, preferring to eat, sleep, and play in a twenty-square-block area of Harlem.

Cronin's assignment was to lay out Pickett's schedule so that Stone could determine the best time and location for the hit. Tonight Cronin had discovered where that spot would be—on Charles Street, a quiet, residential street—at one in the morning, as Pickett walked the long block to the taxi stand. Cronin had become quite proficient at following people, and he almost enjoyed it. It was like hunting—finding the prey, stalking it, and finally . . . Finally what? Executing a man who was not a criminal?

Following the others had been easy. He'd watched them with the detachment of a scientist observing mice negotiate a maze. He felt no anger when he lost them and no elation when he found them again. The enjoyment came from something more elusive—something Cronin couldn't admit even to himself. The enjoyment came from the omnipotence he felt knowing that the man he watched was going to die, and only he, Walter Cronin, knew it.

But Nathan Pickett was different. In some curious way Cronin knew that as long as he was tailing the senator, he was protecting him. While he was there, Tecci and Beals wouldn't be waiting in the shadows of Charles Street. Because they didn't know where to find Pickett. Only he knew, and he wasn't ready to tell them yet.

22

IT WAS A SUNDAY NIGHT, AND THE FOUR-TO-TWELVE TOUR HAD BEEN quiet. All the teams were back in the NET office. Sergeant Kakavos looked at the calendar. "Holy shit. Today's the twenty-ninth. Christmas is less than a month away! I better start thinking about what I'm going to get the old lady."

Cronin took a calendar out of his drawer and stared at it. Sometime between now and Christmas, Pickett would be dead, unless he, Walt Cronin, did something about it.

He left the NET office just after midnight and walked around the corner to where his car was parked. If his mind hadn't been so preoccupied, he might have noticed another car pull out behind him. But he was deep in thought, once again rehashing his limited options. No matter how he thought about it, he kept coming back to the one option that was open to him, the one option he didn't want to consider—IAD. Going to Internal Affairs was

his only choice. He had to think about Nancy and the baby. If he ''turned''—
the very word made him almost physically ill—he might be able to
salvage something; somehow make it right by saving Pickett's life.

If he turned . . . To a policeman, the lowest scum of the earth is a cop
who gives evidence against brother officers. Names like Phillips, Leuci, and
Winter were still spoken of with bitterness in station-house locker rooms.
They had turned on their own kind and they would never be forgotten. It
was one of the supreme ironies of the job that a policeman remembered the
names of ''traitors'' but would be hard-pressed to remember the names of the
last three cops killed in the line of duty.

Occupied by such thoughts, Cronin drove aimlessly through the cold
streets, trying to get up the courage to make the call. He found himself on
the Grand Central Parkway and turned off at the Union Turnpike exit.
Preoccupied, he never noticed the other car, which had been following him
since he'd left the NET office. Along a deserted stretch of road in front of
St. John's University, he spotted the lights of an outdoor telephone booth.
He pulled over and glanced at his watch; it was three-thirty. He'd been
driving around for more than three hours. He considered calling Nancy, but
she'd be asleep. Besides, he already knew what she'd say. Before he left for
work, she'd begged him to call IAD. He promised he would, but now that
the time had come, he couldn't bring himself to do it.

He sat in the car nervously drumming the steering wheel with his
fingers. All he had to do was dial the number. Then everything would be out
of his hands. The terrible burden he'd been carrying for months now would
be lifted from him. Someone else would know. If he called IAD, there'd be
no holding back; he'd have to tell them everything. But what choice did he
have? He got out of the car.

Just as he finished dialing, a powerful arm snaked around his neck,
yanking him away from the phone. Stunned and gasping for air, he saw
Tecci pick up the receiver and listen. Cronin heard the voice on the other
end of the line say, ''Internal Affairs Division, Sergeant Romano. May I
help you? Hello? Is anyone there?''

Furtively looking up and down the deserted street, Tecci hastily replaced
the receiver. ''What are you doing, Cronin?'' Tecci slammed the telephone
with his hand, causing the bell to ring. ''What the *fuck* are you doing?''

Beals, still holding Cronin tightly, reached inside Walt's jacket and
wrenched his off-duty gun from its holster. ''Get in the car.''

In the car, Tecci, nervously licking his lips, adjusted the rearview mirror
so he could see Cronin. ''What gives, Walt? What were you gonna do back
there? Blow the whistle on us?''

''Of course not!''

Walt Cronin tried to laugh but instead emitted a hoarse cackle. Frantically, he tried to think of something to say that would defuse the situation.

"I was doing it for my old partner in the Ninth. He's been having trouble with his sergeant—a guy named O'Toole. Maybe you know him? A real hard-on."

Tecci eyed him in the rearview mirror. "I never worked the Ninth."

"He's a real ball-breaker . . . everyone knows him . . . yeah, a real ball-breaker . . ." Cronin knew he was babbling, but he had to keep talking. He had to convince them he wasn't calling about them. "Everybody knows him. I was gonna drop a dime on him, you know? Say he was screwing some bimbo in the precinct—not that anyone would screw for that old bastard—maybe get IAD on his case so he'd leave the guys alone, you know? That's all. I swear to God!"

Beals, sitting in the back with Cronin, grunted. "Hey, Steve, in 'Nam, when a guy had a hard-on for an officer, he'd toss a grenade in his tent and frag the son of a bitch. This is the NYPD version of fragging—you call IAD."

Tecci fingered the gold chain around his neck. "Yeah. Like calling down an IAD strike on the guy!"

"Cronin."

Walter Cronin turned his head. Beads of perspiration glistened on Beals's forehead, and his eyes, usually half closed, were wide, like those of a frightened horse. "I don't believe that bullshit. You were going to hand us up. Or have you already done it, motherfucker?" His fist came out of the darkness, catching Cronin over his ear. The force of the blow drove his head into the doorpost.

He blinked to clear his vision. "Jesus! What'd you do that for?"

Again the fist came out of the darkness. This time it crashed into his nose. Blood squirted over the front of his jacket and he tasted hot, salty liquid filling the back of his throat. Instinctively, Cronin put his hands up to protect his face, but the next blow hit his ribs, driving the air from his lungs. He doubled over, striking his head on the back of the front seat. Beals grabbed his hair and yanked his head back.

"You motherfucker. You were going to IAD."

Again the fist came from the darkness. This time Cronin felt no pain, just a blinding sparkle of light.

He was in a playground watching his little girl build sand castles and he was sublimely happy. Just watching her at play filled him with joy. She squealed in delight and tossed sand up in the air with her shovel. Suddenly, she tottered to her feet and started to run toward him, but between them was a long row of metal swings crashing wildly into each other. She didn't see the danger. With arms outstretched, she tottered toward him.

"No!" he yelled, running toward her. A metal swing struck him on the side of the face. "Go back!" Reeling from the blow, he stumbled and fell to the ground, his face scraping against the hard gravel. He tried to get up, but hands kept pushing him down. Comforting him? The hands became more insistent. Forcing him down. Suddenly, someone was punching him. Why? Where was his daughter? The blows rained down on him in quick succession. The ringing in his ears grew louder and everything went black.

Rhythmically, the lights danced across the black sky in a familiar pattern. Slowly the sky dissolved into his bedroom ceiling. He was home! Thank God! But where was the baby? What would he tell Nancy? The ceiling continued to dissolve into . . . the roof of a car. He was on the floor looking up, and his whole body ached. He ran his tongue over his puffy lips and tasted the pungent saltiness of blood. The headlights from oncoming cars momentarily illuminated Beals's sweaty face.

"What're we going to do with him, Stevie? Take him to the Chief?"

"We can't. He's out of town."

"Maybe we should call Hardy?"

"No," Tecci snapped. "Hardy's a fucking wimp. Besides, he can't decide anything without the Chief."

In his semiconscious state, Cronin felt the car speed up. He had no idea where he was or even how long they'd been driving around, but the soft whine of the engine was soothing and comforting. He wished it would go on forever.

What was the worst thing they could do to him, kill him? Never! No one kills a cop and gets away with it. Besides, Stone would never permit it. So what's left? A good beating. I'm gonna get my ass kicked good. Okay, I can live with that. I'll be told to keep my mouth shut. I can live with that too.

Even in his pain and fear he felt relief. At least he was out of it. He would no longer be part of their madness. *I must have been nuts to think of going to IAD. I'll keep my mouth shut, get a transfer and just go back to being a cop again. Maybe I'll even be able to go back to the Ninth. . . .*

The car stopped. Tecci opened the back door and grabbed his collar. "Okay, Cronin, get out."

He half fell, half crawled out of the car. Moist sand ran through his fingers. He smelled the salt spray and knew they were on a beach. He couldn't see the water, but he could hear it lapping against the shoreline somewhere ahead in the inky blackness. With blurry vision and a throbbing head he stiffly got to his feet.

Tecci hissed, "Cronin, I always thought you were a fucking wimp. The Chief made a mistake bringing you in with us in the first place. Now we're going to have to rectify that mistake."

Cronin braced for the blows. But instead Beals jerked his hands behind his back and snapped handcuffs on him. Then he put his foot in Cronin's back and sent him sprawling into the damp sand. Suddenly very cold, he began to shake uncontrollably; the sand gritted in his chattering teeth.

Tecci roughly pulled him to a kneeling position. "Give me his gun," Cronin heard him say.

"Stevie, maybe we should wait for the Chief."

Cronin was heartened by the uncertainty and fear in Beals's voice.

"Shut up, for Chrissake. What else can we do? We can't let him go. He'll go to IAD!"

"No I won't," Cronin pleaded. "I swear to God I won't say a word. Just let me go. Please."

"Shut up, Goddamn it." Tecci punched him, sending him sprawling onto the sand again.

Beals threw his arms around Tecci to prevent him from jumping on the prostrate body. "Stevie, for Chrissake, he's a cop. We can't waste a cop."

"What else can we do? You tell me. If he talks, we'll go to jail for murder! You know what happens to cops in prison! There's no other way, man."

Cronin, lying helplessly in the cold sand, looked up into Tecci's eyes and knew he was going to die. Just then his sphincter muscles let go and he soiled his pants. Slowly Tecci raised the snub-nosed .38 and pointed it between his eyes.

Desperately, Cronin tried to remember if he'd loaded the gun. It wouldn't be the first time he'd forgotten. More than once he'd gone to the range and forgotten to load for the street. Later, in the locker room, after he'd gotten over the shock of carrying an empty gun, it was good for a laugh. "Can you believe it? I've been on patrol for a week with an empty gun! Damn!"

Dear God, he prayed, *let the gun be empty.* He stared at the black hole of the muzzle, wondering if there was a bullet there waiting to tear into his skull. Far off a dog barked, then the night became very still, except for the softly hissing surf and his pounding heart. With his whole being he concentrated on the muzzle swaying ever so slightly, like a cobra about to strike.

Just when he was sure they were only going to scare him, a blinding yellow-orange flash brighter than the sun erupted from the muzzle.

Walter Cronin's body twitched in the wet sand and then was still. The dog howled.

SHANNON GROPED FOR THE TELEPHONE IN THE DARKNESS. "YEAH?"

"Lieutenant Shannon? Detective Corey from the District." His tone was apologetic. "Bennett wanted you notified."

Shannon rubbed his eyes wearily. "What have you got?"

"A cop was murdered tonight in Queens. Shot execution-style."

Shannon bolted upright. "Do they have a perp?"

"No. No arrest yet."

"How was he shot? What kind of gun?"

"I don't have much info, Loo. I'm just making notifications."

Shannon called Rose and made arrangements to meet him by the diner at Francis Lewis and the Long Island Expressway. He arrived within the hour, and Rose was waiting for him with two containers of coffee. They drove to Rockaway in silence. Shannon turned onto Beach Channel Drive, a road running through Rockaway, a once famous resort area popular with the Irish, now eclipsed by Jones Beach and the Jersey shore. During the summer months the beach was still crowded with inner-city people unable, or unwilling, to drive out to Long Island. But out of season, except for a small year-round population, Rockaway was virtually deserted.

Shannon pulled in behind a cluster of radio cars. The sun, hanging low and undefined like an angry bruise in the sky, did nothing to alleviate the damp chill in the air. A priest, pale in his black overcoat, clutched his black bag containing the instruments of Extreme Unction and stumbled across the sand toward a waiting radio car that would return him to the sane world of incense and marble churches.

The two lieutenants trudged across the dunes to where a small group of detectives stood talking in hushed tones. This morning there was none of the usual bantering and joking. Not even laughter could drive away the ghosts that haunted policemen forced to look upon the body of a murdered brother officer. Shannon recognized the small, wiry sergeant from the One-hundredth squad. "Hello, Creegan."

The dour sergeant nodded and looked warily at Rose.

"Lieutenant Rose," Shannon said by way of introduction. "He's temporarily assigned to the Chief of Detectives office. Bennett sent us out to have a look." The less said the better.

Creegan, a cigarette dangling from his lips, squinted at his clipboard. "Here's what we got so far. Walter Cronin, shield number 4527, assigned to NET." He looked up. "That's that new super-duper narc squad. He did a four-to-twelve last night and was last seen leaving the office around midnight. His car is missing. We've put out an alarm."

"How was he killed?" Shannon asked.

Creegan took a last drag of his cigarette and flipped it away. "His hands were cuffed behind his back and he was shot once in the head. Probably his own gun; it's missing. The cuffs are his, we checked the serial number. There are some tire tracks over by the road. We took a cast." He looked around in disgust and shrugged. "There're tire tracks all over this goddamn beach, but who knows? I guess you wanna see the body?"

They followed Creegan over a dune covered with scrub oak and littered with old tires and broken bottles. High in the sky a lone sea gull screeched at the intruders on his beach. A large rectangular area was cordoned off with orange tape. The blanket-covered body, looking like a bleak, abstract sculpture, lay in the center. The forensic technicians, dusting sand from their tools, were packing up. "They're done," Creegan said, nodding toward them. "We're just waiting for the morgue wagon."

Carefully, they stepped over the tape and approached the body. Shannon knelt down and pulled the blanket away. Walter Cronin's eyes were wide open and his mouth was twisted in a silent scream. The wet black hole in the center of his forehead no longer leaked. Wet sand clung to the left side of his bloody face and eyelid.

"Jesus Christ," Rose muttered softly.

Cronin's face and lips were bloody and swollen and there were dark bruises on his face. His nostrils and the corner of his mouth were caked with dried blood.

Rose walked around behind the body and crouched to look at the hands. "No cuts or bruises. He didn't have much of a chance to put up a struggle." He stood up and looked off into the hazy horizon. "He still has his watch and wedding ring on. It wasn't a robbery."

Gently, Shannon pulled the blanket back over the body and without thinking tucked it around the legs so the wind wouldn't get under. He was suddenly reminded of the times he'd tucked his own child in after he came home from a four-to-twelve. Bone tired, he stood and gazed up and down the beach. In one direction there was a house about two hundred yards away. In the other direction, about a quarter of a mile away, was an old burned-out car. A desolate spot, but strangely peaceful. The waves lapped softly on the beach, and patrolling sea gulls, with a remarkable economy of effort, glided along the water's edge in search of breakfast. Once the haze burned off, it promised to be a beautiful winter day. As they turned away to find Creegan, Shannon wondered what it must be like to die on a beach like this.

BY EIGHT-THIRTY THEY WERE SITTING IN HUGO BENNETT'S OFFICE.

"What about the car?" Bennett asked.

"They found it an hour ago on Union Turnpike. Crime scene is dusting for prints."

"Where did he work?"

"NET."

"The C.O. is Pat Stone, the boy wonder. Any chance Cronin's death had anything to do with his assignment in NET?"

"The squad's looking into it," Rose answered.

Bennett studied Shannon. "Well, what do you think? Does this homicide fit your pattern?"

"Yes and no. The shot to the head is the same, but all the others were killed without a struggle. Cronin took a hell of a beating before they killed him. There are a couple of possibilities. One, he may have been an intended target. Why? I don't know. Then there's the possibility he accidentally found out about them and they had to kill him.''

Bennett turned to Rose. "Was he a Field Associate?"

Rose shook his head. "No. I checked."

"The funeral is Wednesday," Shannon said. "We're going to take some photos and collect license-plate numbers."

Bennett's bushy eyebrows went up. "You think the killers will show up for the funeral?"

Rose looked him right in the eye. "They might be standing in the uniformed ranks right alongside the Police Commissioner."

Bennett frowned but said nothing. They all knew—Rose could be right.

"Rose wants to talk to Mrs. Cronin." From Shannon's tone it was clear he didn't agree with the idea.

Bennett's eyebrows went up again. "Do you think that's wise? If the PBA gets wind you're interrogating a cop's widow, they'll lynch you."

Rose shrugged. "We have to take the chance. Maybe she knows something. The detectives handling the case won't ask the right questions because they don't know what we know. We're also going to enter data on every arrest Cronin was part of. Just in case."

"Good." Bennett sighed. "That should keep the little Puerto Rican busy for a while. I think he's trying to get into my secretary's pants."

23

P ATRICK S TONE HAD GONE TO F LORIDA TO MAKE ONE LAST PITCH TO Victor Cabrera. But it was a waste of time. Cabrera was adamant. Pickett had to go. And soon.

Stone was due in the office in less than an hour, and his plane had landed late. As he rushed through the airport, his eye caught a glimpse of Walter Cronin's face on the front page of the *Daily News*. The headlines above the photo screamed SPECIAL NARC COP MURDERED. He snatched up a paper and skimmed the sketchy article on page three. His eyes locked on the words, "The officer was shot execution-style." He rushed for a phone.

"Narcotics Enforcement Team," Tim Hardy answered in a strained voice.

"Tim, what happened?"

"Chief! Am I glad you're back! Those crazy bastards—"

"Not now." Hardy's tone told him all he needed to know. "Tonight, eight o'clock, everyone at your place. We'll discuss it then.'' He assumed a professional tone. ''What's going on at the office?''

''It's a madhouse. The phones haven't stopped ringing. Everyone's looking for you. I told them you were skiing upstate and would be back this morning.''

''Good. Has the P.C. called?''

''No, but the First Dep's office did. They want a full report forthwith on all Cronin's arrest activity since he came into NET. Public Information called. You have to be available for a press conference this morning at eleven.''

Stone looked at his watch; it was almost ten. ''I'm at Kennedy. I should be there within the hour. And Tim, take it easy. I'll handle everything.''

On the ride into the city he reread the story. The article made no mention of clues or witnesses, but that meant nothing. The department never revealed important information like that to the press. He tried to piece together what had happened. Tecci and Beals had murdered Cronin. But why? Cronin had been acting strange lately, but what had he done to make them kill him? It was clear from Hardy's tone that he was on the verge of panic. Tecci and Beals were the key. They would have the answers.

Stone stared out the window as the taxi sped across the Queensborough Bridge and tried to assess the damages. Apparently, the department knew nothing, or else IAD would have arrested Hardy and the others. The damage, at least for now, was containable.

He tossed the paper aside and turned his attention to what he planned to say as the outraged commanding officer of a slain policeman.

The station-house block was rendered impassable by the logjam of radio cars and TV equipment trucks parked in front of the station. Stone abandoned the taxi halfway down the block and went the rest of the way on foot. Waiting inside the sitting room, reporters and technicians noisily went about setting up their cameras and lights.

He snuck up the back stairs and entered a strangely subdued NET office. It was jammed with cops, and telephones rang incessantly, but no one spoke above a whisper. Stone saw Hardy across the room but ignored him. They'd talk tonight. Right now he needed the facts from someone who was thinking straight. Acknowledging grim nods from a group of cops, he motioned to John Carlin to follow him into his office.

Stone sat down and flipped through the dozen telephone messages on his desk. ''Okay, John. Fill me in.''

Stone's administrative lieutenant referred to his yellow pad filled with minuscule, precise handwriting. ''Walter did a four-to-twelve last night. It was a quiet night. No arrest activity. He left at midnight, and that's the last anyone saw of him. He was found on a beach in Rockaway around four this morning by some insomniac walking his dog.'' Carlin's cool demeanor broke and, in a rare display of emotion, he said, "Captain, the kid was assassinated. Some son of a bitch handcuffed him and shot him in the head."

But Stone wasn't listening. He was watching Hardy through the open door. His sergeant's hair wasn't combed and he needed a shave. Apparently, he'd come right to the office after hearing the news. A steady stream of cops stopped at Hardy's desk to pat him on the shoulder or to whisper a word of condolence in his ear. But Hardy took no notice of them. His eyes were locked on Stone, pleading for a chance to talk to him alone.

Stone got up and kicked the door shut. "Where are we now, John?"

"The Queens Chief of Detectives and the Borough Commander are somewhere in the building, and they're madder than wet hens. They wanna know where you've been."

"I'll take care of them. What else?"

"The media people have been waiting downstairs, and they're getting restless. They want a statement. About five minutes ago the Deputy Commissioner from Public Information called. Apparently, one of his drinking cronies from the press called to complain about the long wait. He wants to know the reason for the delay."

"Fuck the DCPI," Stone said. "I'm not going to answer questions in front of TV cameras until I know exactly what's going on."

Carlin made no comment. It wasn't his job to tell his C.O. he was making a mistake butting heads with the influential DCPI. "I just got off the phone with the detective handling the case," he continued. "They don't have much, but I can fill you in on what he told me."

Stone was relieved. There was no evidence—at least so far. He grabbed a pad. "Okay. Start from the beginning."

Fifteen minutes later Stone, flanked by a stony-faced Borough Commander and the Queens Chief of Detectives, stood before a blinding wall of klieg lights and TV cameras. The Borough Commander, after chewing out Stone for being "missing in action," had ordered him to handle the press conference. His decision came as no great surprise; chiefs volunteered to do press conferences only when the news was good—a major arrest or a seizure of a large quantity of narcotics. The dirty, messy job of explaining a cop's death could be left to someone like Patrick Stone.

Standing at a podium in the packed sitting room, he gave a terse account of the circumstances surrounding Walter Cronin's death. Lieutenant Carlin, standing on the outer fringes of the crowd, marveled at Stone's performance. Fifteen minutes ago his captain didn't even know what had happened, but now, after the short briefing upstairs, he sounded as though he'd been personally working on the case since it had begun.

Stone, careful not to give away the few details the department had to work with, fielded the press's questions truthfully and frankly. Then one reporter asked, "Captain Stone, who do you think did this?"

Stone's eyes, scanning the crowd, locked on Hardy. "We don't know the answer to that question yet." He looked away and made eye contact with several reporters in the front row. "But I guarantee the department will apprehend the killer and bring him to justice."

Stone's voice dropped to almost a whisper; the reporters had to lean forward to catch his words. Even the photographers stopped snapping pictures.

"As a Narcotics Enforcement Team cop, Walter Cronin was a soldier fighting in the front lines to protect the citizens of this city. He gave his life for what he believed in—justice and a safer city. I want the decent, law-abiding citizens to know that he didn't die in vain. He has left a legacy for his brother officers. Every cop in NET, every cop in the New York City Police Department, will remember Walter Cronin. The memory of his sacrifice will serve as a rallying cry for the rest of us. The war that the mayor and the Police Commissioner have declared against the narcotics dealers in this city goes on. And the cops who are fighting this war will see to it that Walter Cronin's ultimate sacrifice is vindicated."

During the stunned moment of silence following Stone's remarks, the Borough Commander and the Queens Chief of Detectives exchanged looks of grudging respect. The egotistical son of a bitch had captured the hearts and minds of a roomful of hard-bitten reporters, and in the process managed to give credit to the mayor *and* the Police Commissioner at the same time. No easy feat.

The only one in the room not taken in by Stone's emotional words was Tim Hardy. Slumped against a wall, he reacted with utter disbelief to Stone's performance. The Chief *knew* who killed Cronin. How could he stand up there and tell such a story? Watching his commanding officer calmly display just the right mixture of sorrow, anger, and indignation, Hardy was, for the first time, suddenly afraid of Patrick Stone.

THAT EVENING IN HARDY'S APARTMENT, PATRICK STONE SUCCESS- fully masked his fury. He was so close to bringing the Victor Cabrera chapter in his life to a close, and now those two fools had to go and murder Cronin. After this weekend's unpleasant meeting with Cabrera, it was imperative that he complete this assignment as quickly as possible. But he couldn't proceed until he heard what Tecci and Beals had to say. Hardy was so full of nervous energy, he couldn't sit still. Stone grabbed Hardy's arm and pulled him into a chair. "Tim, get a grip on yourself. I don't want you to panic them when they get here."

But Hardy, who'd been in shock since he'd heard of Cronin's death, was too distraught to heed Stone's words.

The door bell rang and Tecci and Beals shuffled in, looking drawn and tired. Tecci, in contrast to his usually sharp appearance, looked disheveled. Beals, as usual, displayed no emotion.

"Sit down," Stone said, "and start from the beginning. Leave nothing out."

Tecci licked his lips. "Can I have a beer?"

"No. Tell me what happened."

"You told me to keep an eye on him, right? Well, me and McKay followed him last night after work."

"Why last night?"

"He was acting really weird. He wouldn't talk to us, or anyone in the office. I noticed his hands were shaking, and McKay saw him staring at a calendar. He looked like he was coming apart. So we decided to follow him after the tour was over. It's a good thing we did."

"Where did he go?"

"Nowhere. I mean, he just drove around. Up to the Bronx, down to lower Manhattan, he just drove around. Finally, in Queens, he pulled over to a telephone and tried to call IAD."

"Mother of Christ!" whispered Hardy.

Stone ignored him. "How do you know he was going to call IAD?"

"I heard the guy on the other end of the line. He said, 'IAD.' "

Hardy's face was ashen. "Did he tell them anything?"

"He never got a chance. McKay pulled him away before he could talk."

"Maybe it wasn't his first call to IAD," Hardy said.

"I doubt that," Tecci replied. "He was working up his nerve."

"Then what?"

Tecci avoided Stone's steely eyes. "We didn't know what to do. We couldn't let him go. I mean, he might have called IAD again. We couldn't call you. . . ."

"Why didn't you call Hardy?"

"We didn't think of it. I mean, it was something else! Who figured he'd call IAD? It blew my mind! All I could see was us getting busted and sent to prison. I didn't see any other way out."

"You didn't see any other way out, so you killed him?" Hardy was incredulous.

"Well what the fuck would you have done?" Tecci shouted.

Hardy's face reddened and his lower lip trembled in anger. "I wouldn't have murdered him!"

Stone got to his feet and went to the window. "Enough," he said. "We have to find out if we have a problem. Tim, you have a contact in IAD. Give him a call and feel him out. See if they're working on anything in connection with Walt's death. In the meantime, everything's on hold."

"And then what?" Hardy asked.

"If we haven't been compromised, we'll resume our tail on Pickett."

Hardy groaned. After Cronin's death, he was certain Stone would call the hit off. "Chief, it's madness to—"

Stone turned away. "This meeting is adjourned."

TECCI AND BEALS LEFT QUICKLY, BUT STONE STAYED FOR COFFEE. Hardy, so frightened he could barely think straight, made a desperate attempt to change Stone's mind.

"Chief, things are out of control. Those crazy bastards murdered Walt Cronin and there's no telling what they'll do next. In the name of God let's drop the whole thing now—"

"We can't. Victor is on my case. He thinks we're taking too much time with Pickett."

"Who cares what Victor wants?" Hardy realized he was shouting, and dropped into a chair, his face ravaged and his breath short. "It's *our* necks on the line. Jesus, you know the department is going to investigate Cronin's death with a fine-tooth comb. There may be a witness somewhere, maybe they dropped something, left fingerprints."

Stone, well aware of the stupidity of Tecci and Beals, had already thought of that. But his greater concern was Hardy. The man was becoming unglued, and Stone couldn't afford to have three jumpy people on his hands; he had to hold them together just awhile longer.

"Chief, let's drop the whole thing. Why not quit while we're ahead?"

"No," Stone said softly. "Pickett has to go."

24

NANCY CRONIN LIVED IN A MODEST TWO-FAMILY HOUSE IN A PART of Queens where the neatly edged lawns were tiny and people still swept up the street in front of their homes. When she opened the door, Rose held up his ID card and said automatically, "Lieutenant Rose, Internal Affairs."

Shannon, standing behind him, repressed an oath. He hated being identified with IAD, and was sure the interview was a bust before it started. Most cops' wives had as much loathing for IAD as their husbands did. But to his surprise, Nancy Cronin let them in.

The living room, furnished with heavy Colonial pieces, was tiny; the baby's playpen, filled with stuffed toys, took up most of the room. Cutouts of turkeys and Pilgrims were Scotch-taped to the window. Neatly arranged family photographs, including one of Walter Cronin in his uniform, were displayed on top of the TV. The proud, smiling face looked nothing like the battered one Shannon had seen on the beach, and he turned away from the photo uneasily.

In other circumstances Nancy would have been considered pretty, but now her face was drawn and there were dark smudges under her eyes from the five sleepless nights since her husband's murder. She fidgeted with a small handkerchief, continually twisting it in her hands. At times, in the middle of a sentence, she fell silent and simply stared off into space. Shannon was sure that if she had anything to say, she had already said it to the investigating detectives. In short, he didn't expect much from this interview.

"How are you getting along?" he asked.

"Fine," she said. She didn't mention the nights spent staring down into the crib, wondering what she was going to tell her daughter about her dead father. Since Walt's death, life had become a perplexing blur. There were so many maddening, inconsequential details to attend to if life were to go on. Thank God for the solicitous men from the Pension Section and the PBA. They'd spent hours at her kitchen table patiently explaining her benefits—a strange term to be used in connection with Walt's death. They showed her page after page of numbers, signifying how much she would receive and for how long. Firmly, but gently, they reminded her to be sure and put some money away for a rainy day and her daughter's education. They helped her fill out the dozens of incomprehensible forms that officially declared that Walt was dead and would not be coming back. They were very kind, but to Nancy they were like shadows coming and going with voices barely heard, talking about the future, about hope, about life. Those words no longer held meaning for her.

"Mrs. Cronin," Rose said, "we're investigating your husband's death. We were wondering if there was anything you could tell us that might help us."

She looked blankly at the two lieutenants. Their faces were indistinguishable from all the other policemen who had come to visit her. "What do you mean?"

"Well, for instance, did Walt ever talk to you about the job? Did he ever mention having a problem with anyone? A prisoner, anything like that?"

Nancy peered out at them through the veil of numbness that had descended upon her since Walt's death. In the aftermath of his murder, overwhelmed with grief and faced with the immediate needs of her infant daughter, she had blocked out Walt's terrible tale of theft and murder. She welcomed the daily demands on her time because it didn't give her the chance to think about his death and its tragic implications.

Now these two policemen were asking the same painful questions. This lieutenant from . . . *Internal Affairs* was forcing her to think, to remember. Something deep within her wrenched itself loose, and slowly she felt herself emerging from the depths of denial. *Internal Affairs?* His question was making her remember, pulling her back to reality. Nancy fought the pull, but it was irresistible. Little by little the blessed numbness of grief began to fall away as she returned to the harsh, cold world of the living. The emotions she'd so carefully suppressed since Walt's murder gave way. Now, pain flooded through every cell in her body, and she wept uncontrollably for the first time since his death.

When she was done weeping, Shannon, who'd made some instant coffee in the kitchen, handed her a cup. She looked at Rose with red-rimmed eyes. "Didn't you say you were from Internal Affairs?" Rose nodded. "You investigate other policemen, don't you?" It was more a statement of fact than a question. What she said next gave them both a start. "Then you already know about Walt."

"Mrs. Cronin," Rose said, "why don't you tell us about it."

She stared at the untouched cup in her hands, and as if noticing it for the first time, put it down. "I didn't understand a lot of what he told me. All I know is, he was in bad trouble. He'd taken money, apparently several times, and"—she paused, tears filling her eyes—"and God help him, he was involved in . . . in the deaths of some people."

"Mrs. Cronin, these people Walt was involved with, did he work with them?"

She shook her head, trying to remember, but it was so difficult. Walt's rambling confession the night before he died had come out in a confused torrent of despair. "I don't know. He didn't say—at least I don't think he said. What he said didn't make much sense to me."

"Did he say how many there were?"

"He might have. I just can't remember. I just know he didn't want any part of them, but he didn't know what to do."

"How long had this been going on?"

She shook her head. A tear spilled down her face and stained the collar of the simple dark dress she wore. She took a handkerchief from her pocket and wiped her cheeks. "I don't know."

It was frustrating. She was the only person with any information, and she couldn't—or wouldn't—remember. Rose looked to Shannon for support, but Shannon's eyes were on Nancy Cronin. He said nothing.

"What made Walt change his mind?" Rose persisted.

"They wanted to kill someone. Walt said he wasn't a bad man. He wanted no part of it."

"Did Walt mention a name?"

She twisted her handkerchief. "He's a black politician. That's all I know."

Rose leaned forward. His face was taut and there was suppressed excitement in his voice. "Was the name Nathan Pickett?"

"It sounds familiar . . . but I'm just not sure."

"Why did they want to kill this man?"

"It had something to do with a drug commission. It was going to cause trouble for someone, and they were supposed to . . . get rid of him. Oh, God—Walt went to you for help. Why didn't you protect him?"

Rose felt a chill. Had the corruption they were uncovering crept into IAD too? "Mrs. Cronin," he said firmly, "Walt never contacted us. If we'd have known, we would have helped him."

She bit her lip. "He told me he was going to call IAD the night he . . ."

The two men glanced at each other, now knowing why Walter Cronin was dead. He was going to blow the whistle on them, and they found out about it.

Rose attempted a few more questions, but it was no use. The widow didn't know—or couldn't remember—anything else. He was satisfied at least that she wasn't intentionally concealing anything. He stood up and gave her his card. "If you think of anything else, no matter how insignificant, please call me."

At the door she called, "Wait. There was something else. The leader of the group had some sort of title."

"A police title?" Shannon asked.

She frowned, struggling to remember. Then she said, "I think Walt called him 'Chief.' "

Shannon felt as if he'd been punched in the stomach. Minutes ago he had refused to believe cops were involved in these murders. Now, not only were cops involved, she was saying that a department chief might be the leader!

Shannon thanked her again and urged her to go inside, out of the chill December wind.

When Nancy Cronin first said that her husband had been involved in these murders, he'd been struck dumb. He'd let Rose ask all the questions while he struggled to come to terms with himself. With a mixture of loathing and respect, he'd watched Rose expertly push and coax her in his attempt to gain more information. He wanted to ask questions, but none had come to mind.

They stopped at a phone and Shannon called Velez. "Luis, I want the names of everyone in NET. Then wait till we get back. You're going to be working overtime tonight."

When Shannon got back in the car, a troubled Rose said, "Don't make any plans tonight, Brian. You and I have something to do."

"What?"

"She said Walt was supposed to have called IAD the night he was murdered."

"So?"

"So no IAD investigation was started."

"How do you know?"

"I have a buddy assigned to the Action Desk. I called him the morning after Cronin's murder to see if IAD had anything. They didn't."

Rose hadn't told him about the call to IAD. Shannon felt a flicker of annoyance. What else had Rose kept from him? "So? What are you getting at?"

"So someone in IAD might be involved with this group."

"IAD?" Shannon said it contemptuously.

"In spite of what you think, Brian, cops in IAD are just like cops in the rest of the job. They don't have a lock on honesty."

"How are you going to check it out?"

"All calls to IAD are taped. The building is quiet on the late tour. We'll go there around two and listen to the tapes. If Cronin called IAD that night, he'll be on tape."

Shannon, who was about to put the car in gear, stopped. "What do you mean 'we'? *I'm* not going there."

"There'll be hours of tapes. I can't do it alone."

"Goddamn it, Rose, I'm not going. You're in IAD. *You* go."

"Brian, for Chrissake. We have to know if Cronin called IAD that night. I need your help."

Shannon was furious. He snapped the car in gear. "All right, Goddamn it."

Rose smiled at Shannon's discomfort. "If you're afraid of someone recognizing you going into the building, maybe I can come up with some Groucho glasses and a mustache."

IN THE OFFICE, THEY DESCRIBED THE NANCY CRONIN INTERVIEW TO A dubious Velez. "So you're saying the bad guys are in NET?"

"I don't know," Rose said. "Cronin's wife didn't know if he worked with them or not, but it makes sense."

Shannon reached for a cigarette. The hell with quitting. He had too much on his mind. "The thing that bothers me is, who's the Chief? A department chief? Stone? Or is it just a title?"

Velez said, "I'll get a list of department chiefs and feed their profiles into the computer."

"Do we agree that NET is where the bad guys are?" Rose asked.

Glumly, Shannon stared at the IAD lieutenant. From the beginning, Rose had been willing to believe that cops were involved. Shannon hadn't, and was certain a reasonable explanation would be found and the killers would turn out to be imposters. Now that flimsy illusion had been shattered by a grieving widow.

"Luis," Shannon said, "I want every NET cop's profile in the computer—previous commands, arrest activity, disciplinary records, the works."

"How about photos?"

"Yeah. Get photos. I'll set up a photo array for Mrs. Gordon and Wanda Little."

"Don't forget the blue van," Rose added.

Velez started writing it down. "Okay, I'll run the NET roster through DMV to see who owns a blue van. By the way, just before you guys got back, I finished running everything on the partial plate. Thank God, the Albany computers stayed up long enough for me to get the final run."

"Anything?" Shannon asked.

"Nada. I took all the possible plate numbers and pulled out all the blue vans. Then I isolated those in New York City by borough. Blue is a real popular color."

Shannon knew it had been a shot in the dark, but he still felt a pang of disappointment. "So what *do* you have?"

"A long list of blue vans broken down by borough."

"We'd have to go out and eyeball every one of them," Rose said.

"The hell with that," Shannon said. "We have more important things to do."

"Pickett?"

"Exactly. It looks like he's the next target."

Velez tossed a folder at Shannon. "I got the NET personnel roster from a department printout, but it doesn't give a breakdown by team. How are you going to find out who Cronin worked with?"

"I don't know." Shannon scanned the names. "We can't exactly walk into the NET office and ask for a list of team assignments."

Velez looked at Rose. "What about you, Loo? You could ride in wearing your IAD black hat."

"I thought of that, but it's too risky. We don't want anyone in NET to know they're being looked at by IAD, or anyone else."

"Could it really be Stone?" Shannon's tone was a mix of incredulity and despair.

"It would be hard to imagine a less likely candidate," Rose said. "He's a bright guy on the fast track. Why would he risk that?"

Shannon agreed. "And NET has a rep for honesty. It doesn't fit."

"Wait a minute, guys," Velez interjected. "That shrink said the leader would be a smart, charismatic guy. Stone fits the bill."

"So do a lot of people on the job," Shannon objected.

"Yeah, but only Stone worked with Walter Cronin."

The two lieutenants looked at each other. "He's right," Rose said. "Until something better comes along, Stone is a prime suspect."

Shannon jammed his cigarette out in the ashtray. "I'd *still* like to talk to Captain Stone."

LARSON HUNCHED OVER HIS DESK AND GLARED AT SHANNON AS HE RE-counted his interview with Nancy Cronin. When he finished, the Chief of Detectives strolled to the window, fiddled with the vertical blinds, and gazed out on the city below. To the left of the imposing Municipal Building, he could see the dome of City Hall rising above the trees in the park. Larson's gaze wandered to the ugly, rusting sculpture squatting in front of One Police Plaza. "How's Mrs. Cronin?"

"She's doing okay."

Larson sat down on the edge of his desk and carefully adjusted the sharp crease in his trousers. "Any chance that something snapped? You know, maybe in her state of mind she's trying to get revenge on the department. Maybe she blames the department for her husband's death. Something like that?"

"She's grieving, Chief, but she's not crazy."

"Who said anything about crazy? Distraught, I mean. Maybe she's distraught and her imagination is running away with her."

Restless, he returned to the window again. His eyes fell on City Hall, the eggshell-white building that wouldn't look out of place in a New England town. If this is true, he thought, it'll be the biggest bombshell ever to hit the department. The mayor will go ape-shit when he hears about it.

"Shannon, you and that IAD lieutenant have been working on this case for over three weeks now, and you haven't come up with shit. What the hell have you been doing?"

Shannon bridled at Larson's tone. It had been a long time—twenty-four days, to be exact—since they'd begun. Normally, after this much time he would have come up with something, but this wasn't a normal case. He was investigating three difficult homicides under the worst possible conditions. Operating under Larson's self-imposed restrictions, Shannon hadn't been permitted to call upon the department's vast resources and expertise. Instead he was forced to sneak around, looking over his shoulder while he interviewed witnesses and collected information secondhand.

He'd been in touch with DeNoto, but he wasn't permitted to talk to the detectives who'd caught the other two murders. It was an investigator's nightmare: three detectives investigating three murders that they didn't know were related. Without seeing the big picture, how would they know which leads to pursue or what questions to ask? It was homicide investigation by committee, and it was driving Shannon to distraction. Normally a case like this—with its potential for damaging political fallout—would have had a

task force working on it. Instead, it was being investigated by only him—
and one IAD lieutenant.

Carefully, he said, "We're taking a close look at everyone in NET."

Larson sat down at his desk and absentmindedly realigned his pen and
pencil set. "Why are you so sure NET cops are involved?"

"I didn't say I was sure," Shannon said. He was getting weary of
Larson's penchant for putting words in his mouth. "That's where Cronin
worked. I don't know a hell of a lot about NET, but I know they concentrate
on major drug dealers. And that means big money and high stakes."

Larson *did* know all about NET. He made it his business to keep track of
current events in the department. NET was the P.C.'s pet project, and he'd
handpicked Patrick Stone to head it up. Most of the chiefs were afraid of
Stone; fast-rising stars always gave the old chiefs *agita,* but not Larson.
He'd seen hotshots come and go. Larson had been watching Stone's career
with great professional interest. Happily, the young, hard-charger was moving too fast, making too many arrests, and garnering too much publicity. It
was only a matter of time before he stepped on his cock, and another rising
star would be looking for a police chief's job in Iowa. He chuckled to
himself. If NET was involved in this, the P.C. would be looking for another
job too. It was an appealing thought. "What's the complement of personnel
in NET?" he asked.

"A small unit. One captain, one lieutenant, four sergeants, and twenty
cops. We're collecting data on everyone in the unit from the captain on
down. It'll take some time, but Velez is going to input every arrest made by
NET since its inception. If we can, we'll interview some of the people
they've arrested."

"You're going to find shit, Shannon. Stone is a schmuck, but he has a
reputation as a straight shooter. You're pissing into the wind."

"I don't think so. Mrs. Cronin couldn't say if these men were in NET,
but we think there's a good chance they are." Shannon saw an opportunity
to make another pitch for opening up the investigation. "I'm at a real
disadvantage, Chief. I can't just walk into the NET office and ask for roll
calls and rosters and begin interviewing everyone. Unless you want to make
this case official."

Larson didn't take the bait. "I'll let you know when this case becomes
official, Lieutenant."

It was the response Shannon had expected, but it didn't make him feel
any better. "There's another problem I have with NET."

"What's that?"

"There's no chief. The C.O. is only a captain."

"How many chiefs in the department right now?"

The number changed from month to month, but Shannon had just checked a current department roster. "Thirty-six, including the 'super chiefs,' and two on terminal leave."

Larson mentally reviewed the list of deputy chiefs and assistant chiefs he knew personally. There were some bright ones and some morons, but none who were capable of murder. He was certain of it. "Maybe he's not a real chief. Maybe it's just a title. So you think the politician is Pickett?"

"Yes."

"It's no secret he's planning to move on to bigger and better things. A well-publicized drug commission would be a big boost to that bastard's career. He's been putting the department on the spot for weeks. The son of a bitch deserves to be assassinated."

He stood up. "Talk to Pickett. Don't tell him what's going on, for Chrissake, but feel him out. See if he knows anything. I'm not saying this cock-and-bull story is true, Lieutenant, but we'll see. Maybe this is some stunt Pickett dreamed up for publicity that went sour. I want you to get off your ass and come up with something concrete. If you can't do the job, I'll find someone who can."

For a moment Shannon considered telling Larson up what portion of his anatomy he could shove this case, but he held his tongue.

"Oh, and one more thing." The Chief of Detectives' eyes narrowed grimly. "Remember what I said about this investigation being confidential. If word of this leaks out, I'll put you and the hump IAD lieutenant out of the job so fast you'll find your ears around your ankles. That's a promise."

After Shannon left his office, Larson sat back with his feet up on the desk and studied the photo in which he was shaking hands with a smiling Mayor Barry Kessel. "Timothy, my boy," he said, "you're walking through a fucking mine field and you'd better watch your step. One mistake and your career goes up in smoke. You don't want to wind up a square badge emptying wastebaskets in a bank, now do you?" He drummed his manicured fingernails on the desk and then reached for the phone. "Chief Larson here. If the commissioner has a moment, I'd like a word with him. It's urgent."

Ten minutes later the Chief of Detectives was shown into the P.C.'s office by an auburn-haired policewoman. Larson wondered if Mara was getting into her pants and made a mental note to check it out.

The view from the Police Commissioner's office was identical to Larson's, except the P.C. was one floor higher. The fourteenth floor of One Police Plaza was the pinnacle of the department. It was the place Larson fully expected to occupy in the not too distant future.

Commissioner Mara, sitting at an old oak desk—the same one used by Teddy Roosevelt when he was the Police Commissioner—watched his dapper Chief of Detectives come through the door. Larson, whose condescending attitude was rankling, never missed the opportunity to remind Mara—in the most diplomatic language possible—that Mara was in the big leagues now, and not back in Pennsylvania. Mara didn't trust his Chief of Detectives, whom he considered both dangerous and useless as the commanding officer of the Detective Bureau. He'd tried on several occasions to replace Larson, but found it impossible. His Chief of Detectives was comfortably insulated by a layer of politicians and influential businessmen.

Mara had learned early on, much to his chagrin, that as powerful as the P.C.'s job was, there were certain things even he couldn't do. Apparently, getting rid of his Chief of Detectives was one of them. The men and women in the department, from police officer to captain, were protected by Civil Service law. That was bad enough, but his senior managers—those above the rank of captain—were protected by something even more powerful— friends in high places. How many times had he tried to force the retirement of an incompetent chief, only to be the recipient of an endless stream of telephone calls from clergymen, politicians, and businessmen who politely asked for a reprieve while at the same time darkly hinting at dire consequences for noncompliance? The convoluted intrigue and political machinations in the department still baffled Mara. Machiavelli, he thought ruefully, must be required reading in the Police Academy executive-development courses.

The commissioner looked at his watch. "Sit down, Larson. I don't have much time, so I'd appreciate it if you made it brief."

THE INTERNAL AFFAIRS DIVISION OFFICE WAS LOCATED IN A FORMER precinct station house on Poplar Street in Brooklyn. The building was a forbidding edifice perfectly suited as the headquarters of the IAD. To cops summoned here for interrogation, it had the depressing pall of a dungeon, and the bars on the windows did nothing to dispel that illusion.

It was just after two when Shannon and Rose pulled up in front of the building. They were buzzed in the front door by a sleepy cop, who grunted a greeting at Rose. After a cursory look at Shannon, he returned to his *Playboy*.

Shannon waited in an office on the third floor, while Rose went to retrieve the tapes. Eyes heavy with sleep, Shannon inspected his surroundings. He'd been on the go since six this morning, and the fatigue was catching up to him. He'd never been inside the IAD building before, and like most cops, felt a mixture of uneasiness and curiosity about the place. Surprisingly, the office looked like any other squad room. It was painted in the same bland shades of blue and green; the same rows of department orders were attached to clipboards hung from hooks on the wall. The desks, with their photos of girlfriends and families, would be interchangeable with desks in any other squad room in the city. Girlie calendars and clever sayings clipped from newspapers and magazines were haphazardly scotch-taped to the walls. To his experienced eye there was only one difference, but a telling one. Every filing cabinet in the room was secured with a long steel bar and lock.

Shannon began to feel claustrophobic. He wanted to go outside and breathe fresh air, but he had to wait for Rose to come back. He found a water fountain in the hallway and ducked his head under the stream of cold water. When he went back into the office, Rose was setting up two tape recorders with earphones attached.

"Here." He slid a stack of tapes toward Shannon. "I don't think Cronin would have phoned while he was working, so we'll begin with calls that came in after his tour ended at midnight. Start listening. We don't have much time. We have to be out of here before the day tour starts arriving."

Shannon pressed the play button and listened. Each conversation began in the same way. "Internal Affairs, may I help you?" But the responses on the other end of the line were all very different. Disembodied voices, in a variety of accents, lodged their many and varied complaints about the New York City Police Department. Some were funny. ". . . the policeman said if I didn't sign over all my worldly possessions to him, he'd give me a ticket, and if I was convicted, I could go to jail for the rest of my natural life. Now that ain't right. He can't—" Others, whispering accusations as though they were afraid to be overheard, were disturbing. ". . . then I seen the cops carrying the TVs and shit right out the broken front window of that appliance store on Bedford. If you don't believe me, ask—"

Shannon fast-forwarded to the next call. As soon as he heard the voice of the next complainant and realized it wasn't Cronin, he fast-forwarded again. Sitting across the desk from him, Rose, with a look of studied concentration on his face, did the same.

It was almost four when Shannon saw Rose stop the tape, rewind it, and play it again. His brow knitted and he repeated the process again. Then he took off his earphones.

"Brian, listen to this." He pressed play, and Shannon heard the telephone ringing on the tape. *"Internal Affairs Division, Sergeant Romano. May I help you? Hello? Is anyone there?"*

There was a vaguely muffled sound on the other end of the line, followed by the sound of the receiver being replaced. The line went dead.

Rose rewound the tape and played it again. He looked at Shannon. "What do you think?"

"I don't know. What time was that?"

Rose glanced at the cassette box. "This tape is the hour between three and four. I'm halfway through, so it's somewhere around three-thirty."

"You think that was Cronin?"

"I don't know." He looked at his watch. "It's getting late. Let's finish up."

It was almost five by the time they'd heard the last of the tapes. Neither Rose nor Shannon had heard anyone that might have been Walter Cronin. As they slipped down the back stairs, they heard the soft murmur of voices in a distant office. A new day was beginning for IAD.

They stopped at a busy diner on Flatbush Avenue. Slipping past truck drivers and office workers beginning their day, Rose and Shannon found a quiet booth in the back and ordered coffee.

Shannon, who was so tired he could barely keep his eyes open, stirred his black coffee. "Was that Cronin?"

Rose's eyes were bloodshot from lack of sleep. "I don't know, but we know Walter Cronin didn't talk to anyone in IAD that night."

"Thank God," Shannon mumbled, "IAD's reputation remains unsullied."

Rose shook his head. "Shannon, I didn't think it was possible, but you're even more sarcastic when you're tired." He slid his half-empty cup away from him. "Let's call it a day. I'm bushed."

Driving east on the expressway, Shannon squinted in the bright morning light. After he caught himself dozing for the second time, he opened all the windows and turned the radio up to full volume. But he didn't hear the music. In his mind, dulled by lack of sleep, he replayed the curiously silent tape over and over again, and the questions that would rob him of sleep when he got home: *Was* that Walter Cronin on the phone? What was he going to say? Did he change his mind, or did they stop him at the moment he was going to come forward?

25

THEY WERE REPAIRING THE BROOKLYN BRIDGE AGAIN. IT SEEMED TO Brian Shannon that it was under constant repair, and by some perverse logic, they always worked on the lanes with the heaviest traffic. His department auto, trapped in a monumental logjam, slowly inched forward. A light December flurry of snow whirled over the bridge.

Shannon, silent since they'd left headquarters, was in a black mood. He wasn't sleeping well. Usually it took dynamite to wake him, but now he woke several times during the night, and found it impossible to get back to sleep. This on-again, off-again, who-knows-what-the-fuck-is-going-on investigation was driving him nuts.

A blast from an impatient driver snapped him out of his reverie. "Rose," he said, "have you noticed anything peculiar about this investigation?"

"I've noticed a lot of peculiar things about this investigation. Which one did you have in mind?"

Shannon deftly slipped in front of a lumbering trailer truck whose horn blasted in protest. "We haven't put anything on paper."

"What do you mean?"

"I mean we haven't made out a sixty-one, a DD5, nothing. Except for the stuff in the computer, as far as this department is concerned, this case doesn't exist."

"That's true, but this isn't a normal case; we spend most of our time slinking around pretending we're not investigating anything. You have a point, though. Today is the sixth. We've been investigating this case for almost a month, and in all our meetings with Larson and Bennett, they've never once asked for any paper."

Rose was distracted by a taxi whose abrupt lane change almost caused a chain-reaction accident. "Look at that son of a bitch!" As they came alongside the cab, Rose stuck his head out the window. "Fucking yellow peril!" he yelled at the startled driver and rolled up his window. "Do you think we're being set up?"

"I don't want to get paranoid, but I know this job. If it ain't on paper, it don't exist."

Reluctantly, Rose had to agree. The department, like all ponderous bureaucracies, had an almost religious reverence for paperwork. Important or petty, it made no difference. Reports were completed in triplicate and dispatched to other offices—whether or not they wanted them, or needed them—to be meticulously filed and forgotten. Nothing was too trivial to be put on paper. The department even required officers to record in their memo books when they defecated. The department referred to it as a "personal necessity"; nevertheless, every officer had to make note of the time he went and the time he returned. As an IAD investigator, Rose relied on paperwork. It was how many internal investigations were conducted. One didn't look for fingerprints or a smoking gun. There were seldom any. One looked for clues in the mountains of paperwork generated by the department. Sometimes it was as clear as tracking a bleeding deer across snow. A careful observer could always find errors and omissions in the host of forms and reports required by the department.

Shannon was right. They were up to their asses in what was potentially the most explosive investigation in the recent history of the department, and not a thing was on paper.

"What do you think it means?" Rose asked.

"I think Larson, Bennett, and the P.C., if he knows, are insulating themselves from this case. If it blows up, they can say 'Gee whiz, I didn't know a thing about it.' "

"You mean something like Ollie North and company?"

"Yeah, something like that."

"Except instead of Fawn Hall, we have Luis Velez."

"Very funny."

"You're right. It's not funny. What do you think we should do about it?"

"I think we should open a case folder and start pumping out some paper."

"What if Larson says he doesn't want any paper on this?"

"We keep copies for ourselves—in a safe place."

Rose, like most cops, knew that putting information on paper could either help you or hurt you. In this case it could only help. "Okay, when we get back to the office we'll start the paper flowing."

Nathan Pickett's office on Pitkin Avenue was in a part of Brooklyn that had long since given up functioning as a neighborhood. Many of the surrounding buildings were burned and gutted; the result of arson-for-profit schemes. Almost every block had its record store with outside speakers blaring the latest soul record at ear-shattering levels day and night.

Thriving smoke shops, which ostensibly sold cigarettes, candy, and newspapers but made their money from the sale of illegal drugs, were in evidence everywhere. Knots of unemployed young men loitered on street corners with little else to do but drink beer and watch the hookers and pushers compete for whatever cash flow was available on the street.

When neighborhood women ventured out to go shopping, they hurried along, looking neither left nor right, and clutched their handbags like determined fullbacks running for daylight. They followed invisible but well-worn paths from home to supermarket to church. These streets were not for idle wandering.

Storefront churches, almost as numerous as smoke shops, were the only peaceful havens for the people trapped in this hostile environment. Every night the infectious sounds of singing, electric guitars, and tambourines wafted through the stagnant air of this forlorn urban wilderness, creating a joyful noise.

Pickett's storefront office had formerly been a barbershop. The old mirrors still hung on the wall, one of which had a sign urging men to use Wildroot Creme Oil. The only furniture in the reception room consisted of a desk and several metal folding chairs on which constituents sat patiently, waiting to speak to their duly elected representative about not enough housing, too much crime, and the plight of assorted loved ones in jail. Pickett's private office was a small cubicle, overflowing with correspondence and, seemingly, every congressional and state government report ever published on fair housing and urban development. It was into this cramped office that Pickett led the two lieutenants.

Shannon studied the man who had become the nemesis of the police department and wondered what the senator's angle was. Was he another charlatan bent on bilking the people he purported to represent, or was he what he claimed to be—a champion of minority causes?

"Sit down where you can, gentlemen." Pickett eased back in a well-worn leather chair. "What may I do for you?" His demeanor was business-like but not unfriendly.

Shannon began. "We're investigating a possible death threat against you."

Pickett's eyebrows went up. "Possible? Don't you know for sure?" His smile was mocking.

"No one was specifically identified," Rose interjected. "We—"

"Well, gentlemen, I can do better than that. I receive several death threats a week, and they mean *me* because they have told me so to my face." He took off his glasses and wiped them with a handkerchief. "You white folks might not believe it, but there are some blacks in this community who would like to see me dead. You see, I don't just harass the police department and the mayor's office, I also go after the drug pushers and the slumlords." He put his glasses back on. "Alas, greed knows no color."

"Have you received any death threats you would consider out of the ordinary?" Shannon asked.

"No, Lieutenant, just the ordinary garden-variety death threat."

Shannon flushed at the sarcasm. "Have you noticed anything unusual? Strange phone calls to your office? Strangers hanging around your home or office? Anything like that?"

"Tell me, Lieutenant, why is the Chief of Detectives office interested in this? I thought this sort of thing was under the purview of the Intelligence Division?"

Shannon, surprised at Pickett's knowledge of police procedures, re-minded himself to be extra careful about what he said. "That's true," he answered. "The Intelligence Division does investigate these threats, but the information was developed by the bureau, so we're doing the preliminary. If there's anything to it, we'll turn it over to Intel."

"I see," Pickett said. But Shannon wasn't sure he bought it. "I am touched by the police department's concern for my safety, but"—Pickett's mocking smile flashed again—"I can assure you, gentlemen, that although there are several people in this city who would like to see me dead—including, perhaps, your own police commissioner—no one is actually trying to kill me. Now if there's nothing else, I have a roomful of people waiting to see me." The senator stood. The meeting was over.

Shannon handed him his card. "If you see or hear anything, please give us a call."

Casually, Pickett tossed the card on top of a stack of papers. "Thank you, Lieutenant. You'll be the first to know."

All through the interview Rose fought against a nagging guilt. He couldn't get out of his mind the image of Pickett in the cross hairs of an assassin's sights. He wanted to tell the arrogant son of a bitch that this wasn't the idle threat of a disgruntled constituent; that he might be the next target of a well-organized group that had already succeeded in carrying out several executions. At the door he turned to Pickett and said simply, "Take care, Senator."

The sincerity in the tall lieutenant's eyes startled Pickett. He'd had many dealings with the police over the years, and his relationship with them had always been adversarial. He had his job to do, and they had theirs.

"Thank you, Lieutenant, I will."

On the way back to headquarters Shannon surprised Rose by suggesting they stop somewhere for a drink. It was the first time he'd suggested doing anything after working hours. "I know just the place," Rose said.

MCSORLEY'S OLD ALE HOUSE LOOKED LIKE IT HAD BEEN CAUGHT IN a time warp. Opened in 1854, it was the oldest saloon in the United States, and its appearance had changed little. If a patron of a hundred years ago were to walk into McSorley's today, he'd feel right at home. A potbellied stove squatted among an assortment of scarred wooden tables and chairs scattered across the sawdust-covered floor. Clumps of dust, probably as old as the saloon itself, clung to unused gaslight fixtures hanging over the bar. The walls were covered with assorted memorabilia of every description, from old campaign buttons to World War One helmets.

They squeezed past a rowdy bunch of college kids and settled into a corner table. Rose ordered four mugs of dark ale, and they sat back to watch the diversity of characters parade in and out. Most were college students from nearby Cooper Union, but there were also a smattering of business types and old-timers from the neighborhood—anachronisms in their own saloon—who sat in corners watching the interlopers and muttering to themselves.

The ale went down smoothly, and soon the small, initial-gouged table was littered with empty mugs. "This place used to be better when they didn't allow women in," Rose pronounced morosely.

"When was that? During the Civil War?"

"No. They changed the rules sometime in the seventies. Goddamn women took it to court," Rose said in disgust.

"I thought you were a liberal and an advocate of women's lib?"

"I am. I was. I don't know." The ale was causing Rose to add more *s*'s to his words than necessary. "Sometimes women go too far, that's all." He drained his mug. "They used to ring that gong behind the bar."

"Who?"

"The bartender."

"Why?"

"To get rid of the women, naturally."

Shannon was having a hard time following the conversation. "What women?" he asked.

Rose looked at him as if he were obtuse. "Women weren't allowed in here," he said with exaggerated slowness. "But sometimes one would wander in and the bartender would ring the gong and everyone would yell, 'No women allowed!' You should have seen their faces. They didn't know whether to shit or go blind!"

"They really did that?"

"Yeah, but now they can come in anytime they want. The place isn't the same." Rose looked around the room as though seeing it for the first time. "This place is depressing. Come on, I'll take you to a classier joint."

For the next several hours they crisscrossed Manhattan. After a couple of drinks in one bar, one of them would remember an even better joint. After the fifth bar they lost track of how many good joints they'd been in.

It was almost three in the morning when they staggered into a dark cheaters' bar hidden in the bowels of SoHo. Except for a few couples huddled in booths and some singles strung out along the bar, the place was deserted. They sat down unsteadily and ordered. When the drinks were served, Shannon raised his glass. "Here's to the CIA, the FBI, IAD, and the TDL."

"I'm not drinking to the JDL," Rose growled.

"TDL," Shannon corrected. "Transparent Detective Lieutenants. That's us."

"Oh, I get it. No one sees us, so we don't exist."

"You got that right. And we're gonna stay invisible unless this investigation turns sour. Then we'll become visible so they can fire our asses."

Rose nodded solemnly. "Yeah. I can see the front page of the *Post*: 'Two Lieutenants Involved in Major Police Scandal!' "

" 'Chief of Detectives Shocked at Subordinate's Behavior!' "

Rose stood up unsteadily. " 'P.C. Forms Task Force to Stamp Out Incompetent Lieutenants!' "

Shannon rose. " 'Two Lieutenants Drummed Out of the Department and Await Execution!' "

Rose looked at Shannon blearily. "I think you've gone too far."

"Yeah, I guess you're right. Besides, if they used rookies for the firing squad, they'd never hit us."

"Not unless they dressed us like a couple of innocent civilians. Then they'd get us right between the fucking running lights!" They cackled and thumped the bar.

After a moment Rose grew serious again. "What are your career aspirations in the job, Brian?" Rose had some trouble with the word "aspirations."

Shannon squinted at his fuzzy reflection in the mirror behind the bar. "To get out of this job with my ass and pension intact, I guess."

"Oh come now, Lieutenant. Let's not be so modest. I'm sure you have higher aspir . . . *goals* than that."

It was Shannon's turn to become serious. "I thought I'd make captain, but I blew the last test. So that's that." Then he added, "I've got my twenty. I should get out. What about you?"

"I didn't blow the last test. In fact I expect to get made soon." He chuckled. "I haven't even told my wife I passed. She doesn't like the police department and she doesn't like policemen. Thinks I oughta grow up."

Shannon felt a momentary stab of envy when Rose said he'd passed the captain's exam. "When you get promoted, I guess you'll stay in IAD? Once a scumbag always a scumbag."

Rose waved his hand in dismissal. "I won't respond to that character assassination. Actually, I think I'm ready to assume command of a precinct."

Shannon snorted. "You're drunker than I thought. With all the shit going on in precincts, a C.O.'s career expectancy is about the same as a platoon leader's in combat."

"Nonsense, I'm a born leader of men. I think—"

"You're a born bullshit artist, Rose." Shannon ordered another round. "You got any kids?"

"Naw. We can't afford them right now. Besides, my wife's career is on the upswing and she has no time to think about that now."

"Shit," Shannon said. "I can't afford them either, but I got one." His voice dropped. "I'm supposed to say something about them being worth it, but I'm not sure anymore. Kids are a big headache."

"Yeah, I guess so." Then Rose said, "My wife is a professional woman."

Shannon set his beer down very carefully. "She's a hooker?"

"A *professional* woman, for Chrissake. She's taken an oath to uphold the principles of Jane Fonda and Gloria Steinem in spite of rain, hail, sleet, husband's wishes, and the maternal instinct."

"You should be proud." Shannon drained his drink. "My wife wants me out of the job."

"Why don't you? You got your time."

Shannon chewed on that for a bit. "I like the job, but I got a feeling someone's greasing the skids and I'm going out of this job on my ass."

"Listen," Rose said, putting his arm around him. "I'll take care of you. I'll be your rabbi. When I get my command, you can be my desk officer."

"You know, for an IAD hump, you're not a bad guy. But if I go out of this job, you're right behind me."

Rose chuckled. "I guess so. That will make my wife very happy."

"Why is it, when we meet our wives they think being a cop is hot shit, but the minute you're married they start lobbying to get you out of the job?"

Rose snorted. "That's because we feed them a lot of bullshit about us being knights in shining armor protecting the world against the forces of evil. After they marry us, they find out that fighting evil is not a nine-to-five job and the forces of evil get paid a hell of a lot more than we do. Their gallant knights come home battered and fall asleep in front of the TV with a half-finished can of beer. And if that's not enough to piss off the wives, they know in the back of their minds that their pathetic little knights might be blown away someday by some wacky son of a bitch strung out on drugs."

"I sort of made a promise to my wife that I'd get out after twenty, but I don't want to."

"Why not?"

Shannon shook his head in bewilderment. "I'll be goddamned if I know."

Rose became serious. "What I said before about fighting crime and being exposed to danger didn't apply to me. This job has been a picnic for me—easy assignments, mostly staff jobs. My wife never had to be afraid of me getting killed. The only way I could have gotten killed was if the elevator in police headquarters collapsed or I fell into a Xerox machine."

Out of the corner of his eye he watched for Shannon's reaction to his confession. Once, in the locker room, he'd glimpsed Shannon's uniform jacket and saw a chest full of medals, including the Police Combat Cross. The job had not been a picnic for Brian Shannon. Apparently he'd spent most if not all of his time as a very active cop, and the disparity in their backgrounds made Rose uncomfortable.

He expected Shannon to ridicule him once again for being an IAD desk jockey, but instead Shannon said, "What the hell, Rose. Everybody's gotta be someplace. Let's have another drink."

Relieved, Rose resumed the conversation. "Rachel wants me out too. She doesn't understand the job. To be more precise, she doesn't give a flying fuck for police work."

Before Rose could say more, he was interrupted by a voice.

"Excuse me," she said, waving her Virginia Slim like a magic wand in Rose's face. "Do you have a light?"

Rose tried his best to focus on the owner of the voice, a diminutive, chubby blonde in her early forties. Her electric-blue eye makeup had faded, but her teased hair was still as rigid as a football helmet. She wore a multicolored dress that looked like it had been designed by a hyperactive child with an unlimited supply of fingerpaint. "Sure," he said, reaching for a soggy pack of matches.

"Thanks," she purred, and exhaled a cloud of blue smoke in his face. "I'm Roxanne, and this"—she beckoned to her friend—"is Leslie."

Leslie, wobbling unsteadily on death-defying high spiked heels—the kind featured in the S&M magazine ads—was about the same age and height as Roxanne, but she had her friend by a good twenty pounds. "Hi," she said breathlessly, rubbing up against Shannon. "What do you fellows do?"

"About what?" Shannon asked.

"About your work." She batted her long eyelashes. Shannon noticed the left one was beginning to slip. "What's your career?"

"We're in shit," Rose told her.

"Pardon?" The eyelashes stopped batting.

"Fertilizer. You know, manure."

"Oh, that must be very exciting." Leslie tried to look excited. "What company are you with?"

"TDL Incorporated," Shannon answered.

"Really?" Leslie looked puzzled. "I don't think I ever heard of it. Is it on the big board? My ex is a stockbroker. I know all those technical terms."

"Nope," Rose said. "This shit's over the counter. I'm the president and he's the vice-president."

"Oh, really?" Roxanne's eyes lit up. What luck! So far this evening she'd met two fags, and one wimp who had to go home to his wife. But now, at this late hour, a president and a vice-president! Things were looking up.

"Do you come here often?" Leslie asked Shannon, who just stared at her, unable to believe she'd actually used that old cliché.

"We're here on a very hush-hush project," Rose whispered.

"Really?" Leslie batted her eyes. "You can tell us. We won't tell a soul."

Rose looked at Shannon. "What do you think?"

Shannon shrugged. "What the hell. Why not?"

"Remember, ladies," Rose cautioned, "this is strictly confidential." They nodded vigorously. "I guess you know that New York City has developed a strain of super rats?"

"Tell me about it," Roxanne said in disgust. "I was married to one for eighteen months."

Rose went on. "There are at least sixteen million in the city."

Leslie squirmed. "Ugh! They're so vile, with their beady little eyes."

"Well," Rose continued, "we've done some research and discovered that New York City rats produce shit that is eighty percent more potent— fertilizer-wise—than the best cow manure in the world. We plan to capture them, breed the little suckers, and start a rat-shit farm that will revolutionize the fertilizer industry."

The girls were speechless.

"Not only that"—Shannon was getting into the spirit of things—"recent tests conclusively demonstrate that rat shit produces the biggest vegetables you ever saw. Grapes the size of cantaloupes! Potatoes bigger than watermelons! You'd have to nuke 'em to get them any bigger!"

"My God," the women said in unison.

"And that's not all." Rose didn't miss a beat.

"There's more?" Leslie asked, wide-eyed.

Rose leaned forward and whispered one word. "Fur."

"Fur?" she echoed.

"Yep. As the old ones die, we skin them and make fur coats out of them."

"Gross! Who would wear a coat made from dead rats?"

"It's all in the marketing," Rose said confidently. "There's nothing more disgusting than a live mink. Have you ever seen one, Roxanne?"

"Just on a coat."

"Rats with nice fur, that's all minks are." He stood up and lurched against the bar. "It's all in the marketing. Who ate the first clam? The first lobster? The first eel?"

"I don't know," she answered, totally confused. "I have no idea."

"Neither do I," Rose admitted. "But the important thing is that someone ate those disgusting things because of a good sales pitch. Imagine a Neanderthal wife slaving over a hot fire in a smoky cave. She serves her husband a half-dozen clams on a rock. He looks at them and makes a face. 'You expect me to eat that?' 'Yeah,' she says. 'Eat! Enjoy! They'll put a little lead in your pencil!' "

"Is that where that saying came from?" Leslie was in awe.

"Why did he eat something as disgusting as a clam?"

"Why?" Shannon blurted out, completely taken in by Rose's sales pitch.

"Marketing," Rose said triumphantly. "You can sell anything if you market it correctly."

"This is true," Roxanne said. "My ex packaged himself very well. He always wore eight-hundred-dollar suits and expensive jewelry, but under it all he was a no-good louse."

"There you go. If we market this the right way, we'll make rat coats the designer craze of the decade. Rats, as you probably know, are of the genus *Rattus,* but they used to be called *Mus.* I like the sound of that better. More cuddly, don't you think? We're going to market the coats under the trade name 'Fun-mus coats.' Catchy, isn't it? And the best part is they're not an endangered species, so we won't have the environmentalists on our case."

"Amazing!" Roxanne said, completely exhausted by the overwhelming sales pitch for rat coats and feces.

When the bar closed, they went uptown to an after-hours joint where they continued to drink and listen to Rose make up even more outrageous stories.

It was almost dawn when Rose announced gallantly that they would drive the girls to their homes in Secaucus. But after a heated discussion with Shannon, it was deemed unwise to venture into the wilds of New Jersey in their present advanced state of inebriation. As Shannon explained it, "If we get bagged by our own guys, we're probably okay—that is, if you don't shoot your mouth off about being in IAD, for Chrissake! But in New Jersey? Who knows what those friggin' foreign cops will do?"

Rose had to agree. Besides, in his condition he wasn't sure he could find New Jersey. At the corner of Second Avenue and Sixty-third Street they poured the girls into a taxi after promising to notify them the moment the Fun-mus coats went into production.

They stood on the snow-sprinkled sidewalk long after the cab had disappeared from sight down Second Avenue. The only activity at this early hour was a small herd of private sanitation trucks noisily feeding on the city's refuse.

"Well"—Rose pulled his collar up against the early morning breeze—"I guess we'll call it a night."

"Yeah." Shannon looked up at the sky, which was beginning to turn a dirty pink. He was very tired and a headache had begun to throb in his temples.

Suddenly they heard singing, and turned to watch a bag lady carrying an American flag, marching down the middle of Second Avenue singing "The Star-Spangled Banner." Taxi drivers whizzing past gave her the finger and yelled cheerful obscenities. A radio car with red lights flashing pulled up alongside her. The driver and the woman had a brief conversation, then the two cops got out of their car and, in the middle of Second Avenue, snapped to attention and saluted the flag. Satisfied, the woman marched onto the sidewalk and disappeared around the corner. The two cops, to the hearty applause of a handful of cabdrivers, got back in their car and drove away.

"What do you think about not telling Pickett?" Shannon asked Rose.

"I think it sucks."

"Yeah, me too."

"Pickett is one arrogant son of a bitch, isn't he?"

"He sure is." Shannon stopped to watch a homeless man with a supermarket cart piled high with junk rummage through a garbage can.

"Rose, we gotta bust this case open soon."

"Yeah, I know. Let's go home and get some sleep."

BY THE TIME THEY WANDERED INTO THE OFFICE THE NEXT DAY, IT was after eleven. Velez, his arms folded, glared at the hung over lieutenants accusingly. "You guys are a disgrace," he said indignantly. "Look at the two of you. Hung over, bloodshot eyes, and you smell like a couple of bar rags. I can't work under these conditions!''

''Shut up,'' Shannon mumbled, and with trembling fingers struggled to remove the lid from his coffee container.

Rose sat down and groaned. ''Velez,'' he said hoarsely, ''try not to let the computer whistle or beep for the rest of the day. Okay?''

''You know what really pisses me off?'' Velez said. ''I was here on time this morning and no one was here to see it!''

$$\mathbf{26}$$

IT WAS GETTING TOWARD FIVE O'CLOCK WHEN SHANNON AND ROSE, who were just beginning to shake off the effects of their hangovers, were summoned into Larson's office. Bennett was already seated.

"Well," Larson said, dispensing with the formalities, "what've you found out?"

"Not much," Shannon said. "Pickett didn't have much to say. He hasn't noticed anything out of the ordinary. At least nothing he wanted to tell us about."

Larson slouched behind his desk, hands cupped in front of him like a gambler playing his cards close to the vest, and eyed the two lieutenants with unbridled hostility. He didn't trust either of them. Shannon, at least, was a detective, but he had a crusader gleam in his eye that made him dangerous. Larson's eyes shifted to Rose, always with the bullshit smile. It was hard to know what was going on behind it. A real sneaky bastard. Typical IAD type. "What else have you got?"

"That's it."

Larson carefully lined up the blotter with the edge of his desk. "If someone is setting up Pickett, they have to follow him. Tail him. See if anyone's watching him."

Shannon and Rose exchanged glances. Larson was suggesting a surveillance which, if done correctly, would require a lot of manpower. "We'll need some help with that, Chief," Shannon said.

Larson's face reddened. "What do you suggest I do, Lieutenant, set up a goddamn task force like we did for the Son of Sam investigation? Should I publish a directive requesting all detectives interested in hunting down murdering cops apply here?"

He got up and poured a cup of coffee, but didn't offer any to the three men. "I thought I'd made it clear. This investigation is off-limits. No one else is to get involved."

"A proper surveillance with only the two of us is impossible." Shannon struggled to keep the anger out of his voice.

Larson flicked some dust from his lapel. "What about the P.R. cop? What's his name?"

"Velez?"

Again the two lieutenants exchanged looks. Velez had been in on the investigation from the beginning, but he'd mostly collected information for the computer.

"I'm not sure Velez will want to get involved in this," Shannon said cautiously.

Larson's eyes bulged. "What is this? A fucking democracy?" He slammed his well-manicured hand on the polished desk. "This is the New-York-fucking-City-Police-Department! He'll goddamn do what he's told."

Later, back in their office, Rose tilted his chair against the wall for a better view of Shannon, who was once again trying to pace the length of the tiny room. "That son of a bitch," Shannon mumbled over and over. He looked at Rose accusingly. "Why didn't you say something in there?"

Rose snapped his chair forward. "I have nothing to say to that Neanderthal."

"That's great!" Shannon threw himself into a chair. "I've got a boss who'd love to dump me out of the bureau, and a partner who doesn't want to get involved." He dug the last cigarette out of a crumpled pack. "Alex," he said, lighting the bent cigarette, "there's no room for spectators here."

That, Rose noted, was the first time Shannon had referred to him as his partner and called him by his first name. Evidently, he'd decided it was time to draw the wagons in a circle, and anyone who could fire a gun would be welcome. "I didn't say I didn't want to get involved. I said I wanted nothing more to do with that schmuck. If we're going to break this case, it will be in spite of Larson.''

Shannon got up and closed the door. ''We're being stonewalled,'' he whispered.

Rose was instantly alert. ''What do you mean?''

''Who else knows about this case? Do you think the P.C. knows?''

''I don't know,'' Rose said. Under normal circumstances the P.C. was kept informed of the progress of all important investigations, but these weren't normal circumstances. ''You may have a point. I called Percell yesterday; he's the one who put me here in the first place. I've always gotten along with him, but when I tried to tell him about Larson's attitude, he cut me off.''

''What did he say?''

''He said I was assigned to the Chief of Detectives office now and any problems I had should be ironed out there. I got the real distinct impression he didn't want to hear from me again. In fact I thought I heard the sound of the umbilical cord being cut.''

''What did you tell Percell about the case?''

''You still don't trust me, do you?''

''You didn't answer my question.''

''I didn't tell him anything. But the fact that he didn't ask me leads me to believe he knows something about it.''

Shannon opened a fresh pack and lit another cigarette. ''I don't trust Larson.''

''I don't trust him either. He's a devious bastard.''

''We're going to have to watch what we say to him from now on.''

''Agreed. Now where does that leave us?'' Rose asked.

''Without a Chief of Detectives we can trust, it leaves us in the peculiar position of trying to put one wagon in a circle.''

Just then Velez came back into the office. ''Hey, what's with the long faces? Run out of names for me or what?''

''Sit down,'' Shannon said. ''We gotta talk.''

Velez pulled up a chair. ''Uh-oh, this sounds serious.''

Shannon came right to the point. ''Larson wants us to tail Pickett and he wants you to help.''

Velez's smile faded. ''Hey, wait a minute, guys. It's one thing to play with the computer, it's another to go out in the street and actually work on other cops. Why don't you get a cop from IAD? All those hard-ons got gold shields. Let 'em earn their grade money.''

''Larson doesn't want anyone else in on this. Unfortunately, you happened to be here when it started.''

''Bullshit, Loo. I came here to work on the computer.'' He turned to Shannon. ''Isn't that right?''

"You're right, Luis. But I don't call the shots around here."

Velez kicked his chair back. "Fuck this! I'm not getting involved in this bullshit. You can stick this job up your ass." He pointed a finger at Rose. "You got a shitload of cops in IAD with gold shields chasing real cops for taking free coffee, and you want me to hunt other cops? No way, man!"

Shannon put his hand on Velez's shoulder. "Take the rest of the day off and think it over."

There was a strained silence as Velez prepared to leave. When he got to the door, Rose said, "Remember, Luis, we're talking about murderers. Just because they carry a shield doesn't alter that fact."

Velez turned. "I don't dispute that, Loo. Someone oughta catch those dudes and put them in the can. But not me." The door slammed behind him.

The next morning Velez came in unusually subdued. There was none of the usual banter about last night's nocturnal conquests. Even more disturbing, he was on time. He mumbled a good morning and went straight to his desk with his usual coffee and bagel. Rose shot a furtive glance at Shannon, who silently raised his eyebrows. Velez finished his coffee, crumpled the bag, and arched it into the wastebasket. "Two points," Rose said lightly. But there was no response from Velez.

For the next two hours the office was ominously silent except for the soft clicking of the keys as Velez queried the computer. Finally, without taking his eyes off the screen, he said, "Okay, I'll do it. But I'll tell you something, Lieutenant Shannon. When this is over, I'm getting out of this fucking job. It sucks."

"Luis," Shannon said quietly, "we're all up to our asses in alligators. Wait'll things calm down before you make any drastic decisions."

Velez studied the tile floor. "What do you want me to do?"

JOSEPH MARA, SITTING IN HIS CHAUFFEUR-DRIVEN OLDSMOBILE AS it sped up the East River Drive toward his home in Riverdale, had a lot on his mind. He stared through the tinted glass, oblivious to the boat traffic on the river, and reflected on his troubling meeting with Larson two days earlier. He still couldn't believe the incredible allegations of cops involved in murder and drugs. Especially in NET!

The multibillion-dollar drug business had become the bane of every police chief in the country. Not only was it responsible for the soaring crime rate, but the temptation of big money corrupted police officers—and in the process wrecked the careers of more than one police commissioner.

The involvement of police officers in illegal drug activity was the ultimate nightmare for a police administrator. No one in law enforcement would admit it publicly, but there was simply too much drug money available; it could compromise, or buy outright, people in the Criminal Justice system. Mara took little comfort in knowing that lawyers, judges, and legislators were just as susceptible to bribery as his police officers. Cops, he knew from sad experience, made the best headlines.

At the last International Associations of Police Chiefs conference he'd attended, that was all they talked about—not in their speeches and press releases, but in hushed tones over drinks in a quiet bar, away from the prying eyes and ears of the press.

J. Edgar Hoover knew the odds against taking on the Mafia and the drug problem. For years he refused to officially acknowledge the existence of the Mafia for one reason only—he knew he couldn't defeat them. In such a contest, second best is not good enough. Besides, Hoover got a lot more public-relations mileage chasing Communists and the KKK.

Unfortunately, the Police Commissioner of New York City didn't have the luxury of denying the existence of a drug problem. That was why he ordered the creation of NET. He wanted a special group of hard-charging policemen to hit the top-echelon drug dealers where it hurt most—their pocketbooks. Stone, his youngest and most able superior officer, was the perfect choice to lead the assault. A man on the way up, a man with unlimited potential, he had everything to lose. If anyone was immune to the allure of drug money, Mara was willing to bet his pension on Stone. But from what Larson had told him, NET cops might be involved; maybe even Patrick Stone. If Stone turned out to be the "Chief," it would represent a serious error in judgment on his part, and one that would be fatal in this unforgiving city.

Once again he reviewed the unhappy litany of possibilities: a full-scale investigation with arrests, ugly headlines, and the likelihood of a special investigation commission. And what about Nathan Pickett, who might be the next target? If Pickett was warned, he'd use the information to his own advantage. On the other hand, if he wasn't warned and he was killed . . . Mara didn't even want to consider the depressing consequences. Never mind becoming the mayor of this city. He'd be lucky to get a job as a security guard in K mart.

Tonight he was going to a black-tie dinner at the Waldorf, where he'd rub shoulders with the movers and shakers of New York politics. He'd been looking forward to the opportunity, until Larson's visit. Now he had more important and immediate issues to attend to. He had to make some crucial decisions, but how could he when there were so many unanswered questions? How many cops were involved? How high up in the department? How many murders had they committed? The Police Commissioner stared glumly out the window and, for the first time since he'd arrived in New York, wished he was back in Philadelphia.

*   *   *

ROSE TOSSED A FLIER ON SHANNON'S DESK. "YOU WANTED TO TALK to Captain Stone? Here's your chance."

The flier announced a retirement dinner for Assistant Chief Dennis Whalen, the Commanding Officer of the Organized Crime Control Bureau.

Rose tapped the paper. "That's going to be a big racket. Whalen's been on the job since they were using muzzle-loading pistols. Everyone will be there—including, I'm sure, Captain Patrick Stone."

Shannon's eyes dropped to the bottom of the flier. "December seventh? That's tonight, for Chrissake! I promised Eileen I'd be home for dinner."

"Don't look at me," Rose said. "I'm IAD. I'd stand out like a nun at an orgy." And he grinned at the sour-faced Shannon.

FOR GENERATIONS, STARRY-EYED BRIDES-TO-BE FLOCKED TO NOBLE'S, one of the largest and best-known catering halls in the Bronx, where, surrounded by the glitter of gaudy chandeliers, tacky red wallpaper, and cascading waterfalls, they were willing to spend their dowries on shamefully expensive wedding receptions for a couple of hundred relatives who barely spoke to one another.

But starry-eyed brides weren't the only ones who flocked to Noble's. Cops, from all over the city, came to run their retirement rackets here. They didn't come for the circular staircases and waterfalls; their reasons were much more prosaic—Noble's had no ties to the New York Mafia families.

Brian Shannon arrived late and in a lousy mood. His Rabbit had come to a dead stop on the Whitestone Bridge, and he had to be towed off. It was half an hour before he got the damn thing started again. The parking lot was full, so he had to park three blocks away. Outside the catering hall two policemen were busy directing traffic. Assigning a uniform traffic cop to one of these affairs was an unofficial barometer of the retiree's prestige and popularity. Deputy Chief Dennis Whalen, a very popular man, was going out a two-cop chief.

The noisy cocktail party was almost over. Shannon, who knew most of those present, grabbed a drink and worked his way around the packed room. Between snatches of half-listened-to conversations he scanned the crowd. He was beginning to think Stone hadn't come when he spotted him by the bar telling a joke to a ring of appreciative listeners.

Later, he watched Stone in a brief conversation with the Police Commissioner. Decked out in a tux, Mara had stopped by on his way to a dinner downtown to wish Whalen well. When it was time to sit down for dinner, Shannon tried to get a seat at Stone's table, but there were none available.

As the waiters were serving dessert, Shannon saw Stone get up and go to the bar. Shannon followed. By the time he caught up to the captain, Stone was talking to Detective Freddy Leahy, the dinner-committee chairman.

Leahy, who tipped the scales at over three hundred pounds, was a first-grade detective with thirty years in the department—the last twenty-nine as a detective. As far as anyone could tell, the only function of "the Perle Mesta of the P.D." seemed to be running promotion and retirement rackets for the bosses in the department. Leahy was on a first-name basis with everyone in the department above the rank of captain.

"Hey, Brian, how you doing?"

"Good, Freddie. As usual, you're running a great racket. I almost didn't get a ticket."

Freddie belched. "This one was easy. Everyone loves Denny Whalen. With some of the others, let me tell ya, it ain't so easy. You don't know what I went through for Ray Dudley's racket last year. You know what a miserable fuck he was. I thought I was going to have to drag people in off the streets. Ya know, like that parable about the wedding feast? No shit. But at the last minute people started buying tickets. Even so, I coulda held his racket in a fucking phone booth and had enough room left over for the Mormon Tabernacle Choir!"

He threw an arm around Stone. "Now *this* guy will be different. I'll have to run his racket in Shea Stadium!"

Stone patted Leahy's huge belly and grinned at Shannon. "Not yet, Freddy. I intend to be around for a long time."

Leahy, who'd been drinking all afternoon while he supervised the dinner preparations, regarded Stone with glassy eyes. "I'm glad to hear that, Pat. Let the fucking Dudleys retire and have heart attacks on Florida golf courses. The job needs bosses like you. Hey, you guys know each other? Brian Shannon, Captain Pat Stone, the C.O. of that Rambo narc squad."

Shannon shook Stone's hand and grinned. "Captain. I've heard a lot of good things about NET. I saw Blackburn's interview the other day."

Stone rolled his eyes. "That son of a bitch caused me a lot of grief because of that interview. My phone rang before they were finished running the closing credits. I got a forthwith to the First Dep's office. I spent an hour convincing him I wasn't feeding Pickett information and that I wasn't going to do a guest appearance on Pickett's commission."

Leahy scowled. "That jig needs a swift kick in the balls." He motioned to the bartender. "What are you guys drinking?"

Both men ordered scotch. As the bartender reached for a bottle, Leahy slammed his ham-hock hand on the bar. "Hey, don't give me that rat-gut shit. I'm paying for top shelf, gimme top shelf."

The bartender, used to being abused by drunken cops, shrugged and reached for the Johnnie Walker Black.

"These fucking humps," Leahy whispered loud enough to be heard in the parking lot. "I pay for premium stuff and they're always trying to pour the cheap shit. You gotta watch these guys every fucking minute."

A burst of laughter distracted the fat detective, who looked like he was about to punch out the bartender. "The speeches are beginning." He tossed a twenty on the bar and headed unsteadily for the dining room. "I gotta get inside. Hey, you know what they're going to give Whalen? A fucking windshield!"

Shannon and Stone laughed. Everyone in the job knew the Whalen windshield story. Years ago, when he was a brand-new sergeant, he'd gotten involved in a stolen-car chase. Someone in the stolen car fired a shot at Whalen, who got so excited he fired six rounds through his own windshield.

Stone sat down on a stool. "I can do without all the bullshit speeches about what a great guy Denny Whalen is. Where do you work, Brian?"

Shannon, relieved that Stone didn't want to go back inside, pulled up a stool. "The Nineteenth squad, but I'm temporarily assigned to the Chief of Detectives office working on a felony-statistics project."

"You poor bastard, you're working for that hard-on Larson?"

"Bennett, actually. I don't see much of Larson."

"I know what you mean. At the Executive Development courses we refer to him as Lamont Cranston."

Stone seemed in no hurry to leave, but Shannon, worried about being interrupted, was anxious to ask his questions. "That was too bad about Cronin."

"Yeah. Walt was a good kid." Stone's face didn't change.

"He didn't have that much time in the job, did he?"

"Less than two years."

"There wasn't much in the papers, but I've been hearing bits and pieces about the case from the chief's office."

Stone appeared interested. "What are they saying?"

"Not much. So far the squad's come up with zilch."

Stone ordered another round.

"It's strange," Shannon continued. "When a cop gets killed, we usually come up with a perp in a couple of days."

"They still don't have any leads?"

"They're playing the disgruntled-prisoner angle—they think it might be someone he arrested."

"I doubt it. He didn't make that many arrests."

"Oh? I thought all your guys were heavy hitters."

"They are, but I used him mostly for undercover work. Cronin looked like he was sixteen. No one ever made him. He was so good, I rotated him among the other teams. As a result, he didn't make many arrests."

Shannon was puzzled. Nancy Cronin had said her husband was assigned to a team. "Well," he said, hiding his surprise, "that throws my theory out the window. The M.O. made me think of professionals. I figured it was a hit ordered by one of those wacky Colombian groups. There's a couple of people downtown who are hinting that Cronin might have been involved in narcotics.''

''That's bullshit.'' Stone's easygoing manner abruptly dissolved. ''Those useless assholes in Police Plaza automatically think anyone who works drugs has to be dirty.'' His anger dissipated as quickly as it materialized. ''Is IAD getting into it?''

''Not as far as I know. It's just talk from the desk-jockey sleuths.''

Stone shredded his napkin and rolled the pieces into balls. ''I'll tell you something. The job's programmed these young cops so they're afraid of their own shadow. When I took over NET, one of the toughest jobs I had was getting my people to forget about the goddamn *Patrol Guide* and just do the job.''

''I know what you mean. A precinct detective can't scratch his ass these days without submitting a DD5. We have inspections in a couple of times a year just to review case folders. It's a real pain in the ass.''

''The job's paranoid. Ever since the Knapp Commission, the brass have been off the wall. They've got more rules than Imelda Marcos has shoes. They've made it damn near impossible for a narc unit to operate efficiently, and the bastards know it. Narc cops can't operate like that. If we're going to keep up with the bad guys, we have to be flexible.''

''I hear you have a pack of real gung-ho people working for you. What's your secret?''

''NET's a special unit, Brian. We go after the big guys with everything we have. As a result, we've developed a reputation as a unit of incorruptible cops.'' Stone took a faded newspaper clipping out of his wallet. ''Look at that. The guy that wrote that story even compared me to Eliot Ness. Does that sound like an outfit where Walter Cronin, or any cop, could take money from the bad guys? I don't handcuff my men with a lot of bullshit rules. I guess the secret to my success is I don't act like a boss; I still think I'm a cop—they just pay me more, that's all.''

Shannon didn't want to press his luck, but he had one more question. ''What do *you* think happened to Cronin?''

There was a burst of applause, then they heard the unmistakable voice of Freddy Leahy asking Chief Whalen to step up to the podium.

''They must be getting ready to give Whalen the windshield.''

Shannon thought Stone was going to break off the conversation and go back inside, but he remained seated and appeared to be lost in thought.

''I've asked myself that same question a thousand times,'' the captain said finally. ''I don't know. Maybe it was mistaken identity. I honestly don't know.''

Shannon decided not to push his luck. He glanced at the neat row of paper balls Stone had lined up in front of him on the bar. ''I guess I'd better be getting back inside. It was good talking to you, Captain.''

"Same here, Brian. Maybe we'll run into each other before the next racket."

"Yeah," Shannon said. "Maybe."

THE GRAND BALLROOM AT THE WALDORF PULSED TO THE SOUNDS OF "New York, New York" played by the Lester Lanin orchestra. Women, dripping with diamonds that threatened to eclipse the gaudy chandelier above, nervously milled about, sipping champagne and praying that no one else showed up wearing the same one-of-a-kind designer gown, while powerful men, uncomfortable in their custom-tailored tuxedos, discussed Wall Street, New York City politics, and discreetly leered at the enticing cleavages of nubile young ladies.

The occasion was yet another in a long series of tedious, fund-raising dinners spawned by the upcoming elections. This dinner, sponsored by the New York Citizens for Justice, was attended by every politician and power broker in the city; each interested in shoring up his foundations in the tricky quagmire of city politics.

The clubhouse hacks were at a loss to understand the strange turns city politics had taken in the last two decades. They longed for the good old days of Tammany Hall and machine politics, when everyone knew exactly where he stood, whom to pay, and how much. But that was a simpler time. Now things were different. The old rules were out. In this age of women's rights, gay rights, and soap-box demagogues, political factions coalesced and divided with dizzying rapidity. Hispanics teamed up with Orthodox Jews, and blacks with women's rights groups. Yet, in the twinkling of an eye, these delicate alliances could be shattered as the mercurial sands of city politics shifted.

It was into this primordial political swamp that unhappy Police Commissioner Joseph Mara plunged. Like everyone else gathered here, Mara had come to cultivate his own political garden. Fortunately, he'd been given a ticket for that evening's event. Police commissioners didn't earn enough to pay $1,000 for the privilege of eating rubber chicken and plastic peas.

Until Larson's bombshell, the possibilities before Mara were limitless. A judgeship perhaps; even the mayor's office itself wasn't inconceivable. There was only one thing that could undermine these bright plans—a major scandal in the department. In spite of Nathan Pickett's ranting, corruption—the perennial nemesis of all police commissioners—was of little concern to him. He had daily briefings with his Chief of Inspectional Services, who assured him that corruption incidents were sporadic and definitely, thank God, not organized. The second biggest headache for a police commissioner was the PBA, the politically powerful police officers' union. In the past, the PBA had made life difficult for his predecessors. But Mara made it a practice to consult with the PBA on major policy decisions. In this way he effectively neutralized them—most of the time. The current exception being the flap over his controversial order on narcotics arrests, which had opened a can of worms with the PBA, thanks to Nathan Pickett.

Right after his meeting with Larson, Mara had called Mario Percell, his First Deputy Commissioner. Of all his high-ranking officers, Mara trusted only Percell. A man with thirty-five years service—most of it in the sensitive areas of internal investigations—Percell, a crusty veteran of department politics, was a good source of wisdom and advice. Percell enjoyed his powerful position and, best of all from Mara's point of view, exhibited no desire to become the Police Commissioner. It was comforting to know at least one man in the department who wasn't angling for his job.

Percell had counseled Mara to let things proceed as they'd been going. He pointed out that the investigation was under the direction of the Chief of Detectives, and if it should blow up, Larson would serve as a buffer for the P.C. Mara relished the idea of throwing Larson to the wolves before they got to him. Although he was a man of action, and bridled at doing nothing about so serious a matter, he reluctantly decided to go along with Percell's advice, at least for the time being. Larson had assured him that only two lieutenants were working on the case, and they'd been told to keep their mouths shut.

Surrounded by a phalanx of plainclothes detectives, Mayor Barry Kessel made his entrance into the ballroom. The mayor looked positively presidential as he waved and, in the tradition of Lyndon Johnson, "pressed the flesh." Even though Kessel was short and had the undistinguished profile of an ex-pug, Mara could feel the excitement sweep the ballroom like an electric charge.

All eyes had turned to the mayor. People jockeyed for position, hoping for a nod, a handshake, or even better—a remembered name. It has been said that the Mayor of New York City is the second most politically important job in the country. Looking at the effect the mayor had on a roomful of the most influential men in the city, Mara believed it. Perhaps, someday— His fantasy was interrupted by a voice from behind him.

"Commissioner Mara, how are you this evening?"

Mara turned to face Nathan Pickett. "Senator," he said calmly, "good to see you."

Pickett's handshake was firm. "I called your office today," he said, not letting go of Mara's hand. "The police manpower problem in Brooklyn has still not been resolved to my satisfaction. The precincts in the black neighborhoods are at least ten percent understaffed. Commissioner, you can't fight drugs in the street without troops."

"Now, Senator"—Mara assumed a soothing tone, but he was wondering how the hell Pickett knew *that,* when manpower figures were confidential— "you know the whole department is down in strength. I'm trying to utilize what resources I have."

Pickett's smile was thin and joyless. "That's bullshit and you know it. You're planning to shift more cops into the Orthodox Jewish community at the expense of blacks."

Goddamn it, Mara thought; he'd just approved those moves this morning. If he found the son of a bitch who was leaking information, he'd spend the rest of his career walking a foot post on Staten Island!

"Nothing has been finalized yet," the commissioner said evenly. "I've been meeting with my Chief of Personnel. We're formulating plans for freeing up police officers from administrative functions and returning them to street-patrol duties."

"Commissioner, this is December seventh. I'll give you until after Christmas. If I don't see results"—he leaned close to Mara—"I'll have a thousand black mothers with baby carriages demonstrating in front of every one of your station houses in Brooklyn. You'll have to bring in more policemen for that, won't you?" Pickett straightened Mara's tie. "Let me give you a word of advice, Joe. When my commission begins in a few weeks, the police department is going to be in for a very rough time. I suggest you do all that you can between now and then to make the department look like it's serious about fighting drugs." Without waiting for a response, he turned and walked away.

Until this afternoon, Mara hadn't believed that Pickett knew anything damaging to the department. But now he wasn't so sure. His thoughts churning, he found his table and introduced himself to the others already seated, a *New York Times* executive and his bored wife, a deputy commissioner buried somewhere in Human Resources, and two gays from the garment district.

Mara picked at his fruit cup and watched the mayor on the dais joke and wave to well-wishers in the audience. What would his reaction be when he was told? Mara sat stiffly in his tuxedo, wishing Nathan Pickett in hell.

27

IN THE BIG APPLE A VISITING PRESIDENT GETS THE FULL TREATMENT. Only the New York City Police Department could muster the manpower necessary to block off traffic at every intersection along the motorcade route from the Waldorf to the Wall Street Heliport—a distance of about five miles and three thousand cops.

With everyone in place, the Secret Service advance man had only to nod to his police counterpart and instantaneously hundreds of cross streets, highway entrances and exits were sealed off. Of course, such action played havoc with Manhattan's midday traffic. It took hours to unsnarl the mess, but it permitted the President to roar down the streets with sirens wailing and red lights flashing, unencumbered by the molasseslike traffic encountered by ordinary New York motorists. It was a genuine thrill, even for the President of the United States, to whiz past the throngs of New Yorkers who lined the motorcade route to get a glimpse of their distinguished visitor.

243

Unless it was a special political event, the mayor kept out of the spotlight on these occasions. But there was an election coming up next fall, and Kessel, flushed by the success of the previous night's fund-raiser at the Waldorf, decided to capitalize on the President's visit.

Presidential motorcades usually contained at least twenty vehicles carrying Secret Service agents, NYPD sharpshooters, presidential staff, press corps, and anyone else with enough influence to get themselves included. Because of this great number of vehicles, confused bystanders usually waved to the first limo they saw, which never contained the President. And on this day, thousands of New Yorkers inadvertently waved and cheered Mayor Barry Kessel, who was riding in the first limo. Hardly anyone noticed a smiling, waving President four limos back.

Barry Kessel stood back from the prop draft as the huge Marine helicopter revved its engines and ponderously lifted off for Newark Airport across the Hudson River. When he saw it was safely on its way, he turned and shouted above the roar of the fifteen police motorcycles. "Joe Mara!" He pointed to his waiting limo. "Take a ride with me."

Inside, with the windows rolled up, it was almost tranquil after the cacophony of sirens, motorcycles, and helicopters. Small and compact like the welterweight boxer he was in college, the mayor moved with the fluid movements of a much younger man. His broken nose, a souvenir of his boxing days at Columbia, endowed him with a pugnacious visage that had come to symbolize his aggressive, scrappy tenure as a two-term member of the House of Representatives.

Some wags claimed he'd won the tightly contested mayoralty race simply because he looked like the meanest son of a bitch in New York City. He may have been the meanest looking, but more than that, he was a savvy, pragmatic politician with a gift for juggling the city's diverse constituencies.

"Your guys did a terrific job," he said to the commissioner.

Mara was relieved. Providing security for a presidential visit was a nightmare. Joe Mara, like everyone else in law enforcement, would never forget Dallas. Protecting a President in a city of seven million people was almost impossible, even with the help and guidance of the Secret Service. A motorcade depended on so many people, and timing was critical. If anyone dropped the ball, it could be a disaster. As the one ultimately responsible for presidential security, the Police Commissioner was probably the only man in the city who hated presidential visits.

"One thing, Joe. You gotta do something about the appearance of these cops. Christ! Some of them look like they work for Pancho Villa! Don't you make them get haircuts anymore?"

Mara had to smile. It was just like Kessel to pay attention to such details. Nothing escaped him. He'd just hosted the President of the United States, but he could still find time to notice a couple of cops along the parade route who needed haircuts. "I'll have an order issued reminding them of our uniform and appearance standards."

Kessel nodded and looked out the window. "Look at the guys on the motorcycles. They look good. Really sharp. Why can't the rest of the force look like them?" Without waiting for an answer, he said, "Before, you said you wanted to talk about something important. Shoot."

Mara was reluctant to discuss such a delicate matter in the backseat of the mayor's limo. "Well, sir, this is serious, and may take some time. Perhaps you'd rather wait till we get back to your office."

"For Chrissake, Joe, there's no better place to hold a private conversation than right here. He can't hear us." He nodded toward the detective chauffeur on the other side of the Plexiglas partition. "You wanna beer?" Kessel leaned forward and took two beers out of the cooler disguised as a jump seat. The mayor, famous for his beer drinking, had had a personal dislike for Billy Carter because, as he once said, "That stupid son of a bitch gives beer drinkers a bad name, pissing all over the place like a damn stray dog." Even at formal dinners, while others sipped champagne or vintage wine, Kessel sucked on a beer. The last time he was at the White House for dinner, the President made sure Barry Kessel was served beer. They both got great press out of that one.

He held up the brown bottle. "New Amsterdam. Great taste, great color," he said, sounding like a beer commercial. "This is the way they used to make beer in this city in the old days. A shame. New York used to have a hundred and twenty-seven breweries. Now they're all gone." He shook his head. "Did you know that beer is mostly water? And New York has the best water in the country. Did you know that?"

Mara nodded, hoping the civics lesson would soon end.

"All those breweries gone. That's a lot of jobs." The mayor became silent, probably brooding on ways to lure the breweries back. "Okay, enough of that." He slapped Mara's knee. "What's up?"

Joe Mara knew the mayor didn't like to beat around the bush, so he hit it straight on. "The day before yesterday, the wife of Walter Cronin, that cop who was murdered in Rockaway, was interviewed." He paused. He was trying to find a delicate way to phrase it, but he couldn't think of one. "She said her husband was involved in drug protection and murder. And he wasn't the only one."

Kessel, who was about to take a drink, slowly lowered the bottle. His eyes fixed on Mara. "Frank," he said, pressing the intercom button, "take a slow ride up the East River Drive. I'll tell you when to turn back. Call the office and tell them where I am." Then he turned his attention to Mara. "Tell me everything, Joe. Don't leave anything out."

By the time the commissioner finished his story, the mayor was on his third beer. Except for some minor questions to clarify a point, he listened in attentive silence. Always the consummate politician, he betrayed no emotion. "Who else knows about this?"

"My First Deputy Commissioner, Mario Percell; Larson and his exec, and a couple of lieutenants."

At the mention of the Chief of Detectives' name, the mayor frowned. Even he was aware of Larson's penchant for prowling the political alleyways of the city. "If even a hint of this hits the papers, Joe, there will be big trouble."

"I agree. There are only two lieutenants working on this, and they report directly to Larson."

"What about reports? Paperwork? If it's on paper, you can bet your ass Nathan Pickett is going to get his hands on it."

"No problem. I've directed that nothing be put on paper and nothing through channels. I have daily briefings with Larson. Everything is verbal."

"By the way, Joe, have you found out who's been leaking information to Pickett?"

"IAD is still investigating, but they haven't come up with anything yet."

Kessel scowled. "Well, give them a kick in the ass. Pickett is using confidential department information to beat the shit out of you in the newspapers. It has to stop."

"I'll put more men on it."

Kessel was still thinking about the Chief of Detectives. "Larson is the last one in the department I'd want to know about this. He's always got his nose up some politician's ass. This is information he may be able to use someday."

"I don't think so, sir. I've told him in no uncertain terms that he's responsible for this investigation. He's in the middle of it. He has to keep his mouth shut."

Kessel looked grim. "Who are these people? How close are you to grabbing them?"

Mara hesitated, and Kessel, who got to where he was by an uncanny ability to read faces, said, "Jesus Christ! You don't know, do you?"

"We're working on it. We just received this information two days ago."

When Mara had first heard about it, his inclination was not to tell the mayor until he knew more. But then he began to worry about Pickett getting the story first. If the mayor was embarrassed, his P.C. might very well be out of a job. Still, he didn't relish telling the mayor—a man who asked endless questions—about a case he knew so little about. "We don't have anything solid yet," he continued, "but we think they may be in the Narcotics Enforcement Team."

"Isn't that the special group you set up a while ago?"

"Yes, sir."

"Christ, Joe, that's a handpicked unit! You had thousands of cops to choose from, and you picked thieves and murderers?"

"I try to—"

"Goddamn it. What about that young captain who runs the unit? What's his name?"

"Patrick Stone."

"What does he have to say about all this?"

Mara took a deep breath. "Again, we're not sure, but he may be part of it."

The mayor swore softly.

"They refer to the leader of the group as 'Chief,' " Mara went on. "Of course, Stone is only a captain." Mara knew he was sounding more ridiculous by the minute, but he continued. "The details are sketchy," he added lamely. "Mrs. Cronin couldn't tell us very much."

He saw the stony look on the mayor's face and added, "We're doing a thorough background check on everyone in NET, including Stone."

The mayor stared out the window. But Mara could see his jaw muscles tightening. "Nathan Pickett. Are you sure he's the target?"

"She didn't name him, but we're almost a hundred percent certain."

"Of all people. If we don't warn him, and something happens to him . . ." He didn't finish the sentence. "On the other hand, if we tell him, we give him my administration on a silver platter."

"For the time being I've decided not to tell Pickett he's a target. But we're keeping an eye on him to see if anyone's following him." Mara didn't know how to interpret the mayor's silence. "Do you think he should be told?"

"It's your call, Joe. Do what you think best. But I'll tell you, nothing had better happen to Nathan Pickett. The key to this problem is a quick resolution. If you get these people first, you may be able to turn a liability into an asset. On the other hand, if Pickett learns of this, he'll blow us out of the water." Kessel pressed the intercom. "Frank, back to the office."

They were passing through the South Bronx. The mayor stared out the window at row after row of burned-out, gutted buildings that looked like newsreels of Berlin after the war, and was reminded of Jimmy Carter's visit to the Bronx more than a decade ago. Carter had walked these streets and promised to rebuild the Bronx. But it was still rubble. Just like his promises.

The mayor broke the silence. "Joe, I don't have to tell you what this can do to a lot of careers in this town, including your own."

The commissioner was only too aware of the ramifications.

Kessel chose his words carefully. "This is a time bomb, Joe. If it's not managed properly, there will be a whole new set of players in the primaries next year. I put you in this job because it's the most sensitive commissioner-ship in the city and you are a competent man." He punched his fist into his open palm. "Find these guys fast and make an arrest. Then you stress the diligent, painstaking police work that went into getting these criminals. The voters in this town aren't very understanding when it comes to corrupt cops. It's going to require careful handling. Think about how you're going to deal with that."

"Maybe I should put more people on this?"

The mayor frowned. "I don't think that's a good idea. You can't afford a leak." Kessel reached for another beer, but the cooler was empty. "Damn, I gotta put a bigger cooler in this car."

On the drive back to City Hall, the mayor rambled on about city politics and the problems of governing a city like New York, but Mara wasn't listening. He was preoccupied assessing what the mayor had told him. Clearly, Kessel wanted quick results, but he didn't want to see anyone else involved in the investigation.

One other subtle fact hadn't eluded him; during the course of their talk the mayor had gone from "we" to "you."

THE ATMOSPHERE IN A POLICE DEPARTMENT FACILITY CAN BE DE-pressing enough in the daytime, but at night, without the distraction of ringing telephones, clicking typewriters, and constant chatter, the shabbiness of the surroundings is even more glaring. The ubiquitous bile-green paint, broken window shades, and cheap metal furniture did nothing to alleviate the sense of squalor. It was after midnight. The men from the four-to-twelve tour had gone home and the NET office was quiet.

Patrick Stone, reviewing arrest reports, watched a gloomy Hardy sitting at his desk in the outer office. "Hey, Tim," he called out, "is there any coffee left?"

Hardy glanced at the pot. "Dregs."

"If there's enough for two, come on in."

Hardy came in with two paper cups and sat down.

Stone took a sip of the hours-old coffee and made a face. It was bitter and lukewarm. "What's up, Tim?"

"I don't know, Chief. Things are such a mess now. I was just thinking about the early days in NET. Those were good times."

Stone, not one to dwell in the past, had also been thinking about the heady days when he'd started up NET. He knew it was the beginning of his move up through the ranks, and he'd vowed to let nothing get in his way. But that was before Victor Cabrera.

"Those were good times," he agreed. "And there will be good times again, Tim. Once we get Pickett out of the way, I'm through with Victor. Mara should be promoting me soon, and then I'm on my way."

Hardy didn't share Stone's optimism. "Chief, please, let's walk away from Pickett."

Stone crushed his cup and threw it into a wastebasket. "I can't."

Something in Stone's voice frightened Hardy. "There's more to this Pickett commission than you told us, isn't there?"

Stone regarded the pale man across the desk from him. "You're right, Tim. There is more to it. Pickett has a couple of witnesses who can expose Victor's operation."

Hardy tried to put his cup down gently, but his hand shook and coffee spilled on the desk. He wiped it away with the back of his hand. "What about us?"

"Us too."

Hardy slumped. "Mother of God. Why didn't you tell us?"

"The less the others know, the better. Tim, what I've told you is strictly between us." He saw the look on Hardy's face and added, "Don't worry. Victor is convinced a hit on Pickett will scare the witnesses into silence."

"What if he's wrong?"

The same thought had occurred to Stone, and he gave his sergeant the same answer he gave himself. "What choice do we have?"

Stone remained in the office long after Tim Hardy, more frightened than ever, had gone. He took a bottle of scotch out of his desk and half filled a dirty glass. Then he turned off the harsh fluorescent lights, and, in the softer light of a green desk lamp, sipped the warm scotch. Once again he thought about Victor Cabrera.

He'd underestimated the Peruvian from the start. He'd thought Cabrera was a simple, crude man, whose success was predicated more on violence and intimidation than finesse and guile. But Stone had been wrong. Cabrera was certainly capable of violence, but he'd captured Patrick Stone without a struggle.

After that uncomfortable dinner at the Plaza six months earlier, Stone had hoped he was done with Victor Cabrera. But a couple of weeks later the Peruvian called to invite him to spend a weekend at his home in Florida. All of Stone's instincts told him to say no, but he'd become obsessed with Victor Cabrera. Who was he? What did he want? And more important, what were the real circumstances of Tina's death? On one hand, he wanted to know everything that happened after they'd dropped him off in San Juan, but on the other, he realized that the less he knew, the better. What nagged him most was Cabrera's silence. It hung over his head like a sword. Reluctantly, he went to Florida to find some answers.

Cabrera's sprawling home, in keeping with the sedate, understated ambience of Palm Beach, was large but not ostentatious. Perched on a hill, the house offered a magnificent panorama of the Atlantic Ocean to the east and the Inter-Coastal Waterway to the west. Stone wasn't the only guest that weekend. There was an eclectic mix of American businessmen and European jet setters who roamed about the house and grounds. But it was only Stone whom Cabrera steered into his study for private, uninterrupted conversations.

Cabrera was intelligent and well-read. His topics, seemingly random, focused on issues of morality and the law. Rather than ask a direct question, he'd seize upon a current front-page topic—the arrest of a politician, the indictment of a Wall Street financier—and discuss the issues from a purely philosophical point of view.

Stone was impressed at Cabrera's mental adroitness. His demeanor, including his speech, was slow and deliberate, which Stone attributed to English being his second language, but his mind was quick. He would make a devastating chess opponent, Stone decided. Indeed, the game they had tacitly entered had swiftly taken on the air of a chess match.

"Tell me," Cabrera said, pouring brandy into Waterford crystal snifters, "do you think bribery should be a crime?"

Stone answered slowly. "I guess it would depend. I'm not a moralist, but there are times when taking a bribe would be wrong."

"Such as?"

"I don't know, say a bribe to turn over government secrets to the enemy."

Cabrera waved his hand dismissively. "Of course, in such a situation there is no doubt. Let me give you a more concrete example. I import and export. Frequently I am forced to bribe port and customs officials just to get them to do their jobs. Is that wrong?"

Stone smiled. "For you or them?"

Cabrera didn't smile. "You know what I mean, Patrick."

Stone ground his half-smoked Cuban cigar into the ashtray. He didn't particularly like them, but it wasn't often he had the chance to smoke a twenty-dollar cigar. "Bribery is a crime, Victor. But things aren't black-and-white. There are always extenuating circumstances."

Cabrera studied him. "Why did you become a policeman? With your intelligence and ambition, you could have become anything."

"As long as I can remember, I've always wanted to be a cop. Where else do you get a front-row seat to life?"

"Will you stay in the police department?"

Stone felt like he was being interviewed for a job. "Yes," he said matter-of-factly, "I'm going to be the Police Commissioner."

Victor's mood seemed to change. He looked even more unhappy, if that was possible. "A man with such lofty goals must be like Caesar's wife."

Stone didn't answer, but his thoughts flashed back to the night on the yacht and he felt a chill.

Cabrera looked at him appraisingly. "You are the most self-contained man I have ever met. You are also, I am certain, a cautious man."

Stone tried, unsuccessfully, to read Cabrera's neutral expression. "I've got big plans, and I'm not going to let anything jeopardize them."

The older man was silent for a long time, as though he were weighing what he would say next. Stone sensed that the chess game they'd been playing was coming to a conclusion. The pawns had long since been sacrificed; they were entering the end game with only their most important pieces. A mistake now would be fatal.

Finally Cabrera said, "Our first meeting was not entirely an accident."

Bishop begins the attack? By this time Stone was sure their first meeting was no accident. Nevertheless, hearing him say it startled him. "Why me?"

Cabrera pursed his lips. "I'm afraid your NET policemen in their exuberance have been severely damaging the business interests of my associates."

The queen was in motion and the all-out attack was under way. But this was no game; his future depended on how he handled himself in the next few crucial minutes. Oddly, he felt a certain elation. Stone, a born competitor, had been sparring with a phantom, and he felt he'd been at a disadvantage. Now that Cabrera had committed himself to a plan of attack, things were different; the elusive Cabrera had become a known quantity. In a contest of wits, Stone was certain he'd emerge victorious over a provincial drug dealer. "Drugs are illegal in New York City, Victor."

The older man shrugged. "True enough. But there are many illegal activities going on in your city."

"Come on, Victor."

"I know that is neither here nor there," he added quickly. "But the world is a very complicated place, Patrick." He refilled their glasses and echoed Stone's words. "Things aren't always black-and-white." Dark eyes that revealed nothing, but nevertheless held a vague menace within, studied Stone. "My friend," he said softly, "opportunity is about to present itself to you."

Stone, his senses heightened by the tension of the moment, swirled the tawny brandy and inhaled its rich oak-scented aroma. The game had come down to check-checkmate, and Patrick Stone, feeling a rush of excitement, was confident he would be the winner. Cabrera held his snifter up to the light and studied the color. "Nothing complicated. Payment in return for leaving me and my associates alone."

Cabrera was suggesting a pad—an organized payoff system. It had been pads that had been the downfall of many cops during the Knapp Commission. Stone wasn't about to make that mistake. "No."

Cabrera looked genuinely surprised. "But why? I'm not asking you to *do* something. I'm asking you *not* to do something. There is absolutely no risk. On the contrary. I can give you information that will advance your career.''

"What could you do for me?''

"I can provide you with information on the movements of other dealers. Seizing their shipments will serve both your interests and mine. The efficiency of your organization need not suffer on my account. I promise you I can give you enough work to keep your entire squad busy.''

Cabrera's proposition was attractive. More than money, the idea of receiving high-level information about large drug shipments appealed to Stone. It was getting more and more difficult to sustain the high level of quality arrests NET was making. More arrests would increase his stature with the P.C., and the added publicity wouldn't do him any harm either. Although he'd been getting sporadic coverage in the press, he'd been looking for a way to increase his visibility. Perhaps Cabrera had the answer. He would make money for doing nothing and, if Cabrera wasn't exaggerating, his information would increase the effectiveness of NET. He was tempted, but it was too dangerous. If one person knew about their arrangement, so would another, and it was only a matter of time before that someone talked. Narcotic traffickers were notorious for selling information in exchange for leniency.

Stone stood up. "I can't help you. It's too risky.''

Cabrera looked disappointed. "I'm sorry you feel that way.'' He rose and went to the bar. "More brandy?''

Stone offered his glass and Cabrera poured more of the expensive brandy. "By the way, Patrick, do you remember Pablo, my cabin steward?''

Stone saw the sword poised over his head begin to fall. He'd never forget the look of horror on the steward's face as he stood in the cabin doorway. Slowly, he put his glass down; a knot was already forming in his stomach. "Vaguely,'' he answered. "Why?'' His voice betrayed none of the inner turmoil he was feeling.

"He lives in a little village outside Chiclayo.'' Cabrera's eyes bored into Stone. "Peru is a very poor country and it is very difficult for the peasants. You should see the conditions in which they live. Shacks, no running water.''

"Get to the point.''

Cabrera looked pained to have to talk about it. "There has been illness in Pablo's family and he is in need of a great deal of money. He's talking about going to the authorities and telling them what really happened on the yacht that morning.''

"What did happen?''

The older man looked sad. "Who could forget? A tragic, accidental death. Nevertheless, the poor fool thinks his information is worth money.'' Cabrera shrugged like a man who has done his best under difficult circumstances. "You know how these peasants can be. I told him there was nothing to be gained by going to the authorities. I am sure you would be completely exonerated. But the publicity . . ." He let Stone imagine the rest.

"I don't suppose you'd be able to stop him from talking?"

Cabrera pursed his lips. "There is a charming expression in your country: one hand washes the other. Did I get it right?"

Calmly, Stone reviewed his options. If he called Cabrera's bluff, and the story of Tina's death came out, he'd be finished in the job. Innocent or guilty, the department would never tolerate a scandal.

"Besides, Patrick, it wouldn't be the first illegal thing you've done."

The hairs rose on the back of Stone's neck. "What's that supposed to mean?"

Cabrera returned to his chair and motioned Stone to sit down. "Recently, your men arrested one of my couriers. There was a considerable difference between the amount of money he was carrying and the amount you submitted as evidence. You were present at that arrest. If such large amounts of money were being withheld, you would have to know."

Stone forced an easy smile. "Victor, your courier is full of shit. He's ripping you off and blaming the police."

"I think not. My employees know better than to lie to me about such things. Besides, it is not the first time." Before Stone could protest, Cabrera continued. "But that is water under the bridge. Your actions tell me that you are a practical man who will listen to a solid business proposition."

Stone assessed his position, looking for a way out, but Cabrera seemed to have boxed him in. Losing his job was bad enough, but if Cabrera produced witnesses to the thefts of the money, he'd go to jail for sure. Cabrera had him. He'd have to do what Cabrera wanted, but he'd do it on his own terms. If he could dictate the conditions, he could at least minimize his risk of exposure.

"All right, here's the deal, Victor. Take it or leave it. You pay me for leaving your operation alone, period. I don't transport goods for you and I don't expedite or protect your operation in any way. If your people get busted by anyone else, they're on their own."

"Agreed."

"You give me information on other dealers. I do what I want with the information." Again, a nod. Then he issued the final condition—the one that made the deal palatable for him. "Our arrangement lasts only as long as I'm in NET. Once I leave NET, you and I part company."

The unit was doing so well, Stone was confident it was only a matter of time before the P.C. promoted him away from NET and Victor Cabrera. Ironically, if Cabrera's information on other drug dealers was good, it would only hasten that day.

In spite of Stone's initial misgivings, their arrangement worked well. Cabrera told him which operations were his, and Stone saw to it that NET stayed away from them. But the information he supplied on the others provided more than enough activity for NET. Stone's incessant drive for more and more arrests surprised even his workhorse cops. But they didn't know what he knew: The more successful NET was, the quicker he'd be able to break his tie to Victor Cabrera.

Stone was brought out of his thoughts by the sound of a siren outside his window. He looked down and saw two sector cops dragging a man kicking and screaming into the station house. He looked at his watch. He'd been sitting at his desk for almost an hour. He drained the rest of his scotch, angry at himself for daydreaming. There was no point in dwelling in the past. There was much to be done, and he needed to focus his attention on the future. Victor Cabrera and Nathan Pickett were the last two obstacles in his path. Soon they would be out of the way and he'd be back on track. Buoyed by this thought, he took a last look around the office, shut off the lights, and left for home.

28

Alex Rose, on his way to pick up a ballistics report, was waiting in the Police Academy lobby for an elevator when he ran into Pete Sprizzo—the lieutenant who had broken him in at IAD. Known as the "guided missile"—because once he locked on to a target, nothing could deter him—Sprizzo had a reputation in police union circles as a "hard-nosed scumbag, but a fair one." And *that* was the highest praise an IAD cop could hope to get from the rank and file.

It was supposed to be a secret, but Rose knew that Sprizzo had transferred to the Inspectional Services Bureau to work in the Field Associate program. Sprizzo, built like a fireplug, grabbed Rose's hand in a death grip.

255

"Alex, you old bastard. I thought someone shot you. Where the hell have you been?"

"Just keeping a low profile, Pete." Sprizzo was a personal friend of Percell, and Rose wondered if he knew about his transfer to the Detective Bureau. "What are you doing here?"

"The usual. Giving corruption lectures to the recruits."

Rose knew about the lectures. He also knew that Sprizzo, and the handful of others involved in the Field Associate program, used this opportunity to recruit cops for the program.

"How about you?" Sprizzo asked. "What have you been doing?"

"I was in the neighborhood so I thought I'd go up to Ballistics and see an old friend. But he can wait. Come on, I'll buy you a drink." If anyone knew about a Field Associate in NET, it would be Pete Sprizzo.

"I could use a drink, but I just finished talking about corruption to a bunch of impressionable kids. It wouldn't do for them to see me sitting in a gin mill. You can buy me a cup of coffee."

They sat at a booth in the back of the luncheonette, away from other cops, and played the whatever-happened-to-what's-his-name game. While Sprizzo talked about old cases, Rose tried to think of a way to bring up the delicate topic. Sprizzo was an old friend, but Rose knew when it came to discussing confidential department business, he was as tight as a clam. During a lull in the conversation, he saw his opening. "Pete, I want to ask you a very important question."

Sprizzo picked up his cup. "You can ask, but I may not answer."

"Fair enough. Do you have a Field Associate in NET?"

Sprizzo slammed the cup down on the table. "For Chrissake, Alex, you know better than that."

"I'm not being nosy, Pete. It's important."

Sprizzo's eyes were cold. "Let me tell you something, Alex. I have a lot of respect for anyone who'll agree to be a Field Associate, and I swear to every one of them that their identity will be known only to me. Do you really expect me to answer that question?"

"Pete, do you know where I'm working now?"

"No."

Rose studied the lined face of his old mentor. He'd never met a more honest man in his life, and he doubted Sprizzo was capable of lying to him.

"I've been transferred, temporarily, to the Detective Bureau. A lieutenant from the bureau and I are working on a case that could blow this department wide open."

"That's a new one on me. IAD and the bureau working on something together."

"It's a long story, and I can't go into it. All I can say is that time is critical and right now we have zilch."

"You know the drill, Alex. You want to talk to one guy, you interview the whole command. That way no one knows who your target is."

"I can't do that."

"Why?"

"I can't tell you why."

Sprizzo's stern face broke into a grin. "Listen to us. A couple of hair-bag cops whispering secrets like bad actors in a Grade B spy movie." He motioned to the waiter for the check. "I gotta be getting back."

"Does that mean no?"

The older lieutenant's grin vanished. Those dark eyes, eyes that had thrown a chill into more than one cop on the receiving end of an interrogation, bored into Rose. "Yes, there's one in NET. He was just transferred there a few weeks ago."

"Pete, I have to talk to him."

Sprizzo started to get up. "Forget it, Alex. It's out of the question."

Rose grabbed Sprizzo's sleeve and pulled him back down. "For Chrissake, Pete, you know me better than that. I wouldn't ask you if there was some other way. I have to talk to him."

Sprizzo's tone became businesslike. "First of all, Lieutenant, if I decide he'll be debriefed, I'll do the debriefing."

"You can't."

"Why?"

"You don't know what to ask."

"You'll tell me."

"I can't."

"Fuck you—"

"Pete, all I can say is you have to trust me on this." He didn't want to bring Percell's name into it, but he was afraid Sprizzo was going to turn him down. "Talk to Percell. He knows what's going on. See what he says."

Sprizzo gazed at the ceiling, the conflict evident in his face. Obviously, Rose's case was serious, but on the other hand, so was the confidentiality of the Field Associate. "He's not going to want to talk to you," Sprizzo said. "He's a nervous wreck just talking to me."

"Pete, you can charm the balls off a brass monkey. Tell him it's crucial."

"Let me think about it."

Rose wasn't happy with the answer, but it was better than no. "Okay. Take your time. I'll call you tomorrow."

Sprizzo stood and looked down at Rose. "You're a persistent bastard, aren't you?"

"What can I say, Pete. I had a good teacher."

"You're in the wrong line of work, Rose. You should be selling used cars."

29

SHANNON AND VELEZ, OUT CHASING A LEAD THAT WENT NOWHERE, got back to the office as Rose was leaving.

"Oh, I didn't think you guys were back, so I was cutting out early."

Velez was amused at the guilty look on Rose's face. "That's okay, Lieutenant. You don't have to explain. I won't write you up this time, but don't let it happen again."

Rose put his arm around Velez. "That's what I like about guys who get laid a lot, they have such understanding dispositions."

He went back inside with them. "I might as well tell you what I found out about Stone's financial picture."

"Anything good?" Shannon asked.

"I didn't come up with a hell of a lot."

"I thought you IAD guys were experienced at doing financial background checks on cops."

Rose smiled. "I *found* all the records I wanted. But there's no smoking gun. He has a savings account with a couple of thousand in it. I looked at his checking-account activity over the last year. Nothing special. No big amounts in or out."

"Where does he live?"

"An apartment in Bayside. Pays eight-fifty a month. Easy enough to afford on a captain's salary."

"Why not?" Shannon said with a straight face. "He's single. What else does he have to spend it on?"

"What kind of car does he own?"

"A late-model Corvette."

"Hey, those things cost a bundle."

"Yeah, but it appears to be his only luxury. Again, on his salary he could afford the payments."

"So what are you saying?"

"I'm saying there's nothing in his financial picture or his lifestyle to indicate an infusion of unexplained money."

Velez sighed. "Now what?"

"We keep digging."

ROSE, DISCOURAGED BY THE LACK OF RESULTS AFTER ALL THIS TIME, was glad that he was going home to an empty apartment. He was in no mood for forced conversation about the wonderful world of advertising.

Rachel greeted him at the door. "Hurry up and change. I've already made reservations. If we don't hurry, we'll be late."

"I thought you were in Chicago!" he blurted.

"I was, but we finished up early." She put her arms around him. "I rushed home to be with my poor orphan husband."

Alex felt like a heel. Rachel was self-centered, but she could be thoughtful at the most unexpected moments. One time he'd mentioned a Giant game he wanted to see, and the next day, with a big smile, she handed him a ticket for a seat on the fifty-yard line. He was the one who was supposed to bring home unexpected gifts, but it was she who slipped the occasional books and cuff links under his pillow.

They went to one of those small, pretentious pseudo-French restaurants that infested the north shore of Long Island. They tried so hard to imitate their bigger cousins in the city, but the only similarity between them was their inflated prices. Rose, who had a deep dislike for all restaurants French, harbored a belief that French waiters were schooled in being obnoxious. How else to explain their attitude?

At the restaurant Alex continued the argument that started in the car. "Of course I appreciate you flying back early, but you know how I feel about French restaurants. Why couldn't we just stay home and bring in Chinese?''

She wrinkled her nose. ''Please, Alex, you know I detest Chinese food. Besides, this place got a terrific write-up in the Sunday *Times*.''

''I don't care if it was written up in the Bible!''

She looked around in embarrassment. ''For God's sake, Alex, keep your voice down. I work all day too. Do you think I enjoy coming home and slaving over a hot stove?''

''Rachel,'' he whispered, ''you haven't slaved over a hot stove since you failed home economics in junior high. Everything we eat comes in cardboard boxes and gets zapped in a microwave.''

She looked hurt. ''I told you I wasn't into cooking when I married you.''

''I don't care about the food. It's just that sometimes I want to be at home alone with my wife. Is that too much to ask?''

''No.'' She patted his hand, mollified. ''That's sweet. By the way, what's going on? Why are you working all these crazy hours anyway?''

''I've been temporarily assigned to the Detective Bureau. We're working on a—''

''Alex, this is almost part of my job, you know? My God, everyone in the office talks about the latest 'in' restaurants. You don't expect me to sit there and say, 'I wouldn't know about that. My husband and I stay home every night and eat Chinks!' ''

In spite of his anger, Alex laughed. Her biting wit and aggressiveness contrasted sharply with her soft beauty. When they were first married, he wondered how long it would be before he took her beauty for granted. So far that time hadn't come. He still got a great deal of pleasure from watching her jump up naked from the bed to run into the bathroom or put on a robe. She had the sort of lean body that looked erotic in bright sunlight, or soft moonlight. Sometimes he'd just lie awake in bed watching her dress—a practice that caused them both to be late for work on more than one occasion.

Rachel looked up from her menu. ''What are you going to have?''

''I don't know,'' he mumbled. ''How do you say lo mein in French?'' She kicked him under the table.

The maître d' offered Rose the wine list, a heavy tome that looked like a Ph.D. dissertation. As usual, the wines were ordinary and overpriced. Rose handed it back to him. ''We'll have a carafe.''

The maître d's nose actually cranked up a couple of notches. ''Of course, if monsieur wishes. Red or white?''

''Red.'' Rose resisted asking him what year it was.

The man returned shortly, and as Rose expected, poured a sample with great theatrical flourish. Without touching the glass, Alex squinted at it and said in his best Texas drawl, "The color looks 'bout right to me. Fill the son of a bitch up."

Dinner was a torturous affair. The waiters and busboys hovered around them like gnats, hardly giving them a minute alone. The maître d' passed their table, and Rose leaned toward Rachel. "You know what?" he whispered. "I'll bet that guy was born in the Bronx. No kidding. I think I went to high school with him. His name is Howie Lipshitz and his father was a tailor on Fordham Road. I remember old Howie failed French 101. That's why he has such a lousy accent."

Rachel started giggling. She loved it when he made up these wild stories. On their first date he told her that their taxi driver was a Nazi war criminal. He made up an entire history for the poor man on a short ride across town.

"Rachel, I'm not kidding. When he comes back, listen closely to his accent. Tell me you don't hear Yiddish overtones. Paris by way of the Bronx. The only left bank he ever saw was the left bank of the Harlem River."

Of course, when the hapless maître d' returned, the first words out of his mouth brought gales of uncontrollable laughter from Rachel, while Alex traded perplexed looks with the nonplussed man.

Finally Rachel shook her head. "Pay the bill and let's go home," she said.

They went home and made love, but something unsaid hung between them; even their lovemaking seemed forced.

Rose returned to the bedroom with two glasses of sherry and they sipped their drinks in silence, each wondering what the other was thinking. It was at times like this that doubts long suppressed came to the fore; a dangerous time for reflecting.

"Rachel, did you mean what you said at that party?"

"You mean about not quitting my job? I don't know, Alex. There's so much going on right now that I can't think about it."

"You're thirty-two."

"Well don't make it sound like I'm ready for a nursing home."

"Don't get so touchy. It's just that you don't have forever to make a decision about this. You remember the trouble your friend Marsha had having a baby."

"Alex, she was thirty-eight."

"And in six years you'll be thirty-eight."

"Can we drop this?"

"No. You don't want to give up your job, do you?"

"The way I'm going now, the sky's the limit." She saw the look on his face and softened her tone. "Alex, there's still plenty of time to think about having a family."

He knew she was lying; perhaps even to herself. The excitement in her eyes when she spoke about her job said it all. She had no intention of giving up a career to have a family. He wasn't surprised at her answer. What did surprise him was the way he felt about it; he was relieved. A child was a commitment, and without that responsibility, he and Rachel could go their separate ways. With a start he realized it was the first time he'd allowed the thought of divorce to enter his mind.

"Why don't you get out of the police department?" Rachel said.

"Because I like the job."

As soon as he said it he realized it was the truth. Why? He'd never taken the job seriously before. Sure, it was exciting sometimes, but he never saw it as a vocation the way Brian Shannon did. To Shannon the job was everything. Rose never understood that kind of devotion. All his life things had come easy to him. His family had money, he was bright in school, good at sports, and never had the usual adolescent problems with girls. But in spite of all this, he was dimly aware that something was missing. Part of the problem, he suspected, was that he never took anything seriously. He found it impossible to commit himself to a cause or idea the way others did. Was it fear, or was he shallow, as his father had once suggested? Why did he suddenly like the job? Because he was investigating murderers who were cops?

"You could get a job on Wall Street with your father and brother. Lead a normal life and make ten times the money. And you'd have prestige, not like—"

"Not like being a lousy cop? Is that what you were going to say?"

"Even your parents don't like you being a cop."

"I know. It's simply not done in the best Jewish families. My son the policeman," he said sarcastically, "doesn't have the same ring as my son the doctor, or my son the lawyer."

"Oh, stop it, Alex. I'm sorry, but I agree with them. Being a policeman is such a . . . a . . . I don't know what. You can do better than that."

"What could be better than being a lieutenant of police?"

"Stop making jokes. I'll admit when I met you I was impressed. All the guys I dated were boring, uptight college types preoccupied with making a success of themselves. You were different. You were so relaxed and easygoing. You made police work sound like the most entertaining job in the world. But it's like watching a boy who was a star basketball player in high school. Everyone's impressed, but if he grows up and still spends all his time in the schoolyard playing basketball, then he becomes something to be pitied."

"You mean now that I'm all grown up, I should put away the toys of a child."

"Yes, exactly. Cops are like kids playing cops and robbers."

An image of Walter Cronin's body curled on a lonely beach flashed into his mind. "It's not that way at all, Rachel. When we were kids playing cops and robbers and you got shot, you could yell 'new man' and you were alive again. Cops can't do that."

He could tell by her look that she had no idea what he was talking about. A cop's life—*his* life—was something totally alien to her. She was interested only in her job, her career, her world. There was room for nothing else.

"Alex, sometimes I'm embarrassed to say my husband's a policeman. I'm meeting a different class of people now. To them a cop's a novelty— like a circus performer. I . . . I really think you should leave the police force. Besides, you're getting worse. You're always preoccupied, or on the telephone with that Shannon guy."

"How would you know, Rachel? You're not around that much yourself."

"Please, Alex, let's not get into that again."

"What if I don't want to leave the police department?"

"I'm serious about this, Alex. Think it over carefully."

"Do I hear a threat?"

"I'm very tired. Let's talk about this tomorrow." She turned the light off.

He remained awake long after her breathing told him she was asleep.

EARLIER THAT EVENING, ABOUT THE TIME ALEX ROSE WAS HAVING dinner with his wife, Nathan Pickett got out of the cab on Charles Street and briskly walked up the steps of the brownstone.

That morning, remembering the odd visit from the two lieutenants four days earlier, Pickett had reluctantly decided to take their advice. When he'd left his home, he'd scanned the streets looking for . . . what? There wasn't a sign of anyone on his quiet residential street at eight A.M. When he pulled up at his office, he did the same thing, but it was even more ludicrous. Pitkin Avenue teemed with pedestrians, trucks and cars. How could he hope to spot someone following him in a crowded city like New York? Later in the day he was scheduled to speak at a rally outside the Board of Education headquarters on Livingston Street, where hundreds of people would be present. It was impossible. Those two cops meant well, but they'd been watching too many spy movies.

Had Pickett looked to his left as he went up the stairs, he might have seen a car with its headlights off coast into a parking spot at the top of Charles Street.

That afternoon McKay Beals had resumed the tail that Walter Cronin had begun eight days before. Beals had picked up the senator as he left his Pitkin Avenue office. After Pickett disappeared into the brownstone, Beals slid over to the passenger's side. Stone had taught him that a man sitting in a parked auto looks less suspicious if he's sitting in the passenger's seat.

He scanned the street. Satisfied that nothing was out of the ordinary, he slid down in the seat and lit a joint. Smoking marijuana calmed him when he was nervous, and this Pickett deal was making him very nervous.

He recalled his conversation with the Chief earlier in a bar at the South Street Seaport. "Today's the thirteenth," Stone had said. "I have to know the location soon."

"I'm only one guy," Beals protested. "I'll be lucky if I don't lose him in traffic. Besides, how much am I going to find out in one day?"

"You won't know until you do it, will you? Meet me back here when you're done."

"I don't know when I'll be finished."

Stone, who'd been lining up rows of rolled-up napkin balls, scattered them off the bar with an impatient sweep of his hand. "It doesn't matter. I'll be here."

Beals, giving way to the warm, mellow feeling coursing through his body, tried to forget about Stone. Through half-lowered lids he studied the expensive brownstones and apartment buildings on the block; a far cry from the squalor of Pitkin Avenue. A jogger wearing a dirty gray sweatshirt with NYU across the front passed in front of him and he was reminded of Thomas Rowe.

It had been just after eleven when they'd pulled into the parking lot by the Verrazano Bridge where, Cronin had reported, Rowe came to run every night. Tecci squinted at his watch. "He should be along soon. Let's go."

Dressed in sweat suits and sneakers, careful not to attract undue attention, they jogged slowly along the path away from the parking lot and the bright lights.

About two hundred yards from the parking lot, they stepped into a clump of bushes. Beals studied the darkness, looking for the now familiar outline of Thomas Rowe, whose short legs and loping gait made him easy to spot. As part of their dress rehearsal a week earlier, they'd stood among the same bushes and watched him run by. As Rowe's squat form receded into the darkness, Tecci had raised his index finger, pointed it in the direction of Rowe, and said softly, "Pow."

Tecci was the first to spot him. He tossed his cigarette into the water. "Here he comes."

Just as Rowe was upon them, they stepped out of the shadows and blocked the path. Rowe had tried to run past them, but Tecci grabbed him by the collar and yanked him to a stop.

"Hold it, pal." Tecci flashed his shield. "Don't get excited. Narcotics. We just wanna talk to you."

"Jesus." Rowe was breathing hard from his run. "You gave me a fright. I thought you guys were muggers."

Tecci led the man to a nearby bench. "Sit down. We just want to ask you a few questions."

Beals remained standing. It was his job to keep an eye out for other joggers. He glanced up and down the path. They were alone.

"Victor sent us," Tecci said.

Rowe stiffened at the name. "What is this? I'm an attorney. You have no right to—"

"Disbarred attorney," Tecci corrected. "The Bar Association frowns on their members laundering money."

Rowe, who had been put through the wringer by the U.S. Attorney's office during the five months of his trial, was no longer frightened by law enforcement people. "Listen, if I'm under arrest, take me to see a judge. I'll be out so fast it'll make your head spin."

"Must be very lucrative laundering money." Tecci fingered the expensive jogging suit.

"Enough to buy and sell you, asshole." Rowe stood up. "Come on, let's go see the judge."

Beals made a movement, and Rowe felt something cold and hard pressed into his stomach. "Sit down," the black man said.

Rowe looked at the gun in astonishment, and slowly sat. "You guys aren't real cops. This is a rip-off, right?" He was more confused than frightened. If they were robbers, how did they know about Victor? He struggled to mask his fear. "All right, we're all adults. Put that goddamn gun away before someone gets hurt. Here, take my watch and ring."

Tecci whispered in his ear, "We don't want your watch."

The bastards! He had five hundred in his pocket, but he was hoping they'd settle for the ring and watch. "All right, I have a few bucks, take that—"

Without warning Beals squeezed the trigger. The silencer made the report sound like a muffled pop. Rowe's head snapped back. Tecci, still holding onto him, relaxed his grip as he felt the body go limp.

Beals glanced around nervously. "Come on. Let's get the fuck out of here."

Tecci's eyes swept the area to make sure they were leaving nothing behind, but there was only Rowe's body, slumped on the bench as though he were sleeping. They jogged slowly back to the parking lot, where they did some more loosening-up exercises. Only when they were certain they'd attracted no attention did they climb into the car and drive away.

Beals took the last drag on his roach and threw it out the window. He was watching an old black guy, probably the super, hauling cans out to the curb in front of the building Pickett had entered. Beals left the car and walked down the block toward him. "Yo," he said, "I saw a black dude go in there a while ago. Looked real familiar. Maybe I've seen him on TV or something?"

The super smiled, revealing two missing front teeth. "That's Nathan Pickett, some hotshot from Brooklyn. The dude has himself some steady white pussy up there."

"Is she fine?"

The man spat. "Ain't my idea of choice; ugly as homemade sin, you ask me. She's a teacher at that college up by Washington Square Park."

"That guy looks like a stud. I'll bet he gets some every night."

"Every *Thursday* night like clockwork—in by six, out by one. 'Spect he don't get home, his mama kick his ass."

"Only on Thursday night?"

"Sometime he here on other nights, but *always* Thursday."

Beals started to walk away. "Sounds like she's one fine woman."

"Excuse me, boss. You got a cigarette?"

Beals tossed him the pack. "Keep them."

"Thank you, boss."

"No," Beals said. "Thank *you*."

It was two-thirty by the time he got to the bar. Stone was still there. Beals slid onto the bar stool next to him. "I think I found the spot."

Stone's eyes lit up. "Where?"

"Charles Street in the Village. He's got a girlfriend lives there. I talked to the super. He says Pickett visits her every Thursday night. . . . Chief, this is the last one."

Stone didn't even blink. "Don't worry, Mac. This is the last one for all of us. That's a promise."

30

VELEZ BOUGHT A PACK OF CIGARETTES IN A BODEGA DIRECTLY across the street from Pickett's office. Outside, he lit one. Squinting through the smoke, he could barely make out the image of Pickett behind the dirty window talking to two women. Velez checked his watch; it was almost four-thirty.

The young cop had left his car a block away. He made certain he didn't stay too long in one place. Nothing aroused suspicion in this neighborhood more than a strange car parked too long in the same place. From his carefully selected vantage point he'd be able to see Pickett leave.

Since Velez had agreed to take part in the investigation, he'd been tailing Pickett. Surveillance is a boring yet demanding task. There is the need constantly to change one's profile—move the car, change a hat, put a jacket on, take it off. Then there's the pressure to stay close enough to the subject so he isn't lost, but not close enough to be spotted. Long tedious hours of waiting can suddenly be interrupted by a frantic Keystone Cops chase to stay with a quick-moving subject. And in between one eats cold hot dogs, drinks bitter coffee, and tries to ignore the urge to urinate.

Surveillance also takes a great deal of patience, and Velez was losing his. Hyperactive by nature, he felt trapped by the long, confining hours. Personally, he thought it was a waste of time. He had a hard enough time trying to keep up with Pickett in traffic, never mind looking for suspicious people at the same time. He'd give it one more day, then he planned to tell Shannon what he thought of the whole idea.

Back in his car, he stopped in mid-yawn to watch a pretty girl in very tight jeans cross the street in front of him. He was admiring the snug fit of her jeans when he was suddenly distracted by a dirty brown Buick parked diagonally across the street from him.

It was dusk, that time between day and night when visibility is poorest. He strained to see the faces inside the automobile, but all he could make out was the flickering glow from inhaled cigarettes. But he did notice something; the two occupants kept turning their heads as if looking for something. Or someone. With a jolt, it suddenly occurred to him that they could be waiting for Pickett. Velez slid farther down in the seat and automatically jotted down the plate number.

The car door opened and two Hispanic men got out.

Velez relaxed. They weren't cops. Even from here, in the bad light, he could see they were stone junkies. The driver, an emaciated man wearing a dirty yellow windbreaker, kept shrugging his shoulders as though his shirt didn't fit properly. The other man, a little taller but just as thin, moved with slow, exaggerated movements—a sure sign he was tripping out and his brain was short-circuiting.

Velez watched them with bemused detachment, but then the man in the yellow windbreaker tugged at something under his jacket. Velez was instantly alert. He'd seen the movement enough times to know the man had adjusted a gun.

The two moved across the sidewalk and entered a smoke shop. Velez bolted upright and reflexively reached for the radio. But there was none. He was in his own car. "Jesus Christ," he mumbled, slamming the steering wheel. "A stickup going down right in front of me and I got no radio, no backup, nothing!"

Frantically, he craned his neck, looking up and down the street for the telltale red roof lights of a radio car. It would be useless looking for a telephone in this neighborhood; they were either vandalized or inoperative.

He started the car and drove slowly past the smoke shop. The lighting was poor, but he saw several people inside. At the corner he gunned the engine and roared down the avenue in search of a radio car. At every intersection he braked sharply, looking right and left down the side streets. "Goddamn it!" he yelled. "You can never find a cop when you want one!"

He drove another four blocks, then snapped the steering wheel and made a screeching U turn that sent two teenagers scurrying for the safety of the sidewalk, but not before they gave him the finger and the verbal equivalent in case he didn't understand sign language.

Approaching the smoke shop again, he was relieved to see the Buick still parked in the same place. Now the questions started. Should he wait outside and take them when they came out, or should he go in after them?

Velez cut his engine and glided up next to the Buick, effectively blocking it at the curb. He removed his .38-caliber revolver from his ankle holster and cursed himself for not having his more accurate service gun with him. The off-duty gun was convenient to carry, but its short barrel made it notoriously inaccurate.

Taking a couple of deep breaths, he got out of the car. He walked slowly past the smoke shop and casually glanced inside. In the dim light he saw the yellow jacket with his back to the door, facing several other people. Just past the entrance he stopped against the building line and reviewed his tactics. Get in fast . . . element of surprise . . . stay low . . . duck to the left. Or was it right? He couldn't remember. He took one last look for a radio car, barged through the door, and yelled, "Police!"

As the man in the yellow jacket whirled, Velez saw a blur of shiny metal in his hand and he fired. The air erupted in a quick succession of explosions and muzzle flashes. Yellow jacket was thrown back violently against the counter and slowly slid to the floor, a look of shock and certain death on his face.

Above the ringing in his ears Velez heard rapid clicking sounds and was startled to realize it was he squeezing the trigger on empty chambers; he'd fired all five bullets! In that moment, with curious detachment, he knew he was dead. In the few seconds it took for the gunfight to begin and end, he realized he didn't know where the other man was. Before he could react, he was pounded in the back by two sharp blows.

He was seven years old again in Central Park. The big kids were playing softball, and Velez, crossing the outfield, didn't see the hard-hit line drive heading for him. The ball struck him in the back, and the jeering, hooting players yelled at him to get off the field. He fled in tears, more from embarrassment than pain.

This time the pain was much greater. He'd cried then, but now he bit his lip. The force of the blow took his breath away and drove him to his knees.

The last thing he saw as he pitched forward into darkness were terror-stricken customers diving for cover.

OF ALL THE POLICE RADIO CALLS, A 10–13—''ASSIST PATROLMAN''—provokes the most visceral response. A 10–13 means a cop is in trouble, and never is the "us-against-them" syndrome more evident. A 10–13 means a cop has been attacked, and that means every cop in the city has been attacked. A 10–13 becomes a living Rorschach test, as every cop imagines the worst that can happen to him.

On this night in Brooklyn the nightmare started with the terse transmission, "Ten-thirteen . . . assist police officer . . . shots fired . . . 173 Pitkin Avenue . . . what units responding?"

Some cars acknowledged, while others, too far away to respond, waited anxiously for the disposition. Sometimes the disposition comes from a cop on the scene: "Call it off, Central . . . no further assistance required." At other times the dispatcher announces: "That ten-thirteen is unfounded. All units resume patrol." But not tonight.

The frantic voice of the officer driving the car in sector 77 Boy ruptured the uneasy silence. "Officer shot . . . on the way to Kings . . . Jesus Christ . . ." He was shouting into the mike and part of his transmission was garbled. In his excitement he held the key open and every cop in Brooklyn North sat grimly listening to the wail of the siren and the screech of tires mingled with the shouts of the men in 77 Boy.

At times like this the dispatcher's main function is to get the necessary information. "What unit is this?" she said with deliberate calmness. "Ten-five, you're coming in broken up."

A cop in the Seven-nine Precinct, infuriated by her dispassionate tone, shouted into his mike, "He said Kings County, for Chrissake, Central. Have surgeons standing by!"

The dispatcher's voice, now with an edge in it, persisted. "All other units please stay off the air unless you have an emergency message. What unit responding to Kings County?"

By now the cops monitoring the radio had heard enough. The tone in 77 Boy's voice had told them everything they needed to know. One of their own had been shot and would need blood. One by one the radio cars scattered over Brooklyn North streamed toward Kings County Hospital as if drawn by an irresistible magnet. Assignments and routine radio calls would go unanswered tonight. Petty jealousies between uniform cops and detectives were forgotten. Precinct boundaries ceased to exist. Patrol cars with sirens screaming and lights flashing hurled toward the one morbid scene no cop wants to witness.

The incessant sound of sirens, like mourning banshees, filled the air as more and more radio cars screeched to a halt outside the emergency room. A patrol sergeant stood at the door and tried futilely to get some of the cops to return to patrol. But of course no one listened.

Inside was chaos. On a normal night the emergency room at Kings County resembled a Vietnam field hospital, but tonight in addition to the usual carnage, they had a shot cop. A nervous captain, who'd just arrived, shouted to the cops pouring through the doors, "Call it off, for Chrissake. No more units needed."

Other patients were left lying on stretchers as harried nurses tried to herd the growing cluster of cops out of the way. But the cops, nerves taut with fear and rage, either snarled defiance or simply ignored the nurses' pleas.

Police Officer Gene Forti, blood splattered across the front of his uniform, sat on a wooden bench and tried to steady his red-stained fingers long enough to light a cigarette. He had sat in the backseat of 77 Boy and cradled Velez's body during the eternal ride to the hospital. Some cops stood apart from him, unwilling to be near a man who had touched death, while others tried to comfort the distraught officer.

A nurse entered and announced, "Anyone with type AB follow me. If you're not sure, come anyway."

Several cops, glad to have something useful to do, nervously shuffled down the corridor.

The duty captain, who was responsible for investigating the night's events, was anxious to begin putting the pieces together before the brass showed up and started asking questions to which he had no answers. "Sergeant," he said, pointing to the blood-splattered cop on the bench, "bring that man over here. I gotta start getting something on paper."

The nurse said, "You can't talk to that man now, Captain. He's going into shock. Sue, give me a hand with this one." The other nurse took one look at the cop shivering on the bench and nodded. Together they led the dazed cop into a curtained cubicle.

The unhappy captain shook his head. "Damn! I forgot to call Operations!"

The sergeant was an old-timer. "I already called, Cap."

"Thanks, Sarge," the captain said, still feeling miserable, and wishing he'd taken the night off.

The sergeant peered into the room where Velez lay. The body was barely visible behind the cluster of green-clad doctors and nurses hovering over him, but the sergeant had been in enough emergency rooms to recognize the frantic battle to save a dying man. Tubes leading from plastic bottles carried clear and red fluids into Velez's arms and nose. Blood-soaked clothing cut away from the body lay in a haphazard pile on the floor amid hastily discarded bandage wrappings and bloody gauze pads. The sergeant studied the erratic, jagged lines on the screen, which monitored the vital signs of a body fighting for life. On the other side of the table a respirator pumped rhythmically for overburdened lungs slowly filling with blood. Occasionally, the monitor's alarm sounded and someone made an adjustment until the beeping stopped. Doctors swore loudly if an instrument fell or a nurse didn't respond quickly enough. The sergeant ambled outside to light a cigar. It was going to be a long night.

When the doctors judged Velez stable enough to move to surgery, they came through the doors in a rush. "Watch it! Out of the way!" they shouted as they raced Velez and his life-support system toward the elevator bank. Each cop standing in line to give blood reacted differently. Some stared, others turned away, while a few slipped outside for a breath of stagnant Brooklyn air.

The captain was on the telephone with the Borough Commander. "Info is still sketchy, Chief, but . . . What? . . . Oh . . . Off duty . . . Yeah . . . I don't know . . . Yeah, it was a smoke shop . . . Him? . . . We don't know yet . . . No, we didn't find any on him . . . Certainly, Chief, as soon as I know."

One by one the police officers who'd given their blood for a brother officer drifted back to their respective precincts to resume their everyday mundane chores—responding to family fights, parking violations, and loud radios.

Now it was the press's turn. Camera crews jostled each other and jockeyed for the best camera angles. Bright lights flashed as camera crews set up test shots and light levels.

Shannon and Rose shoved through the milling reporters and identified themselves to the belligerent cops guarding the doors to the emergency room. Inside, the last of the cops were giving blood. The captain sat at the nurse's station writing notes on a clipboard.

"Captain, I'm Lieutenant Shannon from the Chief of Detectives office, and this is Lieutenant Rose."

The captain looked up at them. His eyes were red with fatigue. "Yeah?"

"Velez worked for me. What happened?"

"I thought he worked in the Four-four?"

"He was working for me on a temporary assignment."

The captain swore. Now he'd have to change his report. He'd never get the damn thing written if they kept changing the information on him.

"Do you know what happened?" Shannon asked again.

The captain removed his glasses and rubbed the bridge of his nose.

"There was a holdup in a smoke shop on Pitkin Avenue. Somehow Velez got into the middle of it. He killed one perp, but apparently didn't know there was another. He took two slugs in the back."

"What's his condition?"

The captain replaced his glasses. "I don't know. They took him up to surgery over an hour ago. By the way"—he glanced about, looking even unhappier—"the P.C. is here somewhere." Then he remembered his role as the investigating officer and said to Shannon, "This man worked for you, Lieutenant. What was he doing in this neighborhood? Was he using drugs, or what?"

Before a surprised Shannon could stop him, Rose was across the table and had the startled captain by the throat. "He wasn't buying drugs, you fucking moron, he was doing police work."

Shannon dragged Rose off the desk and shoved him away from the captain. "Cool down, for Chrissake. You're not helping things."

"Lieutenant," the captain squeaked when he caught his breath, "I want your name and command. I'm going to prefer charges." He adjusted his glasses. "You're suspended," he hissed. "I . . ." His voice trailed off as he tried to remember if he had the authority to suspend a lieutenant. Goddamn, he hated this job. The Borough Commander was on his ass with all kinds of questions he couldn't answer. The P.C. was here and might ask him questions, and now this crazy lieutenant attacked him for no reason! He felt a bowel movement coming on—the second one tonight. Why had he ever taken the captains' exam? He'd been happy as a lieutenant in the Pension Section. *It was my wife, goddamn her! She made me take the test.* He forgot about Rose and raced down the corridor in search of the men's room.

A doctor in a wrinkled green gown stepped off the elevator. "How is he, Doc?" Rose asked.

The doctor, a short, round-faced Filipino, peered at Rose through thick glasses. "We are doing everything we can for him. He has lost a great deal of blood and his vital signs are marginal. The X rays show extensive bleeding, and we are doing an exploratory to ascertain the extent of the damage."

The litany of medical procedures wasn't what Rose wanted to hear. "Is he going to be all right?"

The doctor averted his eyes. "It is too soon to tell. Now if you will excuse me . . ." He brushed past Rose, anxious to get away from these big angry cops with guns.

The captain returned. While sitting on the bowl, he'd decided he did have the authority to suspend a lieutenant, but he didn't want to face the mountain of paperwork that would surely follow. Ignoring Rose, he addressed his questions to Shannon. "Is he married? Who's next of kin?"

With a shock, Shannon realized he didn't know who the next of kin was. In fact he knew next to nothing about the impish young cop.

Down the hall a door opened and the P.C. and Chief of Detectives emerged from the hospital administrator's office. A young deputy inspector yelled to the cops guarding the door, "Okay, let them in."

The doors opened and a stampeding herd of reporters with cameras, lights, and trailing wires converged on the commissioner. The klieg lights clicked on, bathing the corridor in a harsh glare. Strobe lights flashed as photographers, anxious to make the deadline for the morning edition, cranked off picture after picture. Even in a news-jaded city like New York, a shot cop was headline material.

The P.C. raised his hands. "Okay, ladies and gentlemen, settle down. I have a statement to make and then I'll take your questions."

Immediately, the murmuring stopped and only the whirling of the electric-drive cameras was heard. Mara began, "At approximately five-thirty this evening, off-duty Police Officer Luis Velez, who is assigned to the Forty-fourth Precinct in the Bronx, was shot while attempting to terminate an armed robbery. Officer Velez shot and killed one of the perpetrators, but was himself shot by a second perpetrator who is still at large."

"What's his condition?" a reporter shouted.

"The doctors are still operating. We don't know yet."

"Why was he in a smoke shop? Was he making an undercover buy?"

Mara shook his head. "No. The officer was off duty. He was not acting in an official capacity."

A nervous inspector whispered something in the P.C.'s ear. "Of course," Mara added quickly, "a police officer is technically on duty twenty-four hours a day, so when he witnesses a felony in progress, he is expected to take proper police action."

The barrage of questions continued. "What's proper police procedure?" "Why did he go in there alone?" "Why didn't he wait for a backup?"

The commissioner raised his hands for silence. "Our officers are trained to request assistance in these circumstances. We don't know why this wasn't done."

A female reporter known for her outspoken anti-police views stuck her microphone in the P.C.'s face. "Commissioner Mara, Senator Pickett alleges that the police department has been compromised by drug money. It's common knowledge in this neighborhood that this smoke shop was selling illegal drugs. Was this officer shaking down the owners or was he buying drugs for himself?"

The P.C. flinched and a gray-haired chief standing behind him looked like he was going to be physically ill. Earlier, Mara, as well as most of the brass in the room, had come to the same conclusion. The old guard was more than willing to believe that any cop under thirty was a closet junkie. It was only after Larson whispered in his ear, that Mara learned who Velez was and why he came to be on Pitkin Avenue this night.

"An official investigation is under way," the commissioner said, trying to head off further questions of this sort. "That's all I have for you. As soon as we know more, you'll be informed. Thank you."

After a few more half-hearted attempts to question the P.C., the lights were turned off and the TV crews rushed back to their studios to prepare for the eleven o'clock news.

Larson stood behind Mara. "Commissioner, the two lieutenants are down the hall. Do you want to talk to them?"

"No I don't," Mara hissed. "They've screwed up enough for one night." He poked a finger into Larson's silk tie. "You told me they were the only two working on this investigation. I want to know who's responsible for letting this cop Velez get involved."

Larson nodded gravely. "I'll get on that right away, Commissioner. I'll give it my personal attention."

The commissioner and his entourage departed, leaving Larson alone to ponder whom to blame for this fiasco. On his way out he snapped at Shannon, "I want you two in my office tomorrow morning 0800 hours sharp."

Later, in the hospital cafeteria, Rose fed coins into the coffee machine. "Sugar?"

"Black," Shannon answered.

They sat down at a dirty table and cleared a space amid the day's accumulation of paper plates and cups. The cafeteria was empty except for a small group of white-clad hospital workers laughing and joking at another table. Shannon sipped the hot, bitter coffee. "What did you think of the P.C.'s performance?"

"He's a hell of an actor."

"Do you think he knows?" Shannon persisted.

Rose angrily hurled the untouched cup into the wastebasket. "If he doesn't, it's time somebody told him."

Velez's shooting had jarred Rose out of his complacency. Until now he'd insulated himself from the emotional impact of the investigation with sarcasm and humor. Certainly, murder was a serious matter, but there was something antiseptic about the death of strangers, merely names on a piece of paper. Investigating murder was just an exciting game. But now, for the first time, he realized that he and Shannon were in a life-and-death struggle, and Luis was upstairs in an operating room fighting his own personal battle for survival.

They returned to the waiting room and took turns going for coffee. At fifteen minutes after four Shannon looked at his watch; he'd forgotten to call Eileen. He was about to, but thought better of it. Middle of the night telephone calls to a cop's house can be heart-stopping.

Rose tried to get comfortable in an orange imitation-leather chair. Except for the porter waxing the floor, the corridor was deserted. With eyes that felt like they had sand in them, he watched as the buffer swung gently back and forth in a smooth, graceful arch.

A hand shook him. He opened his eyes and stretched. "Damn, I must have dozed off. What time is it?"

Shannon, pale from lack of sleep, stood over him. "Luis is dead."

31

BRIAN SHANNON PUT IF OFF AS LONG AS HE COULD, BUT TONIGHT WAS the last night of the wake.

As he entered the funeral home he was assailed by the sweet, sickly smell of flowers. Ignoring the coffin surrounded by flowers, he approached the frail woman sitting in the front row. Juanita Hernandez sat in her plain black dress with her eyes fixed on the body of her dead nephew. She was around fifty, but looked older. Raising Luis and her own three children in the hostile environment of El Barrio had sapped her energy and strength. Life in Spanish Harlem was a constant state of siege. Violence waited in the streets, the hallways, and sometimes even the home.

"He was a good boy," she told Shannon in a heavy Spanish accent. "Always very smart in school. One hundreds in all his arithmetic papers. Other boys made fun of Luis because he was so smart. Every day he fought. Once I went to get him after school . . .'' Her eyes misted at the memory. "He was so mad. Only ten, but he said to me, 'Mama, don't you ever come for me again. I can take care of myself.' So independent, my Luis.''

"I only worked with Luis for a short time," Shannon said softly, "but I liked him very much. He was a fine man and a good police officer." The words sounded hollow and pretentious, but she seemed to take comfort from them.

She fingered her rosary. "Lieutenant Shannon, why did Luis have to die? He was so smart. He could have done so much." Her eyes drifted past him and settled on her own vision very far away.

He started to answer, to offer an acceptable platitude that would make her feel better about her dead nephew, but nothing came out. A steel band tightened around his chest and he couldn't breathe. Numbly, he patted her hand. In a daze he made his way to the back of the room and collapsed into a folding chair. He put his head down and waited for the spell to pass.

Finally his breathing returned to normal. He sat quietly in the rear, watching the mourners file past the casket. It was an odd mix who came to pay their last respects. Some were cops, and some were street people—friends from the old neighborhood. It was obvious that a few were drug addicts; friends of Luis's who had gone down a very different road.

Some recognized Shannon was a cop and stared at him in unbridled hatred. To them he epitomized "the man"—white, well-fed, and surviving at the expense of token minority cops. Luis's death had only confirmed their suspicions—"the man" would not allow bright kids from the ghetto to succeed in the white man's world. Even the slowest-witted junkie recognized something special in Luis, and now he was dead.

When Shannon felt he was in control again, he stepped forward and knelt before the casket. Dressed in his blue uniform and ribbons, Luis didn't look like the cocky kid who came in late every morning with outrageous tales of sexual conquest. Staring at the sallow, passive face, Shannon fervently hoped the stories were true.

Shannon tried to pray for Luis, but the childhood prayers he knew by rote sounded foreign and meaningless. Who was he praying to? A God he didn't believe in? What was he praying for? That God would somehow restore life to Luis? In his crushing despair he was rapidly losing faith. It seemed that every building block in his life was turning to sand. His relationship with his wife and child, his faith in the police department, and his belief in God, were all crumbling. He was adrift with no reference points to guide him. In the end, kneeling there with his eyes tightly shut to keep in the tears, he prayed to Luis, a dead cop.

*   *   *

IT WAS JUST AFTER ONE WHEN HE PULLED INTO THE DRIVEWAY. THE house was dark except for a light in his bedroom; Eileen was still awake. He went into the kitchen and retrieved the Black Bush from under the kitchen sink. The bottle had been a Christmas present from Eileen—something to use on happy, special occasions. He held the bottle up to the light and saw that it was almost empty. But he couldn't remember the last time he was happy. So how the hell did it get so empty?

He downed the first shot and poured another. He estimated there were about four shots left. He already had a head start, so there should be enough left to dull his mind for sleep. He didn't want to think and he didn't want to dream—especially to dream. For the past several nights he was having the same dream. He was in the Chief of Detectives office and Larson, with a sarcastic smile on his face, was throwing reams of paper at him. "Here's another sixty-one, Shannon. You call yourself a detective? Another man executed because of your incompetence. How many are going to die because of you?" Shannon always bolted upright in bed, ending the dream there.

He just wanted to sleep. He didn't want to think of Luis, the investigation, or Pickett. As he was pouring his third shot, he looked up and saw Eileen standing in the doorway.

"Have a hard day at the office, Junebug?"

"Yeah. Lately every day's a hard day at the office. How're you doing?"

"Fine. How are you?"

He eyed the bottle. "If the Black Bush holds out, I'll be just fine too."

"Since when have you taken to drinking whiskey in the kitchen?"

"I do seem to have picked up some bad habits, haven't I?"

Eileen filled the kettle. "Want some tea?"

"Good Lord, no. On top of Black Bush? That would be a mortal sin."

Eileen gave him a bemused look. "Are you drunk?"

"No, but not for the lack of trying. I had a few drinks in a gin mill in the Bronx. I think they must water the stuff down. I didn't even get a buzz. I couldn't stay, though. I was putting a real damper on the festivities. The locals aren't used to having cops drinking in their gin mills."

"What were you doing in the Bronx?"

"I had to do something."

Eileen fixed her tea and sat down. "Brian, you look like hell."

"Well, thank you very much."

"You know what I mean. You haven't been sleeping right. What do you do when you get up?"

"There are some terrific movies on at three A.M. The commercials are even better. Where's Kathy?"

"It's after one in the morning, Brian. She's in bed. Where else would she be?"

"That's right. Sometimes I lose track of the time. Sometimes I lose track of myself. How's Kathy?"

"Fine. Nothing's changed since you saw her this morning."

"Good. She looks just like you. Do you know that? When is that concert?"

"Thursday."

"That's only four days away. Is she nervous?"

"Sure. You'll be there, won't you?"

"Absolutely. I wouldn't miss it."

"Come on, Junebug. Drink up and let's go to bed. You're beat."

They went to bed, but neither of them went to sleep. Eileen, with her back to him, said softly, "How did it go at the wake tonight?"

There was a long silence, then he said, "How did you know about that?"

"Alex Rose called. He was concerned about you. He seems like a nice guy."

"Rose is a nosy bastard from IAD who should mind his own business. He's a yenta and a lousy detective."

"He thinks you blame yourself for Velez's death."

Brian didn't answer.

"Brian," she began tentatively, "I'm sorry . . . so sorry. From the way you spoke about him, I know you liked him."

"Yeah." His voice was husky. "Luis was a good kid. He—" Then, to his horror—he'd never cried in front of Eileen before—tears welled up in him. "Eileen . . . I just . . . don't know . . . anymore . . ."

"Brian . . ." Unable to speak herself, she pulled him to her and felt the wetness on his cheek. They held each other tightly and they wept; Brian, for Luis Velez and the futility of his death, and Eileen, because for the first time she had personally glimpsed the isolation and grief of his job.

THE BUSES BEGAN TO ARRIVE IN A STEADY DRIZZLE THAT HAD WASHED away all the color from the morning. Somberly, the police officers from Luis Velez's precinct filed off the bus and buttoned up their blue uniforms against the rain. They collected under the dripping awning of a bodega to talk in hushed, self-conscious whispers while waiting for the funeral to begin. Curious women and men sat at their tenement windows and looked down on the strange assortment of uniforms and police cars assembled below. Police cars from Nassau and Suffolk counties were already there. Later, more buses and police cars from states as far away as Pennsylvania would be arriving. The fellowship of policemen transcends county and state lines when a member of the fraternity dies. They came to Police Officer Luis Velez's funeral to demonstrate this solidarity and pay their last respects.

One of the perks of dying in the line of duty is an inspector's funeral—a sad ritual meant to honor the dead and console the living. Everyone—from the mayor to the Police Commissioner to members of the slain officer's command—attends.

Row after row of multicolored uniforms representing scores of local law enforcement agencies is an impressive sight. And when the Emerald Society's lone piper in solemn half-step leads the uniformed contingent up the street to the plaintive tune of "Amazing Grace," there's a great deal of blinking and throat clearing in the ranks of tough, cynical cops.

Later, when the family, numbed with grief and shock, is led into the church, each man in the ranks will steal a furtive glance at the bereaved family and try to imagine how his family would react to his own death.

Inside the church the chaplain will talk about service, loyalty, and the supreme sacrifice. He will share intimate anecdotes about a man he has probably never met. Finally, there is the ritual of incense and prayers, and it's over. The six uniformed pallbearers in their white gloves carry the flag-draped casket to the waiting hearse, and when the door slams, it signals the end of another aborted career.

The department will put up a plaque to the memory of the slain officer, and for a while the men who knew and worked with him will talk in reverent tones about what a great guy he was—funny, droll, cheap—but above all, a good cop. Eventually, some of his friends will retire and others will be transferred, and their replacements, who every day will walk past the commemorative plaque, won't know who he was. In time the slain officer will be forgotten by everyone except his family—his wife, who will remember him during those long, lonely nights, and his children, who will remember him especially on those special occasions like Father's Day, Dad's school dinners, and the countless times when such events remind them that they have no father.

Police Officer Luis Velez's inspector's funeral was like all the other cops who'd been murdered in the line of duty. The mayor and the Police Commissioner, standing side by side in front of the ranks of cops, looked suitably grieved. During the homily the chaplain spoke of the tragedy of such a young death, while at the same time praising Velez's ultimate sacrifice—a sacrifice that should be an inspiration to policemen everywhere.

The rain let up as the melancholy procession left for the cemetery. The ranks were dismissed, and some cops, opening their collars and loosening their ties, drifted over to the PBA canteen for a soft drink and a stale baloney sandwich, while others, in need of greater stimulation, wandered into the nearest saloon to talk about the job and tell war stories. Every man there needed a diversion—something to allay the disturbing feelings of guilt triggered by the dark, selfish thought that brings both shame and relief to the minds of policemen at a time like this: *Thank God it wasn't me.*

Shannon and Rose followed the procession to Woodlawn Cemetery in the Bronx. After the short graveside ceremony, they offered their condolences to Velez's aunt and drove straight to the OTC Pub.

The Irish bartender poured an extra drink for himself. "This one's on me, gentlemen," he said solemnly. "God rest the poor officer."

After the bartender went to the other end of the bar, Rose asked, "How did the wake go last night?"

"All right. I got a chance to talk to Luis's aunt. She's a terrific woman. I don't know how women like that raise kids in neighborhoods like the Bronx."

"It's not easy, but a lot of them do."

"Yeah." Shannon cradled his head in his hands. "Rose, I don't feel like a cop anymore. I looked at the faces of those guys today, and I wasn't sure I could trust any one of them."

Rose drained his glass. "I was watching the mayor's face and wondering if he knows what's going on. But I couldn't tell."

"It's like it's us against the rest of the department," Shannon said. "I don't like the feeling."

"That's because we don't know who to trust anymore. We can't trust Larson. Bennett? I'm not sure. And we don't know how many guys we're looking for. Maybe it's a few guys in NET. Maybe it's the whole goddamned command."

Idly, Shannon spun the ice cubes in his glass. "When I heard Luis had been shot, I thought they'd done it. Jesus, cops killing cops. That's hard to deal with." His face twisted in anger. "What was the point? Why would he try to stop a holdup in a smoke shop? It doesn't make any sense. A fucking smoke shop! There are hundreds of them in the city, and every one of them is dealing dope. Why did he risk his life for that?"

"Why do we do anything we do? One night when I was a rookie I was assigned to a radio car with an old-timer. He must have had thirty years on the job. I had eight months. Remember in the old days, old-timers wouldn't talk to you until you had at least three years on the job? He was really pissed because I was assigned to his car. He even bitched to the sergeant, but there was nobody else, so he was stuck with me. He didn't say one word to me the entire night. The radio was quiet, so it was a long night. We were just heading in at the end of the tour when we got a run—'Man with a gun.' Outside the door we heard all kinds of yelling and screaming. The old-timer just looked at me. I guess he was trying to decide how badly this asshole rookie in his new blue suit and shiny leather was going to fuck up. My mouth was so dry I couldn't spit. All he said to me was, 'We're going in, watch yourself.' He shoved me to the side, put his foot to the door, and was the first one into the apartment."

"Was there a gun?"

Rose smiled at the recollection. "Yeah, an old double-barrel shotgun. The guy was so surprised at our explosive entrance that he just stood there with his mouth hanging open. The old-timer walked up to him, yanked the gun out of his hand, and cold-cocked him with his jack. I found out later he had three kids.

"Why did he go through that door first? Why did either of us go through that door, for that matter? Because we get paid to do it? They don't pay us enough to do that. Christ, one asshole rock musician in drag can make more in one night than a cop can in a whole year! I don't know why he went in then, and I still don't know. But every day, somewhere, a cop goes through another door."

Shannon gulped his drink. It was his fourth, but it had absolutely no effect on him. He wanted to forget Velez, the murders, the whole damned department, but the alcohol wasn't doing its job. Instead of slipping mercifully into the numbness of intoxication, his mind, if anything, was more acute. He stood up. "Come on, let's get out of here. We're wasting time."

BACK AT THE OFFICE, SHANNON RUMMAGED THROUGH VELEZ'S DESK. "I don't know what any of this crap is. There must be a couple of dozen diskettes here. Everything he programmed into the computer. We're going to have to look this stuff over carefully."

Chief Bennett, carrying his coffee cup like it was nitroglycerine, came in. He sat down and promptly splashed coffee on his clean shirt. "I'm sorry about Velez, Brian. I hope you don't feel responsible for what happened."

Shannon's mouth was set in a straight line. "We're all big boys. We do what we gotta do."

"I had a talk with Larson this morning," Bennett said abruptly. "He's on a witch-hunt. He needs a human sacrifice because of the Velez shooting."

"Why?"

"The P.C.'s on his back. It seems Larson told him there were only two of you working on this investigation and then Velez was killed. The P.C. is afraid this thing will get out to the press. He's got a point. If they—"

"Fuck the media, fuck the P.C., and fuck Larson," Shannon said bitterly.

Bennett kicked the door shut. "Take it easy. I know how you feel, but you know this job. It doesn't run on morals and principles, it runs on pragmatic politics. If this case isn't handled properly, it'll mean the careers of a lot of people in this city."

"What about us?" Shannon asked.

"Lieutenants are expendable," Rose said dryly.

Bennett gave him a sharp look. "We don't need the sarcasm, Rose." Then he said, "I owe you guys an apology. I tried to put some distance between myself and you because I knew this was a hot potato. But what the hell''—he ran his fingers through his thick red hair, making it even more unruly—''worse comes to worse, I'll throw my papers in early. From now on I want to be kept informed of everything you do. If you need anything, come to me.''

Rose studied Bennett with renewed respect. In spite of the bravado, he was indeed putting his career on the chopping block. This investigation was a classical no-win situation. All they could do was try to keep the casualties down.

''So what's your next move?'' Bennett asked.

''We'll pick up where Luis left off,'' Rose said without hesitation. ''We'll tail Pickett.''

Shannon thumbed through Velez's spiral notebook. It was filled with notes written in a small, neat hand. ''Christ,'' he mumbled, ''what a waste.''

32

"POWER BOATS! YOU GOTTA BE KIDDING," ROSE SAID DERISIVELY.

Shannon switched the headlights off. They were parked where they could watch the cab waiting in front of the brownstone. Automatically, they scanned the street and cars for the telltale signs of someone, or something, out of place. But Charles Street was quiet.

After yesterday's meeting with Bennett, they'd spent the rest of the afternoon sorting through Velez's records. At dawn they'd waited a discreet distance from Pickett's home. They had been following him ever since.

As they crossed the Brooklyn Bridge, Rose spotted a sloop motoring up the East River and remarked about the joys of sailing. And the argument was on. They had found yet another area of disagreement.

"How fast does a sailboat go?" Shannon demanded.

Rose was cautious. "A small one? Maybe four or five knots."

Shannon snickered. "At that rate it would take you all day to get across Long Island Sound."

"Well if you're in such a big hurry, you should take a plane. *Getting* there is half the fun of sailing."

"You can't fish off a sailboat," Shannon added smugly.

Rose looked at him like he'd lost his mind. "Why? Don't fish swim in the same water with sailboats?"

"The sides of a sailboat are too high—"

"Freeboard," Rose corrected.

"What?"

"The side of a boat is called freeboard."

"Whatever. You can lose a fish raising him that high out of the water. Besides, the hooks get tangled on all those ropes . . ."

"They're called lines. You hang people with ropes. You use lines on a boat. You stink potters know as much about seamanship as that fireplug. Heads up, here they come. Hey, how about that! Senator Pickett has a white girlfriend."

The couple climbed into the cab, and Rose noted that Pickett didn't look around before he got in.

"Look at that dopey bastard. He's not looking. He'll never spot a tail if he doesn't look for one."

The taxi edged through the narrow streets of the Village and turned up Sixth Avenue. Once they were safely positioned behind the taxi, the argument resumed. "So you're a big fisherman, eh, Brian?"

"Yeah." His tone was defensive. "I like to fish. It's relaxing. Last summer a sailboat passed me, and everyone on deck was yelling and tugging on ropes—excuse me, *lines*. It looked like they were in the middle of a fucking mutiny. That's not my idea of a relaxing day on the water." He slowed down to allow a car to get between them and the taxi.

"They were racing," Rose said patiently. "When you're cruising you just set the sails and—watch it! He's turning onto Fiftieth Street."

Shannon edged into the right lane. "Yeah, I got him. Look at that red Toyota up ahead."

"What about it?"

"It's been with us since Fourteenth Street."

Rose grabbed a pen. "Get closer so I can get the plate number."

Shannon eased past a stretch limo. Now there were only two cars between them. One pulled to the side and the plate was visible. Rose keyed the mike. "Nine-six-one to Central."

"Go ahead," the dispatcher said.

"Ten-fifteen on New York registration seven-five-zero-Boy-Tango-Charlie."

"Stand by. The computer is down."

"Thank God for modern technology," Rose muttered.

The taxi pulled over at the corner of Fifth Avenue and Fiftieth Street. Pickett and the woman got out. "You stay with the Toyota," Rose said, opening the door. "I'll meet you back at this corner."

As Rose was getting out, a man wearing a tan leather jacket and a baseball cap emerged from the Toyota. Shannon tapped the horn and pointed. Rose nodded in acknowledgment.

The couple turned onto Fifth Avenue and disappeared. The man in the leather jacket walked to the corner, stood as if uncertain which way to go, and then casually strolled after Pickett.

The light changed and Shannon and the Toyota were swept away in the flow of traffic. Rose arrived at the corner just in time to see Pickett and the woman turn into the Rockefeller Center promenade. At the same time, he saw the man in the leather jacket staring intently into the window of an Italian shoe store. Suddenly the man turned his head and looked in Rose's direction. Following the cardinal rule of surveillance—never make eye contact with the subject—Rose stepped briskly to the curb and pretended to hail a cab. To his amazement a taxi, ignoring the frantic waves of more prosperous-looking passengers, screeched to a halt in front of him. Recalling Murphy's Law, he reluctantly got in. As he did, he glanced out the rear window; the leather jacket was gone. "Never mind," he said, climbing out of the moving taxi as the angry driver roundly cursed him in Arabic.

Rose, scanning the sidewalk, didn't see the leather jacket and decided he must have disappeared into the promenade. He tried to spot him in the crowd, but it was impossible. Rockefeller Center, aglow with its dazzling Christmas display of lights and decorations, was a favorite tourist attraction at this time of the year. With Christmas only seven days away, the promenade was filled to capacity. Rose waded into a human sea of men, women, and children all making their way, imperceptibly, toward the other end, where the Christmas tree with its thousands of colored lights towered over the statue of Prometheus.

Eventually, he made it to the edge of the ice-skating rink. Here he could get a better view of the surrounding area. Below on the blue-white ice, skaters with varying degrees of proficiency glided or stumbled their way around the rink. In the center a trim woman in her sixties, wearing a shocking pink skirt, executed some reasonably good spins and jumps. Even from this distance Rose could see she must have been a beauty in her day. He scanned the crowd on the opposite side, and there, just to the right of Prometheus, stood Pickett and the woman, arm in arm, smiling down at the skaters below.

He started to make his way toward them while at the same time looking for the leather jacket. He was pushed and jostled by tourists jabbering in a dozen foreign languages. For a moment he lost sight of them, but then saw them heading up the stairs leading to Fiftieth Street. Unexpectedly, the leather jacket emerged from the blue smoky haze of a chestnut vender's cart and quickly climbed the stairs behind Pickett and the woman.

With a greater sense of urgency, Rose elbowed his way through the crowd. In spite of the chill in the air, he was sweating by the time he caught up to the couple on Sixth Avenue. Frantically, he looked for the leather jacket, who had once again disappeared. He ducked into a doorway, removed his gun from his ankle holster and stuffed it in his pocket.

Halfway down the block the couple stopped in front of a nondescript Italian restaurant to read the menu in the window. They had a short conversation and went in. Rose glanced at his watch. Almost an hour had passed. He took a last look around for the leather jacket and rushed back to Fifth and Fiftieth.

Shannon was waiting with a glum look on his face. "How'd you do?" he asked Rose.

"The guy in the leather jacket was definitely following them. I'm not sure, but he may have made me. I lost him coming out of the promenade on Fiftieth."

"That's great!"

Rose, cold and angry at himself for losing his man, lashed out at the rebuke in Shannon's tone. "Fuck you, Shannon. You think it's easy tailing someone in a mob? What about you? What did you find out about the guy in the Toyota?"

"It came back stolen," Shannon said in disgust. "When I got the ten-sixteen, we were on Third Avenue and Fifty-eighth. Traffic was all screwed up. He made the light and I got caught in a spillback. By the time I got untangled, he was gone."

"Oh, so the super sleuth lost his man too!"

"Don't break my balls."

Rose snapped the gun back into his ankle holster. "Our friends are having dinner in a joint off Sixth Avenue. What did you get on the plate?"

"They don't match the Toyota. If the car is theirs, they're not very smart."

Rose rubbed his neck to relieve his splitting headache. They'd been with Pickett since seven this morning and had eaten almost nothing. "When we get back to the office we'll check the vehicles of everyone in NET to see who owns a Toyota. What do you wanna do now?" He hoped Shannon would suggest they call it a day.

Shannon started the car. "Let's wait by the restaurant. We'll follow Pickett home. These guys might still be hanging around."

Cautiously, they made a pass through the block, looking for the Toyota or the leather jacket. Seeing neither, they took up a position at the top of the street, where they had a good view of the restaurant entrance. Shannon reached behind him for a bag. "I bought coffee and Danish."

A starving Rose opened the bag. "What kind did you get?"

"I got you prune."

"I hate prune."

"Take mine."

"What is it?"

"Cheese."

"I hate cheese."

"Fuck you, then starve." Shannon bit into the stale cheese Danish.

"At least we were right about Pickett." Rose pried the lid off his container. "He's the target."

"Yeah. Did you get a good look at the guy in the leather jacket?"

Rose took a sip of his cold coffee and made a face. "Damn, this tastes like gasoline."

"Then you must have gotten the tea by mistake. The coffee is supposed to taste like kerosene."

Rose poured the container out the window. "No, I didn't get a good look at his face. He was about five-eight; looked like blond hair under the cap."

Shannon eyed two men walking on the other side of the street. When he was satisfied they were merely pedestrians, he continued. "That sounds like the same guy who was seen outside Wanda Little's apartment."

"Yeah."

They sat in silence, punctuated occasionally by a dispatcher's message, and waited for Pickett and his girlfriend to come out. Neither spoke, but they were both fantasizing about the same thing—a plate of pasta primavera, veal medallions, and a bottle of wine.

Eventually, Pickett and the woman emerged and the two starving lieutenants followed Pickett to Charles Street, and finally, at one in the morning, to his home in Brooklyn.

Shannon was hungry and bleary-eyed when he pulled into his driveway at two-thirty. But he couldn't sleep. He sat in the den with a can of beer and a piece of cold chicken and watched another rerun of *A Walk in the Sun*. But he couldn't concentrate on the assault on the farmhouse because he kept thinking about the man in the leather jacket. A killer? A cop? Or both?

He was awakened in the chair at seven by the sound of Eileen getting Kathy off to school.

TENSION, AS PALPABLE AS A FOG, HUNG IN THE AIR OF HARDY'S apartment. Listlessly, they drifted in, first Beals and then Tecci. The three barely spoke.

Tim Hardy couldn't shake the uneasiness, the impending sense of doom that had begun to fill his every waking moment. Uncomfortable in the presence of the two men, Hardy kept glancing at his watch. The Chief was late; it wasn't like him. Finally, the bell rang.

Since that tumultuous meeting two weeks ago, when Tecci admitted killing Cronin, Stone had wisely decided not to hold any more meetings for a while. It was a decision Hardy found encouraging. He hoped Stone was having second thoughts about Pickett. But when he'd been told to set up this meeting for tonight, he knew the Chief was going ahead with it.

Outwardly, Patrick Stone seemed the same. But to Tim Hardy, who knew him intimately, Stone had changed since Cronin's death.

Patrick Stone took a scotch from Hardy and turned to Tecci. "You followed Pickett last night. Tell me about it."

As Tecci began his report, Hardy's unsettled mind drifted back to the first time he'd met Patrick Stone. Tim Hardy's twenty-year career had been uneventful. After fifteen years as a patrol cop in a quiet Queens precinct, he made sergeant, and in one of the unexplained quirks of the job, was assigned to the Narcotics Division—an assignment many sergeants senior to him and more experienced would have given their eyeteeth for.

He hated it from the start. By nature he required stability and routine in his life, but the Narcotics Division was anything but routine. As a team leader he was responsible for a group of young, ambitious cops whose only goal was to make detective. He could barely keep up with them, let alone control their behavior, which frequently bordered on the illegal. Totally frustrated, he was about to ask for a transfer back to patrol, when Patrick Stone, a young police officer, was assigned to his team. In a matter of weeks Stone, the newest and most inexperienced member of the team, had become their informal leader. Following his lead, the team's arrests and convictions soared. During that time Hardy and Stone became friends. Perhaps it was because they were so unalike. Stone was impetuous and daring, while Hardy was conservative and deliberate. Stone instinctively grasped a problem and quickly came up with workable solutions, while Hardy pondered endlessly on too many alternatives. Their relationship was like father and son, except Stone played the father to Hardy's son.

Tecci was describing his tail of Pickett. ". . . they were sight-seeing at Rockefeller Center like a couple of tourists!"

"Then where did they go?" Stone asked.

Tecci picked at a hangnail. "I don't know, Chief. I broke off contact."

"Why?"

"I'm not sure." Tecci's restless eyes flicked from Stone and settled on his hangnail. "I thought . . . I don't know . . . it was just a feeling . . . maybe I was being followed."

Hardy shot forward in his chair. "Who was following you?" His worst fears were realized; someone was on to them.

Tecci fingered the gold chain around his neck. "I didn't see anyone for sure. I don't even know if I was followed or not. It was just a feeling."

"You were in Rockefeller Center with hundreds of people!" Hardy said in exasperation. "You can't just have had a feeling. What made you think you were being followed?"

"I don't know," Tecci snapped. He felt cornered by Hardy's incessant questions. "I told you it was just a feeling."

Stone turned to Beals. "What about you? Do you think you were followed?"

"After I dropped Stevie off I went on to Queens. I didn't notice anything."

"Did you look?" Hardy persisted. "Did you check your rearview mirror?"

Beals's face was as immobile as an African mask. Only the eyes displayed a smoldering anger. "Shit no. In midtown Manhattan? You got a hundred cabs climbing up your ass and you want me to look for a tail? How you gonna notice?"

Hardy couldn't suppress his nervous anger any longer. His fist slammed down on the table, upsetting a beer can. "Goddamn it! This whole thing is getting sloppy. You may have been followed. What if they got your plate number!"

"It's my girlfriend's car," Beals said softly. "And I was using stolen plates. There's no way anybody can trace those plates to me."

"Back off, Hardy," Tecci said. "We know what we're doing. I used my brother's van, and I had stolen plates on it too. Neither the vehicles nor the plates can be traced back to us."

Hardy was convinced they were going to be caught. In spite of his promise to himself not to voice doubts in front of them, he said, "Chief, I think we should call the whole thing off." There was a desperate tone in his voice. "At least for the time being. We're starting to make mistakes, and sooner or later these two are going to fuck up badly."

Tecci came off the couch like a shot. "What are you talking about, Hardy? You haven't done a goddamn thing since Cronin was killed. You got no balls."

Only Stone's firm hand clamped on Hardy's forearm prevented him from attacking the more powerful Tecci. "Sit down. Both of you," Stone said. Tecci slid back onto the couch and sulked.

It was evident to Stone that everyone's nerves were frayed. As a group, they were beginning to unravel. It was essential that he hold them together for just a little while longer. For the first time in his life, Patrick Stone felt uncertainty and loss of control, but he displayed none of it to the others.

"Tim, you spoke to your contact in IAD. What did he say?"

Hardy stared at the floor and his voice was strained. "I asked him if there was anything special going on with the Cronin investigation. He said no. The homicide was being investigated just like any other murdered policeman."

Stone weighed the possibilities. It was risky, but time was running out. Today was December nineteenth. He came to a decision. Avoiding Hardy's gaze, he said, "Mac has come up with some good information on Pickett. He found out that he visits his girlfriend every Thursday night and leaves around one. If that's true, he'll be there tomorrow night. Steve, you and McKay will be waiting for him."

Tecci's eyes narrowed. "Tomorrow? What about a dry run?"

"You don't need it," Stone said. He couldn't afford to wait another week. Pickett might go on vacation, or change his routine; it had to be done tomorrow. "McKay has seen the street," he added, "it's quiet."

Tecci was puzzled. This wasn't the way they'd done it before. He turned to Beals. "Mac, did you scope this out?"

"No. I was only there once." Beals looked at Stone. "The super said he comes by every Thursday night, but he was there last night. Maybe he ain't coming back tomorrow night."

Stone wouldn't be deterred. "We'll proceed on the assumption that he will."

Tecci didn't like being rushed. "What the fuck is going on?"

"What's the problem?" Stone said softly. "Mac says it's the perfect spot. Tomorrow night, when he walks up the block, you kill him."

STONE LEFT WITH THE OTHERS. HARDY, ALONE IN THE KITCHEN, TRIED to sort out what was happening. They were rushing headlong into disaster. It all started with the money, Hardy thought ruefully. If they only hadn't taken the money. He thought back to that first time.

Stone, as he did from time to time with all the teams in NET, accompanied Hardy, Tecci, and Beals on a stakeout. It was just another routine intercept of a mule, and they took him in a parking lot at LaGuardia Airport without a hitch. Later in the station house, when they were alone vouchering the money, Stone casually removed two stacks of bills and slipped them into his briefcase. "I've decided NET needs a slush fund," he said in response to the shocked look on their faces.

Tim Hardy was struck dumb at seeing a man he trusted and admired stealing money. But Stone, true to his word, didn't keep the money for himself. Instead he made the money available to the team for expenses the department couldn't or wouldn't cover.

Like all bureaucracies, the department demanded endless forms com-

pleted in triplicate—even for small cash expenses. It was so much easier to
go to Stone, explain the need for the money, and get it from him. After a
while it seemed the most natural thing to do, even though the existence of
the fund was known only to Hardy, Tecci, and Beals.

Stone's illegal fund provided a useful service. The inability to pay
adequate compensation to their confidential informants has always been a
sore point with New York cops. There wasn't a city narc who hadn't had
a good C.I. bought out from under him by a federal counterpart with a
seemingly unlimited expense account. The hard truth was that C.I.'s weren't
motivated by loyalty; they went to the highest bidder. And in a price war
with the feds, city cops always came up second best. Now Hardy's team had
the money to compete with the feds on an equal footing, and they stopped
losing their C.I.'s.

The team had just begun to become comfortable with this arrangement
when Stone added a twist. One day he took the usual amount, but then did
something that shocked all of them. He distributed packets of money to
Tecci, Beals, Hardy, and himself. "To cover personal expenses," he explained to the startled men.

Tecci and Beals, neither of whom needed much convincing, quickly
learned to appreciate the extra money, but such was Stone's power over
them that neither man would dream of taking a dollar without his permission.

Once, Hardy had asked Stone why they'd started taking money.

Stone's gaze never faltered. "You know why, Tim. I've told you
enough times."

"I know it started as expense money." He knew it was stealing, but he
didn't know how to phrase it. "You've got more to lose than any of us.
You're on your way to the top. Why risk all that?"

Stone's eyes flashed. "I'm not risking anything, Tim. I am going to the
top. This department is run by morons and incompetents, and I've got more
on the ball than all of them put together. The job's not a religious vocation; I
didn't take any vows of poverty. Besides, we're only taking from thieves.
There's plenty of money; the drug dealers won't complain, and every
member of your team has been handpicked. The rest of NET is virgin pure.
Who's going to suspect NET people of taking money? It's the perfect
setup."

And it was the perfect setup. Under Stone's careful direction, they took
money, but never enough to arouse suspicion. Hardy had even learned to
ignore the defendants' surprised glances, which turned to knowing smirks,
when the amount of money placed in evidence was read out in court. The
first time it happened, he expected one of the defendants to shout out in
protest, but they said nothing. They merely smiled—a smile that said *You
may be a cop, but you're no different than us.*

The money was one thing; the killing was something else. If it hadn't been for the Bay View Motel incident, there wouldn't have been an excuse for the killings. Hardy didn't realize it then, but that night they all sold their souls to the Devil, and Patrick Stone was the broker.

Their peculiar friendship had given Hardy the illusion that he'd eventually make Stone see the light. But now, after tonight, even that flimsy illusion was shattered.

At some level he realized he'd severed the delicate connection between him and the Chief. It took tonight's events to see that their friendship, while strong, had never been on an equal footing. The truth of their relationship, a truth he'd chosen to ignore, was that they were like master and servant—and the servant was never to question the master. Tonight he'd violated that unspoken rule, and things between them would never be the same again.

Stoically, Hardy accepted the unpleasant truth. In spite of what Stone had become—or had always been—Hardy still felt a deep loyalty toward him. No matter what, he knew he'd never betray Patrick Stone; especially after what Stone did to save his job.

In those days the pressure of supervising a narcotics team had become unbearable for him. The ever-present danger, the arrest quotas, and the skating on the edge of illegal activity were all taking their toll on him. The only thing that helped was booze. At first he only drank on his days off. Then he started drinking after work, and finally, during the tour. The cops in his team, glad to be rid of an incompetent, nervous boss, dropped him off at a bar at the beginning of the tour and came back to collect him at the end of the night. Sometimes he was so drunk they had to take him home and put him to bed.

One night Hardy, in a drunken stupor, pulled his gun and fired five shots into the row of bottles behind the bar. Fortunately, it was late and the bar was empty. But the bartender, frightened and angry, was just about to call 911 when Stone, newly assigned, came in with the rest of the team. Stone talked him out of making a beef and paid for the damages out of his own pocket. Then he took Hardy back to his apartment, and for the next six days and nights he stayed with Hardy while he went through the agony of withdrawal.

Hardy remembered waking in a fog and seeing Stone, unshaven, standing over the bed; a welcome beacon in a storm of anxiety. Finally, it was over. Hardy was exhausted and drained; but he was sober.

Stone fed him soup. "You're never going to do this again. You don't need booze as long as I'm here."

Hardy smiled weakly. "How did you get to be so goddamn self-confident?"

"Did you ever hear the story of Icarus, the guy who made wings out of feathers and wax? His old man cautioned him not to fly too close to the sun. Naturally, the kid didn't listen, and he plunged to his death. The story's supposed to say something about pride, but that's not the way I saw it. I must have been nine or ten the first time I heard that story. You know what I thought? I thought Icarus was a jerk. If that had been me, I'd have found some way to fly right into the goddamn sun.''

Hardy fed off Stone's optimism, and his strength, as well as his confidence, returned. Back at work, nothing was said. Hardy was still the boss, but in rank only. Stone, a natural leader, made the decisions for the team. No one objected because he had an uncanny instinct for sniffing out drugs. Within months Hardy's team led the division in arrests. Those were happy, exciting days.

Hardy sipped his coffee, but it had become cold and bitter. Restlessly, his eyes flicked to the clock on the wall. Coffee was not what he wanted now. He licked his dry lips, and the memory of the burning, soothing whiskey made his mouth water. The panic, the old half-remembered panic, began to well up in him once again. He grasped the edge of the table and squeezed so hard his knuckles turned white. He held his breath and willed himself to remain seated.

He didn't know how long he stayed like that, but soon the spell broke and he rose. Like a disinterested observer he watched himself put on his coat and hurry through the door.

On the way down the stairs he made himself the same pathetic promise that all alcoholics make even as they plunge headlong off the wagon: I'll have just one drink.

33

EVEN BEFORE TIM HARDY OPENED HIS EYES, HE KNEW HE WAS IN a strange bed in a strange room. As consciousness slowly seeped into his alcohol-soaked brain, he began to experience the nauseating anxiety that comes when one awakens from a blackout.

Hardy lay still with his eyes shut tight and tried to recall the events of the night before. Or was it the week before? The dull, throbbing headache forming in the back of his head rumbled like an approaching tropical storm, waiting for him to open his eyes so it could burst forth in all its malignant fury. His cottony mouth tasted of cheap liquor and too many cigarettes. He concentrated on keeping his head perfectly still in the vain hope that the headache would die aborning. Somewhere nearby the sound of a motor whirled and stopped.

Then he heard another sound. It was in bed with him; the sound of rhythmic breathing. Involuntarily, he moaned and tried desperately to remember last night. The body in the bed shifted and the breathing rhythm altered slightly. The subtle change in tempo prompted the lurking headache to surge dangerously. Hardy knew from past experience that containing a headache in suspended animation depended upon everything in his immediate environment remaining perfectly stable. Any change in his precarious equilibrium, no matter how slight, could throw his whole world out of kilter and send the headache careening through his brain. With super-human effort he willed it into submission.

He felt the breath of the unseen body against his bare shoulder. It was then that he realized he was naked. He ran his tongue over his dry lips. His throat was parched and he had an incredible thirst. He couldn't lie here forever; there was only one thing to do; let the pain begin. He sighed in resignation and opened his eyes. The headache, fueled by the bright sunlight streaming into his bloodshot eyes, erupted. The searing, blinding pain made him blink, and his hands went involuntarily to his head as he tried, unsuccessfully, to subdue it into manageable form.

His first sight was of a dirty ceiling. A light, a single plain white globe, hung from the end of a thin electric cord. Lying at the bottom of the translucent globe he could see the dead bodies of assorted insects and roaches. Slowly, he turned his head to confront the unseen body next to him. All the jokes about drunken salesmen waking up in strange motels with 250-pound linebackers flashed through his mind. The jokes weren't funny anymore.

She wasn't a linebacker, but she was close. Even the bed sheet couldn't conceal her enormous bulk. She lay facing him with her mouth half open; a thin, glistening thread of saliva ran from her mouth to the wet pillow. Her blond beehive hairdo sprawled half unraveled on the dirty pillow, and one ample breast cascaded from her tattered nightgown.

Subterranean tremors rolling through his stomach started a chain reaction releasing gastric juices to fuel his heartburn. It had the effect of pouring gasoline on a fire. He gasped and sat upright; the sudden movement signaled the headache to surge to a maddening crescendo.

Hardy moaned softly and squinted at his surroundings. Sunlight mercilessly glared through broken slats in the venetian blinds. For so small a room, it was unbelievably cluttered. A couple of overstuffed chairs flanked a table covered with a faded, frilly red covering, which in better days could have been a shawl. Dozens of photographs, yellowed with age, crowded the tabletop. Every inch of available wall space was covered with photos torn from magazines of celebrities, from Errol Flynn to Mick Jagger. "My God," he said aloud, "I shacked up with a bag lady!"

She rolled over on her back, let out a loud snort, and woke up. She struggled up on one elbow and with one easy motion tucked her jiggling breast back into her nightgown. "Hi champ." Her voice was gravelly. "Is there anything left to drink?"

At the mention of drink, Hardy's stomach clenched and another shot of gastric juice squirted on the fire. "Where am I?" he asked, cradling his head in his hands.

"My place." She reached for the empty vodka bottle and turned it upside down. "Shit," she mumbled, and fell back on the bed.

In spite of Hardy's conscious effort to remain as motionless as possible, the throbbing headache banging through his blood vessels took his breath away. Stiffly, like a man in a neck brace, he turned toward her. "Where is your place?" he asked patiently.

"Rivington Street." She folded her hands behind her head and stared at the ceiling.

"Manhattan?" He didn't remember leaving Astoria. But then again, he didn't remember leaving the bar either.

"Yeah." She raised herself on her elbow again and fixed him with a curious stare. "You're something else, champ," she said cryptically.

Again his stomach knotted. If only he could remember! "What day is it?" he asked suddenly.

She had to think for a moment. "Thursday."

Thank God, he thought. It's the next day. I only blacked out for one night. Suddenly, he thought about Scrooge, the Charles Dickens character. When Scrooge woke up and discovered it was still Christmas, he was overjoyed because the spirits had done it all in one night. Me too, Hardy thought giddily. The spirits did it to me in one night too. Me and Scrooge. He began to chuckle, but the physical movement stirred up the beast inhabiting his head and it gnawed on his nerve endings. His laughter dissolved into a whimper.

"I never seen anyone put away the booze like you. You kept saying you had a secret and you couldn't tell no one."

Hardy's stomach rolled and the room tilted. He had to hold on to the side of the bed to keep from falling. "What did I say?" he moaned. By now his careful plans to remain calm had become undone. His headache, completely out of control, raged and crashed through his brain like a short-circuited pinball machine. His stomach clenched, knotted, and surged with a life of its own. The pain was literally blinding. He tried to focus on her but saw only black and yellow spots drifting in his field of vision.

"What else did I say?" he asked slowly.

"Nothing." She shook her head. "Let me tell ya something, buddy. You oughta leave off the sauce, ya know? You couldn't get it up last

night for shit. I tried. Believe me I tried. It was like trying to raise
the dead.''

Hardy stood up very slowly. "You got a bathroom here?"

"Down the hall. A community john. You gotta piss? Use the sink."

He staggered to the sink. The room rolled and pitched and he almost
collided with the photo table. After he relieved himself he saw a tube of
toothpaste and squirted some in his mouth.

She lay in bed and watched him dress. "You in the Navy, right?"

"Why?" He reached over to tie his shoelaces and forgot the effect of
gravity on a cerebral thunderstorm. He brought his head up too quickly;
pinwheels floated everywhere.

"You kept saying the chief this and the chief that . . ."

He held his breath. "What did I say about the chief?"

"My husband was in the Navy. A chief petty officer on one of them
aircraft carriers. The prick used to come home with more crabs than the
Fulton Fish Market. I remember—"

"What did I say about the chief?" Hardy shouted. He had to physically
restrain himself from jumping on the bed and strangling everything out of
her at once. "What did I say?" he shouted again.

"Nothing." She pulled the sheet up around her protectively. "That's it.
You weren't making no sense. By the time you met up with me, you
couldn't hardly talk, for Chrissake. You were mumbling all night, but I
couldn't make it out. Hey, we all got things bothering us that we don't want
no one to know. I ain't one to pry."

Hardy studied her simple, blowsy face and believed her. He tucked his
shirt in his pants. "I gotta go." There was an awkward silence. He almost
said it was nice meeting you. Instead he asked, "What's that motor I keep
hearing?"

She looked puzzled. "Oh, that." She pointed to the wall behind the bed.
"The elevator shaft. I been living here so long I don't even hear it no
more."

As he opened the door she called out, "Hey champ." Even her red-
rimmed eyes couldn't conceal the loneliness. "Do you think you could get it
up now? Do ya wanna try?"

"I gotta go," Hardy mumbled, and stumbled out into the urine-soaked
hallway.

Hardy went home, showered, and fell into a fitful sleep. He woke in the
early afternoon with a milder version of the same headache, an upset
stomach, and gut-wrenching anxiety; today was the day Pickett was going to
be murdered. He dialed Stone's number, but there was no answer. Restlessly, he moved about the apartment trying to find something to occupy his
mind, but it was no use. He couldn't concentrate on anything, and the walls
were closing in on him. He had to get out.

Soon he was aimlessly wandering the streets. Although he'd lived in Astoria for more than twenty years, he'd had little contact with the neighborhood or the people in it. When he was married, his wife did all the shopping. After she'd left, he ate wherever he happened to be when he got hungry. His home-cooked meals usually consisted of frozen and canned goods.

Now, walking the streets for the first time in years, he was surprised to see how the area had changed. Astoria had once contained more Greeks than Athens, but they'd been replaced by a new wave of immigrants—Orientals and Hispanics. In spite of the cultural changes, Christmas lights stretched across Broadway, and most of the stores, including the Korean fruit markets, displayed colorful holiday decorations. Hispanic housewives haggled with Korean fruit vendors, neither of whom seemed to understand the other. He felt like an alien in his own land. Soon he found himself standing in front of an old, run-down church. Hardy couldn't remember the last time he'd seen the inside of a church.

Quietly, he slipped into a pew. The sweet, familiar smell of incense permeated the air, and the cavernous interior echoed occasionally as worshipers moved about the church. A sound like gentle whistling came from the comically loud whispered prayers of old women hunched over their beads, earnestly praying to vacant staring statues.

The church was decorated for Christmas. Clusters of poinsettia plants flanked the main altar. At a side altar an elaborate nativity scene, complete with angels, shepherds, and animals, awaited the birth of Christ.

Hardy closed his eyes. Images and shadows of childhood flooded into his consciousness—a stern Sister Mary Paul prodding a smirking Billy Conlon; he and Frankie Forgione in the sacristy, hurriedly drinking sacramental wine but remembering to save enough for Father Dunn with the drinking problem; boys in identical white shirts and ties standing in endless lines next to prissy girls dressed in identical blouses and plaid skirts. All of them so young, so solemn, so foolish.

He was crying. Quickly, he wiped the tears with the back of his hand and turned furtively to see if anyone had seen him. Except for a few scattered women intent on their prayers, he was alone. His gaze was drawn to the shadowy crucifix dominating the altar. How many times, to ward off boredom, had he studied the tortured figure on the cross and tried to imagine what Christ was like? During those moments of childish meditation, he dwelled on the dark, mysterious questions that lay hidden like cancerous secrets in the mind of a thirteen-year-old boy. So many unanswered questions about the world, eternity, and sin. Mostly sin. Some of the nuns in their misguided zeal filled them with dire warnings of sin and damnation, infecting them with undeserved guilt. In their eternal search for evil, the nuns found ways to sin that didn't exist. And like a Chinese water torture, their incessant indoctrination bore into impressionable young minds and hearts until Hardy and his classmates were almost mad with guilt.

His thoughts were interrupted by the sound of someone briskly walking down the aisle; the squeak-squeak of the shoes echoed through the church. The priest, his black cassock flowing behind him, swept into the confessional, and in a moment the green light came on, signaling he was ready to hear confessions.

Hardy recalled the confessional with a mixture of dread and relief. The dread of confessing unspeakable sins in the darkened chamber, expecting at any moment to be denounced by the priest, and the relief when the verdict was mumbled: three Hail Marys and three Our Fathers.

The door slid open and the priest inclined his head toward Hardy. Still in his early twenties, the priest was losing his hair. His hands resting on his lap held a copy of *Sports Illustrated*. "Bless me, Father, for I have sinned," Hardy whispered hoarsely.

The priest waited expectantly, and when Hardy failed to continue, asked gently, "How long has it been since your last confession?"

Hardy's answer was barely audible. "Years. It's been years."

The priest seemed to visibly slump in his seat. It was going to be a long afternoon. The feature story on Phil Simms would have to wait.

Hardy stumbled through his confession. Thirty-five minutes later it was over. "Is there anything else you'd like to add?" the priest asked.

Hardy wiped his eyes. He felt better than he had in a long time, but he was painfully aware that he hadn't confessed the one sin he should. "Father," he began tentatively, "is it ever permissible to take a human life?"

The priest's fingers, idly toying with the pages of the magazine, became still. "What do you mean, my son?"

"The commandment says thou shalt not kill. But aren't there exceptions?"

"Well, there's war," the priest began. "During war men—"

"I don't mean that." Hardy searched for the proper words. "Aren't there times when someone's life could—should—be taken?"

The priest exhaled slowly. In the three short years since his ordination, he'd been asked about the morality of euthanasia several times. Troubled himself by the question, he'd sought the counsel of his pastor, a sour old monsignor, at supper one evening. The pastor admitted that the question came up frequently. After all, he pointed out, it affected the people in parishes like this the most. Lower-middle-class people had parents to take care of, and a prolonged illness often meant interminable pain and suffering for the patient as well as bankruptcy and family disruption for the survivors.

Although the old pastor was well versed in the arguments pro and con for euthanasia, he supported the church's position unequivocally. "This is not war," he had said, stabbing his knife into the butter. He looked at the young priest over his wire-rimmed glasses. "The answer is found in the fifth commandment: Thou shalt not kill." And the subject was closed. But the young priest, who was of another generation, couldn't so easily seek refuge in Church dogma. The issue of euthanasia went to the very heart of his belief system, and he didn't know the answer. How was he going to counsel someone else?

He racked his brain to think of the right way to phrase his answer, which would give the Church's position yet at the same time offer consolation to the petitioner. "My son," he began, "we don't always know, nor do we understand, the will of God. Sometimes, someone close to us is stricken and in great pain. It seems as though God has abandoned us. We pray and ask God to take the soul of the suffering person, but sometimes he doesn't." He took a deep breath. "But even under these circumstances, we cannot take a sacred life."

Hardy's voice came through the screen like the lash of a whip. "What if the person is evil? What if he deserves to die?"

The priest jerked his downcast eyes toward the faceless voice behind the mesh screen and tried to see what manner of man would ask such a question of a priest. Instinctively, Hardy leaned back into the shadows.

"That is murder," the priest pronounced in a whisper. "There is no question about that."

"But what about the right of society to protect itself?"

"There are laws," the priest countered, now frightened by whoever was on the other side of the screen. "We cannot take the law into our own hands."

"The law doesn't work," Hardy shouted through the screen, and stumbled out of the confessional.

"Wait, wait," the priest whispered desperately. He'd handled it all wrong. This was a tormented soul who needed help, and he was arguing with him. He stood up and the magazine slipped to the floor. By the time he came out of the confessional, Hardy was almost at the back of the church. "Wait," the priest called out in despair. "Let me talk to you. Please!"

But Hardy had already burst through the doors, and the sound echoed through the church like the report of a rifle shot. Just as quickly it died away, leaving the church silent once again, except for the sound of whispering women and a trembling priest.

Hardy rushed blindly down the street, angry at himself for his stupidity. What did he expect? Forgiveness? Understanding? Across the street he caught sight of a temple he could worship in, one which would give him the comfort and solace he required. Without questions. Without recriminations. A bar has more answers any day. He opened the door and was immediately assailed by the familiar, comforting smell of stale beer and cigarettes.

34

LATE IN THE AFTERNOON, PATRICK STONE CALLED TECCI FROM A
bar in midtown. "Is everything set?"

"Yeah, Chief. Mac and I are ready. But what if he doesn't show? Who
knows how reliable that super is?"

"He'll be there." Stone willed him to be there. He just wanted to get
this over and done with. He gave Tecci the telephone number of the pay
phone he was using. "Call me here when you're finished."

"It could be late."

"I'll be here."

Stone took his drink to a table in the corner. It was just past five and the
bar was empty, but soon office workers would be coming in, and by nine
the place would be jammed. And that's what Patrick Stone wanted tonight—
noise, music, inane conversations—anything to stop him from thinking.

Tonight's outcome would determine his future. If all went well, the last man who could cause him trouble would be dead and the slate would be wiped clean. The turmoil of the last couple of months had been a valuable, if painful, learning experience for him. He'd been forced to reassess himself, and for the first time in his life, he didn't like what he'd seen. Supremely self-confident, he'd always thought he could do anything, fix anything. But his experience with Victor Cabrera had taught him a bitter lesson: there were events that even Patrick Stone couldn't control. He was forced to admit that it was only a combination of luck and careful manipulation of Hardy and the others that would allow him to break away from Cabrera tonight.

He ordered another drink and, as he tore off pieces of his napkin and rolled them into balls, recalled his final slide into the clutches of Victor Cabrera.

He was well aware of the danger in getting too deeply involved with Cabrera, but as their arrangement proceeded smoothly, he grew more relaxed and confident. It was the perfect setup. Cabrera told him when he was making a shipment, and Stone kept NET away. At the same time, the information Cabrera provided allowed NET to make some spectacular drug seizures. Once more in control of his destiny, he began to enjoy the challenge of walking a tightrope between two so divergent worlds. Indeed, he successfully maintained his balance until that September day, in the middle of lunch, when Cabrera cut the wire.

Stone had taken up Cabrera's offer to join him on a Caribbean cruise. On the second day at sea, Victor Cabrera poured more champagne into Stone's glass and asked casually, "Patrick, would it be possible for you to eliminate someone?"

Stone put his fork down. "What do you mean?"

"I am speaking hypothetically, of course, but it seems to me that a person in your position should be able to eliminate someone quite easily under the color of official police action." He cracked a lobster claw and extracted the meat with one easy motion of his fork. "For instance, if in the process of making an arrest, someone were to, let us say, resist, he could be shot. No?"

Stone sipped his champagne. "No. New York City is not Peru. There are very strict rules regarding a policeman's use of a gun, and all homicides are investigated thoroughly; especially if a cop does the shooting."

Cabrera poured more champagne. "But I detect in your tone that it is possible. How could it be done?"

Stone sat back and dabbed the butter from his mouth with his napkin. Like many cops, he was intrigued by the idea of the perfect crime. The conventional wisdom was that there was no such thing as the perfect murder, but every cop knew that was nonsense. There were thousands of unsolved homicides in New York City, and by definition all were perfect crimes. There were three reasons why a murderer was caught—motive, physical evidence, and witnesses. A homicide detective's first task was to establish a motive. Whoever gained by the death of the victim automatically became a suspect. But what if a person killed for no motive? There would be no reason to suspect him.

Most murders were unplanned and done in haste, causing the murderer to leave damaging evidence—fingerprints, blood, or weapons. But with careful planning, no physical evidence would be left. In his panic the murderer often runs from the scene, or in some way arouses the suspicions of witnesses. Again, with careful planning there should be no untoward behavior to draw undue attention. Patrick Stone gazed at the black eyes across the table. "A cop could pull it off if he was careful and planned it thoroughly."

Cabrera buttered a roll and frowned. "You think it would be that easy?"

"That easy and that difficult. It would require careful planning, the right location, and the proper means of carrying it out. If—and that's a big if—he were able to fulfill all those requirements, he could commit the perfect murder."

After lunch they adjourned to the yacht's rear deck and took shelter from the blazing sun under a candy-striped awning. While stewards brought more champagne and an enormous bowl of fruit, Stone watched three of the most beautiful women he'd ever seen swimming nude off the stern. After the steward left, Cabrera said, "I would like you to do it." His tone was so matter-of-fact that Stone thought he was joking. But his eyes, those coal-black eyes with the flat, predatory expression of a shark, said otherwise.

"Don't look so shocked, my friend. We are both adults. Surely you don't object on moral grounds."

Stone didn't object on any grounds except self-preservation. The perfect murder was an intriguing, seductive idea. He knew most homicides were solved by luck and accident, and not, as the TV detectives would have you believe, by electronic microscopes and painstaking lab analyses. In a city like New York, where more than fifteen hundred murders were committed a year, there simply wasn't enough time or money to employ the full arsenal of forensic aids available to law enforcement. Only the noteworthy or promising murders were likely to be investigated with full vigor.

Cabrera lit a dark, almost black, cigar. "Actually, I have four people in mind," he said, squinting at Stone through the pungent smoke.

"Four?" Stone repeated in surprise. The idea of the perfect crime, which had just begun to germinate in his mind, evaporated. "Forget it. One perfect murder, maybe, but the odds of getting away with four are astronomical." Stone tossed a grape into the clear blue water below. "You had me going there for a minute. It would have been an interesting intellectual exercise to plan the perfect murder.''

''Don't give up so easily, my friend.''

''Victor, I said forget it.'' He'd become suddenly uneasy. He'd allowed Cabrera to dangle forbidden fruit in front of him and he'd been tempted.

''We have a serious problem, Patrick.''

Something in Cabrera's tone made Stone's mouth go dry. ''What does that mean?''

''Do you know who Nathan Pickett is?''

''Sure. He's been sticking it to the Board of Education in the papers; something to do with student-teacher ratios in ghetto neighborhoods.''

''Don't look so smug, my friend. Senator Pickett is going to turn his attention to the police department next, and his main focus will be drugs.''

Stone saw his whole world crashing down around him, but he remained outwardly calm. ''So?''

''My sources tell me he has a couple of witnesses who can implicate several people in both my country and yours.''

Stone, who had no idea Cabrera's operation was that big, masked his surprise. ''Do you know who he is?''

''Not yet.''

Stone relaxed. *They* didn't have a problem, Cabrera had a problem. He popped a grape into his mouth. ''Don't get your balls in an uproar. This isn't the first crime commission and it won't be the last. Most of them are all bullshit and bombast anyway. Just lay low and ride it out.''

''I may be able to, but I don't think you can.''

A knot formed in Stone's stomach. ''What has this got to do with me?''

Cabrera's smile, totally devoid of humor, was more of a grimace. ''I know you have tried to keep a low profile, Patrick, but you are not unknown to some of my associates.''

''Such as?''

''Tiny Leonard.''

''I don't know a Tiny Leonard.''

''Remember that rather large black man I introduced you to the first time you came to my home?''

Vaguely, Stone remembered him. Unlike the other guests, he was a loud, crude man, whom Stone did his best to ignore. He remembered wondering why someone like Leonard had been invited to such a gathering.

''Mr. Leonard is my major distributor in Harlem.''

Stone threw the cluster of grapes on the table. ''Good Christ, Victor! You introduced me to a fucking drug dealer?''

Cabrera feigned surprise. ''I thought you knew who he was.''

''Do you think I know every two-bit drug dealer in the city?''

"Tiny is something more than that. He represents several million dollars' worth of business to me every year."

Stone cursed himself. If Cabrera was telling the truth, Leonard could indeed cause a problem. The easiest way to flip a drug dealer was to ask him if he could hand up a cop. Leonard couldn't implicate him in anything criminal, but merely saying he'd met a police captain at a party in Florida would be enough to start Pickett's people on a witch-hunt. Even if they found nothing, Stone's career would be ruined. How would it look to the department if the commanding officer of the premier narcotics enforcement unit was consorting with a known drug dealer?

"Who are the others?"

"The two who have been delivering payments to you—Nelson Marbridge and Tom Rowe."

Unlike Leonard, the art dealer and the lawyer—whom Stone had met several times—had class. Marbridge was a flaming fag, but he was an intelligent and witty man. Because they didn't appear to be part of Cabrera's operation, he'd foolishly consented to them being the middlemen in several payoffs. "How much do they know?"

"Too much, I'm afraid. Nelson has been a conduit of drugs and money for years, and Rowe, from time to time, has taken care of my finances."

"How much do they know about me?"

The black eyes locked on Stone. "They gave you money. How much more do they have to know?"

Stone turned to watch one of the girls climb up on the swim platform. The sun glistened off her naked, bronzed body. He'd come here for the women, but now that was the furthest thing from his mind. If Pickett got to any one of them and they talked, there was a good chance he'd go to jail.

"By a strange coincidence," Cabrera said, "they are also a danger to me. Of all my associates, they are the three I cannot trust."

Suddenly, it all fell into place for Stone. "You bastard. You deliberately introduced them to me. That way, if they became a danger to you, they'd be a danger to me as well."

Cabrera didn't speak, but his silence said it all. With a sickening jolt the final piece of the puzzle fell into place. "And you murdered Tina, didn't you? You hot-loaded the cocaine, knowing it would kill her. All to set me up. You're a fucking lunatic."

Cabrera's immobile face showed no emotion. "Patrick, you are a very naive man. In your neat little world of cops and robbers everything is so simple. But you're living in a fantasy. You thought you were smarter than me, but you are not. I didn't get to where I am by being a foolish man. I do whatever I have to do to survive. And so will you."

Stone felt as though he'd suddenly been plunged into a nightmare world where everything was turned upside down. One moment he was in total control of his well-planned life, the next he was seeing that life crumble before his eyes. "Who's the fourth?" he asked numbly.

"Nathan Pickett."

Stone, his nerves stretched to the breaking point, erupted. "Are you out of your fucking mind!"

The girl, drying herself, looked up, startled at his outburst. Cabrera said something to her in Spanish and she ran into the cabin. He came halfway out of his seat and the veins in his thick neck stood out. "Don't you ever talk to me like that again."

Stone, in his blinding anger, refused to be cowed. "Don't threaten me, Victor."

For a moment he expected Cabrera to summon his bodyguards, who were never very far away. But he sat back and smiled. "Let us not quarrel, Patrick. We have a common enemy."

"Maybe, but I'm not killing anyone."

Cabrera didn't even blink. "You know you are very photogenic?"

"What's that supposed to mean?"

"I have you on videotape."

"Victor, you're full of shit." Frantically, Stone tried to think if that was possible.

"Now, now. I have to run my operation like a business, and every big business needs insurance. Does it not? The tapes of you accepting money would be quite damaging."

"You're bluffing."

Cabrera leaned over the table and plucked a small metallic device from the floral arrangement. He dangled it in the air. "I've taken the precaution of videotaping and recording our conversations." He tossed the bug on the table. "Expensive, but quite effective."

Stone knew that. He'd seen the device before; the FBI used the same model.

"Why are we quarreling?" Cabrera continued. "Our interests are not dissimilar, we simply disagree on methodology."

Stone tried to read Cabrera's self-satisfied smile. Was he bluffing? If he wasn't, just one of those tapes could put him in jail. His mouth went dry. Like all cops who'd seen the inside of a prison, he had a morbid fear of being locked up with criminals who would know he was an ex-cop. He cursed himself for being so careless. He'd underestimated Cabrera. Under that flabby, sleepy exterior was a clever and vicious man, who used his bland manner to lull others into making mistakes.

"You're bluffing. You can't show those tapes. They're as damaging to you as they are to me."

"Not really. If you recall, I never personally gave you anything."

Cabrera was right. Only Marbridge and Rowe had delivered the payments. He tried to recall where he'd accepted money—once in a hotel room, another time at the airport, then one time . . . what was the use? Cabrera could have taped him any one of those times, and just once would be enough.

Ruefully, he recalled attending a department seminar on the technical and legal aspects of videotaping corrupt police officers. They'd shown actual evidence tapes of policemen taking money. One was even heard to whisper that they had to be careful because IAD was in the precinct. Stone, as well as the others in the audience, hooted at their stupidity. But corrupt cops didn't have a monopoly on stupidity. Two weeks later on the six o'clock news, he saw, along with millions of other Americans, the FBI surveillance tapes showing the Abscam congressman stuffing money into his pockets. Watching those tapes then, he couldn't believe anyone could be that careless. But now, at last, he knew how it could happen: Whether you're a congressman or a cop, you simply refuse to believe that someone might videotape you.

Cabrera ground his cigar into an ashtray and gazed at Stone in disdain. "I am well-insulated and perfectly safe back in Peru. There is no chance that I could be extradited. I have obtained insurance against that eventuality as well. The worst that could happen to me is that I could never return to the United States. Big deal, I will never get to see Disneyland." He threw back his head and laughed.

"My friend," he said in his soft Spanish accent, "you have done very well by me, have you not?"

"I have no beef there. But I'm telling you, even if I were willing, you can't hit a high-profile politician like Pickett. All hell would break loose. We're talking New York City, not some goddamn banana republic. It's too risky."

"Patrick, you're a good businessman. That's why I do business with you. You're smart and careful—attributes I prize highly. But you don't know anything about dealing with the competition. When somebody threatens to get in your way, he must be crushed. Pickett, unfortunately, is the most dangerous of politicians; he will not listen to reason."

"Have you tried?"

"Of course. Overtures have been made. It is always better to solve a problem with money. I dislike violence and only use it as a last resort. Unfortunately, Mr. Pickett is after something more than money."

"What's that?"

"Right now he will settle for the publicity his drug commission will bring. Later, he intends to be the first black President." The older man's face darkened. "I do not care if he becomes king, but he will not satisfy his ambitions at my expense."

His attention was drawn to a small sloop gliding by. The passengers on the much smaller vessel gawked and pointed at them. Cabrera smiled and waved back. "Pickett and the others," he said softly, "must be disposed of. If you don't get rid of them, I'll be forced to send the tapes to your superiors."

Stone needed time to think this through. Stalling, he said, "What time frame are we talking about?"

"Pickett must be disposed of before Christmas."

"Before Christmas! That's only three months."

Cabrera ignored Stone's protest. "The commission is due to begin the first of the year. If nothing else, his death will send a message to anyone who might be thinking of testifying."

Slowly, Cabrera rotated his cigar to keep the ash burning evenly. "Let us take it one step at a time. You have a fine mind, Patrick. I am confident you will come up with a plan. And I'm sure I don't have to tell you it will be more than worth your while."

"Victor, you're talking murder."

"It is something that must be done, and I would prefer that you handle it. You're clever, resourceful, and you won't make mistakes. Go home, my friend, and think about it. We'll talk again."

The first thing Stone did when he got back to New York three days later was to run a criminal-record check on Tiny Leonard. From reading Leonard's lengthy rap sheet, it was clear that Cabrera hadn't exaggerated. The fat man had been convicted of everything from grand larceny to felony sale of controlled substances. Stone could just imagine the P.C.'s reaction if it came out that his favorite captain knew someone like Tiny Leonard.

Cabrera had him in a vise. But the thought of getting involved in murder was out of the question. He had to get away from that madman, but trying to get free of Cabrera was like trying to climb out of a sand pit—the more one struggled, the more firmly one was trapped. With the threat of three witnesses and the tapes hanging over him, how could he say no? On the other hand, how could he say yes?

At first Stone put Cabrera's proposition out of his mind completely. Then, in spite of himself, he began to give it some thought. At odd moments—standing in the corridor outside a courtroom, reviewing the wording of an arrest warrant, eating lunch—he'd suddenly find himself thinking about the best weapon to use, the perfect location, the optimum time of day. He'd drive these thoughts from his mind, only to have them reappear three hours or three days later.

He gave Cabrera his answer one glorious tropical evening in St. Thomas. The yacht had just pulled into the quay and he and Cabrera stood on the bridge watching the deckhands skillfully tie the large vessel to the pier. Off to the west, half hidden by a mountain, the sun set the sky ablaze with multihued reds, oranges, and pinks. To the east a squall line retreated over the horizon, black against the brilliant sky. Cabrera appeared to take no joy in the beauty surrounding him. With an impassive look that defied interpretation, he leaned on the railing and looked at the pastel-colored houses dotting the hillside. Just then the engines stopped, plunging the evening into silence. "Well, Patrick," he said, "what is your answer?"

Stunned by the suddenness and finality in Victor's tone, Stone realized the game had come to its conclusion: check-checkmate. But who was the winner? He turned the question over in his mind again. It was deceptively simple, but one with wide-ranging implications. The pros and cons, which he'd dwelt on night and day, were very clear. Still . . .

Out of the corner of his eye he saw a flash of white. He turned to see a large bird with outstretched wings dive into the sea. Moments later it returned to the surface, triumphantly holding a squirming fish whose silver scales sparkled in the fading light. As the bird flew away, each beat of the wings caused droplets of water to fall like a shower of diamonds to the water below.

"Yes," Stone said.

35

SHANNON AND ROSE ARRIVED BACK AT THE OFFICE LATE IN THE afternoon. They'd gone to interview the owner of the stolen Toyota license plates. But it was a wild-goose chase. All the owner could tell them was that he'd parked the car in midtown to go to a Broadway show, and when he came out, his plates were gone.

"What are we going to do with all this?" Shannon stood over Velez's work area, staring down at a pile of floppy disks, printouts, and assorted folders. He turned on the computer, and an intimidating, unblinking blank screen stared at him. "Do you know how this thing works?"

"A little." From the start Rose had been curious about the computer. In spare moments he'd looked over Velez's shoulder, and as a result had learned something about it. Velez, in order to stop Rose from pestering him with endless questions, had even prepared a brief set of operating instructions.

Shannon sat down in front of the terminal. "The day he was killed, he told me he'd finished inputting the list of names from the Early Intervention Unit and all the data on cop shootings in the last two years. He was really pumped up about it. He planned to run correlations the next day. Do you know how to do that?"

"I'm not sure. I'd have to look at the instruction sheet."

Later, Shannon was sorting through a stack of folders when he came across one marked *Cronin*. He opened it and perused the history of Walter T. Cronin as recorded in military and police department personnel records, memo books, and photocopies of papers in his possession at the time of his death. Random images emerged from the neatly typed reports—a bank teller before he became a police officer; a PFC in the Armored Division; a cross-country runner at St. Francis High School; hobbies—reading, jogging, softball; married at Holy Flower in Queens; a memo-book entry that said he worked the last St. Patrick's Day parade and gave out two summonses for illegal consumption of alcohol.

Snatches of information, the sum total of Police Officer Walter Cronin's life, all the facts, times, dates, and places typed on the appropriate forms. But nowhere was there anything to explain how a former altar boy-athlete-soldier-policeman became involved in murder. Obviously, the answers weren't to be found in these neatly typed forms. There were no boxes to check to indicate he was crazy, stupid, dedicated, or fanatical. That information was buried with Walter Cronin forever, unless he and Rose were able to find it somewhere else.

Shannon closed the folder. "That's it for the day. I gotta get home early. My daughter's in a concert tonight."

"I'll stick around a little while longer. I'm expecting a call."

Rose's uncharacteristic evasiveness raised Shannon's antenna. "Who?"

Rose busily shuffled papers on his desk.

"Rose, what's going on?"

Alex Rose took a deep breath and sat back. "There's a Field Associate in NET."

Shannon slid into a chair. "Goddamn," he mumbled. "When did you plan to tell me? We're working on this—"

Rose put his hands up. "Brian, hold it. You know how the program works. There are only two men in this department who know the identity of a Field Associate—his control and the Chief of Inspectional Services."

"How did you find out?"

Rose didn't answer. Shannon leaned forward, his face red with anger. "You IAD hump. You still don't trust me."

"It isn't that. I don't even know if he'll talk to me yet. At this minute his control is trying to set up a meeting."

Shannon wasn't satisfied with Rose's excuse. "So what's next?"

"I'm waiting for a call to find out if he'll talk to me."

"Do you think he'll know anything?"

"I don't know. He's only been assigned to NET for a few weeks. But what the hell, we gotta pull all the stops. According to the control, the kid's assessment so far is that NET's a straight-arrow outfit. Everyone wants to make collars."

"I thought Stone handpicked his own people. How'd a Field Associate get in?"

"Pure luck. What helped was Stone's penchant for picking young guys. Most of the Field Associates are young. Or so I understand," he added weakly.

"I'll bet you do."

"Go home, Brian. Enjoy the concert. I'll fill you in tomorrow."

While Rose was waiting for his telephone call from Lt. Pete Sprizzo, he searched through his cluttered desk and finally found Velez's instruction sheet. He sat down at the computer and, reading from the instructions, tentatively entered a command. A menu appeared on the screen. He selected "correlation search," and the screen asked for a "list one" and a "list two."

He typed in PD SHOOTINGS and NET ROSTER. One correlation appeared on the screen:

NAME: PO STEPHEN TECCI
SHIELD NO.: 4186
COMMAND: NET
COMPLAINT NO.: Q–69232
LOCATION: BAY VIEW MOTEL (QUEENS)
REMARKS: WHILE MAKING AN ARREST PO TECCI SHOT AND KILLED ONE
EDUARDO LLERANDEZ. JUSTIFIABLE HOMICIDE.
CASE PROFILE: SEE FILE 8–371

Following the instructions, Rose pressed the proper series of commands, and a copy of the Complaint Report appeared on the screen. He started to read it when the telephone rang.

It was Sprizzo. "Okay, Alex, he'll see you. Meet us at the Blue Star luncheonette on Canal and Broadway."

Rose was elated. "I owe you one, pal. I'll be there in fifteen minutes."

THE MOOD AT DINNER WAS A PLEASANT CONTRAST TO RECENT FAMILY GATHERINGS. Except for Kathy, who was so excited she could barely eat.

Unable to sit still any longer, she rushed off to get ready, but she came back to the table three times to announce that they had to be there at seven-thirty sharp.

Brian swallowed the last of his beer as Eileen cleared the table. With a straight face, Brian said to his daughter, "What's the rush? The concert doesn't start until eight-thirty. If we leave at eight twenty-five, we'll have plenty of time."

She looked at him agog and could only utter, "Oh, Daddy," and rushed off to comb her hair again.

With her mother's green eyes and small, upturned nose, Kathy was developing into a beautiful young lady, and tonight she was going to sing a Bach solo—in *German* no less!

THE FIELD ASSOCIATE, WHOM LIEUTENANT SPRIZZO INTRODUCED SIMPLY as Ken, was about twenty-three years old, with a smooth, baby face that looked like it needed shaving about once a month. By prior agreement, Sprizzo left after making the introduction.

"I appreciate your seeing me," Rose said. "I just want you to know your identity is safe with me."

The baby-faced officer looked relieved. "Thanks. Lieutenant Sprizzo said you were a good guy and could be trusted. Doing this isn't easy, you know? My father's retired from the job—thirty years in the Three-oh. He doesn't know what I'm doing. Sometimes, I wonder if I should tell him."

Rose could imagine the kid's father—a hairbag precinct cop who'd come on the job in a very different era. If Rose, who was in the internal affairs business, didn't understand why cops became Field Associates, he knew Ken's father wouldn't either. "I wouldn't tell him if I were you," he said. "The less people who know about it, the better. But I'm sure your father would be proud of you. It takes a lot of guts to do what you're doing." The young cop seemed grateful for Rose's words.

"Ken, have you ever heard of anyone taking money in NET?"

He didn't appear surprised by the question. Rose imagined Field Associates were asked that question all the time.

"No, sir, never. We're all in NET to make collars. It's a great way to get into the bureau."

"Ken, you don't have to call me sir."

"Yes, sir."

Both of them laughed.

"Did you ever work with Walter Cronin?"

"No, sir. I mean—no. As part of my orientation, I worked with a few teams, but not his. I knew him to say hello, but that's it. He seemed like a real nice guy. It was a shame.''

A bell went off in Rose's head. "He was assigned to a team?"

"Yes, sir. Everyone's assigned to a team."

"I thought Cronin did undercover work and was assigned to different teams?"

"I don't know about that, but as far as I know, he was assigned to Sergeant Hardy's team."

"Is Steve Tecci in Sergeant Hardy's team?"

"Yeah."

"Who else?"

"A guy named Beals."

"Black or white?"

"Black."

"Tall or short?"

"He must be at least six-three."

"How about Tecci?"

"I'm five-ten, I guess he's about two inches shorter than me."

"What color hair?"

The young cop laughed. "We're always kidding him about it. Who ever heard of an Italian with blond hair?"

Rose had heard enough. Tecci and Beals fit the description of the two men seen outside Wanda Little's apartment. He had to get back to the office and read the report of the Bay View shooting case.

Outside the luncheonette Rose thought of one last question. "By the way, Ken, did you ever hear anyone in NET called Chief?"

THE DISHES WERE CONSIGNED TO THE DISHWASHER, THE HAIR WAS sprayed into submission, and Kathy Shannon was finally ready for her public. They were leaving when the phone rang. "Daddy," Kathy pleaded, "let it ring please. We'll be late."

He started for the den. "It's okay. Go ahead out to the car, I'll be right there."

It was Rose. "Brian, I have something."

"Can you make it fast? I'm on my way out the door to a concert."

"Oh, I forgot. I'm sorry . . ."

"What's up?"

The door bell rang insistently. Shannon looked out the window and saw Eileen and Kathy standing in the driveway. Kathy was stamping her feet against the cold.

"I spoke to the Field Associate," Rose said.

"And?" Shannon glanced at his watch.

"He's a good kid, nervous, but very observant."

"Yeah, so?" Rose seemed to be talking slowly on purpose.

"He's been working with different teams as part of his orientation, so he's met most of the guys in NET."

Shannon lit a cigarette. "Rose, can you get to the point?"

"When we were leaving I asked him one last question. I asked him if he ever heard anyone called Chief."

"And?"

Rose's voice was so low, Shannon had to press the phone to his ear. "He said he heard a sergeant call Captain Stone that once. He thought that odd with him just being a captain and all."

Shannon sagged. "Christ!"

The door bell rang again, and he slammed the door closed with his foot. "Who's the sergeant?"

"Name's Hardy. He's home. I just called. Said I was selling aluminum siding—"

Kathy opened the door. "Daddy—"

"Wait in the car," Shannon snapped. She burst into tears and ran down the hallway.

"Listen, Brian. I know this is a bad time, but there's more."

Shannon, infuriated at Rose's habit of giving out information a little at a time, exploded. "Goddamn it, Rose, what is it?"

"Before I got the call to meet the Field Associate, I was playing around with the computer. I found out that NET cops were involved in a shooting. The Grand Jury called it justifiable homicide, but except for an unconscious perp, the only witnesses to the shooting were all cops."

"Who were the cops?"

"Tecci, who did the shooting, Captain Stone, Sergeant Hardy, another cop named Beals, and—are you ready for this?—Walter Cronin."

"Christ! That must be the group."

"Right. Another thing: Stone told you that Cronin wasn't in a team. He lied to you. The Field Associate said Cronin was in Hardy's team."

Instead of elation, Shannon felt drained. After almost five weeks of chasing threads of evidence that led nowhere, they'd finally gotten a break. But now that they had this information, they'd have to do something about it. Tonight.

"Brian, we don't have the luxury of time. We don't know when they'll go for Pickett. I called all of them. The only one home is Hardy. We have to talk to him tonight."

Goddamn it! Why tonight? Why couldn't Rose have talked to the Field Associate this morning, or tomorrow? He pushed the curtain aside and saw Eileen and Kathy getting into the car. He held the receiver so tightly his hand was cramped. The engine started and the headlights came on.

"Brian? Are you there?"

The horn sounded in the driveway.

Brian Shannon stared at the photograph of his daughter. A solemn little girl in a lacy white Communion dress, squinting in the bright sunlight. So many years ago, and he wasn't there to see it. He was working a strike detail and couldn't get the day off. He'd missed so many things. "Where does he live?"

"Astoria."

"I'll meet you at the diner, foot of the Triborough Bridge. Give me forty-five minutes."

Rose heard the anguish in Shannon's voice. "Brian, I'm sorry. Maybe—"

But Shannon wasn't listening. He'd replaced the receiver and had gone outside to tell his daughter he wouldn't be going to her concert.

SHANNON PULLED UP IN FRONT OF THE DINER AT EXACTLY NINE-fifteen.

Rose slipped into the car. "I'm sorry, Brian. I forgot about the concert."

"Stuff it. Where does Hardy live?"

They parked around the corner and walked into Hardy's tree-lined block, a mix of apartment buildings and two-family homes. Outside Hardy's apartment Rose put his ear to the door. "I hear a TV," he murmured.

Shannon removed his gun from his holster and put it in his more easily accessible jacket pocket. "Let's do it."

Rose rang the bell, and the sound of the TV stopped. Instinctively, they moved to either side of the door, and Shannon felt a knot forming in his stomach. He strained to hear a sound coming from the apartment—footsteps, voices, anything. Seconds seemed to stretch into hours.

Except for the sound of a muffled TV coming from another apartment, the hallway was quiet. Suddenly, there was a burst of laughter; someone must be watching a comedy, Shannon thought. His mouth was dry. They'd done this all wrong. The sergeant inside the apartment knew they were here and he was going to come out shooting. They didn't even know how many people were in there with him. They'd planned this like rookies. He'd allowed the amateur from IAD to get him into this and now— He started to look for cover when the door bolt snapped open. It sounded like a round being fed into a chamber.

The door opened. Tim Hardy, looking disheveled and in need of a shave, stood there in his undershirt, baggy slacks, and socks. He looked from one to the other with bloodshot eyes, and it was clear from his expression he knew they were cops. Rose saw something else in the drawn, hungover face: a combination of fear, dread, and relief. After years in IAD he'd come to recognize that haunted look on the faces of cops who suddenly realized they'd been caught; the look of abject and total despair was hard to forget. Rose stuck his shield in Hardy's face. "We're here," he said, "to talk to you about some murders."

Hardy stepped back as though he'd been struck. The tension and anxiety of the past several weeks overwhelmed him like a tidal wave. The moment he'd been dreading, yet almost hoping for, was here. He wouldn't have to carry the terrible burden any longer. It was over. His breathing came in sharp, irregular gasps. His shoulders shook and a guttural, primitive sound akin to a bark tore from his throat. He stood before them a man stripped of his humanity, his dignity, and he wept.

The lieutenants reacted in different ways. Shannon, still clutching the gun in his pocket, was embarrassed. But to Rose, who'd arrested cops before, the sight of a grown man crying was nothing new. He put his arm around the broken man and led him to a chair.

In time Hardy regained his composure and became calm, almost placid. "Sergeant Hardy," Shannon began tentatively, "why don't you tell us about—"

"Just a minute," Rose interrupted. "Sergeant Hardy, I'm going to read you your Miranda rights."

Shannon, who'd never interrogated a cop before, looked at Rose in surprise. He'd forgotten for a moment that everyone—even a Supreme Court justice—has the right to have the Miranda warnings read to him. Besides, they weren't talking to a policeman any longer; they were interrogating a felon who would stand trial for his crimes, and it was important that neither Hardy, nor anyone else in this group, got away with murder because of a technical violation of criminal procedure.

Rose was a different person now. No smiles, no jokes, his attention was focused on the suspect sitting before him. Hardy nodded silently as Rose recited the Constitutional rights against self-incrimination, and Shannon, listening to the familiar recital, waited for those infuriating, final words from Hardy: "I want to talk to my lawyer."

Once those words were uttered, information-gathering came to a painful, screeching halt. A cop's ultimate frustration is fulfilling the Miranda requirements, knowing that the suspect, heeding the warnings, will stop talking and the best source of information will be lost forever.

But to Shannon's surprise, Hardy smiled sadly. "I don't need a lawyer. It doesn't matter anymore."

Now came the hard part. Interrogating a suspect, even an agreeable one, was like trying to control the direction of a soap bubble; a harsh movement or forced change of direction can cause it to burst. Questions had to be carefully thought out and just as carefully phrased. A murderer might be willing to describe in graphic terms how he dismembered a body, but then let the interrogator ask a seemingly innocuous question and the bubble bursts. The subject stops talking, looks at you as though seeing you for the first time, and you see the curtain come down over his eyes. You *know* what he's going to say next: "I want to talk to a lawyer."

Rose opened with a safe gambit. "Sergeant Hardy, why don't you just start at the beginning?"

Hardy's smile was ironic. "Is thirty pieces of silver still the going rate?"

"It seems to me you made considerably more than thirty pieces of silver."

"That's true, Lieutenant. But I can't tell you anything. I'm sorry."

Shannon tried a different approach. "Sarge, you're in a lot of trouble. Don't make it worse."

Hardy's sad smile faded. "I don't think I can make it any worse than it is."

Shannon was furious. Like many detectives, he sometimes fell into the trap of ascribing superhuman powers to the people he was after. How else to explain the lack of hard evidence and the fact that the perp has been able to elude him all this time? But when the arrest is made, the detective is invariably disappointed. No Dr. Moriarty, his perpetrator is just another ordinary human being—tall or short, smart or dumb—but no different from the thousands of other nondescript criminals found in station houses throughout the city.

Looking at Hardy, Shannon could scarcely believe that this balding, insignificant man had been responsible for so much trouble and grief. Shannon was too much of a professional to lose his temper, but he wanted nothing more than to beat the living shit out of Sergeant Hardy.

"Okay." Rose stood up. "You'll have to come with us." He wasn't concerned about Hardy's silence. He'd seen this reaction before. Arrested in familiar surroundings, a cop was inclined to tough it out. It was later, when he was taken to a police facility, that he became a different person. The experience of handcuffs, fingerprints, and cell bars was devastating, especially to a man who made a living arresting others. The finality of a slamming cell door had a way of reorganizing a man's priorities.

"I understand," Hardy said. "Just give me a minute to put on some clothes." He started for the bedroom.

"Wait," Rose said. "I'll go with you."

In the bedroom, Rose said, "Sergeant Hardy, can I have your gun and shield now?"

Hardy paled. "They're in that drawer." He indicated a night table.

Taking a cop's gun was sometimes more traumatic than the arrest itself.

Pop psychologists like to expound on the theory that cops don't want to give up their guns because of some underlying fear of emasculation. The real reason is more prosaic.

The two most important pieces of property a rookie receives when he comes into the department are his gun and his shield. From day one, and for the rest of his time in the department, he is continually threatened with dire consequences if he loses either. After a time the gun and shield become a part of him, like his wallet and the clothes on his back. Every time a cop stands up he pats his body for his three most important possessions—his gun, his shield, and his wallet. And in that order.

The powerful pull of ownership is never more apparent than when a policeman retires from the job. Every retiree is shocked by the unexpected sense of loss when he drops his shield on the desk and knows he will never wear it again. For an arrested cop, turning over his gun and shield is the ultimate metaphor for loss—the loss of job, the loss of self-respect, and most important, the loss of fellowship with other policemen.

Rose retrieved the shield and two guns buried under handkerchiefs and socks. Before he'd left the office, he checked Hardy's force record card and recorded the serial numbers of his guns. He checked them now. They matched.

Rose sat on the bed as Hardy took an inordinate amount of time to select a shirt, tie, and slacks. As they were leaving the bedroom, Hardy asked if he could use the bathroom. From his first days in the Police Academy a cop is cautioned to watch his prisoner at all times, especially when he goes to the bathroom. It's embarrassing watching a man relieve himself, so some cops wait outside. As a result, more than one prisoner has taken that opportunity to exit the criminal justice system prematurely through the shithouse window.

Rose made a quick check of the bathroom. The window was too small to climb out, and Rose saw that it was more than a forty-foot drop to the ground. "Okay," he said to Hardy, "but don't be long."

Rose came into the living room and sprawled on the couch next to Shannon. They were both exhausted. It had been a long search, a long day, and now it was almost over. In spite of Hardy's initial reluctance to talk, they were both convinced they'd be able to get through to him later.

"After we bring him downtown," Rose said, "we'll go after the others."

Shannon, his head resting on the back of the couch, wasn't listening. Something Hardy had said was nagging him. Was it something he'd *said,* or the *tone* of his voice? His manner—placid, calm, despair . . . *Despair.* "Christ," he said, jumping to his feet. "He said it doesn't matter anymore." Shannon raced for the bathroom.

The sound of the shot reverberated through the apartment. In one movement Shannon put his shoulder to the door and the jamb gave way in long, jagged splinters. Hardy, seated on the toilet bowl, slumped to one side, the gun still in his hand. Blood spurted from a powder-blackened hole in his temple. As though he'd planned not to make a mess, the streaming blood—in stark contrast to the white porcelain—puddled in the sink. The body twitched spasmodically.

"Oh shit." Rose slumped against the splintered doorframe. "Oh shit. I thought I had all his guns."

Rose couldn't have known that Tim Hardy had rehearsed his ritual suicide several times in the past few days. He'd sit on the edge of the tub, finger the cold, heavy .45 Colt, and ponder the technical difficulties of suicide. Where was the best spot? The mouth? The temple? Finally, after much deliberation, he settled on the temple. He'd seen enough suicides to know temple shots were sure and effective. Knowing that he had the means to take his life gave him some respite from the ever-present anxiety gnawing at his belly. The gun was his safety net. If the fear and pain became too great, Hardy had a way out.

Each time, he returned the gun—a souvenir from the Army—to its hiding place under the sink. He told himself he'd never actually use it, and he believed it. It wasn't until he opened the door and stood face to face with the two lieutenants that he knew he would take his life. Somehow, some way, he would end the agony this night. Oddly enough, he wasn't afraid. His only concern was that the tall, by-the-book lieutenant wouldn't let him stay in the bathroom alone. It was only when Hardy turned the lock in the bathroom door that he knew he was free.

"Look!" Rose said hoarsely.

Shannon whirled and saw Rose staring in disbelief at the bathroom mirror. Tim Hardy's last desperate act of atonement was one word neatly printed with soap: TONIGHT.

BEFORE THEY LEFT HARDY'S APARTMENT, SHANNON CALLED THE Detective district office. The detective answering the telephone laughed. "You gotta be kidding, Loo. Larson is at a lobbyists' convention in Albany."

"Do you have a number?"

"Naw, the chief never leaves a number when he goes out of town."

Shannon dialed Bennett's number. No answer. He slammed the receiver down. "We're batting a thousand."

Rose called Pickett's home. His wife said he was at a meeting—she didn't know where—and wouldn't be home until late. Rose gave her his pager number and brusquely asked her to have Pickett call as soon as she heard from him.

Rose redialed Stone, Tecci, and Beals, but got no answer. He slammed the telephone down. "Goddamn it! This is crazy! Now that we know who we're looking for, we can't find anyone."

Shannon was pacing up and down again. "The hell with them. We gotta find Pickett. He's the important one. Where the hell can he be?"

"Hey, maybe he's with his girlfriend," Rose suggested. "The one who lives on Charles Street."

Shannon looked at his watch; it was almost ten-thirty. "Let's go. It's worth a shot."

Rose stopped. "What about Hardy?"

Shannon didn't even hesitate. "He'll keep. First we have to find Pickett."

36

THEY PARKED THE CAR ON BLEECKER AND ENTERED CHARLES STREET on foot. As they hurried down the street, they carefully scanned the sidewalks and parked cars.

Upstairs, on the second floor, Shannon rang Julia Nussbaum's bell. There was no answer.

In frustration, Rose slammed the door with his hand. "Now what?"

"We'll keep calling the others," Shannon said glumly. "We'll go for the first one we find home." He wasn't happy with that idea, but he couldn't think of a better one. "In the meantime, we'll watch the building from the street."

As they walked back to their car, Rose raised the inevitable question. "Do you think it's time to let the rest of the department in on this?"

They both knew there would come a time when they would have to go official with this investigation. But they hadn't thought about the mechanics of it.

"I'd rather have Larson or Bennett do it," Shannon said.

"But they're not here," Rose reminded him. "We could call Emergency Service to stake out the block," he suggested.

"And after the guys in the flak jackets and shotguns arrive, what do we tell them? *Maybe* there's going to be an assassination tonight? *Maybe* it's going to be on this street?"

Rose scratched the stubble on his chin. "Yeah, I see what you mean. Too many maybe's."

"Besides, how would we keep the press away?" Shannon lit a cigarette and stared at it in disgust. "This is the second one today. I almost made it through the whole day without one." He popped open the glove compartment and handed a portable radio to Rose. "They're set on a confidential channel."

Rose toyed with the squelch knob. "Does this work?"

"What the hell. It's better than two tin cans on a string."

Shannon was only half kidding. They both knew that relying on a shaky form of communication tonight was dicey. Because of the great number of radio transmissions bouncing around the city's air, it was not unusual to pick up telephone conversations, taxi dispatchers, and an occasional police broadcast from Ohio, but not the transmission of your partner down the street.

"If I get into trouble," Rose said, trying to sound cheerful, "I'll fire a shot in the air. If I get into real trouble, I'll fire two. You stay here. I'll go down to the other end of the block and watch from there."

At the far end of the block he selected a suitably darkened doorway with a good view of the street and Nussbaum's brownstone. He popped open the cylinder to make sure the gun was loaded. Since Velez's death, he'd taken to carrying his bigger and more accurate service revolver. He blew a dust ball from under the hammer and wiped the excess crud away with his handkerchief. He couldn't remember when he last used this, or any other gun. Although every member of the department was supposed to qualify twice a year, Rose usually found an excuse not to go. The truth was, he didn't particularly like guns, and the trip to the range in Rodman's Neck in the Bronx was a pain in the ass. Now he wished he'd gotten more practice. In spite of his tenseness, he laughed out loud. He felt like Sam Spade waiting for Sydney Greenstreet to show up with the Maltese Falcon. It was so melodramatic, it was almost funny.

The damp breeze coming off the nearby Hudson River made him shiver, and the sky, a bright pink, meant snow or rain was not far away. He envied Shannon sitting in a warm car. Christmas lights blinked on and off in apartment windows across the street, but huddled in the doorway, cold and uncomfortable, Rose felt no holiday cheer. There were menorahs displayed in several windows, but the owners couldn't seem to arrive at a consensus of how many lights should be lit tonight. Rose, a nonpracticing Jew, had no idea which one was correct. He stuck his head out and surveyed the street. No cars, no people; the street was deserted. He thought about the M.O. of the past murders. They were all done with small-caliber guns, but that didn't mean the killers weren't packing heavy artillery. The thought of going up against an automatic weapon, or a shotgun, made him shiver again. Quickly, his eyes scanned the surrounding area for a good source of protection. The vestibule door behind him was made of glass. "Can't hide behind that," he muttered, and was suddenly reminded of Billy Boyle. When they were kids playing cops and robbers, he and Billy had a running argument as to whether you could shoot somebody through glass. Billy had insisted, sometimes to the point of tears, that you could. Rose steadfastly maintained that you couldn't. They argued endlessly over their imperfect understanding of the applied laws of physics. "You were right, Billy boy," Rose murmured. "I acknowledge my error." Maybe it was why, armed with this certain knowledge, he thought, Boyle had joined the Fire Department.

Rose was not overjoyed with the prospect of using a car for cover in the event of gunplay. He remembered only too well a demonstration at the range where the instructors graphically demonstrated the inadequacy of an automobile as a protective shield by blowing a depressing number of holes through it with a wide variety of weapons.

Then there was the problem of civilians. In New York City, regardless of the time—day or night—there were always people on the street. Because of the crowded streets, the NYPD had promulgated the most restrictive law enforcement gun-use laws in the country. He noted with disgust that the only safe backdrop for firing was a short twenty-foot brick wall across the street. Great! Now all he had to do was convince the combatants to stand in front of the wall so he could shoot at them.

He was too old for this John Wayne crap. If the shit hit the fan, he resolved to keep his ass down until the shooting stopped, and he assumed Shannon would have the good sense to do the same. He'd been to enough inspectors' funerals, and he didn't want to go to another one; especially as the guest of honor.

The radio crackled. "Rose . . . do you hear me?"

"Yeah, I'm in a doorway at the end of the block. Anything yet?"

"Nope. Quiet at this end. I made more calls. Still no one home."

Rose looked at his watch. It was eleven-thirty. "We've been here almost an hour. How long do you want to wait?"

"Awhile longer."

Worst-case scenarios had been haunting Shannon for the past hour. Maybe Pickett hadn't come here at all, and if he did, maybe he wasn't coming back. Maybe Stone's people took Pickett out somewhere uptown. He could picture Bennett at the scene, standing over Pickett's body and wondering where the hell his hotshot lieutenants were. For the second time tonight Shannon felt a panic attack coming on. The whole investigation was coming apart. Hardy was dead, a hit team was on the loose, and Pickett was out there somewhere in the city, oblivious to the danger that stalked him.

Shannon had shut the engine off and the car was getting chilly. He was about to start the motor when a cab turned into Charles Street. Following close behind the taxi, a blue van pulled up to the corner, paused, then turned into Charles Street. "It's Pickett," he whispered into his radio. "And they have company."

Cautiously, Rose stuck his head out and saw the cab stop in front of the brownstone. Pickett and the woman emerged and hurried inside. The van slowed, but continued down the street. As it passed, Rose stepped farther back into the darkness and whispered into the radio. "The plate light is out. I couldn't read the number. Too dark to see the driver, but the passenger was black."

"Was it the same guys we saw uptown?"

"Couldn't tell."

"What do you think?"

Rose stamped his feet to ward off the chill. "As long as Pickett is off the street, he's safe. Let's jump the van when it comes back."

Shannon's instinct was to protect Pickett, but Rose had a point. The senator was safe as long as he remained in the apartment. "We'll take whoever comes first. If it's Pickett, we grab him and take him home. No more secrets."

As time passed, it got colder in the car, but Shannon didn't want to attract attention by turning on the motor. When he'd first seen the van, he'd considered requesting assistance over the radio, but the call would have brought a flood of radio cars screeching into the block, possibly alerting whoever was in the van. He could have made a telephone call requesting unmarked cars only, but that would have taken time and he didn't want to leave Rose alone. Unhappy with the alternatives, he'd have to wait for Pickett or the van occupants to make the first move. He pulled his collar up and carefully scrutinized every vehicle and the few pedestrians who entered the street.

Rose came back on the radio. "Brian, do you read me?"

"Yeah."

"It's almost one, and I'm freezing my ass off. I don't think they're coming back. Let's collect Pick—"

"Hold it," Shannon said urgently.

The blue van pulled up to the corner, slowed, and then turned into the block. The vehicle—reminding Shannon of a shark, quietly, but relentlessly circling its prey—coasted to the curb in front of a fire hydrant. The headlights went out.

"They're back," he whispered into the radio. "Off the corner on the south side of the street."

Rose watched from his darkened doorway. "I see them." His heart was pounding and he was finding it hard to concentrate. He needed action, something physical; anything but standing in this doorway, cold and uncomfortable. "Let's take them. Give me some time to get up the block. When I'm almost there, you come down and block them on the street side. I'll take the driver, you take the passenger."

Rose started up the block with no idea of what he was going to do when he got there. The van was too far away to see anyone inside, but his eyes never left the dark-tinted windshield that looked like the cold, impersonal eyes of a large insect. The gun he gripped in his pocket felt heavy and unwieldly. In spite of the chill in the air, rivulets of sweat slid down his back. He was alone on the street.

Rose had just passed the brownstone on the opposite side of the street, and didn't see Pickett appear at the top of the stoop. With its headlights still off, the van edged away from the curb. Rose, unsure of this new development, hesitated.

From his vantage point at the top of the block, Shannon saw Pickett at the same time the van did. "Rose," he yelled into the radio, "he's on the *street*! Pickett is on the *street*!"

Rose whirled and saw the tall senator buttoning his overcoat as he walked up the block. He stepped off the curb and yelled, "Pickett! Get down! Get down!"

At first the senator, thinking Rose was a drunk, ignored him. But then he got a better look at the figure in the darkness and recognized the lieutenant who had given him the warning in his office. He didn't understand what the lieutenant was shouting, but out of the corner of his eye he saw a vehicle coming down the block without lights. All at once he understood. He should get down, out of danger, but his body refused to respond.

Rose, realizing that Pickett was frozen, started to run toward him. He was in the middle of the street when he heard the van accelerate. Cursing himself for getting caught out in the open, he drew his gun, spun, and aimed at the center of the darkened windshield as the giant insect loomed larger in his field of vision. Just then the headlights flashed on, blinding him. Instinctively, he pumped off six quick shots. The vehicle swerved like a horse avoiding a swarm of angry hornets and sideswiped several parked cars; the shrill screech of tires and ripping metal filled the quiet street. The van careened off the autos and headed directly toward him. He dove for the safety of the sidewalk, but the van's large sideview mirror caught his right shoulder and tossed him like a rag doll over the hood of a parked car. With tires spinning and rubber burning, the van fishtailed down the street.

*   *   *

TECCI, WHO WAS BEHIND THE WHEEL, HAD BEEN THE FIRST ONE TO see Pickett appear on the stoop. "There he is," he whispered to Beals. "Right on time."

Slowly, he eased the van away from the curb and started down the street. They'd already made their plan. Tecci was to call Pickett over for directions. When he was close enough, Beals was to lean over and shoot Pickett at point-blank range.

Tecci gripped the steering wheel with sweaty hands. "For Chrissake, Mac, make sure you don't shoot me."

"Don't worry. Just keep your head back."

Suddenly, a figure darted out into the street.

"Who the fuck is that?" Tecci screamed.

They'd been so intent on watching Pickett that neither of them saw Rose coming up the block on the other side of the dark street.

Beals rolled his window down. "He's yelling something to Pickett. Christ! He's warning him to get down. Get him, Steve! Knock him down!"

Tecci stomped on the accelerator and the van shot forward. The man, now in the middle of the street, whirled.

"Oh, shit!" Beals shouted. "He's got a gun!"

Tecci yanked on the headlight switch and watched in horrified fascination as the man crouched and brought the gun up. Tecci didn't hear the report of the gun over the engine noise, but he saw the barrel jump with each muzzle flash. Four tiny holes appeared in the windshield.

Beals's head slammed into the rear of the seat and he stiffened. "I'm hit!" he screamed. "I'm hit!"

Tecci, concentrating on keeping the van under control, rapidly closed the distance. At the last moment the man dove to the side, but Tecci heard a satisfying thump as the body glanced off the side of his vehicle.

"It's a fucking trap!" he yelled to Beals. "We walked into a setup!" Tecci stomped on the accelerator and sped through the intersection.

Shannon had seen the van hit Rose. He screeched to a stop by the prostrate Rose and flung his door open. "Are you okay?" he shouted.

"Yeah, I think so." Rose grimaced and staggered to his feet, holding his shoulder. "But this coat is ruined."

Once Shannon saw Rose was all right, his fear quickly turned to anger. "What the fuck were you doing in the middle of the street, you asshole? Goddamn useless cop chaser, you're not worth a *shit!*" He slammed the car in gear. "Get in, they're getting away."

Rose hobbled over and barely had time to close the door before the vehicle bolted forward. As they sped by Pickett, who was still rooted to the same spot, Shannon yelled, "Get back inside and stay there!"

Rose shouted into the radio. "Nine-six-one to central."

"Go ahead," a sleepy dispatcher answered.

"This unit in pursuit of a vehicle wanted in connection with the attempted murder of a police officer. Blue Ford van heading south on Washington at Christopher . . . two male occupants . . . New Jersey registration . . . Victor-Thomas-Mary-four-nine-Nora." Pain shot through Rose's shoulder when he tried to wipe the blood from a deep gash in his forehead. Then he looked down at his torn slacks. "Shit!"

"What?" Shannon's eyes were riveted on the van's red taillights in the distance.

"I landed in shit!"

"What are you talking about?" Shannon snapped, his nerves already stretched to the breaking point.

"I got dog shit all over me!" Rose yelled in disgust. "Some son of a bitch didn't clean up after his dog. The dirty bastard. It must have been a Great Dane too."

Shannon hooted. "I thought that smell was you. I thought you shit your pants!"

Rose laughed, feeling light-headed. "Are you kidding? I may never shit again."

Like most department vehicles, Shannon's couldn't get out of its own way. Rose thumped on the dashboard yelling "Faster, faster," while Shannon, between obscenities, yelled that he had his foot to the floor. Several times they lost sight of the van, only to see it again as they screeched around a corner. In this manner they squealed through the narrow Greenwich Village streets. At every intersection Shannon braked and looked left as Rose, straining to see if there was oncoming traffic, looked right. A terse "Go" from Rose, shouted over the wail of the siren, signaled it was all clear on his side.

Rose continued to broadcast the location and direction of the van so other radio cars in the area could intercept it. But at one in the morning there weren't many radio cars in the lower end of Manhattan, and the few there were, arrived at the cutoff point too late.

There is nothing cops like better than a good car chase, especially when it breaks up the monotony of a long late tour. On the other hand, there is nothing the department brass likes less, because invariably radio cars manage to collide with each other, citizens, and assorted immovable objects, but seldom the bad guys.

A Borough Commander's worst fear consisted of a radio car in pursuit of another vehicle careening through crowded city streets as a cop, firing a lucky shot, takes out the driver, causing four thousand pounds of uncontrolled metal to plow into a school bus full of handicapped children. As a result of this collective nightmare, the department issued an order, carved in granite: thou shalt not chase autos, and thou shalt *definitely* not fire at moving vehicles.

As more and more cars happily joined the chase, a nervous probationary captain assigned to supervise Manhattan South sat at the corner of Fifth Avenue and Fourteenth Street, biting his nails and listening to the chase hurtling through his zone of responsibility. He knew he should get on the air and call it off, but he hesitated. He clutched the steering wheel and stared wide-eyed at the radio speaker as though it were a rattlesnake that had just crawled out from underneath the seat.

"No-Balls" Newman, as he was known in Manhattan South, knew from past experience what would happen if he called the chase off. For the rest of the night he'd have to endure on-the-air taunts from every smartass cop in Manhattan South. And unauthorized transmissions, he knew only too well, were also against department regulations. Finally he decided that having his name besmirched by a bunch of schmucks was preferable to getting his ass chewed out by the Borough Commander, who ate probationary captains for breakfast.

Quickly, before he had a chance to change his mind, he grabbed the mike. "Central, this is the patrol supervisor. I'm directing that this chase be called off."

Captain Newman, already hardened to the slings and arrows of outrageous fortune, wasn't prepared for what followed. Rose, in great pain and caught up in the excitement, heard the captain's transmission with a mixture of astonishment and fury. His response was direct and to the point. "You fucking moron!" he screamed into the mike. "This van has to be stopped!"

Several other radio-car wits, seizing the opportunity to engage in cathartic release, took turns describing in graphic terms their assessment of Newman's masculinity, parentage, and his proclivity toward incestuous relationships with his mother—assuming he had a mother.

Even the radio dispatcher was disappointed. It was no fun sitting at a radio console hour after hour doing nothing more exciting than dispatching cars to "disorderly youths" and "loud radio" runs. He liked a good chase as well as the next guy, but orders were orders. "All units on patrol . . . be advised the chase is called off . . . authority PBMS patrol supervisor . . . time . . . 0130 hours."

Rose stared at the mike. "Are you fucking people crazy?" he shouted as their car plunged into the Battery Tunnel alone in pursuit of the van.

37

When Tecci had sped away from Charles Street, he'd looked in his rearview mirror. "Mac," he said, "someone's following us."

Beals moaned softly, and Tecci tore his eyes from the road for a quick glance at his partner. Beals was clutching his chest. Blood trickled through his fingers, and his eyes were growing cloudy.

"Hang on, buddy," Tecci said. "I'll get us out of this. I'll outrun whoever's following us and then I'll get you to a doctor. You're gonna be okay."

But Beals's only answer was a gurgling death rattle. Small, frothy pink bubbles appeared at the corner of his mouth.

Tecci, operating on instinct alone, shot into the Brooklyn Battery Tunnel. Skillfully, he wove in and out of lanes, ignoring the angry horn blasts of other motorists. As he roared out of the tunnel, he saw that the toll plaza was clogged with cars. There was nowhere to go, but then he spotted an unused toll gate at the far left side of the plaza. Yanking on the wheel, he cut across a line of cars and, to the accompaniment of blaring horns, sped through the tollgate, shattering the wooden barrier.

"How was that, Mac?" He glanced at his partner to get his reaction.

McKay Beals was dead.

POLICE OFFICERS ROCCO SANTANGELO AND STANLEY LEIBOWITZ, assigned to the Brooklyn Highway Unit, were sitting in their radio car enjoying a late-night snack. It had been a slow night, and the radio, on a different frequency from Manhattan, was quiet. At forty-one, Santangelo was the old-timer in the car. He sipped his Sanka and looked askance at his partner, a twenty-three-year-old with a cast-iron stomach, who was boring his way through an enormous meatball hero dripping with greasy tomato sauce. It had been many years since Santangelo had been able to eat like that on a late tour. He was getting *agita* just watching the kid.

Leibowitz was newly assigned to the Highway Unit. Before the recruits were sent to motorcycle school, they were assigned to radio-car duty with seasoned veterans for several weeks.

Plenty of young cops wanted to get into the Highway Unit. After all, what was more macho than wearing leather and sticking a big Harley between your legs? But the moment of truth for these neophytes always came the first time they partook in a high-speed chase. Cranking up a radio car to 100 miles an hour in pursuit of a speeder can be a soul-searching experience. Between the potholes and repavement patches, the car is airborne more than it's on the ground. Then there's the moment of truth when you pull up next to a car doing 90 mph, not knowing if the driver is drunk, crazy, or brain dead. A driver's reaction is often unpredictable. When overtaken, some gape at the police officer in utter surprise and slam on the brakes—right in the middle of the highway. Others change lanes—sometimes into the same lane as the pursuing radio car. Still others, terrified, just keep driving until they are overtaken and herded to the side of the road like a runaway horse.

Leibowitz, a high-strung kid, wasn't thrilled to be riding with Santangelo, who enjoyed a reputation for being one crazy son of a bitch. Santangelo held the department record for the most speeding summonses issued in a single tour; he also held the record for the most radio cars totaled in a single year. Some wags he worked with tried to get him into the *Guinness Book of World Records,* but the publisher wrote back a polite letter saying they were sorry, but there was no category for "The Most Police Vehicles Wrecked by a Single Cop in a Single Year."

Santangelo, who'd been grounded for most of the year, had just gotten his wings back earlier in the week. His commanding officer, a psychology major at John Jay College and a man who prided himself on being an expert in interpersonal relations, called Santangelo into his office and gave it to him straight. "Rocco," he began reasonably, "this is your last chance." At this point in his prepared speech the captain lost his resolve to remain aloof and detached, because it suddenly occurred to him that his career would crumble as surely as the front end of the next totaled radio car. With eyes afire he bellowed his final warning. "If you get into one more accident, I'm going to tear up your driver's license, rip your fucking heart out, and transfer you so far from here you'll be the only cop wearing leather in the Gobi Desert! Is that clear?"

Santangelo sipped his coffee and tried to ignore the hero eater next to him. As he often did when things were quiet, he slipped into his favorite daydream—driving race cars. Santangelo knew in his heart he would have made a great Indy 500 driver, right up there with his hero, Mario Andretti. But being a poor Italian kid from Brooklyn, he had to settle for the next best thing—becoming a New York City cabdriver. It wasn't until a motorcycle cop clocked him doing 93 mph on Flatbush Avenue that he knew he wanted to be a cop. It was a revelation akin to a religious experience; motorcycle cops had a license to speed!

Most of the department autos, including the eight-cylinder models used by the Highway Unit, were a sorry lot. Constant use and abuse made them sluggish and prone to frequent breakdowns. Santangelo, in violation of department procedures, took his department vehicle to a friend's hot-rod shop, where in addition to tuning the car to perfection, they added a little something here and a little something there, until the wheezy old department auto was metamorphosed into a machine that could go from zero to 80 in the blink of an eye. The only accessory missing was the parachute.

Santangelo had positioned his vehicle that night at the top of the eastbound ramp at Bay Eighth Street. From this vantage point he could monitor traffic unobserved. For an old pro like him, spotting a speeder was a piece of cake. From years of experience he had the ability to estimate the speed of a car to within plus or minus two miles, and his technique was flawless. Eyeball the speed, sweep down the ramp, slide into position at the driver's blind spot, clock him for a quarter of a mile, hit the roof lights, tap the siren, and write the summons before the driver knew what hit him. It was like falling off a log. Santangelo was an artist.

He was suddenly brought out of his reverie by the sight of a blue van rocketing by at 80 mph. Instinctively, he snapped the gear-shift lever into drive and stomped on the accelerator. Like a space-shuttle lift-off, the vehicle trembled but remained momentarily motionless as the rear wheels spun in the loose road sand. Finally they hit asphalt and the car catapulted forward. Leibowitz made a grab for his can of Classic Coke perched on the dashboard, but he wasn't quick enough. It flipped onto him and the soda fizzed onto his lap. The rookie tried to rise, but the seat belt held him in place.

He glanced at the rapidly climbing speedometer needle; they were doing 72 mph and they weren't even off the ramp yet! Involuntarily, he squeezed his hero and a large, greasy meatball squirted down the front of his shirt. "What should I do with my sandwich?" he yelled above the whine of the engine and squealing tires.

"Throw it out the window," Santangelo yelled as he concentrated on negotiating a power turn onto the parkway.

Without taking his eyes off the speedometer, Leibowitz threw the sandwich out the window. In his panic he'd neglected to open the window, and the greasy, tomato-laden meatball hero bounced back into his Coke-soaked lap. But by now Leibowitz's hair could have been on fire and he wouldn't have noticed. In sheer terror he gripped the dashboard with both hands and swore that if God would only get him out of this alive and away from this crazy schmuck, he would go to temple every Friday night. For a kicker he promised never to eat another ham sandwich as long as he lived, which he fervently hoped would be longer than the next five minutes.

Santangelo roared onto the parkway and almost sideswiped Shannon, who had been trying his best to keep up with the van. The Highway cop glanced in the rearview mirror. "I think there's a department auto behind us. I wonder why we didn't hear a chase on the radio?"

Leibowitz was unable to turn around. His eyes were locked on the speedometer needle inching toward 90 mph.

Santangelo studied the van ahead of him with professional interest. No fishtailing. Nice and steady. No drunk here. Must be stolen. He flipped on his roof lights, hit the siren, and watched the van's taillights to see if the driver hit the brakes. Nothing. "All right!" he screamed exuberantly. "We got us a goddamn *chase*!"

Leibowitz groaned and tightened his seat belt. By now the Coke had reached body temperature and wasn't too uncomfortable, but he was getting the urge to urinate. "I'll put the chase over the air," he said hoarsely, and pried one hand from the dashboard.

"Don't do that," Santangelo yelled. "We're not allowed to do chases." The young officer's hand snapped back onto the dashboard as the needle crept toward 100 mph.

Santangelo was impressed. "Son of a bitch is a real good driver," he said with grudging admiration. "He's really flying."

Police officers were allowed to take a shotgun on patrol only when they were alone, but Santangelo *always* took one. "What the hell," he'd tell anyone who'd listen, "I'm riding with a rookie. I might as well be alone!"

There was a rack to lock the shotgun under the seat, but Santangelo never used it. He was convinced that by the time he unlocked the damn thing, he wouldn't need it, or he'd be dead. So against department regulations, he kept the gun barrel wedged in the rear seat with the stock resting on the back of the front seat next to his head. "Hey kid," he said, "grab the shotgun and lock and load one."

Leibowitz tore his eyes away from the speedometer to look at Santangelo. "Are you *crazy*?" he screamed, convinced he was riding with a madman. "You wanna shoot someone for *speeding*? You're out of your mind!"

"Can't be too careful," Santangelo said. "There are a lot of crazy bastards on the roads these days."

"I know," Leibowitz nodded in vigorous agreement, "I know." But he didn't touch the shotgun. In the event of an accident, which he was certain would occur, he didn't want to add a shotgun wound to his other injuries.

WHEN SHANNON AND ROSE HAD ROARED INTO THE BATTERY TUNNEL, they were far behind the van. Traffic was light, but they couldn't gain ground. Shannon wove in and out of traffic, occasionally sideswiping the wall, but he couldn't make the car go any faster. "We have a chance to catch them at the toll booth," Rose yelled.

Shannon nodded. There was always a tie-up at the toll booth. They came out of the tunnel just in time to see the van crash through a closed gate. "Goddamn!" they said in unison, and sped through the same gate, scattering wood chips as they went.

They'd followed the van onto the Brooklyn-Queens Expressway toward Staten Island, and then eastbound onto the Belt Parkway. Just when Shannon was beginning to wonder where the hell all the Highway cops were, a blue-and-white shot out in front of them. "About time!" he yelled excitedly.

"All right!" Rose thumped the dashboard. "Here comes the cavalry!"

But their exuberance was short-lived. Shannon looked at the rising temperature gauge. "Shit. I think the engine is having a meltdown."

Rose grabbed the radio. "Central, notify the Brooklyn South dispatcher that a Highway car is pursuing a van wanted in connection with the attempted murder of a police officer."

"What unit calling?"

"The same unit that called before," Rose shouted. "Nine-six-one."

"Nine-six-one," the dispatcher answered testily, "that chase was called off. Resume patrol."

Rose stared slack-mouthed at the mike. Then, in a fit of frustration, he yanked on it and stared dumbly at the loose wiring dangling in his hand.

The smell of burning oil filled the car. "Son of a bitch," Shannon muttered. "The engine's seizing up."

Up ahead Rocco Santangelo planned his final attack. He knew there was roadwork around the bend a couple of miles ahead. If he timed it just right, he could get alongside the van as they were going into the turn and force the vehicle into the construction barriers.

He stomped on the accelerator, pleased with the smooth performance of the engine. Slowly, he inched up on the van until his front wheels were parallel to the van's rear wheels. He remembered the chariot race in *Ben Hur* and wondered if he could rig spikes on his hubcaps. The air turbulence rocked the lighter police car, and Leibowitz was finding it hard to swallow. The needle started pegging off 110 mph. The rookie squeezed his eyes shut.

They were almost at the curve. Santangelo made his move. He punched through the gap and came up even with the van. The van driver, seeing the lane up ahead was closed, tried to move left, but Santangelo was there. The two vehicles caromed off each other, once, twice. Then Santangelo cut his wheels sharply to the right. The air was filled with the crunching sounds of metal and squealing tires as the vehicles bounced off each other. The van's brakes locked and a plume of smoke rose from the burning tires. It tore through a row of barriers, exploding wood and yellow lights in all directions. Out of control, the van fishtailed off the road and struck a concrete barrier, catapulting Beals's body through the windshield.

The radio car skidded to a stop. Santangelo was out before it stopped rocking. Shotgun in hand, he ducked behind a drill compressor. "All right, scumbag," he yelled. "Come out with your hands in the air."

The driver's door opened and a man started to get out. Even in the poor light and swirling dust, Santangelo clearly saw the flash of metal in the driver's hand. Sighting over the shotgun barrel, he watched the hand coming up toward him and he pumped off three quick rounds. The first round of "double-O" buck, containing twenty-seven 9mm lead balls, blew the door window out. The second round caught Tecci in the face and neck, throwing him back into the van. The third round went harmlessly over the roof.

By now Leibowitz had disengaged himself from his seat belt and was out of the car with his gun drawn. Covered by Santangelo, the shaken young cop approached the vehicle and shined his flashlight into the interior. Half of Tecci's face was blown away. An eyeball, hanging by a tendon, stared out through red, glistening flesh. Then police officer Stanley Leibowitz looked down, and the flashlight illuminated the police shield clutched in Steve Tecci's outstretched, bloodied hand.

When Shannon and Rose limped up in their hissing, steaming car, they found Rocco Santangelo, the shotgun at his feet, staring vacantly at the van and mumbling over and over again, "I killed a cop . . . Jesus Christ . . . I killed a cop . . ."

Behind the van, leaning on the bumper for support, Leibowitz was hunched over, discovering that a meatball hero comes up much faster than it goes down.

38

IT WAS EARLY AFTERNOON IN THE OTC PUB, AND MOST OF THE LUNCH crowd had long since stumbled back to the office to finish out the day in a pleasant martini fog.

The two sat at the far end of the bar sharing the leaden effects of postinvestigative depression. Rose, his dislocated shoulder in a sling, was the first to speak. "I hear Stone is seeing the P.C. today."

"Yeah, that's what I hear. What the hell, it's only been a week."

Bitterly, Shannon recalled the unsatisfactory conclusion to their investigation. That night, less than an hour after they'd caught up to the van on the Belt Parkway, they'd finally reached Bennett on the telephone and went to his home.

The chief, in fire-engine-red pajamas and plaid robe, looked even more outrageous than usual. His sleep-tossed hair, wilder than ever, made him look like a cranky Viking. In the kitchen he poured some freshly made coffee for the grateful lieutenants. Saying little, he scowled as he listened to Shannon describe the night's ironic turn of events.

When Shannon was done, he looked expectantly at Bennett. "Well, Chief, when do we pick up Stone? I think we should do it right now."

Bennett ran his fingers through his hair and frowned. Then he glanced at Rose. "You look like hell." The gash on Rose's forehead had stopped bleeding, but specks of dried blood clung to his pale face, and his clothing was spattered with blood. "How're you feeling?"

"I'm okay, but my shoulder hurts."

Bennett turned to Shannon. "Call an ambulance."

"No," Rose said abruptly. "I'm not going anywhere until we're finished with this."

"I wanted to take him to the hospital," Shannon interjected, "but he wouldn't go."

Bennett pulled his robe about him. "Suit yourself," he said, and drank from his cup.

Shannon and Rose watched in giddy fascination as drops from the bottom of the wet cup dripped silently onto the food-stained bathrobe. Rose whispered, "It's nice to see some permanence in a confused world, isn't it?"

"What?" Bennett asked, putting his cup down with a splash.

Shannon shook his head. "Nothing. Where do we go from here?"

"Go home," Bennett said. "Get some sleep." He saw the puzzled looks on their faces. "I can't make the decision on Stone. It'll have to come from Larson. Go home the both of you, but don't take the phone off the hook. I may need you in a hurry to come back and make the arrest."

But there was no arrest. No urgent telephone call summoning them back to wrap up the investigation with the final act—the arrest of Captain Patrick Stone.

The next morning Shannon stormed into Bennett's office. "What happened?" he demanded.

The chief looked embarrassed. "I gave the information to Larson."

"And?"

"And he went to the P.C. with it."

"And?"

Bennett's eyes evaded Shannon's glare. "And that's it. I'm not privy to what was discussed in the commissioner's office," he added lamely.

Shannon wouldn't let him off the hook that easily. "Are you telling me there's not going to be an arrest?"

Bennett busied himself shuffling papers. "It looks that way."

"Why?" Shannon exploded.

Bennett didn't answer. Unwilling to remain skewered by Shannon's accusing gaze, he had gotten up from his desk and left the room.

Shannon gulped down the remainder of his drink and signaled for another round. "What was the point of it all?" he asked Rose.

"What do you mean?"

"All the time, effort, and aggravation, and for what? One week later and still nothing has happened. If I hadn't dragged Velez into this—"

"Knock it off, Brian. You've been a cop long enough to know there's no percentages in playing Monday-morning quarterback. We all know the risks of the game. Luis was a tough, spunky cop. He knew the risks better than most."

"Thank you, Professor Rose," Shannon said dryly. "I think you missed your calling. You should be teaching Police-amatic Bullshit 101 at John Jay."

Rose tried to change the subject. "What are you going to do now?"

"I don't know. Go back to my squad, I guess. The felony project has been canceled indefinitely." He laughed humorlessly. "I don't think Bennett wants me around anymore. Not after I told him what I thought of him and Larson. That's okay with me. I'm up to here with those no-balls paper-pushers in the Puzzle Palace. What about you? What are you going to do?"

"I guess we're both on the shit list. I've been on sick report, but no one called me. I don't know where I'm supposed to report when I come back."

Shannon chuckled. "That's funny, Rose. Even IAD doesn't want you. That makes you lower than whale shit, and that's at the bottom of the ocean. Of course, I can see why they don't want you back. Let me see if I can remember all the charges and specs you have coming to you." He ticked them off on his fingers. "Insubordination, assault on a superior officer, unauthorized radio transmissions, destruction of department property, and loss of a prisoner. Is that about it?"

"Yeah," Rose said. "I think you got them all. I still think you belong in IAD, you have the killer instinct; you always go for the old jugular. Anyway, fuck 'em. I expect to make captain with the next batch of promotions."

Shannon looked away and for a brief moment envy flickered in his eyes, but then it was gone. "That's great," he said sincerely. "You going to stay in the job?"

"Yes," Rose answered, surprising himself. "I am."

Shannon studied him. "Why?" He asked the question as though he needed to be convinced himself.

Rose tried to think of a good reason, but he couldn't come up with one. Instead, he cited the unspoken challenge that seduces good men to remain in a no-win situation. "Maybe I can change some things in this department, make a difference."

Shannon slammed his glass on the bar. "What a fucking mess."

"The job?"

"This whole case." He ticked off the names. "Luis, Cronin, Hardy, Tecci, Beals. All dead."

"Don't forget the victims."

"They were all scumbags; they deserved it."

Rose laughed. "I'm glad to see this experience hasn't shaken your faith in Old Testament justice."

"The only one left alive is the bastard who started the whole thing," Shannon said softly. "What's going to happen to him?" He was silent for a moment, then he said abruptly, "I'm getting out of the job."

"Hey, Shannon, take it easy. I know it's dramatic tossing your gun and shield on Larson's desk, but that futile gesture will have just about as much impact as pissing in the East River. We don't mean a thing to this department."

"You got that right," Shannon said bitterly. "I can't count all the Christmases, birthdays, and anniversaries I've missed because of this job. And for what? This job is like a leech. It sucks the lifeblood out of you, and when there's nothing left, it spits you out. I'm a selfish bastard. I was having a great time playing cops and robbers, but I never saw what it was doing to my family."

Shannon toyed with his glass. "I've been thinking about something that shrink Altman said. He said cops must have the ability to split their minds so they don't bring the job home with them. I've lost that ability; maybe I never had it. For a long time I've been bringing the job home with me, and it's almost wrecked my marriage. I didn't see it because I was too busy playing super sleuth."

"Brian, don't make it sound like you were playing a game." Rose suddenly thought of his own marriage.

"But it was a game, wasn't it? Hide-and-seek. It took us a little longer than it should have, but we tagged the bad guys and now the game is over. Everybody goes home."

Idly, Shannon lined up coins on the bar. "A guy I fish with once told me a funny story. He'd just bought an anchor, and as he went forward to tie it to the anchor line, he slipped and fell overboard. Suddenly, he's sitting on the bottom in fifteen feet of water cradling his brand-new anchor. He didn't want to let go, but he was running out of breath. Realizing his choice was drowning or losing the new anchor, he reluctantly let go and swam to the surface.

"The job has been my anchor, and I've been holding on to it for twenty-three years. I don't want to let go either, but I've run out of breath. I guess it's all part of growing up, but you have to learn when to let go. Of

course, knowing that doesn't make it any easier. I can't shake the nagging
feeling that I've failed; that I've given up. What the hell, I'll live."

He started to raise his hand to order another drink, but changed his
mind. "That's it for the day," he said with finality.

Rose put his hand on Shannon's arm. "I don't want to sound corny, but
the job needs guys like you. We've got plenty of deadwood and guys in
mental retirement. If this job is going to get any better, it has to have people
who know what has to be done and who are willing to do it."

Shannon pulled his arm away. "Not me. Not anymore. This job has
beaten the shit out of me for the last time. *I* am a victim of police brutality."

"Brian, you're a good cop. I've learned a lot from you. Everything has
always come easy for me. I've never had to struggle for anything in my life.
Maybe that's why I never took this job too seriously. It was just a place to
go every day, have a little fun. You see things differently. You're the most
dedicated and tenacious man I've ever met. You have a single-minded
purpose that I envy. Unfortunately, I think some of that has rubbed off on
me. For the first time in my life something has become important to me: this
job. I know it's run by schmucks who are afraid to make decisions, but
guys like you and me can change that."

Shannon gave him a look of disgust. "No we can't. This department is
like a glacier. It moves slowly, but it sweeps away everything in its path. It
runs over guys like you and me and doesn't even notice. Why do you think
the smart people get out of the job? Because eventually they realize they're
pissing into the wind."

"And they're fucking cowards," Rose said vehemently.

Shannon shook his head. "What're you smoking?"

"They're cowards because they gave up and they were the ones who
could have saved this job. They ran away and left the job to morons like
Larson. That's why the job is in the shape it's in. The talented guys leave
and empty suits like Larson fill the void. They get to run the job by default,
and that's bullshit. Guys like you and me have to take the job away from the
Larsons."

Shannon was unmoved. Alex Rose, amateur detective, was getting
religion. "Give me a break, Rose."

"Say what you want, but you know I'm right."

"Right about what?" Shannon snapped. "Look at yourself. Prince
Charming. You've said it yourself. This job has been a fucking hobby for
you. You're a dilettante playing at being a cop. I've been in this job for
twenty-three years and I busted my ass for everything I've gotten. Nothing
ever came easy for me—not studying, not promotions, nothing. I've given it
my best shot, but I can't afford the cost anymore. My home life is a
shambles because of this fucking job. And what has the job given me? I'm
on Larson's shit list. I may lose my squad. And what about Captain Stone? I

thought we were going to lock him up? What happened? No collar. No department charges, not even a forced retirement. They'll probably promote the son of a bitch!''

"I don't like it any better than you, but that just underscores what I've been saying. If nothing happens to Stone, it means the P.C. is another empty suit. That's the kind of guy we have to drive out of the job.''

Shannon studied Rose. "You're serious, aren't you? That old whore— the job—has seduced you. You're ready to mount a crusade—tilt at windmills and police commissioners.''

He was making light of Rose's newfound convictions, but he understood the feeling. After all, he'd had it for twenty-three years. Rose was right about one thing: there were too many incompetents running the job. But could he or Rose do any better? Maybe the view from the fourteenth floor was different for a reason. Even in his bitterness he suspected there was more to running the New York City Police Department than he, pontificating from a bar stool, could imagine. It was easy to criticize when you didn't have to do it.

Shannon stood up. "I gotta get home. I have a lot of fence-mending to do. Tonight, and every night from now on, I plan to have dinner with my family. After New Year's I'm going to take Eileen away somewhere for a couple of days—maybe Montauk.''

"It's pretty cold out there this time of the year.''

"I don't expect to be outdoors much. When I get back, I'll write my résumé. Then on Sunday afternoon I'll sit down with a bottle of Black Bush, the *New York Times,* and look for a sane, normal job in the real world.''

Rose tried to smile, but his heart wasn't in it. Inside, he felt like he was attending another inspector's funeral. "If that's what you really want, Brian, go for it.''

"Hey Rose,'' Shannon said cheerfully, "when you make captain, you're going to need a good accountant. I'll give you a special discount on your tax returns. I'll even toss in a second set of books free.''

"Not on your life. The last thing a Jew needs is a goyim Mick accountant.''

"Okay, suit yourself.'' He looked at his watch. "I gotta stop back at the office to pick up a couple of things before I go home.'' They stood facing each other in awkward silence, then Shannon said, "I just want to say I was wrong about you, Alex. In spite of being an IAD hump, you turned out to be a pretty good detective after all. If it weren't for you talking to the Field Associate and—''

"Can it, Brian. It was pure luck. Isn't that the way most homicides are solved?''

"Yeah, I guess so, but a good detective makes a lot of his own luck. Listen, Alex, we'll get together in a couple of weeks, have dinner, a couple of drinks.''

Rose shook Shannon's hand. "Yeah, I'd like that." But they both knew the call wouldn't be made.

Rose stood by the door and watched Shannon cross the street to his car. The wind, channeled by the tall buildings and narrow streets of lower Manhattan, formed whirlwinds of dust and debris in the fading light. Shannon got into his battered Rabbit and tried to start the engine. It cranked but wouldn't catch. He got out, opened the hood, and banged something with a wrench. Then he got back in and the engine coughed to life.

Rose remained at the door long after the Rabbit was out of sight, thinking about what Shannon had said earlier. *You have to learn to let go.* It had taken Shannon a long time to understand that. Now it was Alex Rose's turn to face the truth. His marriage was a fraud. It suddenly occurred to him that he didn't have to equate its success with his success as a human being. There was a hell of a lot more to define his life than a marriage. *It* was a failure, but *he* wasn't. He'd have to accept his share of responsibility, but there was no need to shoulder the burden alone.

He'd discovered a lot about himself in the last six weeks. For one thing, he didn't share Shannon's cynicism. In spite of everything that had happened, he was optimistic about the department and himself. He knew what he wanted, and he was prepared to fight for it. For the first time his life had real purpose and meaning.

"Another?"

Rose turned away from the window and looked at the little bartender, who was holding his empty glass.

"Yeah, Frankie. Why not? I feel like celebrating."

39

WHILE SHANNON AND ROSE WERE SAYING THEIR GOOD-BYES IN THE OTC Pub, Captain Patrick Stone, dressed in full uniform, was being shown into the Police Commissioner's office.

Joe Mara was still incensed at having to meet with Stone under these circumstances. Incensed and ashamed. All his life he'd viewed himself as a moral and ethical man, traits that others sometimes interpreted as intolerance and rigidity. The product of Irish-American parents, Mara was raised to believe in God and the innate, if fallible, goodness in man. These qualities, the sum total of Joseph Mara, made him at times naive—a debilitating handicap for a man in his chosen profession.

Mara had never before encountered anything to challenge his comfortable belief system. Until now. This investigation, with its subtle nuances of right and wrong, virtue versus expediency, had thrown his world off its neat, precise axis. In the tidal wave of the investigation's aftermath, his belief system—everything he stood for—was put to the test.

The morning after the attempted murder of Pickett, the P.C. went to see Kessel. In the mayor's office, surrounded by the ghosts of the city's history, he recounted the dismal conclusion to the investigation. Kessel, as always when serious issues were being discussed, listened silently and attentively.

"Who's left?" he asked when Mara had finished his story.

"Patrick Stone."

The mayor toyed with his enormous cuff links—solid gold, embossed with the emblem of the City of New York—a gift from a Middle East foreign minister. "What do you want to do, Joe?"

Kessel, Mara noted glumly, was still using "you" and not "us." He knew what the mayor wanted: a low-key solution, some way to ease the impact of this scandal in the public eye. But in the aftermath of the carnage, it no longer seemed possible. "I want to arrest Patrick Stone for murder," he said. "I'm sure when we look into it further, we'll find much more to charge him with."

Kessel swiveled his chair toward the window and gazed down at a tranquil City Hall park below. Some homeless men, whom he'd tried, but failed, to have removed from the park, sprawled on benches, while well-dressed citizens hurried to and from their jobs in the rows of glass buildings towering over the park. New York, a city of never-ending contrasts. These people, all of them—from the dotty old lady feeding pigeons, to the park maintenance man listlessly stabbing at litter with his sharpened stick, to the Wall Street worker smoking a joint as he listened to a street band—were all voters. Each would hear about this and make a judgment. What would they decide? After so many years in politics he knew better than to predict what went on inside the minds of New Yorkers. Joe Mara, cloaked in his mantle of self-righteous indignation, didn't have to worry about votes, coalitions, or in-party feuds. He was a Police Commissioner, a peculiar breed of itinerant administrator. He could take his show on the road and find employment anywhere. Kessel had read once that the average tenure for a police chief was three years. With more than forty thousand police agencies in the country, Mara had many opportunities to choose from. What did Barry Kessel have? The job of mayor was nontransferable, and even if it were, he'd still opt to be the mayor of this crazy city. If he sought another job, it would be something higher. He was only fifty-four. There was still plenty of time. Perhaps . . .

Reluctantly, he spun his chair around and faced his Police Commissioner. With his chin tucked in and his head jutted forward, Kessel looked like a boxer about to move in and finish off his opponent. "What kind of evidence do you have against Stone?"

Mara squirmed. Kessel, the marksman, had once again hit the bull's-eye unerringly. "Not a lot," he answered. "A Field Associate heard Hardy refer to Stone as 'Chief,' and Stone frequently accompanied Hardy's team on arrests." He didn't bother to tell the mayor that Stone went out with all his teams.

Listening to himself recite the pathetically slim evidence against Stone made him realize how inadequate it really was. The truth was, there was no direct link between Stone and the murders. The only witnesses who could implicate him were dead.

"Are you certain Stone is the 'chief'?"

Every instinct told Mara that Stone was, but his training demanded hard facts—evidence, witnesses, admissions. He had none of these. "I'm almost sure. There isn't much now, but—"

"Joe." Kessel's tone was that of a man of infinite patience who was prepared to take whatever time was necessary to explain a simple truth to a dense listener. "You're grasping at straws. We're both lawyers. You know you can't get a conviction on such flimsy evidence. You think he's guilty, and maybe he is. But you don't get convictions on belief alone. You need hard, solid evidence."

The commissioner bridled at Kessel's condescending tone. "I'm not a judge. I'm a cop. My job is to arrest people. Let the D.A. make the case. I'll put the resources of the entire department into this. We'll find—"

"For Chrissake, Joe, grow up."

Mara felt himself redden. He'd never been spoken to by the mayor in that tone of voice.

"You're letting your emotions run away with you. Don't you realize you're sitting on what is potentially the biggest scandal in the history of the police department? Christ! Not even the Knapp Commission found death squads, and here it is almost twenty years later and the department's still living under the shadow of its findings."

The mayor stood up and paced the spacious office. "Arresting Stone will only lend credence to what Pickett has been saying all along. He'll call for another Knapp-type commission. Pickett, and his buddies in the media, will have a field day. They'll trot out every dreary police scandal back to the turn of the century. Then the PBA will get a bug up its ass." He stabbed a finger at Mara. "You know what happens if they pull a job action. We've been through them before. But never mind the PBA. What about all the good, honest cops out there just trying to do their jobs? These scandals are always demoralizing. Their neighbors read the headlines about thieving cops and look at them and say, 'Bought a new car? I wonder where he got the money? A fur coat for the wife? I wonder . . .' Damn it, Joe, I don't have to tell you this, *you* should be telling *me*."

Mara didn't know where the mayor was going with this speech, but he was sounding more like the head of the PBA than the mayor of New York City. "Everything you say is true, but there's a larger issue here. Stone is guilty of murder, and I'm not going to let him get away with it."

Kessel slumped back into his chair. "Joe, this isn't a morality play. We're talking practical politics. You have to see the big picture. It's not simply right and wrong, good versus evil. I don't want the son of a bitch to get away with murder either, but let's keep things in proper perspective. What's to be gained? How do you weigh locking up one guy—and probably losing him in court—against all the headaches and problems it'll cause?" In spite of Kessel's effort to sound reasonable, the irritation came through. "You're a good cop, Joe. But you don't know a damn thing about politics. Nobody ever appointed me. I've been elected to every job I've ever had. Over the years I've learned a thing or two about human nature and politics. Trust me on this. We can't jeopardize a lot of careers to satisfy one uneasy conscience."

Mara listened to Kessel with mounting anger and frustration. Clearly, the mayor, who had decided that the resulting political fallout would be unacceptable, didn't want Stone arrested. Mara knew he was being backed into a corner. At stake was an issue that transcended the pragmatism of politics. Murder was not something Joe Mara was willing to dismiss, no matter what the cost. As the Police Commissioner he had to run his own shop. When he'd taken this job, he'd made that very clear to Kessel. To his surprise, he heard himself blurt out, "I don't agree with you. Perhaps I should resign." As soon as he said it, he was sorry.

The mayor's face was a blank. "Of course that would be your decision," he said quietly. "But the timing would be most unfortunate. Some might view your resignation as an admission of responsibility for all this. How it would affect your career . . . ?" He let Mara finish the sentence in his own mind.

A knot tightened in Joe Mara's gut. He'd tried to bluff an old pro and he'd been called on it. But now he had no choice; he'd have to resign. He opened his mouth to speak, but instead of announcing his resignation he said, "How would you suggest I handle this?"

With that desperate, pathetic question, Joe Mara felt a part of himself die. He'd betrayed everything he stood for with that simple query, but he couldn't bring himself to retract it. He'd worked too hard to lose it all now. He wouldn't—couldn't—give it up.

Barry Kessel had seen men sell themselves before, and like a true professional, softened the fall. "Joe," he said, getting up, "I know you feel strongly about this. The son of a bitch should go to jail, but it just isn't in the cards." He patted Mara's shoulder. "Talk to Stone; get him to resign. He'll go quietly."

Talk to him? Mara was aghast. He wanted nothing to do with the bastard. "Why the hell should I talk to him?"

"Joe, who else can? You're the boss. It has to be you." Kessel returned to his desk and began shuffling through some papers. The meeting was over.

Mara was disgusted at his behavior. All his life he'd been an aggressive, take-charge guy, but he'd allowed Barry Kessel to destroy all that. Fighting back the anger, he said, "I'll talk to him and I'll try to get him to resign." After a long pause he added, "But if I find one decent piece of evidence against him, I'll have Patrick Stone arrested."

The mayor's face darkened. "I thought we'd agreed that would be unwise? The political problems—"

"I wasn't thinking about politics," the commissioner answered.

Kessel sighed. He had no patience with anyone who wasn't prepared to play the game all the way. Perhaps his assessment of Joe Mara had been wrong. Maybe his Police Commissioner wasn't as smart as he'd thought. "Joe, I want you to think about this carefully. I can't have a Police Commissioner who doesn't support my political philosophy."

"And what exactly is your political philosophy, Mayor?"

Kessel's face was expressionless. "You rock the boat and all you do is sink the ship."

"SIT DOWN," MARA SAID CURTLY.

The commissioner studied the man seated opposite him. Patrick Stone's lean, youthful looks made him appear young and innocent. He looked so benign, it was hard to believe he was responsible for all those deaths. Mara was astounded at the man's sheer chutzpa. Looking at Stone—so earnest, so at ease—one would think he was about to receive an important promotion instead of . . . instead of what? Ruefully, he recalled the last time Patrick Stone had sat in that seat. He'd been so grateful when Stone announced he was going to make that drug arrest. Indeed, NET's spectacular seizure, and the next day's press conference, had bumped Pickett off the front page; at least for one day. With chagrin he recalled how he actually toyed with the idea of promoting Stone to deputy inspector. Now Mara wondered how he could have been so wrong.

He opened Stone's folder and glanced through it once more. Since he'd scheduled this meeting, he'd read it through a dozen times, hoping to understand Stone. But all he saw was an impressive collection of documents attesting to a promising future for a young, intelligent police captain—highest written marks on the sergeant's, lieutenant's, and captain's exams; and a leave of absence for a fellowship at Harvard—for which, Mara recalled glumly, he'd been responsible. Nowhere in Patrick Stone's folder was there evidence of his malignancy.

Once again Mara was reminded of how inadequate were the administrative indicators of a policeman's career potential. Yet, every day he promoted, transferred, and sometimes fired men almost solely on the basis of a few scraps of paper. For a man who had almost made a religion of scientific management, the truth was devastating. The system was crazy. Absolutely crazy. And he had no solutions.

If men like Stone could slip through the system, they were in a lot of trouble. The question that had haunted him from the beginning of this affair returned: Of the thirty thousand men and women in the department, were there any more like Stone? Mara shuddered involuntarily. A policeman's job is pure power; he literally has the power of life and death. What kind of men and women are we attracting? What kind of signals are we sending to our future leaders? Do we have the proper safeguards in place to filter out future Stones? So many questions; so few answers. He closed the folder, threw it on the desk and said: "Why?"

Stone was attentive and alert. "Excuse me, Commissioner, why what?"

"I personally selected you to command NET because I thought you were smart. How in God's name did you think you'd get away with this madness?"

"Commissioner, I'm afraid I don't follow you."

Patrick Stone was in control now, unlike the night he'd found out about Tecci and Beals. He'd waited in the bar for the call from Tecci that never came. Several times during the long night he'd checked the telephone to make sure it was working. As the hour grew late, the bar emptied out. Soon he was the last one left. With mounting anxiety he'd called Tecci's and Beals's home numbers and had gotten no answer. Finally the bartender said he was closing, and Stone went home.

When he walked in his door, the telephone was ringing. Relieved, he picked it up, expecting to hear Tecci's voice. Instead, a strange voice said, "Captain Stone? This is Inspector Farrell from Queens Detectives. I've been trying to get you all night. Two of your men—police officers Tecci and Beals—have been killed. You'd better get over here right away."

The inspector, who had only sketchy details, refused to discuss anything on the telephone. Stone called Tim Hardy. There was no telling what he'd do when he heard Tecci and Beals were dead. He let the telephone ring for five minutes, but he couldn't wait any longer. Inspector Farrell was waiting.

All through the night and into the next morning Stone remained in the 106th station house, answering questions for the Borough Commander, detectives, ADAs, and an inspector from IAD. Through it all he maintained his composure; displaying just the right amount of sorrow and perplexity. But all he thought about was—*Where was Tim Hardy?* Every time the door opened, he half expected it to be IAD, coming to place him under arrest.

But the brass, who seemed stunned by the unusual circumstances of the two officers' deaths, were sympathetic toward him.

At seven o'clock Inspector Farrell came into the precinct C.O.'s office where Stone was sipping from a container of coffee. "Stone, this is incredible, but I've just been told that the body of one of your sergeants has been found. Sergeant Timothy Hardy committed suicide in his home sometime last night."

Stone assumed a stricken look, but for the first time since he'd heard about Tecci and Beals, he relaxed. Hardy, the only man left who could incriminate him, was dead. He was sorry for Tim Hardy. As for the others? He only wished they'd carried out their assignment before they themselves were killed. But Cabrera would understand. He'd tried. What more could he do?

Now Mara met the young captain's unwavering gaze. For an intelligent man, Stone's eyes were strangely vacant, as though he were somehow disconnected from the lethal swirl of events around him. "Are you going to tell me, Captain, that you had nothing to do with the criminal activities of these cops?"

Stone toyed idly with the gold braid on his cap. "Sir, I handpicked every one of them, and in that sense I must bear some responsibility. But I had no idea they were engaging in criminal activity. I'm as shocked as you are."

Mara assumed a conversational tone. "It was all so pointless, don't you think, Captain? I mean a bunch of stupid men led by an equally stupid egomaniac." The commissioner, carefully watching Stone's reaction, thought he detected a flash of anger in the eyes. Perhaps his hunch about Stone had been correct. Maybe he'd found a weakness. He probed further. "I can have a grudging respect for intelligent criminals, I think most cops can, but these pathetic fools . . ." He let the sentence die in the air, a challenge.

Stone's fingers stopped toying with his hat. "I don't think they were stupid," he replied. "Of course I don't know much about it."

Mara's tone was mocking. "They're all dead, and they never got to Nathan Pickett."

Stone was about to defend them, but he stopped himself. He'd almost let Mara goad him into an admission. He looked at the commissioner with renewed respect; Mara wasn't as stupid or naive as he'd thought. But Mara was wrong. *They* hadn't been stupid. It was Victor Cabrera. If only he'd listened, none of this would have happened.

Stone read the disappointment in the commissioner's face. It was evident he was hoping for an admission. "Commissioner," Stone said, closing that door forever, "perhaps you're right. Maybe they were stupid. The department's selection process leaves a lot to be desired, doesn't it?"

Mara felt himself redden. The son of a bitch was playing with him.

Sitting up ramrod straight behind his desk, he began the next phase of his attack. From studying Stone's folder, he thought he'd hit upon Stone's Achilles' heel—pride. Patrick Stone was ambitious, but more than that, he was an inordinately proud man. He had a driving compulsion to excel, to be the best at everything he did. Valedictorian of his high school class, captain of the football team; he had to demonstrate that he was superior to everyone around him. Rank and status were everything to him. He was incapable of taking orders from anyone to whom he felt superior, and that was everyone in the police department, including, no doubt, the Police Commissioner himself.

"Captain Stone," Mara said, "you are a disgrace to the uniform you wear. If I had my way, you'd be under arrest at this very moment." He thought he detected a flash of relief in Stone's face. "I wish I could bust you back to police officer, but, unfortunately, Civil Service laws preclude that option. But I'll tell you what I can do." Mara spoke slowly so he could savor the moment. "Effective immediately, you are relieved of your command of NET."

At this pronouncement, Stone's confident smile faded. Mara, seeing the change, was elated. He dug the knife deeper. "I'm going to transfer you to a borough office where your most important assignment will be to look for sleeping cops and sign memo books. I will personally see to it that you are assigned to every half-assed strike and demonstration in this city. And I'll be watching you. If you step out of line, make one mistake—a lateness, out of uniform—anything, no matter how petty, I'll have you brought up on charges. I intend to make you the laughingstock of the department. As to your future here? Forget it. You'll remain a captain forever, but you will have the opportunity to watch younger, less able men rise above you."

As Mara spoke, Stone had grown pale and his mouth set in a grim straight line. The humiliation of such an assignment was evident on his face. Mara, seeing he had Stone on the ropes, moved in for the kill. "On the other hand, you have another option. You may resign." He sat back, satisfied he'd delivered the coup de grace.

Stone was in turmoil. He'd considered the possibility that they knew about, or at least suspected, his involvement. But lacking evidence, he assumed the department would close ranks in its efforts to avoid adverse publicity, and things would go on as before. But now? To be just another uniformed captain again; to be subordinate to younger, less intelligent superiors; to police mindless demonstrations and endless uniform details without the hope of advancement—it was a bleak scenario.

He fought to control the rage welling within him. After the years of study; the endless hours wallowing in the slime and soul-deadening world of drugs; lying and manipulating to placate Victor Cabrera; and all for one purpose—to rise to the top of the greatest police department in the world—was it all going to end with a few contemptuous words of dismissal?

Reeling, he struggled to think of a way out; some way to salvage his career. The cost of getting to this plateau had been too great. He couldn't—wouldn't—give it up. There was only one answer. From what Mara had said, it was clear that they had no evidence. They were powerless to do anything to him. Besides, he had time on his side. He was a young man—he'd still be here long after Mara was gone. Then he'd make his move. With his talent and skills, he was bound to advance. This wasn't defeat, it was merely an inconvenient delay in his career timetable.

He stood up and straightened his uniform jacket. "Commissioner Mara," he said gravely, "I think you're making a mistake, but I accept the transfer. When do I begin?"

It was Mara's turn to be stunned. He'd taken Stone's initial silence as a sign of defeat, and wasn't expecting this response. He was wrong! He hadn't found Stone's weak spot after all. Patrick Stone, this living reminder of his own personal failure, was going to stay in the department, and there wasn't a thing he could do about it. Without evidence there was no case, and all the speculation in the world wouldn't win a conviction.

Mara cleared his throat. "You'll be notified," he said tersely. "Now get out of my office."

Captain Patrick Stone saluted smartly and walked out the door.

FOURTEEN FLOORS BELOW THE POLICE COMMISSIONER'S OFFICE, Shannon waited for an elevator in the lobby where, in the spirit of municipal ecumenism, a menorah and a Christmas tree stood side by side. Idly, Shannon watched the security detail check IDs and the packages of visitors. It was business as usual. The job went on unaware of the drama that had played itself out over the last several weeks. Shannon gazed around the brick-walled lobby and tried to calculate how many times he'd come and gone through these doors. It had been a fast twenty-three years, sometimes routine, sometimes exciting, but never dull. He was sorry to see it end this way.

Just then the elevator door opened and Brian Shannon stood face-to-face with Patrick Stone. Resplendent in his captain's uniform, Stone flashed the same confident smile that Shannon had disliked from the first moment they'd met.

"Hey, Brian, how're you doing?"

All the anger and frustration that Shannon had struggled to contain burst forth at the sight of Patrick Stone. Shannon didn't plan it, nor did he remember throwing the punch, but he felt the satisfying impact of his fist hitting Stone's face.

The captain bounced off the wall and tumbled over an ashtray stand. Immediately, three startled cops grabbed Shannon. One cop reached for his handcuffs, but Stone, lying sprawled on the floor, stopped him. "Forget it, officer," he said, stumbling to his feet. The blood gushing from his nose dripped onto his shield and rows of decorations. Someone handed him a handkerchief. He dabbed at his nose and waved them away. "It's all right. It's just a misunderstanding."

The cops exchanged uneasy glances and backed off, leaving Stone and Shannon alone. The two men stood facing each other in silence. Then Shannon saw Stone's expression change from puzzlement to understanding; he knew why Shannon had hit him. Shannon was gratified to see another change in Stone's eyes. That infuriating self-confident gleam had been replaced by one of fear.

"It's not over, Stone," Shannon said. "It's not over yet." The elevator door opened and he stepped in.

ONE WEEK AFTER NEW YEAR'S DAY, THE MAYOR, MAKING AN APPEAR-ance at a retirement dinner for a judge, literally bumped into Senator Nathan Pickett. "Nate," he said, awkwardly grabbing Pickett's arm, "excuse me."

Nathan Pickett was the one loose cannon in this whole sordid affair. Kessel thought he'd have a hard time with his stubborn Police Commissioner, but Mara, in spite of his face-saving threats, had finally fallen in line.

Since the shooting, Kessel had been waiting for Pickett to drop the other shoe—perhaps a press conference called to expose a police cover-up, or a telephone call from the FBI requesting a confidential interview. With trepidation, Kessel had watched Pickett's press conference on TV. The senator repeated the same old charges and allegations, but said nothing about the attempt on his life. Kessel was relieved, if puzzled. What bothered him most was that he didn't know the extent of Pickett's knowledge of events. The senator knew, no doubt, that someone had tried to kill him, but did he know the circumstances surrounding the attempt? In the business of politics, knowledge was power. If Pickett knew the real story, he could destroy the mayor. But so far the senator had remained uncharacteristically silent.

Kessel's ex-boxer's instincts told him to go after Pickett to find out what he knew. But his political experience told him to lay back and wait. Let Pickett bring the fight to him.

Now the time had come.

"Good evening, Mr. Mayor." Pickett peered through his glasses. "I trust you're well?"

"Very well, Senator. Very well indeed," the mayor answered with forced lightness. "I must congratulate you on your drug commission hearings. It's all I've seen in the headlines today."

"There's more to come. Tomorrow I have a surprise witness who's going to cause shock waves in some very high places. By the way, Mr. Mayor . . ." Pickett took off his glasses and wiped them with a handkerchief. "The street crime in this city is appalling. You really must do something about it. Why, just recently I was almost shot dead on the street." He put his glasses back on and focused on the mayor's face, his expression impassive.

The other shoe. Kessel didn't even blink. With the aggressiveness that had earned him a collegiate boxing championship, he moved in swinging. "It certainly is dangerous," he said, "especially for politicians who must visit their—constituents?—at all hours of the night. Is Professor Nussbaum a political advisor, Nate?"

Pickett's eyes narrowed. "Have you been spying on me, Barry?"

"No, not at all. But it is my business to know what goes on in this city."

The tall senator, assessing the effect that revelation would have on his career, scowled. "What do you want, Kessel?"

"Fairness, Nate. Get off the city's back. Your commission is making it sound as though New York invented drugs. You know goddamn well we're doing the best we can with the limited resources we have at our disposal."

"You're breaking my heart, Barry. What do you want me to do, terminate the commission tomorrow?"

"No. Just shift the focus to where it belongs—the federal government. You know as well as I do that Washington has been cutting funds for law enforcement. Between the loss of federal funding and a shrinking tax base, I'm facing a serious monetary shortfall. I'll tell you something else, Nate. For the sake of your career it's time you moved on to national matters. I admire the way you've used local issues to put you in the spotlight, but take an old pro's advice—move on. You don't want to get bogged down in local issues that have no solutions. I could see myself endorsing someone like you for the Senate. We need a man who will fight for the interests of the big cities."

Pickett's expression was neutral, but he was considering Kessel's words. The commission was not as successful as he had hoped. It *was* getting publicity, but all of it local. And two of his star witnesses, a middleman to a Peruvian drug kingpin and a former bank official, whose testimony would have provided media fireworks, had vanished. The mayor might have a point. If he shifted the blame for the narcotics problem to the federal government, he'd attract national coverage. And Kessel's veiled allusion to an endorsement was also interesting. Barry Kessel was a powerful force in city and state politics. His support would be invaluable.

"Perhaps you're right, Barry. If we're going to defeat the narcotics problem, it will have to begin in Washington."

Kessel's heart pounded in his chest. *Got him!* The brief, verbal spar, over so quickly, left him exhausted but elated. He felt the tightness leave his stomach. He didn't know how much Pickett knew, but it no longer mattered. He was willing to make a deal.

Once again Barry Kessel felt safe and secure in his world. As long as men were willing to iron out their differences, life could go on in an orderly, predictable fashion. In the ethereal world of political power, the scales had shifted imperceptibly, and Barry Kessel, once again, was indisputably the most powerful man in New York City.

THE DAY AFTER PICKETT'S SECOND-STRING WITNESS DESCRIBED THE inner workings of a major drug cartel that reached from Peru to New York, Chief Duffy, the commissioner's aide, knocked on the door. Usually a jovial, easygoing man, Duffy entered the office ashen-faced. "Commissioner, I think you should see this." He held in his hands a bundle wrapped in brown paper.

"What is it?"

"Videotapes, sir. The package was addressed to you. I started to review them myself, but . . ." He cleared his throat. "They concern Captain Stone. I've never—"

Mara was instantly alert. "Who sent the package?"

"There's no name, but it's postmarked Peru."

Mara felt the electricity shock him, and something else—apprehension. Could this be the evidence he needed to bring Stone down? And if it was, would he use it? He'd already wavered once. Would he again?

Joe Mara, alone in his office, viewed the videotapes in horrified fascination. For the most part the picture was grainy and the sound was poor, especially in the airport restaurant. But the conversation on the boat deck between Patrick Stone and a man called Victor was startlingly clear. That conversation alone was enough to charge Patrick Stone with conspiracy to commit murder, bribery, and a host of other charges. The tape ended when the man plucked the microphone out of the floral arrangement.

Mara, emotionally drained, swiveled in his chair and gazed out on the hazy skyline of lower Manhattan. As the Police Commissioner, he was responsible for the safety and protection of more than seven million people. It was a heady experience for a boy from Pennsylvania.

In the past several weeks his career had taken more than one unexpected turn. Joe Mara was no longer the same man who'd listened impatiently to his Chief of Detectives tell him about cops involved in illicit drugs and murder.

Mara had always viewed right and wrong in terms of black and white. But now he realized it wasn't that simple. Politics, career, and expediency added layers of shading, and the distinction between right and wrong became much more difficult to see.

On the other hand, maybe there was only one definition of right and wrong. Perhaps anything else was simply a rationalization to obscure the truth. If he acted against Patrick Stone, his career could be ruined. But if he did nothing, his integrity would be destroyed forever.

Mara, turning from the window, had made up his mind. He pressed the intercom button. "Duff, get Mario Percell in here forthwith. Then call the District Attorney and tell him I have to see him immediately on a matter of great importance. And Duff . . . tell him to have a videotape machine set up in his office.''